FANNY HILL
OR,
MEMOIRS OF A WOMAN OF PLEASURE

JOHN CLELAND

FANNY HILL

OR,
MEMOIRS OF A WOMAN
OF PLEASURE

Introduction by Gary Gautier

Notes by Audrey Bilger,
Claremont McKenna College

THE MODERN LIBRARY

NEW YORK

Grateful acknowledgment is made to the following for permission to
reprint previously published material:

COPYRIGHT CLEARANCE CENTER: Excerpt from "Fanny Hill's Mapping of
Sexuality, Female Identity, and Maternity" by Gary Gautier from
Studies in English Literature, 1500–1900, vol. 35, issue 3, Summer 1995.
Copyright © 1995 by Johns Hopkins University Press. Reproduced with
permission of Johns Hopkins University Press in the format
Trade Book via Copyright Clearance Center.

THE ESTATE OF CHARLES REMBAR: Chapter 13 from *The End of Obscenity* by
Charles Rembar. Copyright © 1968 by Charles Rembar. Reprinted by
permission of the Estate of Charles Rembar.

LIBRARY OF CONGRESS CATALOGING-IN-PUBLICATION DATA
Cleland, John, 1709–1789.
[Memoirs of a woman of pleasure]
Fanny Hill; or Memoirs of a woman of pleasure/John Cleland ;
notes by Audrey Bilger.
p.   cm.
ISBN 0-375-75808-9
1. Prostitutes—Fiction. 2. England—Fiction. I. Title: Fanny Hill.
II. Title: Memoirs of a woman of pleasure. III. Title.
PR3348.C65 M45 2001
823'.6—dc21   2001030431

Modern Library website address: www.modernlibrary.com

Printed in the United States of America

4 6 8 9 7 5

John Cleland

John Cleland, whose notorious tale of the prostitute Fanny Hill
endures as the most famous erotic novel in English literature,
was born in Kingston-on-Thames, Surrey, in 1710. He came
from a prosperous middle-class family and grew up on St.
James's Place, in the heart of London's newly fashionable West
End. His father was a Scots army officer and customs official who
enjoyed friendships with Alexander Pope and Richard Steele; his
mother was a cultivated Englishwoman of Dutch Jewish ances-
try who moved in prominent social circles. In 1721 Cleland entered the Westminster School, where he excelled at Latin and
Greek. Named a King's Scholar, one of a group destined for ad-
vancement to Oxford or Cambridge, he abruptly withdrew from
the school for unknown reasons after two years. In 1728 Cleland
enlisted as a common foot soldier in the militia of the East India
Company. During twelve years in Bombay he rose quickly to the
level of civil servant and finally emerged as a well-established
colonial merchant. Scholars assert that he probably composed an
early version of *Memoirs of a Woman of Pleasure*, commonly
known as *Fanny Hill*, while stationed there. Returning to London

in 1741, Cleland became involved in an unsuccessful scheme to revive the defunct Portuguese East India Company and eventually exhausted the small personal fortune he had accrued abroad.

Cleland rewrote *Fanny Hill* and secured its publication while confined in Fleet Prison for debt from February 1748 to March 1749. The Bishop of London immediately censured the work as "an open insult upon Religion and good manners," and James Boswell deemed it "a most licentious and inflaming book." Arrested on charges of obscenity, Cleland attempted to disavow authorship and denounced the memoir as "a Book I disdain to defend, and wish, from my Soul, buried and forgot." Yet *Fanny Hill* continued to appear in clandestine editions and became an underground bestseller. By his own account Cleland existed thereafter in a "low abject condition, that of a writer for Bread." He contributed scores of anonymous articles and reviews to publications such as the *Monthly Review* and the *Public Advertiser*. In addition, he turned out a burlesque, two didactic poems, two quarrelsome medical treatises, a political pamphlet, and several linguistic studies attempting to prove that ancient Celtic was the primitive language of mankind. His three subsequent novels— *Memoirs of a Coxcomb* (1751), *The Surprises of Love* (1764), and *The Woman of Honor* (1768)—lacked the sensual grace and robust irony of *Fanny Hill*. And despite a friendship with David Garrick, the great actor and theater manager, Cleland was unable to stage his plays *Titus Vespasian* (1755), *The Ladies Subscription* (1755), and *Tombo-Chiqui* (1758). John Cleland died impoverished and forgotten on January 23, 1789, at his house in Petty France, Westminster.

In 1966 the United States Supreme Court ruled that *Fanny Hill* was not obscene, prompting critics to reconsider the novel. "The disconcerting thing about the book—as a piece of 'pornography'—is that it has charm," noted V. S. Pritchett. "Fanny goes into prolonged, detailed descriptions of several kinds of sexual adventure and intercourse. In doing so, however, she never utters an obscene word, rarely descends even to colloquialism, never to the clinical; she indeed writes an elaborate literary language that would do credit to any master of baroque and poetic utterance—shall we say Henry James?—spoken in the drawing room." Novelist Brigid Brophy agreed: "*Fanny Hill* turns out to possess, over and above the interest of its material, literary charm, that seems almost too bonus to be true. It is in fact a highly engaging little erotic tale—perhaps the most engaging to emerge from the entire seventeen centuries of European literature that lie between *Daphnis and Chloe* and *Claudine à l'École.*" Erica Jong, who wrote a bestselling adaptation of the novel entitled *Fanny* (1980), praised "the delightful cheerfulness of the heroine, the sheer healthiness and bounciness of its approach to physical love," and concluded: "*Fanny Hill* is one of my favorite books [and a] classic of erotica."

CONTENTS

INTRODUCTION: FANNY HILL'S MAPPING OF SEXUALITY, FEMALE IDENTITY, AND MATERNITY

Gary Gautier

The eighteenth-century British were not only remapping world territories, but were also involved at home in the concomitant remapping of conceptual space to suit the new world of bourgeois capitalism. Through three related language patterns, *Memoirs of a Woman of Pleasure* (1749) confrontationally engages this process by making legible the bourgeois remapping of certain categories constitutive of "woman," and then exposing that remapping as ludicrous. Through metaphors of "prospects" and "flowers," the sexual body is aestheticized and commodified. Through the "seats-and-centers" pattern, female identity in particular is redefined. Through the "mothers-and-daughters" pattern, the maternal bond becomes represented as an economic bond masking as a sentimental one.[1] John Cleland not only remaps these concepts of sexuality, female identity, and maternity, but pins the remapping to an emergent bourgeois ideology, and then politically situates himself as an antagonist to that ideology. In satirizing these bourgeois constructions of gender, Cleland is not at all boxed into a feminist vantage point but rather assumes a vantage point that is generally (though not in every detail) sympathetic to the landed conservatism represented in Henry St. John Bolingbroke, Henry Fielding, and Tobias Smollett, all of whom Cleland praised in *The Monthly Review*.[2]

The word "prospect" has three meanings in *Memoirs*—a view of nature, a view of the sexual body, and a view of a change in material conditions—and through the interplay of these three meanings the sexual body is both aestheticized and commodified.[3] "Prospect," first of all, refers to the aesthetic appreciation of natural scenery. As Ann Bermingham points out, this view of nature as an aesthetic object, taken for granted in post-Romantic times, was relatively new in eighteenth-century England.[4] Whether the shifting sensibility was due to the fashion of the Grand Tour, as Christopher Hussey suggests,[5] or due to the ideological needs of a culture in political conflict, as James Turner argues,[6] *Memoirs* takes the conceptual artifact of the aestheticized "prospect" and uses it to remap the sexual body into the domain of aesthetics.

Charles first refers to the natural prospect when he takes Fanny to Chelsea: "Come, my dear, and I will show you a room that commands a fine prospect over some gardens."[7] The natural prospect is, however, displaced even before the sentence ends by the "prospect" of a sexual landscape, as Charles, "without waiting for an answer ... led me up into a chamber ... where all seeing of prospects was out of the question, except that of a bed, which had all the air of having recommended the room to him." Fanny thus learns this metaphorical use of "prospect" from Charles at the scene of her defloration, but she quickly adopts it into her own vocabulary. The following morning she describes in detail the sexual "prospect" of Charles's body, and refers directly to the sexual "prospect" twice thereafter before finally returning to its use in reference to natural scenery. With repetition, the sexual prospect becomes less and less a metaphor and increasingly a primary association of the word, aestheticizing the sexual body by way of the natural prospect. Notably, this aestheticization is not gender-specific. It refers to both male and female organs.

The aestheticization of the sexual body, male and female

alike, is a recoding of sexuality which meets the needs of the commercial world within which Fanny is working and which was rising to pre-eminence in eighteenth-century England. The aestheticized body is the objectified body, and once objectified, the body can be readily mapped into the bourgeois world of commodity-values. Looking at the sexual body as the point of overlap between the imagery of nature and imagery of mechanical production brings together two strands of *Memoirs* criticism. John Hollander, reviewing Putnam's 1963 publication of *Memoirs*, refers to Cleland's use of "almost standard Renaissance erotic topography,"[8] a view ratified and developed recently by Douglas Brooks-Davies.[9] At the other extreme, Douglas J. Stewart claims that *Memoirs* effects "a near-total displacement" of that standard erotic topography by the imagery of " 'engines,' 'movements' (as in a watch or clock), 'springs,' " and so on.[10]

A less selective reading shows these two fields of imagery to overlap in Cleland's representation of the sexual body. Leo Braudy points us in the right direction when he says that "the language of mechanism and the invocation of nature are . . . complements in *Fanny Hill*."[11] Braudy argues that these two patterns converge into a materialist celebration of the "egalitarian possibilities of sexuality,"[12] and cites Fanny's affair with Will to justify his claim. A closer look at Fanny's evaluation of Will, however, shows something more complex than a celebration. Fanny's coding of sexuality, which favors "the talent of pleasing" over "titles, dignities, honours, and the like," upsets the old, fixed, and oppressive structures of the aristocratic hierarchy, but this same coding creates new problems. Having shaken off the shackles of title, the human being now becomes an object of aesthetic judgment. Fanny doesn't scorn Will because of his rank, but locates "the greatest of all merits" in the ability of this "handsome person" to give sexual pleasure, thus reducing him to a sexual object. The cost of egalitarianism, in the bourgeois vision which Fanny here participates in, is that all individuals, regardless of class or gender, become interchangeable units in some gigantic sociosexual machine.[13]

The vision of the aestheticized body in *Memoirs* has important implications for aesthetics in general. The eighteenth-century boom in aesthetic theory was not coincidentally aligned with the rise of capitalism and the bourgeois world view. Marx suggests that with the rise of capitalism, commodity-value replaces use-value as the standard of material intercourse, and the world of social relations takes on the "fantastic form of a relation between things."[14] Under these conditions, social identity becomes dehumanized, and if one is to salvage human identity, a distinction must be created between "private" and "social" identity. Social identity becomes perceived as superficial, and "real" human identity becomes perceived as private. If this is tentatively seen as a two-step process—the dehumanization of social identity and then the construction of private identity as "real" identity—it is the first step that primarily concerns *Memoirs*. Cleland depicts, and depicts with a satirist's eye, the manner in which the bourgeois cultural context aestheticizes the sexual body, leading to the fantastic coding of sexual relations as relations between things. In *Memoirs*, indeed, the sexual act is often portrayed as an act between autonomous sexual organs, creating an effect which is often comical but comical in a politically motivated way. Through the mediation of *Memoirs*'s satirical form, the comedy is intimately connected to such conservative critiques of bourgeois commercialism as found in Pope's *Dunciad*.

Insofar as the "aesthetic" coding of the sexual body leads to the "commodity" coding, *Memoirs* further calls into question those eighteenth-century aesthetic discourses which led up to Kant's "purposiveness without a purpose." Those discourses tended to present the aesthetic object and aesthetic judgments as isolated from the world of practical relations and from ideological concerns. In the case of imagery of nature, whereas " 'land' and 'country' were once synonymous with 'nation,' "[15] land in the eighteenth-century sense of "prospect" ostensibly detaches itself from politics and lays "claims to something more universal."[16] But that move is itself ideologically motivated, and is exposed as such through the satirical form of *Memoirs*. Once Fanny learns the aestheticized "prospect" coding of the sexual body, she has made the adjustments necessary to become a player in the eighteenth-century marketplace of economic individualists. Aestheticization, far from promoting some pre-ideological category, is merely a preliminary rite of initiation into the world of commodity values. As Fanny comes to naturalize the bodily "prospect" through rhetorical and sexual repetitions, she also comes to see her body as so many units of product. Thus she can say that her "heart" is "pre-ingag'd" to Charles, while Mr. H——— is "possessor of my person."

The movement from aestheticized body to commodified body brings us to the third meaning of "prospect"—the view of material success. "Prospect" is used in this third sense several times, culminating in Fanny's reflections after the death of the rational pleasurist: "I grew somewhat comforted by the prospect that now open'd to me, if not of happiness, at least of affluence, and independence." The implied link between the sexual prospect and the business prospect can, interestingly enough, claim the authority of John Locke. In *Treatises on Government,* Locke suggests that the relationship to self is primarily one of *ownership.* This not only supports Locke's own position on private property, but opens the way for a recoding of the body as commodity and raw material that can legitimately enhance one's business prospects. If Locke points the way toward a bourgeois coding of the human body, *Memoirs* ritualizes that coding, partly through the repeated conflation of nature, body, and business venture behind the sign of the "prospect."

The triple coding of prospect is most clear in the return to the "prospect" of nature in Fanny's last prostitution scene. Here, Fanny is again offered the "prospect" of a "garden." In this scene, "prospect" directly refers neither to the sexual body nor to the prostitutes' payoff. The implication is that, insofar as the conflation of meanings is complete, the recoding of the sexual body is complete. Sexual body and business interests automatically share the space of the natural "prospect." Nature and sex together have been initiated into the world of commodity values by way of the "prospect" pattern.[17]

The "flowers" image is also used in *Memoirs* to aestheticize the

sexual body, but additional meanings extend the range of significance seen in the "prospects" pattern. The climax of the "flowers" pattern is in Louisa's seduction of "*Good-natured Dick.*" Only
in this scene is "flower(s)," which has been used several times as
a metaphor for "maidenhead," used literally. Fanny introduces
Dick by saying: "we had often . . . bought his flowers." Significantly, this literal reference is almost immediately displaced
with the use of "so rare a flower" as a metaphor for penis.[18] The
natural flower is displaced by the sexual flower, and sex becomes
the mediating activity through which we might get back to the
"natural." But it is a special kind of sex. In this scene the reifica-
tion of the sexual body hits its peak. Dick, called "the natural,"
becomes first "man-machine" and then "brute-machine"; Louisa
"went wholly out of her mind into that favourite part of her
body . . . There alone she existed . . . In short, she was now as
mere a machine . . . as the natural himself." Human being is displaced by reified sex organ, and sex organ is coded as a kind of
"machine." As the flower-boy, Dick at least has some kind of social identity, but even that becomes displaced by the flower-
penis. The episode ends with Dick's flowers becoming one unit
in a fiscal transaction, with Fanny and Louisa "taking all his
flowers off his hands, and paying him at his rate." The sexual
body becomes the space across which natural flowers, as well as
the social identity of Dick "the natural," are coded into the
world of commercial transactions.

Thus far the "flowers" pattern has been seen as a supplement
to the "prospects" pattern. Indeed, "prospect" occurs in the Dick
episode as the vaginal field of Dick's metaphorical "flower," and
this kind of networking of concepts certainly increases the
power of the ideological remapping. However, the displacement
of natural flowers by sexual flowers sets us up for the next scene,
in which "flowers" exhibits a meaning unaccounted for by the
"prospects" pattern.

Following the Dick episode, Fanny and Emily go up the river
for their last transaction as prostitutes, whereupon Fanny
launches into one of her reflections on style, which culminates

in her praise of sex as a subject that "is poetry itself, pregnant with every flower of imagination, and loving metaphors." The space of sexual transaction, which has been a kind of recoding ground for the interplay of nature and formative bourgeois conceptual categories, now becomes displaced by one of its own metaphors.[19] Sexual activity becomes a kind of narrative (not "the province of poetry" but "poetry itself"), and the narrative logic that this poetry follows might best be described as the logic of commercial transaction. Nature, prospects, flowers, sexuality: all are remapped according to the narrative logic of bourgeois commercialism.

Whereas the prospects-and-flowers pattern remaps the sexual body, the seats-and-centers pattern allows us to focus more narrowly on the female body and on how female identity is recoded by way of the body. Of the many terms Cleland uses for the vagina—including "home," "spot," and "place"—"seats" and "centers" are peculiarly germane here. First of all, they are gender-specific, referring repeatedly to the vagina but never to the penis.[20] Second, each carries extra meanings which are particularly telling with regard to the emerging bourgeois world view. "Seats" carries the meaning of "county seat," the primary political and economic unit of a residual landed and aristocratic social order; and "center" explicitly refers to the central "article" of a rather bourgeois business deal concerning the commodity-value of Fanny's counterfeit maidenhead. Third, the occurrence of "central seat" in the final sex act of the novel provides textually-specific closure to the pattern.

During Fanny's first night with Phoebe, the pattern begins with Fanny's recognition of her own vagina as "the sweet seat of the most exquisite sensation . . . which had been, till that instant, the seat of the most insensible innocence." Here, Fanny discovers her vagina-centered identity. The innocence which had characterized her vagina, and her being, is seen as the mere *absence* of sensation. Her identity as such is recognizable only retrospectively, from the vantage point of the *present* sensation. This iteration of vaginal identity is reinforced through the concept of "center," which occurs for the first time in the same passage. Fanny feels "a new fire . . . fix'd with violence in that center appointed them by nature." In terms of the vaginal reference, "center" here is perfectly synonymous with seat, but "center" also carries some extra semantic freight which allows us to talk about, for example, Fanny's center of identity. Moreover, with the death of Fanny's parents, and her desertion by Esther in London, Fanny is thrust into what might be called a de-centered existence, "alone, absolutely distitute [*sic*] and friendless ... [and in] helpless strange circumstances." With Phoebe's advances, Fanny finds a narcissistic center of identity in her vagina, as "center of all my senses." Thus in this initial scene of "seats" and "centers," we see Fanny move from a de-centered identity, or an identity as pure absence, to a narcissistic identity centered on vaginal sensations.

The next stage in the development of Fanny's female identity is a recoding of the vaginal "center" upon defloration. What was the vaginal "center of all my senses" becomes the "center of [Charles's] attraction," and the "center of his over-fierce attack." Fanny, as female sexual body, enters the world of social relations, and assumes the patriarchal coding assigned to her within that world. The female, in such a world, has only a quasi-identity which must be "finish'd" by male penetration. She is a sort of *vagina rasa* awaiting male inscription.

A corollary to this notion of female identity is the lack of female space in the eighteenth-century world of social relations.[21] When Esther suggests that Fanny "get into" a "place" as soon as possible, and Fanny more pointedly reiterates her need for "any place ... where I could get into any sort of being," the problem of female space in commercial London is made clear. The desirable place for Fanny in this context is that of a maid. Unlucky at getting such a place, Fanny quickly finds her alternative place in a brothel (a brothel which is superficially matriarchal but which in fact has its *raison d'être* in the servicing of males).

The patriarchal denial of female space was a common theme in the eighteenth century, appearing not only in *Memoirs* but also in such works as *Moll Flanders, Clarissa,* and *The Harlot's Progress.* One possible response to the female's claustrophobic predicament in commercial London might be to dig through older conceptual categories for a more adequate gender coding. Such a strategy can be seen in the two occurrences of "seat" in reference to the "county seat" of "Lord *N*———" in Harriet's defloration tale. The county seat, a primary unit of organization in a land-based economy, carries with it the aura of aristocratic conceptual space. Occurring here in a narrative within a narrative, and in a rather pastoral tale told in an urban brothel, it is twice removed from the real world of social relations in *Memoirs.* The aristocratically coded "seat," with all its conceptual space, may have a certain nostalgia value, but is not presented here as a viable option for women in commercial London.

Fanny's own response to the patriarchal denial of female space can be compared to that of her contemporary, Clarissa Harlowe. Clarissa indeed finds that the gate which marks the end of her father's territory marks the beginning of Lovelace's. Whereas Fanny, however, accepts subjection to Mr. H——— as the natural consequence of rape, Clarissa resists the role of "subjection to ravisher" to the end, perhaps finding the only female space in her world, ironically, in the "coffin." Both Fanny and Clarissa dramatize the socially mandated subjection of the female, but *Clarissa* offers the situation tragically, whereas *Memoirs* presents it as a source of immediate pleasure and, somewhat tongue-in-cheek, as a source of ultimate domestic bliss.

In the world of *Memoirs,* Fanny not only requires male penetration to complete her identity (a patriarchal coding), but needs a bourgeois coding of her body in order to fully have her "place." A variant meaning of "center" fosters such a coding: "When the articles of the treaty had been fully agreed on, the stipulated payments duly secur'd . . . nothing now remain'd but the execution of the main point, which center'd in the surrender of my person up to his free disposal and use." Fanny's vagina becomes center of identity, center of male attention, and center of business transaction, all three meanings becoming conflated into a coherent coding of female identity and female space that suits an emergent bourgeois ideology.

The concluding reference to "central seat" reiterates the conflated coding with an emphasis on subjection: "Think then! as a lover think, what must be the consummate transport of that quickest of our senses, in their central seat too! when after so long a deprival, it felt itself re-inflamed under the pressure of that peculiar scepter-member, which commands us all." The female who buys into the coding and subjects herself to the phallus gets the reward of a presumably benevolent master.[22]

Fanny's identity problems can be seen as not merely those of the female in a bourgeois patriarchy, but also as those of a female deprived of her mother. The orphan motif is used in *Memoirs* to recode maternity itself into the bourgeois patriarchy. Three semantic modes of "mother" (and variants) can be identified in the process of that recoding. First of all, there is the reference to the biological mother. Although over half of the usages of "mother" refer to biological mothers, many are in set-piece introductions to coming-of-age narratives within *Memoirs,* and the adjectival variants—"motherly," "maternal," and "matron-like"—are reserved for the second mode, surrogate mothers. The bulk of the maternity recoding in *Memoirs* is through reference to these omnipresent surrogate mothers, and in one such case we find a reference to "my good temporal mother," which I will treat as a separate mode of the term "mother."

The de-centered position in which Fanny finds herself early in the novel can be seen from this angle in relation to the premature loss of her biological mother. Much of Fanny's narrative suggests an inner longing for an adequate maternal bond. After her parents' death, she is quick to see mother-figures in Esther, Mrs. Brown, the landlady in Chelsea, and Mrs. Cole. When "motherly" is first used in the surrogate sense, as Fanny touts Esther's "motherly care," the maternal bond is already sliding from a bond of sentiment to one of economics—"she taxed me for her protection, by making me bear all travelling charges"—but this is only a foreshadowing of Fanny's experiences in London, where the recoding of maternity begins in earnest.

At the intelligence office, Fanny almost immediately codes Mrs. Brown as "matron-like," and her entrance into Mrs. Brown's household can be seen as the fulfillment of a desire to reenter maternal space. That space seems more "magnificently furnished" than ever, perhaps suggesting Fanny's own rapture at entering a maternal space after a period of deprivation. This maternal space, however, is not what it appears to be. Though a brothel, the house ironically appears to Fanny to be "a very reputable" place. Likewise, the maternal woman who appears to take such a sentimental interest in Fanny has primarily a commercial interest. Fanny has entered a world where not only are daughters commodities produced by mothers, marketed, and sold (the Chelsea landlady, the only biological mother actually present in the story, sells her daughter outright, "for not a very considerable sum neither"), but daughters are also a sort of bourgeois office space for repeated business transactions between mothers and clients. After upsetting Mr. Crofts's efforts, Fanny in fact makes a telling comment: "I dreaded the sight of Mrs. *Brown,* as if I had been the criminal, and she the person injur'd." Fanny's body is the space of contract between Mr. Crofts and her surrogate mother, and her violation of that coding of her body as contractual space results in the kind of irrational guilt a daughter might feel upon anticipating a motherly reproach.

In book 2, the brutally economic coding of maternity seems to soften somewhat, as the "perfectly maternal" Mrs. Cole seems more likeable than the surrogate mothers of book 1. But is Mrs. Cole really more likeable, or is the coding of the maternal relation as economic relation merely becoming naturalized? B. Slepian and L. J. Morrissey cite Mrs. Cole's advice following the sailor scene as evidence that "Fanny's principal teacher is Mrs. Cole" as she learns "the value of reason and self-control."[23] A close look at the scene, however, suggests that such evidence is ambiguous at best: "When I got home, and told Mrs. *Cole* my adventure, she represented so strongly to me the nature and dangerous consequences of my folly, the risques to my health, in being so open-legg'd . . . [that I never] venture[d] so rashly again." Mrs. Cole's advice deals with consequences and health risks—i.e., not on the moral implications of promiscuity, but on the danger of spoiling the product the daughter represents. In other words, a bond often coded in terms of "morals" or "sentiment" is coded in *Memoirs* as primarily a commercial bond, and the coding is subtle enough to seem "natural," and thus to go unnoticed by even careful readers like Slepian and Morrissey.

My argument that *Memoirs* presents a bourgeois remapping of the concept of maternity, and betrays that concept as more deeply economic than sentimental, requires some qualification. Lawrence Stone and others, after all, have argued that sentimental attachment within the family increases dramatically with the rise of bourgeois culture.[24] The difficulty lies not in my reading of *Memoirs* so much as in the cultural significance of *Memoirs.* Within *Memoirs,* there can be little doubt that the maternal bond, constructed largely through surrogate mothers who are also bawds, is more economic than sentimental. The interesting question is why the presentation of maternity takes this form and what that presentation means in terms of social history. One might first suggest that this presentation of maternity is peculiar to pornography, which adopts features of the prostitution subculture such as the appellation "Mother" for such notorious London bawds as Mother Needham. But the satirical form into which *Memoirs* is cast suggests that the conventional apparatuses of pornography and prostitution are not deviations *from* but rather representations *of* emerging bourgeois culture. In a world of commodity values, where concrete human relations take on the form of relations between things, the rhetoric of sentiment may well become the crucial cover for social relations which are increasingly alienated and drained of emotional content. From this vantage point, the argument that bourgeois families are more emotionally bonded than families from other eras, or other cultural configurations, is most interesting for what it says about the *ideological need* for sentiment which drives the discourses of bourgeois culture. As an empirical claim about concrete human relations, it seems doubtful, and perhaps other readings of social history are possible.[25] If one looks at Samuel Richardson and the

Cult of Sensibility, one sees increased sentimental bonding in bourgeois culture. If, however, one looks at *Memoirs* through the lens of its satirical form, and ahead to J. Alfred Prufrock as the representative character type bourgeois culture ultimately produces, it appears conceivable that histories which highlight increased emotional bonding in bourgeois culture are highlighting the fabric of an ideological cover which stands at a measurable distance from social reality.[26]

Memoirs, through its satirical form, not only uses the bourgeois remapping of maternal relations to cast a general shadow over the sentimental claims of bourgeois society, but again shows how such a remapping becomes naturalized through repetition. After Mr. Norbert's death, Fanny has achieved some measure of financial independence, but now feels pointedly the "vacancy from any regular employ of my person." Hence, in a move which appears quite natural in the context of *Memoirs,* she returns to her surrogate mother, and becomes the space of transaction between Mrs. Cole and Mr. Barvile.

In the Barvile episode Fanny refers to Mrs. Cole as "my good temporal mother." "Temporal" only occurs one other time in the text, in connection with the homosexual scene. That scene is thus brought into an uneasy contiguity with the mothers-and-daughters pattern,[27] and a networking of references gives a new twist to the "maternity" recoding. The word "temporal," first of all, carries with it both the connotation of divine authorization and the connotation of someone in an intermediate or interim position. Had Fanny been the "temporal instrument" of vengeance against the homosexuals, the implication is that she would have been the temporal instrument of divine justice. By the same token, the identification of Mrs. Cole as "my good temporal mother" places her into the role of a surrogate mother authorized, as it were, from above. In fact, the Barvile scene ratifies the authority of the surrogate mother, while the homosexual scene shows that the mother herself holds a very tenuous and intermediate place in the world of *Memoirs.*

Fanny prefaces the Barvile episode with the comment that

her "good temporal mother" kindly used "all the arguments she could imagine to dissuade me: but as I found they only turn'd on a motive of tenderness in me, I persisted in my resolution." Considering the financial benefits awaiting the shrewd Mrs. Cole, the sincerity of her dissuasive arguments is doubtful. In any event, Fanny herself refers to the rest of the paragraph as a "preamble of encouragement." It seems that Mrs. Cole's hidden agenda is to keep her "only daughter," as she fancies Fanny, under full maternal control. The supposedly dissuasive arguments are part and parcel of her strategies of subjection, and the adjectival attribution of "temporal mother" marks the success of those strategies.

The diction of the Barvile episode ratifies the suggestion that the "temporal mother" role involves a crucial element of subjection. Although Fanny characteristically draws metaphors from the professions of her partners, Barvile has no expressed profession, and the episode is played out in the religious vocabulary of guilt, penitence, and subjection.[28] The sexual act is a "ceremonial" effected by "instruments of discipline" and "lashes" of "the rod." Barvile's penis is "asham'd," and "legions of . . . spirits" possess Fanny's vagina. Fanny at first "repent[s]" and then becomes "careless how much my flesh might suffer."

Meanwhile, Mrs. Cole, who had watched "from her stand of espial" and "to whom this adventrous [*sic*] exploit had more and more endear'd me, look'd on me now as a girl after her own heart, afraid of nothing." The implication is that the "temporal mother" of eighteenth-century London has a peculiar interest in the subjection of the daughter, an implication seconded by Fanny's remark that Mrs. Cole was known to preach "very pathetically the doctrine of passive obedience." In a world where the concrete human bond called "maternal" is displaced by a purely economic relation, strategies of subjection covertly displace sentiment in the foreground of maternal behavior.[29] I should add that I am not much interested in the empirical veracity of such claims about eighteenth-century maternal relations. What is important to me is the manner in which *Memoirs* participates in the ideological construction of bourgeois reality, and politically situates itself relative to that construction by way of its satirical form.

The homosexual scene, after which Mrs. Cole discourages Fanny from being the "temporal instrument" of vengeance, is noteworthy for the loathing it elicits in Fanny and Mrs. Cole, the woman of whom Fanny says "there were no lengths in lewdness she would not advise me to go." In a book, moreover, which apparently finds Phoebe's lesbianism rather harmless, if not altogether satisfying, the homophobia calls attention to itself. Homosexuality is the one variant of sexuality which apparently must be "abjected" from Fanny's world.[30] Each recoding of conceptual space involves the exclusionary coding of what is to be considered "filth," "defiling," "abject." Homosexuality, by way of exclusion in *Memoirs*, defines the limits of the bourgeois coding of the "clean and proper" sexual body. Fanny, in fact, frames the passage with an emphasis on abjecting the filth homosexuality presumably represents. She introduces the scene by saying that "I will here set down [the incident], that I may not return again to so disagreeable a subject"; and she ends the scene by "washing my hands of them [the homosexuals]."

Eve Sedgwick notes two crucial developments in the concept of "homosexuality" occurring around the time of the Restoration: "First, the emergence of a distinct gay male subculture; second . . . the formulation of a homophobic ideology in terms that were secular and descriptive enough to seem to offer the English public a usable set of cognitive categories for their day-to-day experience."[31] Although we can presume that there have been sex acts between men from time immemorial, "homosexuality" was codified into a peculiarly modern category with clear edges and a clear social significance only in the late seventeenth century.

The abjection of homosexuality, and the consequent need to silence it (Mrs. Cole says that "the less said of it was the better)", may lie in the fact that it betrays the problematic coding of sexuality, and of maternity, in bourgeois conceptual space. It first of all betrays the fact that sexual relations are coded as transactions

between males, and that the female is at best the space of transaction.[32] Thus homosexuality becomes a visible index which represents the underside of all the supposedly "normal" sexual
transactions in *Memoirs*. It is the abjected self of bourgeois sexuality and must be identified as such in order that Fanny may
"wash her hands" of it.

Mrs. Cole's homophobia can be explained by the fact that homosexuality also betrays the problematic coding of maternity.
The homosexual act is perceived as an act through which the
male appropriates the "maternal" function: "If he was like his
mother behind, he was like his father before." If the daughter
had become the mere commercial space of mother-client transactions, now the mother herself is seen as merely a commercial
placeholder. The emerging ideology calls on the mother not to
guarantee the continuity of landed estates, but to guarantee the
new economic system by providing commercialized female
space.

With this problematic coding of maternity, the two senses of
"temporal" merge. The coding of the mother as "temporal"
grants her the semblance of absolute authority with which to
subject the daughter. But that authority is betrayed as a product
of her "intermediate" position in the larger system of subjection.
The more the maternal bond becomes reified into a purely commercial relation, the more it relies on subjection rather than sentiment (or, subjection under the rhetorical cover of sentiment).
But the more comfortable the mother becomes with the new
coding of maternity, the more she participates in her own coding as commercial space, and provider of commercial space, for
male transactions. Maternity itself becomes coded as a "temporal" function, the mother as a mediary of male exchanges, and
the "bawd" as the symbolic prototype for bourgeois maternity.[33]

With maternity in this precarious position, Mrs. Cole's maternal (i.e., commercial) relations with her "daughters" rather
rapidly dissolve. She loses Louisa in the next scene, and Emily
and Fanny in the following scene. Maternity is virtually threat-
ened with extinction at this point in *Memoirs*, only to be revived

in a rather unsettling way in Fanny's reunion with Charles. In the reunion scene, Charles becomes the anchor for the whole series of surrogate mothers. The scene begins with Fanny's recalling how her vaginal lips owed their "first breathing to this dear instrument [Charles's penis]." After this figural birth, the penis becomes a mother-figure in earnest: "[I] exert[ed] all those springs of the compressive exsuction, with which the sensitive mechanism of that part thirstily draws and drains the nipple of Love, with much such an instinctive eagerness, and attachment, as, to compare great with less, kind nature engages infants at the breast, by the pleasure they find in the motion of their little mouths and cheeks, to extract the milky stream prepar'd for their nourishment." There are two readings of the equation established here between the penis and the maternal breast. The first, in line with Nancy K. Miller's argument that the text as a whole "glorifies the phallus,"[34] would suggest that the coding of maternity in *Memoirs* leads to a ratification of male prerogatives. So long as maternity remains a relation between females, it has no legitimate place in the eighteenth-century world of London as it appears in *Memoirs*. The female mother occupies virtually the same categorical space as "bawd" in this coding. Hence, maternity can only be legitimated insofar as it is appropriated by the male. The daughter must turn to the male not only for sexual fulfillment, not only for completion of identity, but for maternal fulfillment as well. A second and more comprehensive reading would suggest that the male as well as the mother is reified in this passage. Charles's value in the economy of *Memoirs* is that of the usable penis, and in this case, the penis which can be used as a substitute for the missing maternal bond.

Through the mothers-and-daughters pattern, Cleland articulates the threat posed by a bourgeois recoding of "maternity." With the remapping of human beings onto a field of marketable attributes, with the remapping of social relations into relations between things, the maternal bond is in danger of becoming a purely commercial relation, and one which as such relies more and more on subjection rather than sentiment for its cohesive force. The problematic resolution of the pattern suggests that Cleland is at once crystallizing the restructured concept of "mother," and questioning its validity.

Clarifying Cleland's position relative to the configuration of ideologies available to him in the mid-eighteenth century allows us to clarify the position of *Memoirs* in cultural history. Braudy's emphasis, for example, on "the egalitarian possibilities of sexuality" can be seen as the "crystallization" tier of a project which crystallizes and debunks bourgeois ideological structures. The reading best championed by Miller, which argues that *Memoirs* glorifies the phallus, can also be recontextualized. *Memoirs* may indeed leave general patriarchal paradigms intact, but it deliberately mocks *bourgeois* strategies of privileging the phallus. Moreover, the bourgeois glorification of the phallus involves codings of sexuality, female identity, and maternity which are sometimes comical and sometimes troubling but nearly always demonstrably unacceptable in the deeper strata of *Memoirs*.

Memoirs's place in the history of pornography is best articulated by David Foxon in *Libertine Literature in England, 1660–1745*. Despite the rising popularity of French and Italian pornography from 1660–1745, Foxon cites *Memoirs* as "the first original English prose pornography, and the first to break away from the dialogue form into the style of the novel."[35] In the present context, it is *Memoirs*'s more specific status as satirical novel that controls the ideological operations under consideration. Whereas we saw that on the social level of the satire, prostitution was used to represent bourgeois social relations unmasked, on the level of genre we might see the pornographic novel as an unmasking of the bourgeois novel, and pornographic discourse in general as the abjected self of the bourgeois cultural narrative.[36] Stewart, for example, argues that pornography, unlike older forms of obscenity, views people as mere organs, and was "not even ideologically possible before the rise of capitalism."[37] Pornography, as we know it today, may be one of the by-products of the bourgeois cultural narrative, but it is the one which must be abjected, the one which, by way of exclusion, defines the "decent" bour-

geois narrative. Thus *Memoirs*'s satirical use of its pornographic
materials, and its ideological project of crystallization and sub-
version, must ultimately be seen as one moment in a larger and
loosely connected pattern of bourgeois discourses.

NOTES

1. All quantitative data concerning these patterns is from *A KWIC Concordance to John Cleland's Memoirs of a Woman of Pleasure*, ed. Samuel S. Coleman and Michael J. Preston (New York: Garland Publishing, 1988).
2. For the specifics of that praise, see William H. Epstein, *John Cleland: Images of a Life* (New York: Columbia Univ. Press, 1974), pp. 112–6.
3. A more detailed study could be made of relationships between "prospect" and such synonyms as "view" and "landscape." "Prospect," in the present study, is a particularly useful word because it occurs only eleven times in the singular and plural, and its meanings fall rather neatly into three related categories. "View," by contrast, occurs sixty-six times, with much greater semantic variation, including nominal senses extraneous to the present argument (as in the sense of "opinion"), and verbal senses (as in "to look at") which network it into a separate pattern of synonymous verbs ("survey," "stare," "gaze," etc.). "Landscape," on the other hand, occurs only three times (including variant "landskip"), each time in reference to the female body, and hence does not offer the full range of relations seen in the use of "prospect."
4. Ann Bermingham, *Landscape and Ideology: The English Rustic Tradition, 1740–1860* (Berkeley: Univ. of California Press, 1986), p. 9.
5. Christopher Hussey, *The Picturesque: Studies in a Point of View* (London: G. P. Putnam's and Sons, 1927), pp. 2–12 and passim. See also Samuel Holt Monk's chapter, "The Sublime in Natural Scenery," in *The Sublime* (New York: Modern Language Association, 1935), pp. 203–32.
6. James Turner, *The Politics of Landscape: Rural Scenery and Society in English Poetry, 1630–1660* (Cambridge MA: Harvard Univ. Press, 1979), pp. 8–9 and passim.

7. All citations of *Memoirs* are from John Cleland, *Memoirs of a Woman of Pleasure,* ed. Peter Sabor (Oxford: Oxford Univ. Press, 1985).

8. John Hollander, "The Old Last Act: Some Observations on *Fanny Hill,*" *Encounter* 21, 4 (October 1963): 69–77, 74.

9. Douglas Brooks-Davies, "The Mythology of Venerean (and Related) Iconography in Pope, Fielding, Cleland, and Sterne," in *Sexuality in Eighteenth-Century Britain,* ed. Paul-Gabriel Boucé (Totowa NJ: Barnes and Noble, 1982), pp. 176–97.

10. Douglas J. Stewart, "Pornography, Obscenity, and Capitalism," *Antioch Review* 35, 4 (Fall 1977): 389–98, 389–90.

11. Leo Braudy, *"Fanny Hill* and Materialism," *ECS* 4, 1 (Fall 1970): 21–40, 37.

12. Braudy, p. 36.

13. See Ann Louise Kibbie's related discussion of "the interchangeability of metaphoric terms in Fanny Hill's commercial and sexual transactions" ("Sentimental Properties: *Pamela* and *Memoirs of a Woman of Pleasure,*" *ELH* 58, 3 [Fall 1991]: 561–77, 570).

14. Karl Marx, *Capital,* ed. Frederick Engels, trans. Samuel Moore and Edward Aveling (New York: Random House, 1906), p. 83.

15. Turner, p. 6.

16. Bermingham, p. 135.

17. On the eighteenth-century commodification of nature, see George H. Stankey, "Beyond the Campfire's Light: Historical Roots of the Wilderness Concept," *Natural Resources Journal* 29, 1 (Winter 1989): 9–24. Stankey argues that as nature became increasingly perceived as an aesthetic object rather than a threat in the eighteenth century, "the commodity of wild nature came to be highly valued" (p. 16).

18. Here Cleland is upsetting the traditional association of flowers with females, again crystallizing the emerging ideology of egalitarianism, and displaying the objectification of the human being— and perhaps the inherent hypocrisy—commensurate with that ideology.

19. Cf. Michel Foucault's discussion of "the injunction, so peculiar to the West . . . [of] transforming sex into discourse" (*History of Sexuality,* trans. Robert Hurley, 3 vols. [New York: Vintage, 1978], 1:20).

20. Of the sixteen occurrences of "center" (with variants), fifteen refer to the vagina and one to the central article of a business

transaction involving Fanny's counterfeit maidenhead. Of the ten occurrences of "seat" (with variants, including "Queen-seat," which is not cross-referenced in the concordance), six have sexual referents, all of which are vaginal.

21. Epstein cites evidence that Cleland's attitude toward the social injustices suffered by women is self-conscious and sympathetic (pp. 92, 97–9).

22. See Nancy K. Miller's related discussion of the "economy of romance," in which the female sacrifices all in gratitude for the male lover's affections (*The Heroine's Text* [New York: Columbia Univ. Press, 1974], p. 58).

23. B. Slepian and L. J. Morrissey, "What is *Fanny Hill?*" *EIC* 14, 1 (January 1964): 65–75, 68.

24. Lawrence Stone, *The Family, Sex, and Marriage in England, 1500–1800* (London: Weidenfeld and Nicolson, 1977); Leonore Davidoff and Catherine Hall, *Family Fortunes: Men and Women of the English Middle Class, 1780–1850* (Chicago: Univ. of Chicago Press, 1987), especially chap. 7.

25. Barbara A. Hanawalt explicitly takes Stone (among others) to task on this score in *Growing Up in Medieval London: The Experience of Childhood in History* (Oxford: Oxford Univ. Press, 1993), especially pp. 6–7.

26. Tony Tanner, conversely, argues that increased intrafamilial emotional densities do characterize the bourgeois family in fact as well as in rhetoric, but sees this in a darker light than Stone. Tanner describes the bourgeois home as "a hothouse of desire" linked to a "dangerous . . . potentiality for introducing a generalized sense of lack that cannot be filled" (*Adultery in the Novel* [Baltimore: Johns Hopkins Univ. Press, 1979], p. 100).

27. Preston, in the introduction to the concordance, establishes another verbal link between the two episodes. Barvile "lean'd his head against the back of a chair," and one of the homosexuals "lean'd his head against the back of it [a chair]."

28. Insofar as Cleland gives Barvile a "bowl-dish" haircut in the manner of "the *Round-heads*" he may be seen as a designated Puritan. If Fanny represents Pamela-unmasked, Barvile may thus represent Puritanism-unmasked. Including an anti-Puritan episode would not only serve the interests of the pornographer, but would also support my reading of *Memoirs* as consistently derisive toward

bourgeois and progressive cultural formations, and generally sympathetic to landed and conservative ideologies.

29. Although my interest is in maternal relations, more than maternity is at stake. The general eighteenth-century interest in "sentiment," the "pathetic," and the power of "generous tears" (which Ian Watt attributes to Richardson's novels), may in fact betray some anxiety about the slippage of sentiment from the world of social relations in an increasingly commercialized and urbanized England.

30. On abjection, see Julia Kristeva, *The Powers of Horror: An Essay on Abjection,* trans. Leon S. Roudiez (New York: Columbia Univ. Press, 1982). Establishing the "clean and proper" boundaries of one's own ego and one's own sexual body involves a break from the initial unity in maternal identity. The break is characterized by the exclusionary coding of the mother as "defiling" to one's own identity. This abjection of the mother can also be seen as the abjection of the "defiling" aspect of one's own self which clings to the earlier maternal identity.

31. Eve Kosofsky Sedgwick, *Between Men: English Literature and Male Homosocial Desire* (New York: Columbia Univ. Press, 1985), p. 83. Sedgwick refers to Alan Bray's *Homosexuality in Renaissance England* (London: Gay Men's Press, 1982) here and throughout the chapter.

32. The idea of the female as a space of male transaction may be generally characteristic of patriarchal ideologies, but the bourgeois ideology does shift the context. In an aristocratic ideology based on a landed economy, the female is primarily the space of patrilineal generation, the space across which the family estate is perpetuated. In a bourgeois ideology, based on an economy of capital, the female becomes a space across which commercial rivalries and transactions are played out. I would argue that it is this latter coding of female sexuality which is betrayed by homosexuality in the context of *Memoirs.*

33. Although there have always been sex acts for profit, Randolph Trumbach discusses the changing significance of the concept of prostitution in the late seventeenth century ("Modern Prostitution and Gender in *Fanny Hill,*" in *Sexual Underworlds of the Enlightenment,* ed. G. S. Rousseau and Roy Porter [Chapel Hill: Univ. of North Carolina Press, 1988], pp. 69–85). From the 1690s onward, Trumbach cites "a new kind of prostitution" associated with the

commercialized urban centers and categorically separate from the more general "whore," a term which traditionally included adultresses and any other women who were perceived as being promiscuous (p. 73).

34. Nancy K. Miller, " 'I's' in Drag: The Sex of Recollection," *The Eighteenth Century: Theory and Interpretation* 22, 1 (Winter 1981): 47–57, 54.

35. David Foxon, *Libertine Literature in England, 1660–1745* (New Hyde Park NY: University Books, 1965), p. 45.

36. On pornography's relation to the bourgeois or sentimental novel, see Kibbie, esp. p. 570; Steven Marcus, *The Other Victorians: A Study of Sexuality and Pornography in Mid-Nineteenth-Century England* (New York: Basic Books, 1974); Robert Darnton, *The Literary Underground of the Old Regime* (Cambridge MA: Harvard Univ. Press, 1982); James Turner, "The Properties of Libertinism," in *'Tis Nature's Fault: Unauthorized Sexuality during the Enlightenment*, ed. Robert Purks Maccubbin (Cambridge: Cambridge Univ. Press, 1987), pp. 75–87; Myron Taube, "*Moll Flanders* and *Fanny Hill:* A Comparison," *Ball State University Forum* 9, 2 (Spring 1968): 76–80; and Edward W. Copeland, "*Clarissa* and *Fanny Hill:* Sisters in Distress," *SNNTS* 4, 3 (Fall 1972): 343–52.

37. Stewart, pp. 397–8.

FANNY HILL

OR,

MEMOIRS OF A WOMAN OF PLEASURE

Volume I

Madam,

Sit down to give you an undeniable proof of my considering
your desires as indispensible orders: ungracious then as the task
may be, I shall recall to view those scandalous stages of my life,
out of which I emerg'd at length, to the enjoyment of every
blessing in the power of love, health, and fortune to bestow;
whilst yet in the flower of youth, and not too late to employ the
leisure afforded me by great ease and affluence, to cultivate an
understanding naturally not a despicable one, and which had,
even amidst the whirl of loose pleasures I had been tost in, exerted more observation on the characters and manners of the
world, than what is common to those of my unhappy profession,
who looking on all thought or reflexion as their capital enemy,
keep it at as great a distance as they can, or destroy it without
mercy.[1]

Hating, as I mortally do, all long unnecessary prefaces, I shall
give you good quarter in this, and use no farther apology, than to
prepare you for seeing the loose part of my life, wrote with the
same liberty that I led it.

Truth! Stark naked truth, is the word, and I will not so much as take the pains to bestow the strip of a gauze-wrapper on it, but paint situations such as they actually rose to me in nature, careless of violating those laws of decency, that were never made for such unreserved intimacies as ours; and you have too much sense, too much knowledge of the *originals* themselves, to snuff prudishly, and out of character, at the *pictures* of them. The greatest men, those of the first and most leading taste, will not scruple adorning their private closets with nudities, though, in compliance with vulgar prejudices they may not think them decent decorations of the stair-case or saloon.

This, and enough, premised, I go souse[2] into my personal history. My maiden name was *Francis Hill.* I was born at a small village near *Liverpool* in *Lancashire,* of parents extremely poor, and I piously believe, extremely honest.

My father, who had received a maim on his limbs that disabled him from following the more laborious branches of country-drudgery, got, by making of nets, a scanty subsistance, which was not much enlarg'd by my mother's keeping a little day-school for the girls in her neighbourhood. They had had several children, but none lived to any age, except myself, who had received from nature a constitution perfectly healthy.

My education, till past fourteen, was no better than very vulgar; reading, or rather spelling, an illegible scrawl, and a little ordinary plain-work, composed the whole system[3] of it: and then all my foundation in virtue was no other than a total ignorance of vice, and the shy timidity general to our sex, in the tender stage of life, when objects alarm, or frighten more by their novelty, than any thing else: but then this is a fear too often cured at the expence of innocence, when Miss, by degrees, begins no longer to look on man as a creature of prey that will eat her.

My poor mother had divided her time so entirely between her scholars, and her little domestic cares, that she had spared very little of it to my instruction, having, from her own innocence from all ill, no hint, or thought of guarding me against any.

I was now entering on my fifteenth year, when the worst of ills befell me in the loss of my tender fond parents, who were both carried off by the small-pox, within a few days of each other; my father dying first, and thereby hastening the death of my mother, so that I was now left an unhappy friendless Orphan: (for my father's coming to settle there, was accidental, he being originally a *Kentish-man.*) That cruel distemper which had proved so fatal to them, had indeed seized me, but with such mild and favourable symptoms, that I was presently out of danger, and, what I then did not know the value of, was entirely unmark'd.[4] I skip over here, an account of the natural grief and affliction, which I felt on this melancholy occasion. A little time, and the giddiness of that age, dissipated too soon my reflections on that irreparable loss; but nothing contributed more to reconcile me to it, than the notions that were immediately put into my head, of going to *London,* and looking out for a service, in which I was promised all assistance and advice, from one *Esther Davis,* a young woman that had been down to see her friends, and who, after the stay of a few days, was to return to her place.

As I had now nobody left alive in the village, who had concern enough about what should become of me, to start any objections to this scheme, and the woman who took care of me after my parents' death rather encouraged me to pursue it, I soon came to a resolution of making this launch into the wide world, by repairing to *London,* in order to *seek my fortune,* a phrase, which, by the bye, has ruined more adventurers of both sexes, from the country, than ever it made, or advanced.

Nor did *Esther Davis* a little comfort and inspirit me to venture with her, by piquing my childish curiosity with the fine sights that were to be seen in *London;* the Tombs, the Lions, the King, the Royal Family, the fine Plays and *Operies,* and in short all the diversions which fell within her sphere of life to come at; the detail of all which perfectly turn'd the little head of me.

Nor can I remember, without laughing, the innocent admiration, not without a spice of envy, with which we poor girls, whose church-going cloaths did not rise above dowlass shifts, and stuff gowns,[5] beheld *Esther's* scower'd sattin-gown, caps border'd with an inch of lace; taudry ribbons, and shoes belaced with silver! all which we imagined grew in *London,* and entered for a great deal into my determination of trying to come in for my share of them.

The idea however of having the company of a townswoman with her, was the trivial, and all the motive that engaged *Esther* to take charge of me during my journey to town, where she told me, after her manner and style: "*as how several maids out of the country had made themselves and all their kin for ever, that by preserving their* VARTUE,[6] *some had taken so with their masters, that they had married them, and kept them coaches, and lived vastly grand, and happy, and some, may-hap came to be Dutchesses: Luck was all, and why not I as well as another,*" with other almanacs to this purpose, which set me a tiptoe to begin this promising journey, and to leave a place, which though my native one, contained no relations that I had reason to regret, and was grown insupportable to me, from the change of the tenderest usage into a cold air of charity, with which I was entertain'd, even at the only friend's house, that I had the least expectations of care and protection from: She was however so just to me, as to manage the turning into money the little matters that remained to me after the debts, and burial-charges were accounted for, and at my departure put my whole fortune into my hands, which consisted of a very slender wardrobe, pack'd up in a very portable box, and eight guineas, with seventeen shillings in silver, stowed in a spring-pouch, which was a greater treasure than ever I had yet seen together, and which I could not conceive there was a possibility of running out: and indeed I was so entirely taken up with the joy of seeing myself mistress of such an immense sum, that I gave very little attention to a world of good advice which was given me with it.

Places then being taken for *Esther* and me, in the *Chester*-Waggon, I pass over a very immaterial scene of leave-taking, at which I dropt a few tears betwixt grief and joy; and for the same reasons of insignificance, skip over all that happened to me on the road, such as the Waggoner's looking liquorish[7] on me, the schemes laid for me by some of the passengers, which were defeated by the vigilance of my guardian *Esther,* who, to do her justice, took a motherly care of me, at the same time that she taxed me for her protection, by making me bear all travelling charges, which I defray'd with the utmost chearfulness, and thought myself much obliged to her into the bargain. She took indeed great care that we were not over-rated, or imposed on, as well as of managing as frugally as possible: expensiveness was not her vice.

It was pretty late in a summer evening when we reached the town, in our slow conveyance, though drawn by six at length. As we passed thro' the greatest streets that led to our inn, the noise of the coaches, the hurry, the crowds of foot passengers, in short, the new scenery of the shops and houses at once pleased and amazed me.

But guess at my mortification and surprize when we came to the inn, and our things were landed, and deliver'd to us, when my fellow traveller and protectress, *Esther Davis*, who had used me with the utmost tenderness during the journey, and prepared me by no preceding signs for the stunning blow I was to receive; when, I say, my only dependance, and friend, in this strange place, all of a sudden assumed a strange and cool air towards me, as if she dreaded my becoming a burden to her.

Instead then of proffering me the continuance of her assistance and good offices, which I relied upon, and never more wanted, she thought herself, it seems, abundantly acquitted of her engagements to me, by having brought me safe to my journey's end, and seeing nothing in her procedure towards me, but what was natural and in order, begun to embrace me, by way of taking leave, whilst I was so confounded, so struck, that I had not spirit or sense enough so much as to mention my hopes or expectations from her experience, and knowledge of the place she had brought me to.

Whilst I stood thus stupid and mute, which she doubtless attributed to nothing more than a concern at parting, this idea procured me perhaps, a slight alleviation of it, in the following harrangue: "That now we were got safe to *London,* and that she was obliged to go to her place, she advised me by all means to get into one as soon as possible——That I need not fear getting one—there were more places than parish-churches—that she advised me to go to an intelligence-office[8]——that if she heard

of any thing stirring, she would find me out, and let me know.——
——that in the mean time I should take a private lodging, and acquaint her where to send to me,——that she wish'd me good
luck,——and hop'd I should always have the grace to keep myself
honest, and not bring a disgrace on my parentage:" with this she
took her leave of me, and left me, as it were, on my own hands,
full as lightly as I had been put into hers.

Left thus alone, absolutely distitute and friendless, I began
then to feel most bitterly the severity of this separation, the
scene of which had past in a little room in the inn: and no sooner
was her back turned, but the affliction I felt at my helpless strange
circumstances, burst out into a flood of tears, which infinitely relieved the oppression of my heart; though I still remained stupi-
fied, and most perfectly perplex'd how to dispose of myself.

One of the drawers[9] coming in, added yet more to my uncertainty, by asking me, in a short way, if I called for any thing? to
which I replied, innocently, *No;* but I wished him to tell me
where I might get a lodging for that night: he said, he would go
and speak to his mistress, who accordingly came, and told me
drily, without entering in the least into the distress she saw me
in, that I might have a bed for a shilling: and that, as she supposed I had some friends in town (here I fetched a deep sigh in
vain!) I might provide myself in the morning.

'Tis incredible what trifling consolations the human mind
will seize in its greatest afflictions. The assurance of nothing
more than a bed to lie on that night, calmed my agonies; and
being asham'd to acquaint the mistress of the inn that I had no
friends to apply to in town, I proposed to myself to proceed, the
very next morning, to an intelligence-office, to which I was
furnish'd with written directions, on the back of a ballad of *Esther*'s giving me. There I counted on getting information of any
place that such a country-girl as I might be fit for, and where I
could get into any sort of being, before my little stock should be
consumed: and as to a character, *Esther* had often repeated to me,
that I might depend on her managing me one; nor, however affected I was at her leaving me thus, did I entirely cease to rely on

her, as I began to think, good-naturedly, that her procedure was all in course, and that it was only my ignorance of life that had made me take it in the light I at first did.

Accordingly, the next morning, I dress'd me as clean and as neat as my rustic wardrobe would permit me; and having left my box, with special recommendation, to the landlady, I ventured out by myself, and without any more difficulty than may be supposed of a young country-girl, barely fifteen, and to whom every sign or shop was a gazing-trap, I got to the wish'd-for intelligence-office.

It was kept by an elderly woman, who sat at the receipt of custom,[10] with a book before her, in great form and order, and several scrolls, ready made out, of directions for places.

I made up then to this important personage, without lifting up my eyes, or observing any of the people round me, who were attending there on the same errand as myself, and dropping her curtsies nine-deep, made just a shift to stammer out my business to her.

Madam having heard me out, with all the gravity and brow of a petty-minister of state, and seeing, at one glance over my figure, what I was, made me no answer, but to ask me the preliminary shilling, on receipt of which she told me, places for women were exceeding scarce, especially as I seemed too slight-built for hard work; but that she would look over her book, and see what was to be done for me, desiring me to stay a little till she had dispatched some other customers.

On this, I drew back a little, most heartily mortified at a declaration which carried with it a killing uncertainty, that my circumstances could not well endure.

Presently, assuming more courage, and seeking some diversion from my uneasy thoughts, I ventured to lift up my head a little, and sent my eyes on a course round the room, where they met full-tilt with those of a lady (for such my extreme innocence pronounc'd her) sitting in a corner of the room, dress'd in a velvet manteel[11] (*nota bene,* in the midst of summer) with her bonnet off; squob-fat,[12] red faced, and at least fifty.

She look'd as if she would devour me with her eyes, staring at

me from head to foot, without the least regard to the confusion
and blushes her eying me so fixedly put me to, and which were
to her, no doubt, the strongest recommendation, and marks of
my being fit for her purpose. After a little time, in which my air,
person, and whole figure, had undergone her strict examination,
which I had, on my part, tried to render favourable to me, by
primming, drawing up my neck, and *setting* my best looks, she
advanc'd, and spoke to me with the greatest demureness:

"Sweet-heart, do you want a place?"

"Yes! and please you." (with a curtsy down to the ground.)

Upon this, she acquainted me, that she was actually come to
the office herself, to look out for a servant—that she believed I
might do, with a little of her instructions,——that she could
take my very looks for a sufficient character,———that *London*
was a very wicked, vile place,——that she hop'd I would be
tractable, and keep out of bad company,—in short, she said all to
me that an old experienced practitioner in town could think of,
and which was much more than was necessary to take in an artless unexperienced country-maid, who was even afraid of becoming a wanderer about the streets, and therefore gladly
jump'd at the first offer of a shelter, especially from so grave and
matron-like a *lady*, for such my flattering fancy assur'd me this
now mistress of mine was: I being actually hired under the nose
of the good woman that kept the office, whose shrewd smiles and
shrugs I could not help observing, and innocently interpreted
them as marks of her being pleased at my getting into place so
soon: but, as I afterwards came to know, these *Beldams* understood one another very well, and this was a market where Mrs.
Brown (my mistress) frequently attended, on the watch for any
fresh goods that might offer there, for the use of her customers,
and her own profit.

Madam was, however, so well pleased with her bargain, that,
fearing, I presume, lest better advice, or some accident might occasion my slipping through her fingers, she would officiously
take me in a coach to my inn, where calling herself for my box,
it was, I being present, delivered without the least scruple, or explanation as to where I was going.

This being over, she bid the coachman drive to a shop in St. *Paul*'s churchyard, where she bought a pair of gloves, which she gave me, and thence renew'd her directions to the coachman, to drive to her house in ——*street,* who accordingly landed us at her door, after I had been chear'd up, and entertain'd by the way with the most plausible flams, without one syllable from which I could conclude any thing but that I was by the greatest good luck fallen into the hands of the kindest mistress, not to say friend, that the *varsal* world could afford; and accordingly I enter'd her doors with most complete confidence and exultation, promising myself, that, as soon as I should be a little settled, I would acquaint *Esther Davis* with my rare good fortune.

You may be sure the good opinion of my place was not less-ened by the appearance of a very handsome back-parlour, into which I was led, and which seemed to me magnificently fur-nished, who had never seen better rooms than the ordinary ones in inns upon the road. There were two gilt pier-glasses, and a buffet, in which a few pieces of plate, set out to the most shew, dazzled, and altogether persuaded me, that I must be got into a very reputable family.

Here my mistress first began her part, with telling me, that I must have good spirits, and learn to be free with her; that she had not taken me to be a common servant, to do domestic drudgery, but to be a kind of companion to her; and that, if I would be a good girl, she would do more than twenty mothers for me; to all which I answered only by the profoundest and the awkwardest curtsies, and a few monosyllables, such as yes! no! to be sure.

Presently my mistress touch'd the bell, and in came a strap-ping maid-servant, who had let us in: Here, *Martha,* said Mrs. *Brown,* I have just hir'd this young woman to look after my lin-nen, so step up, and shew her her chamber; and I charge you to use her with as much respect as you would myself, for I have taken a prodigious liking to her, and I do not know what I shall do for her.

Martha, who was an arch jade, and being used to this decoy, had her cue perfect, made me a kind of half curtsy, and asked me to walk up with her, and accordingly shew'd me a neat room two pair of stairs backwards, in which there was a handsome bed, where *Martha* told me I was to *lay* with a young gentlewoman, a cousin of my mistress's, who she was sure would be vastly good to me: then she ran out into such affected encomiums on her good mistress! her sweet mistress! and how happy I was to light upon her,—that I could not have bespoke a better,—with other the like gross stuff, such as would itself have started suspicions in any but such an unpractised simpleton who was perfectly new to life, and who took every word she said, in the very sense she laid out for me to take it; but she readily saw what a penetration she had to deal with, and measured me very rightly in her manner of whistling to me, so as to make me pleased with my cage, and blind to its wires.

In the midst of these false explanations of the nature of my future service, we were rung for down again, and I was reintroduced into the same parlour, where there was a table laid with three covers; and my mistress had now got with her one of her favourite girls, a notable manager of her house, and whose business it was to prepare and break such young Fillies as I was to the mounting-block: and she was accordingly, in that view, allotted me for a bed-fellow; and to give her the more authority, she had the title of cousin confer'd on her by the venerable president of this college.

Here I underwent a second survey, which ended in the full approbation of Mrs. *Phœbe Ayres,* the name of my tuteress elect, to whose care and instructions I was affectionately recommended.

Dinner was now set on the table, and in pursuance of treating me as a companion, Mrs. *Brown,* with a tone to cut off all dispute, soon over-rul'd all my most humble and most confused protestations against sitting down with her *Ladyship,* which my very short breeding just suggested to me could not be right, or in the order of things.

At table, the conversation was chiefly kept up by the two madams, and carried on in double-meaning expressions, interrupted every now and then by kind assurances to me, all tending to confirm and fix my satisfaction with my present condition: augment it they could not, so very a novice was I then.

It was here agreed, that I should keep myself up, and out of sight for a few days, till such cloaths could be procured for me, as were fit for the character I was to appear in, of my mistress's companion, observing withall, that on the first impressions of my figure, much might depend; and, as they well judged, the prospect of exchanging my country cloaths for *London* finery, made the clause of confinement digest perfectly well with me. But the truth was, Mrs. *Brown* did not care that I should be seen or talked to by any, either of her customers, or her *Does,* (as they call'd the girls provided for them) till she had secured a good market for my maidenhead, which I had at least all the appearances of having brought into her *ladyship*'s service.

To slip over minutes[13] of no importance to the main of my story, I pass the interval to bed-time, in which I was more and more pleased with the views that open'd to me of an easy service under these good people: and after supper, being shew'd up to bed, Miss *Phœbe,* who observed a kind of modest reluctance in me to strip, and go to bed in my shift before her, now the maid was withdrawn, came up to me, and beginning with unpinning my handkerchief, and gown, soon encouraged me to go on with undressing myself, and, still blushing at now seeing myself naked to my shift, I hurried to get under the bed-cloaths, out of sight. *Phœbe* laugh'd, and was not long before she placed herself by my side. She was about five and twenty, by her own most suspicious account, in which, according to all appearances, she must have sunk at least ten good years, allowance too being made for the havoc which a long course of hacney-ship, and hot waters, must have made of her constitution, and which had already brought on, upon the spur, that stale stage, in which those of her profession are reduced to think of *showing* company, instead of *seeing* it.

No sooner then was this precious substitute of my mistress's lain down, but she, who was never out of her way when any occasion of lewdness presented itself, turned to me, embraced, and kiss'd me with great eagerness. This was new, this was odd; but imputing it to nothing but pure kindness, which, for ought I knew, it might be the *London* way to express in that manner, I was determin'd not to be behind-hand with her, and returned her the kiss and embrace, with all the fervour that perfect innocence knew.

Encouraged by this, her hands became extremely free, and wander'd over my whole body, with touches, squeezes, pressures, that rather warm'd and surpriz'd me with their novelty, than they either shock'd or alarm'd me.

The flattering praises she intermingled with these invasions, contributed also not a little to bribe my passiveness, and knowing no ill, I fear'd none; especially from one who had prevented all doubt of her womanhood, by conducting my hands to a pair of breasts that hung loosely down, in a size and volume that full sufficiently distinguished her sex, to me at least, who had never made any other comparison.

I lay then all tame and passive as she could wish, whilst her freedom, raised no other emotion but those of a strange, and till then unfelt pleasure: every part of me was open, and exposed to the licentious courses of her hands, which like a lambent fire ran over my whole body, and thaw'd all coldness as they went.

My breasts, if it is not too bold a figure to call so, two hard, firm, rising hillocs, that just began to shew themselves, or signify any thing to the touch, employ'd and amused her hands a while, till slipping down lower, over a smooth track, she could just feel the soft silky down that had but a few months before put forth, and garnish'd the mount-pleasant of those parts, and promised to spread a grateful shelter over the sweet seat of the most exquisite sensation, and which had been, till that instant, the seat of the most insensible innocence. Her fingers play'd, and strove to twine in the young tendrils of that moss which nature has contrived at once for use and ornament.

But not contented with these outer posts, she now attempts the main-spot, and began to twitch, to insinuate, and at length to force an introduction of a finger into the quick itself, in such a manner, that had she not proceeded by insensible gradations, that enflamed me beyond the power of modesty to oppose its resistence to their progress, I should have jump'd out of bed, and cried out for help against such strange assaults.

Instead of which, her lascivious touches had lighted up a new fire that wanton'd through all my veins, but fix'd with violence in that center appointed them by nature, where the first strange hands were now busied in feeling, squeezing, compressing the lips, then opening them again, with a finger between, till an Oh! express'd her hurting me, where the narrowness of the unbroken passage refused it entrance to any depth.

In the mean time the extension of my limbs, languid stretchings, sighs, short heavings, all conspired to assure that experienced wanton, that I was more pleased than offended at her proceedings, which she seasoned with repeated kisses and exclamations, such as "Oh! what a charming creature thou art!——what a happy man will he be that first makes a woman of you!————Oh! that I were a man for your sake————!" with the like broken expressions, interrupted by kisses as fierce and salacious as ever I received from the other sex.

For my part, I was transported, confused, and out of myself: Feelings so new were too much for me; my heated and alarm'd senses were in a tumult that robb'd me of all liberty of thought; tears of pleasure gush'd from my eyes, and somewhat assuaged the fire that rag'd all over me.

Phœbe herself, the hackney'd, thorough bred *Phœbe*, to whom all modes and devices of pleasure were known and familiar, found, it seems, in this exercise of her art to break young girls, the gratification of one of those arbitrary tastes, for which there is no accounting:[14] not that she hated men, or did not even prefer them to her own sex; but when she met with such occasions as this was, a satiety of enjoyments in the common road, perhaps too a secret bias, inclined her to make the most of pleasure, whereever she could find it, without distinction of sexes. In this view, now well assured that she had, by her touches, sufficiently inflamed me for her purpose, she roll'd down the bed-cloaths gently, and I saw myself stretch'd naked, my shift being turned up to my neck, whilst I had no power or sense to oppose it; even my glowing blushes expressed more desire than modesty, whilst the candle left, to be sure not undesignedly, burning, threw a full light on my whole body.

"No! (says *Phœbe*) you must not, my sweet girl, think to hide all these treasures from me, my sight must be feasted as well as my touch—I must devour with my eyes this springing bosom, — —suffer me to kiss it—I have not seen it enough————let me kiss it once more——what firm, smooth, white flesh is here—— ————how delicately shaped!——then this delicious down! Oh! let me view the small, dear, tender cleft!—this is too much, I cannot bear it, I must, I must————." Here she took my hand, and, in a transport, carried it where you will easily guess; but what a difference in the state of the same thing!——a spreading thicket of bushy curls mark'd the full-grown complete woman: then the cavity, to which she guided my hand, easily received it, and as soon as she felt it within her, she moved herself to and fro, with so rapid a friction, that I presently withdrew it, wet and clammy, when instantly *Phœbe* grew more composed, after two or three sighs, and heart-fetch'd Oh's! and giving me a kiss, that seemed to exhale her soul through her lips, she replaced the bed-cloaths over us.

What pleasure she had found I will not say; but this I know, that the first sparks of kindling nature, the first ideas of pollution, were caught by me that night, and that the acquaintance and communication with the bad of our own sex, is often as fatal to innocence, as all the seductions of the other: But to go on: ——when *Phœbe* was restor'd to that calm, which I was far from the enjoyment of myself, she artfully sounded me on all the points necessary to govern the designs of my virtuous mistress on me, and by my answers, drawn from pure undissembled nature, she had no reason but to promise herself all imaginable success, so far as it depended on my ignorance, easiness, and warmth of constitution.

After a sufficient length of dialogue, my bed-fellow left me to my rest, and I fell asleep, through pure weariness, from the violent emotions I had been led into, when nature (which had been too warmly stir'd, and fermented to subside without allaying by some means or other) relieved me by one of those luscious dreams, the transports of which are scarce inferior to those of waking, real action.

In the morning I awoke, about ten, perfectly gay and refreshed; *Phœbe* was up before me, and asked me in the kindest manner how I did, how I had rested, and if I was ready for breakfast? carefully at the same time avoiding to encrease the confusion she saw I was in, at looking her in the face, by any hint of the night's bed-scene.—I told her, if she pleased, I would get up, and begin any work she would be pleased to set me about. She smil'd; presently the maid brought in the tea-equipage, and I just huddled my cloaths on, when in waddled my mistress. I expected no less than to be told of, if not chid for, my late rising, when I was agreeably disappointed by her compliments on my pure and fresh looks: "I was a bud of beauty; (this was her style) and how vastly all the fine men would admire me!" to all which my answers did not, I can assure you, wrong my breeding: they were as simple, and silly as they could wish, and, no doubt, flattered them infinitely more than had they proved me enlightened by education and knowledge of the world.

We breakfasted; and the tea-things were scarce removed, when in were brought two bundles of linen and wearing apparel; in short, all the necessaries for *rigging me out*, as they termed it, compleatly.

Imagine to yourself, madam, how my little coquet-heart flutter'd with joy at the sight of a white lute-string,[15] flower'd with silver, scoured indeed, but past on me for spick-and-span new, a Brussels-lace cap, braided shoes, and the rest in proportion, all second-hand finery, and procured instantly for the occasion, by the diligence and industry of the good Mrs. *Brown*, who had already a chapman[16] for me in the house, before whom my charms were to pass in review; for he had not only in course insisted on a previous sight of the premises, but also on immediate surrender to him, in case of his agreeing for me; concluding very wisely, that such a place as I was in, was of the hottest, to trust the keeping of such a perishable commodity in, as a maidenhead.

The care of dressing, and tricking me out for the market, was then left to *Phœbe*, who acquitted herself, if not well, at least perfectly to the satisfaction of every thing but my impatience of seeing myself dress'd. When it was over, and I view'd myself in the glass, I was, no doubt, too natural, too artless, to hide my childish joy at the change; a change in real truth for much the worse, since I must have much better become the neat easy simplicity of my rustic dress, than the awkward, untoward, taudry finery, that I could not conceal my strangeness to.[17]

Phœbe's compliments, however, in which her own share in dressing me was not forgot, did not a little confirm me in now the first notions I had ever entertained concerning my person, which, be it said without vanity, was then tolerable enough to justify a taste for me, and of which it may not be out of place here to sketch you an unflatter'd picture.

I was tall, yet not too tall of my age, which, as I before remark'd, was barely turned of fifteen, my shape perfectly straight, thin waisted, and light and free, without owing any thing to stays. My hair was a glossy auburn, and as soft as silk, flowing down my neck, in natural buckles,[18] and did not a little set off the whiteness of a smooth skin. My face was rather too ruddy, though its features were delicate, and the shape was a roundish oval, except where a pit in my chin had far from a disagreeable effect: my eyes were as black as can be imagin'd, and rather languishing than sparkling, except on certain occasions, when I have been told they struck fire fast enough: my teeth, which I ever carefully preserv'd, were small, even, and white; my bosom was finely rais'd, and one might then discern rather the promise, than the actual growth, of the round, firm breasts, that in a little time made that promise good: in short, all the points of beauty that are most universally in request, I had, or at least my vanity forbid me to appeal from the decision of our sovereign judges the men, who all, that I ever knew at least, gave it thus highly in my favour; and I met with, even in my own sex, some that were above denying me that justice, whilst others praised me yet more unsuspectedly, by endeavouring to detract from me, in points of person and figure that I obviously excelled in.—This is I own, too much, too strong of self-praise; but should I not be ungrateful to nature, and to a form to which I owe such singular blessings of pleasure and fortune, were I to suppress, through an affectation of modesty, the mention of such valuable gifts?

Well then, dress'd I was, and little did it then enter into my head that all this gay attire was no more than decking the victim out for sacrifice, whilst I innocently attributed all to sheer friendship and kindness in the sweet good Mrs. *Brown,* who, I was forgetting to mention, had, under pretence of keeping my money safe, got from me, without the least hesitation, the Driblet, (so I now call it) which remained to me after the expences of my journey.

After some little time, most agreeably spent before the glass, in scarce self-admiration, since my new dress had by much the greatest share in it, I was sent for down to the parlour, where the old lady saluted me, and wished me joy of my new cloaths, which, she was not asham'd to say, fitted me as if I had worn nothing but the finest all my life time; but what was it she could not see me silly enough to swallow? at the same time she presented me to another cousin of her own creation, an elderly gentleman, who got up at my entry into the room, and on my dropping a curtsy to him, saluted me, and seemed a little affronted that I had only presented my cheek to him; a mistake, which, if one, he immediately corrected, by glewing his lips to mine with an ardour which his figure had not at all disposed me to thank him for: his figure, I say, than which nothing could be more shocking or detestable; for ugly, and disagreeable, were terms too gentle to convey a just idea of it.

Imagine to yourself, a man rather past threescore, short and ill made, with a yellow cadaverous hue, great goggling eyes, that stared as if he was strangled; an out-mouth from two more properly tushes[19] than teeth, livid lips, and a breath like a jakes[20]; then he had a peculiar ghastliness in his grin, that made him perfectly frightful, if not dangerous to women with child; yet, made as he was thus in mock of man, he was so blind to his own staring deformities, as to think himself born for pleasing, and that no woman could see him with impunity: in consequence of which idea, he had lavished great sums on such wretches as could gain upon themselves to pretend love to his person, whilst to those who had not art or patience to dissemble the horror it inspired, he behaved even brutally. Impotence, more than necessity, made him seek in variety, the provocative that was wanting to raise him to the pitch of enjoyment, which too he often saw himself baulked of by the failure of his powers: and this always threw him into a fit of rage, which he wreak'd, as far as he durst, on the innocent objects of his fit of momentary desire.

This then was the monster to which my conscientious benefactress, who had long been his purveyor in this way, had doomed me, and sent for me down purposely for this examination: accordingly, she made me stand up before him, turned me round, unpin'd my handkerchief, remark'd to him the rise and fall, the turn, and whiteness of a bosom just beginning to fill; then made me walk, and took even a handle from the rusticity of my gait, to inflame the inventory of my charms: in short, she omitted no point of jockey-ship[21]; to which he only answer'd by gracious nods of approbation, whilst he look'd goats and monkeys at me[22]: for I sometimes stole a corner-glance at him, and, encountering his fiery eager stare, looked another way from pure horror and affright, which he, doubtless in character, attributed to nothing more than maiden modesty, or at least the affectation of it.

However, I was soon dismiss'd, and reconducted to my room, by *Phœbe*, who stuck close to me, by way of not leaving me alone, and at leisure, to make such reflections as might naturally rise to any one, not an idiot, on such a scene as I had just gone through; but to my shame be it confess'd, that such was my invincible stupidity, or rather portentous innocence, that I did not yet open my eyes on Mrs. *Brown*'s designs, and saw nothing in this titular cousin of her's, but a shocking hideous person, which did not at all concern me, unless that my gratitude for my benefactress made me extend my respect to all her cousinhood.

Phœbe, however, began to sift the state and pulses of my heart towards this monster, asking me how I should approve of such a fine gentleman for a husband? (fine gentleman, I suppose she called him, from his being daubed with lace) I answered her very naturally, that I had no thoughts of a husband; but that if I was to choose one, it should be among my own degree *sure!* so much had my aversion to that wretch's hideous figure indisposed me to all *fine gentlemen,* and confounded my ideas, as if those of that rank had been necessarily cast in the same mould that he was; but *Phœbe* was not to be beat off so, but went on with her endeavours to melt and soften me for the purposes of my reception into that hospitable house: and whilst she talked of the sex in general, she had no reason to despair of a compliance, which more than one reason shewed her would be easily enough obtained of me; but then she had too much experience not to discover that my particular fix'd aversion to that frightful cousin, would be a block not so readily to be removed, as suited with the consummation of their bargain and sale of me.

Mother *Brown* had in the mean time agreed the terms with this liquorish old goat, which I afterwards understood were to be fifty guineas peremptory for the liberty of attempting me, and a hundred more at the compleat gratification of his desires, in the triumph over my virginity: and as for me, I was to be left entirely at the discretion of his liking and generosity. This unrighteous contract being thus settled, he was so eager to be put in possession, that he insisted on being introduc'd to drink tea with me that afternoon, when we were to be left alone; nor would he hearken to the procuress's remonstrances, that I was not sufficiently prepared, and ripened for such an attack; that I was yet too green and untam'd, having been scarce twenty-four hours in her house: it is the character of lust to be impatient, and his vanity arming him against any supposition of other than the common resistance of a maid on those occasions, made him reject all proposals of delay, and my dreadful trial was thus fix'd, unknown to me that very evening.

At dinner, Mrs. *Brown* and *Phœbe* did nothing but run riot in praises of this wonderful cousin, and how happy that woman would be that he would favour with his addresses: in short, my two gossips exhausted all their rhetoric to persuade me to accept them; "that the gentleman was violently smitten with me at first sight————that he would make my fortune if I would be a good girl, and not stand in my own light————that I should trust his honour————that I should be made for ever, and have a chariot to go abroad in,"————with all such stuff as was fit to turn the head of such a silly ignorant girl as I then was: but luckily here my aversion had taken already such deep root in me, my heart was so strongly defended from him by my senses, that, wanting the art to mask my sentiments, I gave them no hopes of their employer's succeeding, at least very easily, with me. The glass too march'd pretty quick, with a view, I suppose, to make a friend of the warmth of my constitution, in the minutes of the imminent attack.

Thus they kept me pretty long at table, and about six in the evening, after I was retired to my own apartment, and the tea-board was set, enters my venerable mistress, follow'd close by that satyr, who came in grinning in a way peculiar to him, and by his odious presence confirm'd me in all the sentiments of detestation which his first appearance had given birth to.

He sat down fronting me, and all tea-time kept ogling me in a manner that gave me the utmost pain and confusion, all the marks of which he still explained to be my bashfulness, and not being used to see company.

Tea over, the commoding old lady pleaded urgent business, (which indeed was true) to go out, and earnestly desired me to entertain her cousin *kindly* till she came back, both for my own sake and her's; and then, with a "pray sir, be very good, be very tender of the sweet child," she went out of the room, leaving me staring, with my mouth open, and unprepared, by the suddenness of her departure, to oppose it.

We were now alone; and on that idea a sudden fit of trembling seized me;————I was so afraid, without a precise notion of why, and what I had to fear, that I sat on the settee, by the fireside, motionless, and petrified, without life or spirit, not knowing how to look, or how to stir.

But long I was not suffered to remain in this state of stupefaction: the monster squatted down by me on the settee, and without farther ceremony, or preamble, flings his arms about my neck, and drawing me pretty forcibly towards him, oblig'd me to receive, in spite of my struggles to disengage from him, his pestilential kisses, which quite overcame me: finding me then next to senseless and unresisting, he tears off my neck handkerchief, and laid all open there to his eyes, and hands; still I endur'd all without flinching, till embolden'd by my sufferance, and silence, (for I had not the power to speak, or cry out) he attempted to lay me down on the settee, and I felt his hand on the lower part of my naked thighs, which were cross'd, and which he endeavour'd to unlock. Oh then! I was roused out of my passive endurance, and springing from him with an activity he was not prepar'd for, threw myself at his feet, and begg'd him, in the most moving tone, not to be rude, and that he would not hurt me:———— "Hurt you, my dear! says the brute, I intend you no harm———— Has not the old lady told you that I loved you?————that I shall do handsomely by you?"————She has indeed, sir, said I; but I cannot love you, indeed I cannot!————pray, let me alone———— —yes! I will love you dearly, if you will let me alone, and go away:————but I was talking to the wind; for whether my tears, my attitude, or the disorder of my dress prov'd fresh incentives, or whether he was now under the dominion of desires he could not bridle, but snorting and foaming with lust and rage, he renews his attack, seizes me, and again attempts to extend and fix me on the settee; in which he succeeded so far as to lay me along; and even to toss my petticoats over my head, and lay my thighs bare, which I obstinately kept close, nor could he, though he attempted with his knee to force them open, effect it so as to stand fair for being master of the main avenue: he was unbuttoned, both waistcoat and breeches, yet I only felt the weight of his body upon me, whilst I lay struggling with indignation, and dying with terrors; but he stopt all of a sudden, and got off, panting, blowing, cursing, and rehearsing upon me *old* and *ugly!* for so I had very naturally called him, in the heat of my defence.

The brute had, it seems, as I afterwards understood, brought on, by his eagerness, and struggle, the ultimate period of his hot fit of lust, which his power was too short-liv'd to carry him through the full execution of; of which my thighs and linen received the effusion.

When it was over, he bid me, with a tone of displeasure, get up————"that he would not do me the honour to think of me any more,————that the old b——h might look out for another cully,————that he would not be fool'd so by e'er a country mock-modestly in *England*————that he supposed I had left my maidenhead with some hobnail in the country, and was come to dispose of my skim-milk in town," with a volley of the like abuse; which I listened to with more pleasure than ever fond woman did to protestations of love, from her darling minion: for, uncapable as I was of receiving any addition to my perfect hatred and aversion to him, I look'd on his railing, as my security against his renewing his most odious caresses.

Yet, plain as Mrs. *Brown*'s views were now come out, I had not the heart, or spirit to open my eyes on them: still I could not part with my dependence on that beldam; so much did I think myself her's, soul and body: or rather, I sought to deceive myself with the continuation of my good opinion of her, and chose to wait the worst at her hands, sooner than being turn'd out to starve in the streets, without a penny of money, or a friend to apply to: these fears were my folly.

Whilst this confusion of ideas was passing in my head, and I sat pensive by the fire, with my eyes brimming with tears, my neck still bare, and my cap fall'n off in the struggle, so that my hair was in the disorder you may guess, the villain's lust began, I suppose, to be again in flow, at the sight of all that bloom of youth which presented itself to his view, a bloom yet unenjoy'd, and in course not yet indifferent to him.

After some pause, he ask'd me, with a tone of voice mightily soften'd, whether I would make it up with him before the old lady returned, and all should be well; he would restore me his affections: at the same time offering to kiss me, and feel my breasts. But now my extreme aversion, my fears, my indignation, all acting upon me, gave me a spirit not natural to me, so that breaking loose from him, I ran to the bell, and rang it, before he was aware, with such violence and effect, as brought up the maid to know what was the matter, or whether the gentleman wanted any thing? and, before he could proceed to greater extremities, she bounc'd into the room, and seeing me stretch'd on the floor, my hair all dishevell'd, my nose guishing out blood, (which did not a little tragedize the scene) and my odious persecutor still intent on pushing his brutal point, unmov'd by all my cries and distress, she was herself confounded, and did not know what to do.

As much however as *Martha* might be prepared, and hardened to transactions of this sort, all womanhood must have been out of her heart, could she have seen this unmov'd. Besides that, on the face of things, she imagined that matters had gone greater lengths than they really had, and that the courtesy of the house had been actually consummated on me, and flung me into the condition I was in: in this notion she instantly took my part, and advis'd the gentleman to go down, and leave me to recover myself, and that all would be soon over with me.——That when Mrs. *Brown,* and *Phœbe,* who were gone out, were return'd, they would take order for every thing to his satisfaction,————— that nothing would be lost by a little patience with the poor tender thing,————that for her part, she was frighten'd,—— ————she could not tell what to say to such doings,————but that she would stay by me till my mistress came home. As the wench said all this in a resolute tone, and the monster himself began to perceive that things would not mend by his staying, he took his hat and went out of the room murmuring, and pleating his brows like an old ape, so that I was delivered from the horrors of his detestable presence.

As soon as he was gone, *Martha* very tenderly offered me her assistance in any thing, and would have got me some hartshorn drops, and put me to bed; which last I, at first, positively refused, in the fear that the monster might return, and take me at that advantage: however, with much persuasion, and assurances that I should not be molested that night, she prevailed on me to lie down; and indeed I was so weakened by my struggles, so dejected by my fearful apprehensions, so terrour-struck, that I had no power to sit up, or hardly to give answers to the questions with which the curious *Martha* ply'd and perplex'd me.

Such too, and so cruel was my fate, that I dreaded the sight of Mrs. *Brown,* as if I had been the criminal, and she the person injur'd: a mistake which you will not think so strange, on distinguishing that neither virtue, or principles, had the least share in the defence I had made; but only the particular aversion I had conceiv'd against this first brutal and frightful invader of my tender innocence.

I pass'd then the time till Mrs. *Brown*'s return home, under all the agitations of fear and despair that may easily be guessed.

About eleven at night my two ladies came home, and having receiv'd rather a favourable account from *Martha,* who had run down to let them in: (for Mr. *Crofts,* that was the name of my brute, was gone out of the house, after waiting till he had tired his patience for Mrs. *Brown*'s return) they came thundering up stairs, and seeing me pale, my face bloody, and all the marks of the most thorough dejection, they employed themselves more to comfort and re-inspirit me, than in making me the reproaches I was weak enough to fear: I who had so many juster and stronger to retort upon them.

Mrs. *Brown* withdrawn, *Phœbe* came presently to bed to me, and what with the answers she drew from me, what with her own method of *palpably* satisfying herself, she soon discovered that I had been more frighted than hurt; upon which, I suppose being herself seiz'd with sleep, and reserving her lectures and instructions till the next morning, she left me, properly speaking, to my unrest: for after tossing, and turning, the greatest part of the night, and tormenting myself with the falsest notions and apprehensions of things, I fell, through meer fatigue, into a kind of delirious doze, out of which I wak'd late in the morning, in a violent fever; a circumstance which was extremely critical to reprive me, at least for a time, from the attacks of a wretch, infinitely more terrible to me than death itself.

The interested care that was taken of me during my illness, in order to restore me to a condition of making good the bawd's engagements, or of enduring further trials, had however such an effect on my grateful disposition, that I even thought myself oblig'd to my undoers for their attentions to promote my recovery, and, above all, for the keeping out of my sight that brutal ravisher, the author of my disorder, on their finding I was too strongly mov'd at the bare mention of his name.

Youth is soon raised; and a few days were sufficient to conquer the fury of my fever: but what contributed most to my perfect recovery, and to my reconciliation with life, was the timely news, that Mr. *Crofts,* who was a merchant of considerable dealings, was arrested at the king's suit, for near forty thousand pounds, on account of his driving a certain contraband trade, and that his affairs were so desperate, that even were it in his inclination, it would not be in his power to renew his designs upon me: for he was instantly thrown into a prison, which it was not likely that he would get out of in haste.

Mrs. *Brown,* who had touch'd his fifty guineas, advanc'd to so little purpose, and lost all hopes of the remaining hundred, began to look upon my treatment of him with a more favourable eye; and as they had observ'd my temper to be perfectly tractable, and conformable to their views, all the girls that compos'd her stock, were suffer'd to visit me, and had their cue to dispose me, by their conversation, to a perfect resignation of myself to Mrs. *Brown*'s direction.

Accordingly they were let in upon me, and all that frolic and thoughtless gaiety in which those giddy creatures consume their leisure, made me envy a condition of which I only saw the fair side: insomuch, that the being one of them became even my ambition: a disposition which they all carefully cultivated; and I wanted now nothing but to restore my health, that I might be able to undergo the ceremony of the initiation.

Conversation, example, all, in short, contributed, in that house, to corrupt my native purity, which had taken no root in education,[23] whilst now the inflamable principle of pleasure, so easily fired at my age, made strange work within me, and all the modesty I was brought up in the habit, (not the instruction) of, began to melt away, like dew before the sun's heat; not to mention that I made a vice of necessity, from the constant fears I had of being turn'd out to starve.

I was soon pretty well recover'd, and at certain hours allow'd to range all over the house, but cautiously kept from seeing any company, till the arrival of lord *B——* from *Bath,* to whom Mrs. *Brown,* in respect to his experienced generosity on such occasions, proposed to offer the refusal of that trinket of mine, which bears so great an imaginary value; and his lordship being expected in town in less than a fortnight, Mrs. *Brown* judged I should be entirely renewed in beauty, and freshness, by that time, and afford her the chance of a better bargain than she had driven with Mr. *Crofts.*

In the mean time, I was so thoroughly, as they call it, brought over, so tame to their whistle, that, had my cage-door been set open, I had no idea that I ought to fly anywhere, sooner than stay where I was; nor had I the least sense of regretting my condition, but waited very quietly for whatever Mrs. *Brown* should order concerning me, who on her side, by herself, and her agents, took more than the necessary precautions to lull and lay asleep all just reflexions on my destination.

Preachments of morality over the left shoulder,[24] a life of joy painted in the gayest colours, caresses, promises, indulgent treatment, nothing in short was wanting to domesticate me entirely, and to prevent my going out any where to get better advice; alas! I dream'd of no such thing.

Hitherto I had been indebted only to the girls of the house for the corruption of my innocence: their luscious talk, in which modesty was far from respected, their descriptions of their engagements with men, had given me a tolerable insight into the nature and mysteries of their profession, at the same time that they highly provok'd an itch of florid warm-spirited blood through every vein; but above all, my bed-fellow *Phœbe,* whose pupil I more immediately was, exerted her talents in giving me the first tinctures of pleasure: whilst nature now warm'd, and wantoned with discoveries so interesting, piqu'd a curiosity which *Phebe* artfully whetted, and leading me from question to question of her own suggestion, explain'd to me all the mysteries of *Venus;* but I could not long remain in such an house as that, without being an eye-witness of more than I could conceive from her descriptions.

One day about twelve at noon, being thoroughly recover'd of my fever, I happened to be in Mrs. *Brown*'s dark closet, where I had not been half an hour, resting on the maids settle-bed,[25] before I heard a rustling in the bedchamber, separated from the closet only by two sash-doors, before the glasses of which were drawn two yellow-damask curtains, but not so close as to exclude the full view of the room from any person in the closet.

I instantly crept softly, and posted myself so, that seeing every thing minutely, I could not myself be seen; and who should come in but the venerable mother Abbess herself! handed in by a tall, brawny, young horse-grenadier, moulded in the *Hercules*-stile; *in fine,* the choice of the most experienced dame, in those AFFAIRS, in all *London*.

Oh! how still and hushed did I keep at my stand, lest any noise should baulk my curiosity, or bring madam into the closet!

But I had not much reason to fear either, for she was so entirely taken up with her present great concern, that she had no sense of attention to spare to any thing else.

Droll was it to see that clumsy fat figure of her's flop down on the foot of the bed, opposite to the closet-door, so that I had a full front-view of all her charms.

Her paramour sat down by her: He seemed to be a man of very few words, and a great stomach; for proceeding instantly to essentials, he gave her some hearty smacks, and thrusting his hands into her breasts, disengag'd them from her stays, in scorn of whose confinement they broke loose, and swagged down, navel low at least. A more enormous pair did my eyes never behold, nor of a worse colour, flagging soft, and most lovingly contiguous: yet such as they were, this neck-beef-eater[26] seemed to paw them with a most unenviable gust, seeking in vain to confine or cover one of them with a hand scarce less than a shoulder of mutton: after toying with them thus some time, as if they had been worth it, he laid her down pretty briskly, and canting up her petticoats, made barely a mask of them to her broad red face, that blush'd with nothing but brandy.

As he stood on one side for a minute or so, unbuttoning his waste-coat, and breeches, her fat brawny thighs hung down, and the whole greasy landscape lay fairly open to my view: a wide open-mouth'd gap, overshaded with a grizzly bush, seemed held out like a beggar's wallet for its' provision.

But I soon had my eyes called off by a more striking object, that entirely engross'd them.

Her sturdy stallion had now unbutton'd, and produced naked, stiff, and erect, that wonderful machine, which I had never seen before, and which, for the interest my own seat of pleasure began to take furiously in it, I star'd at with all the eyes I had: however my senses were too much flurried, too much concenter'd in that now burning spot of mine, to observe any thing more than in general the make and turn of that instrument, from which the instinct of nature, yet more than all I had heard of it, now strongly informed me, I was to expect that supreme pleasure which she has placed in the meeting of those parts so admirably fitted for each other.

Long, however, the young spark did not remain, before, giving it two or three shakes, by way of brandishing it, he threw himself upon her, and his back being now towards me, I could only take his being ingulph'd for granted, by the direction he mov'd in, and the impossibility of missing so staring a mark; and now the bed shook, the curtains rattled so, that I could scarce hear the sighs, and murmurs, the heaves, and pantings that accompanied the action, from the beginning to the end; the sound and sight of which thrill'd to the very soul of me, and made every vein of my body circulate liquid fires: the emotion grew so violent that it almost intercepted my respiration.

Prepared then, and disposed as I was by the discourse of my companions, and *Phœbe*'s minute detail of every thing, no wonder that such a sight gave the last dying blow to my native innocence.

Whilst they were in the heat of the action, guided by nature only, I stole my hand up my petticoat, and with fingers all on fire, seized, and yet more inflamed that center of all my senses; my heart palpitated, as if it would force its way through my bosom: I breath'd with pain: I twisted my thighs, squeezed, and compress'd the lips of that virgin slit, and following mechanically the example of *Phœbe*'s manual operation on it, as far as I could find admission, brought on at last the critical extasy, the melting flow, into which nature, spent with excess of pleasure, dissolves and dies away.

After which my senses recover'd coolness enough to observe the rest of the transaction between this happy pair.

The young fellow had just dismounted, when the old lady immediately sprung up, with all the vigour of youth, derived no doubt from her late refreshment, and making him sit down, began in her turn to kiss him, to pat and pinch his cheeks, and play with his hair, all which he receiv'd with an air of indifference, and coolness, that showed him to me much altered from what he was when he first went on to the breach.

My pious governess, however, not being above calling in auxiliaries, unlocks a little case of cordials that stood near the bed, and made him pledge her in a very plentiful dram: after which, and a little amorous parley, madam sat herself down upon the same place at the bed's foot; and the young fellow standing sideways by her, she, with the greatest effrontery imaginable, unbuttons his breeches, and removing his shirt, draws out his affair, so shrunk and diminish'd that I could not but remember the difference, now crest-fallen, or just faintly lifting its head: but our experinc'd matron very soon, by chafing it with her hands, brought it to swell to that size and erection I had before seen it up to.

I admired then, upon a fresh account, and with a nicer survey, the texture of that capital part of man: the flaming red head as it stood uncapt, the whiteness of the shaft, and the shrub-growth of curling hair that embrowned the roots of it, the roundish bag that dangled down from it, all exacted my eager attention, and renewed my flame; but as the main-affair was now at the point the industrious dame had laboured to bring it to, she was not in the humour to put off the payment of her pains, but laying herself down, drew him gently upon her, and thus they finish'd, in the same manner as before, the old last act.

This over, they both went out lovingly together, the old lady having first made him a present, as near as I could observe, of three or four pieces; he being not only her particular favourite on the account of his performances, but a retainer to the house, from whose sight she had taken great care hither to secret me, lest he might not have had patience to wait for my lord's arrival, but have insisted on being his taster, which the old lady was under too much subjection to him to dare dispute with him; for every girl of the house fell to him in course, and the old lady only now and then got her turn, in consideration of the maintenance he had, and which he could scarce be accused of not earning, from her.

As soon as I heard them go down stairs, I stole up softly to my own room, out of which I had been luckily not mist. There I began to breath a little freer, and to give a loose to those warm emotions which the sight of such an encounter had rais'd in me. I laid me down on the bed stretch'd myself out, joining, and ardently wishing, and requiring any means to divert or allay the rekindl'd rage and tumult of my desires, which all pointed strongly to their pole, man. I felt about the bed, as if I sought for something that I grasp'd in my waking dream, and not finding it, could have cried for vexation, every part of me glowing with stimulating fires. At length, I resorted to the only present remedy, that of vain attempts at digitation, where the smallness of the theater, did not yet afford room enough for action, and where the pain my fingers gave me, in striving for admission, though they procur'd me a slight satisfaction for the present, started an apprehension, which I could not be easy till I had communicated to *Phœbe,* and received her explanations upon it.

The opportunity however did not offer till next morning, for *Phœbe* did not come to bed till long after I was gone to sleep: as soon then, as we were both awake, it was but in course to bring our lie-a-bed chat to land on the subject of my uneasiness: to which a recital of the love-scene, I had thus, by a chance been spectatress of, served for a preface.

Phœbe could not hear it to the end without more than one interruption by peals of laughter, and my ingenuous way of relating matters did not a little heighten the joke to her.

But on her sounding me how the sight had affected me: without mincing or hiding the pleasurable emotions it had inspir'd me with, I told her at the same time that one remark had perplex'd me, and that very considerably: "Ay! says she, what was that?" why, replied I, having very curiously and attentively compared the size of that enormous machine, which did not appear, at least to my fearful imagination, less than my wrist, and at least three of my handfuls long, to that of the tender, small part of me which was framed to receive it, I could not conceive its being possible to afford it entrance there, without dying, perhaps in the greatest pain, since she well knew that even a finger thrust in there, hurt me beyond bearing: ————— as to my mistress's and your's————— I can very plainly distinguish the different dimensions of them from mine, palpable to the touch, and visible to the eye, so that in short, great as the promised pleasure may be, I am afraid of the pain of the experiment.

Phœbe at this redoubl'd her laugh, and, whilst I expected a very serious solution of my doubts and apprehensions in this matter, only told me that she never heard of a mortal wound being given in those parts, by that terrible weapon, and that some she knew younger, and as delicately made as myself, had outlived the operation, that she believed, at the worst, I would take a great deal of killing:————— that true it was, there was a great diversity of sizes in those parts, owing to nature, child-bearing, frequent over-stretching with unmerciful machines; but that at a certain age, and habit of body, even the most experienc'd in those affairs could not well distinguish between the maid, and the woman, supposing too an absence of all artifice, and things in their natural situation: but that since chance had thrown in my way one sight of that sort, she would procure me another, that should feast my eyes more delicately, and go a great way in the cure of my fears from that imaginary disproportion.

On this she asked me if I knew *Polly Philips.* Undoubtedly, says I, the fair girl which was so tender of me when I was sick, and has been, as you told me, but two months in the house? "The same," says *Phœbe.* "You must know then, she is kept by a young *Genoese* merchant, whom his uncle, who is immensely rich, and whose darling he is, sent over here with an *English* merchant his friend, on a pretext of settling some accounts, but in reality to humour his inclinations for travelling, and seeing the world. He met casually with this *Polly* once in company, and taking a liking to her, makes it worth her while to keep entirely to him: he comes to her here twice or thrice a week, and she receives him in the light closet up one pair of stairs, where he enjoys her in a taste I suppose peculiar to the heat, or perhaps the caprices of his own country. I say no more; but tomorrow being his day, you shall see what passes between them, from a place only known to your mistress, and myself."

You may be sure, in the ply I was now taking, I had no objection to the proposal, and was rather a tiptoe for its accomplishment.

At five in the evening then, next day, *Phœbe,* punctual to her promise, came to me as I sat alone in my own room, and beckon'd me to follow her.

We went down the back-stairs very softly, and opening the door of a dark closet, where there was some old furniture kept, and some cases of liquors, she drew me in after her, and fastening the door upon us, we had no light but what came through a long crevice in the partition between ours, and the light closet, where the scene of action lay: so that sitting on those low cases, we could, with the greatest ease, as well as clearness, see all objects, (ourselves unseen) only by applying our eyes close to the crevice, where the moulding of a panel had warp'd, or started a little on the other side.

The young gentleman was the first person I saw, with his back directly towards me, looking at a print. *Polly* was not yet come. In less than a minute tho', the door opened, and she came in, and at the noise the door made, he turned about, and came to meet her, with an air of the greatest tenderness and satisfaction.

After saluting her, he led her to a couch that fronted us, where they both sat down, and the young *Genoese* help'd her to a glass of wine, with some *Naples* biscuit on a salver.

Presently, when they had exchanged a few kisses, and questions in broken *English* on one side, he began to unbutton, and, in fine, stript into his shirt.

As if this had been the signal agreed on for pulling off all their cloaths, a scheme which the heat of the season perfectly favoured, *Polly* began to draw her pins, and as she had no stays to unlace, she was in a trice, with her gallant's officious assistance, undress'd to all but her shift.

When he saw this, his breeches were immediately loosen'd, waist, and kneebands, and slipt over his ankles clean off: his shirt collar was unbuttoned too: then first giving *Polly* an encouraging kiss, he stole as it were the shift off the girl, who being I suppose broke and familiariz'd to this humour, blush'd indeed, but less than I did, at the apparition of her now standing stark naked, just as she came out of the hands of pure nature, with her black hair loose and a-float down her dazzling white neck and shoulders, whilst the deepen'd carnation of her cheeks went off gradually into the hue of glaz'd snow, for such were the blended tints, and polish of her skin.

This girl could not be above eighteen. Her face regular and sweet-featur'd, her shape exquisite, nor could I help envying her two ripe enchanting breasts, finely plump'd out in flesh, but withal so round, so firm, that they sustain'd themselves, in scorn of any stay: then their nipples pointing different ways mark'd their pleasing separation: beneath them lay the delicious tract of the belly, which terminated in a parting or rift scarce discernable, that modestly seem'd to retire downwards, and seek shelter between two plump fleshy thighs: the curling hair that overspread its delightful front, cloathed it with the richest sable fur in the universe—in short, she was evidently a subject for the painters to court her sitting to them for a pattern of female beauty, in all the true pride and pomp of nakedness.

The young *Italian* (still in his shirt) stood gazing, and transported at the sight of beauties that might have fir'd a dying hermit; his eager eyes devour'd her, as she shifted attitudes at his discretion: neither were his hands excluded their share of the high feast; but wander'd, on the hunt of pleasure, over every part, and inch of her body so qualified to afford the most exquisite sense of it.

In the mean time, one could not help observing the swell of his shirt before, that bolster'd out, and pointed out the condition of things behind the curtain: but he soon remov'd it, by slipping his shirt over his head; and now, as to nakedness, they had nothing to reproach one another,

The young gentleman, by *Phœbe*'s guess, was about two and twenty: tall and well limb'd. His body was finely form'd, and of a most vigorous make, square shoulder'd, and broad-chested. His face was not remarkable any way, but for a nose inclining to the *Roman*, eyes large, black, and sparkling, and a ruddiness in his cheeks that was the more a grace for his complexion being of the browness, not of that dusky dun colour which excludes the idea of freshness, but of that clear, olive gloss, which glowing with life, dazzles perhaps less than fairness, and yet pleases more, when it pleases at all. His hair being too short to tie, fell no lower than his neck, in short easy curls: and he had a few sprigs about his paps, that garnish'd his chest in a stile of strength and manliness. Then his grand movement, which seem'd to rise out of a thicket of curling hair that spread from the root, all round his thighs and belly up to the navel, stood stiff, and upright, but of a size to frighten me, by sympathy, for the small tender part, which was the object of it's fury, and which now lay expos'd to my fairest view: for he had immediately, on striping off his shirt, gently push'd her down on the couch, which stood conveniently to break her willing fall. Her thighs were spread out to their utmost extension, and discovered between them the mark of the sex, the red-center'd cleft of flesh, whose lips vermillioning inwards, exprest a small rubid line in sweet miniature, such as not *Guido*'s touch[27] or colouring could ever attain to the life, or delicacy of.

Phœbe, at this, gave me a gentle jog, to prepare me for a whisper'd question, "whether I thought my little maiden toy was much less?" but my attention was too much engross'd, too much enwrap'd with all I saw, to be able to give her any answer.

By this time, the young gentleman had changed her posture

from lying breadth to length-wise on the couch: but her thighs were still spread, and the mark lay fair for him, who now kneeling between them, display'd to us a side-view of that fierce erect machine of his, which threaten'd no less than splitting the tender victim, who lay smiling at the uplifted stroke, nor seem'd to decline it. He look'd upon his weapon himself with some pleasure, and guiding it with his hand to the inviting slit, drew aside the lips, and lodg'd it (after some thrusts, which *Polly* seem'd even to assist) about half way: but there it stuck, I suppose, from its growing thickness: he draws it again, and just wetting it with spittle, reenters, and with ease sheath'd it now up to the hilt, at which *Polly* gave a deep sigh, which was quite in another tone than one of pain; he thrusts, she heaves, at first gently, and in a regular cadence, but presently the transport began to be too violent to observe any order or measure, their motions were too rapid, their kisses too fierce, and fervent, for nature to support such fury long: both seem'd to me out of themselves, their eyes darted fires; "Oh! Oh!—I can't bear it—It is too much.—I die.— I am a going—" were *Polly's* expressions of extasy: his joys were more silent; but soon broken murmurs, sighs heart-fetch'd, and at length a dispatching thrust, as if he would have forced himself up her body, and then the motionless langour of all his limbs, all showed that the die-away moment was come upon him, which she gave signs of joining with, by the wild throwing of her hands about, closing her eyes, and giving a deep sob, in which she seem'd to expire in an agony of bliss.

When he had finish'd his stroke, and got from off her, she lay still without the least motion, breathless, as it should seem, with pleasure. He replaced her again breadthwise on the couch, unable to sit up, with her thighs open, between which I could observe a kind of white liquid, like froth, hanging about the outward lips of that recent opened wound, which now glowed with a deeper red. Presently she gets up, and throwing her arms around him, seemed far from undelighted with the trial he had put her to, to judge at least by the fondness with which she ey'd, and hung upon him.

For my part, I will not pretend to describe what I felt all over me, during this scene; but from that instant, adieu all fears of what man could do unto me; they were now changed into such ardent desires, such ungovernable longings, that I could have pull'd the first of that sex that should present himself, by the sleeve, and offered him the bauble, which I now imagin'd the loss of would be a gain I could not too soon procure myself,

Phœbe, who had more experience, and to whom such sights were not so new, could not however be unmov'd at so warm a scene; and drawing me away softly from the peep-hole, for fear of being over-heard, guided me as near the door as possible; all passive, and obedient to her least signals.

Here was no room either to sit, or lie, but making me stand with my back towards the door, she lifted up my petticoats, and with her busy fingers fell to visit, and explore that part of me, where now the heat, and irritations were so violent, that I was perfectly sick and ready to die with desire: that the bare touch of her finger in that critical place, had the effect of fire to a train, and her hand instantly made her sensible to what a pitch I was wound up, and melted by the sight she had thus procured me: satisfied then with her success, in allaying a heat that would have made me impatient of seeing the continuation of transactions between our amorous couple, she brought me again to the crevice, so favourable to our curiosity.

We had certainly been but a few instants away from it, and yet on our return we saw every thing in good forwardness for recommencing the tender hostilities.

The young foreigner was sitting down, fronting us, on the couch; with *Polly* upon one knee, who had her arms round his neck, whilst the extreme whiteness of her skin was not unde-lightfully contrasted by the smooth glossy brown of her lover's.

But who could count the fierce, unnumber'd kisses given and taken? in which I could often discover their exchanging the vel-vet thrust, when both their mouths were double-tongu'd, and seem'd to favour the mutual insertion with the greatest gust and delight.

In the mean time, his red-headed champion that had so lately fled the pit, quell'd, and abash'd, was now recover'd to the top of its condition, perk'd and crested up between *Polly*'s thighs, who was not wanting on her part to coax and keep it in good humour, stroaking it with her head down, and receiv'd even its velvet tip between the lips of not its proper mouth, whether she did this out of any particular pleasure, or whether it was to render it more glib, and easy of entrance, I could not tell; but it had such an effect, that the young gentleman seem'd by his eyes, that sparkled with more excited lustre, and his inflamed countenance, to receive encrease of pleasure. He got up, and taking *Polly* in his arms embraced her, and said something too softly for me to hear, leading her withal to the foot of the couch, and taking delight to slap her thighs, and posteriours with that stiff sinew of his, which hit them, with a spring, that he gave it with his hand, and made them resound again, but hurt her about as much as he meant to hurt her, for she seem'd to have as frolick a taste as himself.

But, guess my surprise, when I saw the lazy young rogue lie down on his back, and gently pull down *Polly* upon him, who giving way to his humour, straddled, and with her hands conducted her blind favourite to the right place, and following her impulse, ran directly upon the flaming point of this weapon of pleasure, which she stak'd herself upon, uppierc'd, and infix'd to the extremest hairbreadth of it: thus she sat on him, a few instants, enjoying, and relishing her situation, whilst he toyed with her provoking breasts.—Sometimes she would stoop to meet his kiss: but presently the sting of pleasure spurr'd them up to fiercer action: then began the storm of heaves, which, from the undermost combatant, were thrusts at the same time: he crossing his hands over her, and drawing her home to him with a sweet violence: the inverted strokes of anvil over hammer soon brought on the critical period, in which all the signs of a close conspiring extasy, informed us of the *point* they were at.

For me, I could bear to see no more: I was so overcome, so inflamed at this second part of the same play, that, mad with intolerable desire, I hugg'd, I clasp'd *Phœbe*, as if she had had wherewithal to relieve me: pleased however with, and pitying the taking she could feel me in, she drew me towards the door and opening it as softly as she could, we both got off undiscover'd, and she re-conducted me to my own room, where unable to keep my legs, in the agitation, I was in, I instantly threw myself down on the bed, where I lay transported, tho' asham'd at what I felt.

Phœbe lay down by me, and asked me archly, if now that I had seen the enemy, and fully considered him, I was still afraid of him? or did I think I could venture to come to a close engage-ment with him? to all which not a word on my side: I sigh'd, and could scarce breathe. She takes hold of my hand, and having roll'd up her own petticoats, forced it half-strivingly towards those parts, where now grown more knowing, I miss'd the main object of my wishes; and finding not even the shadow of what I wanted, where every thing was so flat! or so hollow! In the vexa-tion I was in at it, I should have withdrawn my hand, but for fear of disobliging her. Abandoning it then entirely to her manage-ment, she made use of it as she thought proper, to procure her-self rather the shadow than the substance of any pleasure. For my part, I now pin'd for more solid food, and promis'd tacitly to myself that I would not be put off much longer with this foolery from woman to woman, if Mrs. *Brown* did not soon provide me with the essential specific: in short I had all the air of not being able to wait the arrival of my lord *B——*, tho' he was now ex-pected in a very few days: nor did I wait for him, for love itself took charge of the disposal of me, in spite of interest, or gross lust.

It was now two days after the closet-scene, that I got up about six in the morning, and leaving my bed-fellow fast asleep, stole down, with no other thought than of taking a little fresh air in a small garden, which our back-parlour open'd into, and from which my confinement debarr'd me at the times company came to the house: but now sleep and silence reign'd all over it.

I open'd the parlour-door, and well surpriz'd was I, at seeing, by the side of a fire half out, a young gentleman in the old lady's elbow chair, with his legs laid upon another, fast asleep, and left there, by his thoughtless companions, who had drank him down, and then went off with every one his mistress, whilst he stay'd behind by the curtesy of the old matron, who would not disturb, or turn him out in that condition at one in the morning, and beds, it is more than probable, there were none to spare: On the table still remain'd the punch-bowl and glasses, strow'd about in their usual disorder after a drunken revel.

But when I drew nearer to view the sleeping estray[28]: Heavens! what a sight! no! no term of years, no turns of fortune could ever erase the lightening-like impression his form made on me.

————Yes! dearest object of my earliest passion, I command for ever the remembrance of thy first appearance to my ravish'd eyes,—it calls thee up, present; and I see thee now!

Figure to yourself, *Madam,* a fair stripling, between eighteen and nineteen, with his head reclin'd on one of the sides of the chair, his hair in disorder'd curls, irregularly shading a face, on which all the roseate bloom of youth, and all the manly graces conspired to fix my eyes and heart. Even the languor, and paleness of his face, in which the momentary triumph of the lilly over the rose, was owing to the excesses of the night, gave an inexpressible sweetness to the finest features imaginable: his eyes closed in sleep, displayed the meeting edges of their lids beautifully bordered with long eye-lashes, over which no pencil could have describ'd two more regular arches than those that grac'd his fore-head, which was high, perfectly white and smooth; then a pair of vermillion lips, pouting, and swelling to the touch, as if a bee had freshly stung them, seem'd to challenge me to get the gloves of this lovely sleeper, had not the modesty, and respect, which in both sexes are inseparable from a true passion, check'd my impulses.

But on seeing his shirt collar unbutton'd, and a bosom whiter than a drift of snow, the pleasure of considering it could not bribe me to lengthen it at the hazard of a health that began to be my life's concern: Love that made me timid, taught me to be tender too: with a trembling hand I took hold of one of his, and waking him as gently as possible, he started, and looking at first a little wildly, said, with a voice that sent its harmonious sound to my heart: "Pray, child, what a clock is it?" I told him: and added, that he might catch cold, if he slept longer with his breast open in the cool of the morning air: On this he thanked me, with a sweetness perfectly agreeing with that of his features and eyes: the last now broad open, and eagerly surveying me, carried the sprightly fires they sparkled with directly to my heart.

It seems that having drank too freely before he came upon the rake with some of his young companions, he had put himself out of a condition to go through all the weapons with them, and crown the night with getting a mistress, so that seeing me in a loose undress, he did not doubt but I was one of the misses of the house, sent in to repair his loss of time; but though he seiz'd that notion, and a very obvious one it was, without hesitation; yet, whether my figure made a more than ordinary impression on him, or whether it was his natural politeness, he addrest me in a manner far from rude, though still on the foot of one of the house-pliers, come to amuse him; and giving me the first kiss that I ever relish'd from man in my life, ask'd me if I could favour him with my company, assuring me that he would make it worth my while: but had not even new-born love, that true refiner of lust, oppos'd so sudden a surrender, the fear of being surpriz'd by the house, was a sufficient bar to my compliance.

I told him then, in a tone set me by love itself, that for reasons I had not time to explain to him, I could not stay with him, and might not even ever see him again, with a sigh at these last words which broke from the bottom of my heart. My conqueror, who, as he afterwards told me, had been struck with my appearance, and lik'd me as much as he could think of liking any one in my suppos'd way of life, ask'd me briskly at once, if I would be kept by him, and that he would take a lodging for me directly, and re-lieve me from any engagements he presum'd I might be under to the house. Rash, sudden, undigested, and even dangerous as this offer might be from a perfect stranger, and that stranger a giddy boy, the prodigious love I was struck with for him, had put a charm into his voice there was no resisting, and blinded me to every objection: I could, at that instant, have died for him; think, if I could resist an invitation to live with him! thus my heart beating strong to the proposal, dictated my answer, after scarce a

minute's pause, that I would accept of his offer, and make my escape to him, in what way he pleased, and that I would be entirely
at his disposal, let it be good or bad. I have often since wondered
that so great an easiness did not disgust him, or make me too
cheap in his eyes; but my fate had so appointed it, that, in his
fears of the hazard of the town, he had been some time looking
out for a girl to take into keeping, and my person happening to
hit his fancy, it was by one of those miracles reserv'd to love, that
we struck the bargain in the instant, which we sealed by an exchange of kisses, that the hopes of a more uninterrupted enjoyment engaged him to content himself with.

Never, however, did dear youth carry in his person more
wherewith to justify the turning of a girl's head, and making
her set all consequences at defiance, for the sake of following a
gallant.

For besides all the perfections of manly beauty which were
assembled in his form, he had an air of neatness and gentility, a
certain smartness in the carriage and port of his head, that yet
more distinguish'd him: his eyes were sprightly, and full of
meaning; his looks had in them something at once sweet and
commanding. His complexion out-bloom'd the lovely-colour'd
rose, whilst its inimitable tender vivid glow, clearly sav'd it from
the reproach of wanting life, of raw and dough-like, which is
commonly made to those so extremely fair as he was.

Our little plan was, that I should get out about seven the next
morning, (which I could *readily* promise, as I knew where to get
the key of the street-door) and he would wait at the end of the
street with a coach, to convey me safe off; after which he would
send and clear any debt incurr'd by my stay at Mrs. *Brown*'s, who
he only judg'd, in gross, might not care to part with one, he
thought, so fit to draw custom to the house.

I then just hinted to him not to mention in the house his having seen such a person as me, for reasons I would explain to him
more at leisure: and then, for fear of miscarrying by being seen
together, I tore myself from him with a bleeding heart, and stole
up softly to my room, where I found *Phœbe* still fast asleep, and

hurrying off my few cloaths, lay down by her, with a mixture of joy and anxiety, that may be easier conceived than express'd.

The risks of Mrs. *Brown*'s discovering my purpose, of disappointments, misery, ruin, all vanish'd before this new-kindl'd flame. The seeing, the touching, the being, if but for a night, with this idol of my fond virgin-heart, appeared to me a happiness above the purchase of my liberty or life. He might use me ill, let him! he was the master, happy, too happy even to receive death at so dear a hand.

To this purpose were the reflexions of the whole day, of which every minute seem'd to me a little eternity. How often did I visit the clock? nay, was tempted to advance the tedious hand, as if that would have advanc'd the time with it! Had those of the house made the least observations on me, they must have remark'd something extraordinary from the discomposure I could not help betraying: especially when at dinner mention was made of the charmingest youth having been there, and stay'd breakfast! Oh, he was such a beauty! I should have died for him! they would pull caps for him! and the like fooleries, which however, was throwing oil on a fire I was sorely put to it to smother the blaze of.

The fluctuations of my mind, the whole day, produc'd however one good effect; which was, that through mere fatigue I slept tolerably well till five in the morning, when I got up, and having dress'd myself, waited, under the double tortures of fear and impatience, for the appointed hour: It came at last, the dear, critical, dangerous hour came; and now supported only by the courage love lent me, I ventur'd a tip-toe down stairs, leaving my box behind, for fear of being surpriz'd with it in going out.

I got to the street-door, the key whereof was always laid on the chair by our bed-side, in trust with *Phœbe*, who having not the least suspicion of my entertaining any design to go from them, (nor indeed had I but the day before) made no reserve, or concealment of it from me. I open'd the door then with great ease; love that embolden'd, protected me too: and now, got safe into the street, I saw my new guardian-angel waiting at a coach-door ready open: How I got to him I know not: I suppose I flew; but I was in the coach in a trice, and he by the side of me, with his arms clasp'd round me, and giving me the kiss of welcome.—— The coachman had his orders, and drove to them.

My eyes were instantly fill'd with tears, but tears of the most delicious delight. To find myself in the arms of that beauteous youth, was a rapture that my little heart swam in. Past or future were equally out of the question with me. The present was as much as all my powers of life were sufficient to bear the trans-port of without fainting: Nor were the most tender embraces, the most soothing expressions wanting on his side, to assure me of his love, and of never giving me cause to repent the bold step I had taken, in throwing myself thus entirely upon his honour and generosity: but, alas! this was no merit in me, for I was drove to it by a passion too impetuous for me to resist, and I did what I did, because I could not help it.

In an instant, for time was now annihilated with me, we were landed at a publick house in *Chelsea,* hospitably commodious for the reception of duet-parties of pleasure, where a breakfast of chocolate was prepared for us.

An old jolly stager who kept it, and understood life perfectly well, breakfasted with us, and leering archly at me, gave us both joy, and said, we were well paired, e'faith! that a great many gen-tlemen and ladies used his house, but he had never seen a hand-somer couple;—He was sure I was a fresh piece—I look'd so country, so innocent! well, my spouse was a lucky man!—all which common landlord's cant, not only pleas'd and sooth'd me, but help'd to divert my confusion at being with my new sover-eign, whom, now the minute approach'd, I began to fear to be alone with, a timidity which true love had a greater share in, than even maiden bashfulness.

I wish'd, I doated, I could have died for him, and yet I know not how, or why, I dreaded the point which had been the object of my fiercest wishes; my pulses beat fears, amidst a flush of the warmest desires: this struggle of the passions, however, this con-flict betwixt modesty and love-sick longings, made me burst again into tears, which he took as he had done before, only for the remains of concern and emotion at the suddenness of my change of condition, in committing myself to his care, and in consequence of that idea, did, and said, all that he thought would most comfort and re-inspirit me.

After breakfast, *Charles*, the dear familiar name I must take the liberty henceforward to distinguish my *Adonis*[29] by, with a smile full of meaning, took me gently by the hand, and said, "Come, my dear, and I will show you a room that commands a fine prospect over some gardens": and without waiting for an answer, in which he relieved me extremely, he led me up into a chamber airy and lightsome, where all seeing of prospects was out of the question, except that of a bed, which had all the air of having recommended the room to him.

Charles had just slipp'd the bolt of the door, and running, caught me in his arms, and lifting me from the ground, with his lips glew'd to mine, bore me trembling, panting, dying with soft fears, and tender wishes, to the bed; where his impatience would not suffer him to undress me more than just unpinning my handkerchief, and gown, and unlacing my stays.

My bosom was now bare, and rising in the warmest throbs, presented to his sight and feeling the firm hard-swell of a pair of young breasts, such as may be imagin'd of a girl not sixteen, fresh out of the country, and never before handled; but even their pride, whiteness, fashion, pleasing resistance to the touch, could not bribe his restless hands from roving, but giving them the loose, my petticoats and shift were soon taken up, and their stronger center of attraction laid open to their tender invasion: my fears however made me mechanically close my thighs; but the very touch of his hand insinuated between them, disclosed them, and open'd a way for the main-attack.

In the mean time I lay fairly exposed to the examination of his eyes, and hands, quiet and unresisting, which confirm'd him in the opinion he proceeded so cavalierly upon, that I was no novice in these matters, since he had taken me out of a common bawdy-house: nor had I said one thing to prepossess him of my virginity; and if I had, he would sooner have believ'd that I took him for a cully that would swallow such an improbability, than that I was still mistress of that darling treasure, that hidden mine, so eagerly sought after by the men, and which they never dig for but they destroy.

Being now too high wound up to bear a delay, he unbutton'd, and drawing out the engine of love-assaults, drove it currently, as at a ready-made breach: then! then! for the first time did I feel that stiff horn-hard gristle, battering against the tender part; but imagine to yourself his surprize, when he found, after several vigorous pushes, which hurt me extremely, that he made not the least impression.

I complain'd, but tenderly complain'd; "I could not bear it—" Indeed! he hurt me—still he thought no more than that being so young, the largeness of his machine (for few men could dispute size with him) made all the difficulty, and that possibly I had not been enjoy'd by any so advantageously made in that part as himself; for still, that my virgin-flower was yet uncrop'd never once enter'd into his head, and he would have thought it idling with time and words to have question'd me upon it.

He tries again; still no admittance; still no penetration; but he had hurt me yet more, whilst my extreme love made me bear extreme pain almost without a groan: at length, after repeated fruitless trials, he lay down panting by me, kiss'd my falling tears, and ask'd me tenderly, what was the meaning of so much complaining, and if I had not born it better from others than I did from him? I answer'd with a simplicity fram'd to perswade, that he was the first man that ever serv'd me so: truth is powerful, and it is not always that we do not believe what we eagerly wish.

Charles already dispos'd by the evidence of his senses to think my pretences to virginity not entirely apocryphal, smothers me with kisses, begs me, in the name of love, to have a little patience, and that he will be as tender of hurting me, as he would be of himself.

Alas! it was enough I knew his pleasure, to submit joyfully to him, whatever pain I foresaw it would cost me.

He now resumes his attempts in more form: first he put one of the pillows under me, to give the blank of his aim a more favourable elevation, and another under my head, in ease of it: then spreading my thighs, and placing himself standing between them, made them rest upon his hips: applying then the point of his machine to the slit, into which he sought entrance; it was so small, he could scarce assure himself of its being rightly pointed. He looks, he feels, and satisfies himself; then driving forward with fury, its prodigious stiffness thus impacted, wedgelike, breaks the union of those parts, and gain'd him just the insertion of the tip of it, lip-deep; which being sensible of, he improves his advantage, and following well his stroke, in a strait line, forcibly deepens his penetration; but put me to such intolerable pain, from the separation of the sides of that soft passage by a hard thick body, I could have scream'd out; but unwilling as I was to alarm the house, I held in my breath, and cram'd my petticoat (which was turn'd up over my face) into my mouth, and bit it through in the agony. At length, the tender texture of that tract giving way to such fierce tearing and rending, he pierc'd something further into me: and now, outrageous, and no longer his own master, but born head-long away by the fury and overmettle of that member, now exerting itself with a kind of native rage, he breaks in, carries all before him, and one violent merciless lunge, sent it, imbrew'd,[30] and reeking with virgin blood, up to the very hilts in me: then! then! all my resolution deserted me: I scream'd out, and fainted away with the sharpness of the pain; and (as he told me afterwards) on his drawing out, when emission was over with him, my thighs were instantly all in a stream of blood, that flow'd from the wounded torn passage.

When I recover'd my senses, I found myself undress'd, and a-bed, in the arms of the sweet relenting murderer of my virginity, who hung mourning tenderly over me, and holding in his hands a cordial, which coming from the still-dear author of so much pain! I could not refuse: my eyes, however moisten'd with tears, and languishingly turn'd upon him, seem'd to reproach him with his cruelty, and ask him if such were the rewards of love? but *Charles*, to whom I was now infinitely endear'd by his

compleat triumph over a maidenhead, where he so little expected to find one, in tenderness to that pain which he had put
me to, in procuring himself the height of pleasure, smother'd his
exultation, and employ'd himself with so much sweetness, so
much warmth, to sooth, to caress, and comfort me in my soft
complainings, that breath'd indeed more love than resentment,
that I presently drown'd all sense of pain in the pleasure of seeing him, of thinking that I belong'd to him, he who now was the
absolute disposer of my happiness, and in one word, my fate.

The sore was however too tender, the wound too bleeding
fresh, for *Charles*'s good-nature to put my patience presently to
another trial; but as I could not stir or walk a-cross the room, he
order'd the dinner to be brought to the bed-side, where it could
not be otherwise than my getting down the wing of a fowl, and
two or three glasses of wine, since it was my ador'd youth who
both serv'd, and urged them on me, with that sweet irresistible
authority with which love had invested him over me.

After dinner, and every thing but the wine was taken away,
Charles very impudently asks a leave, he might read the grant of
in my eyes, to come to-bed to me, and accordingly falls to undressing; which I could not see the progress of, without strange
emotions of fear and pleasure.

He is now in bed with me the first time, and in broad day; but
when thrusting up his own shirt, and my shift, he laid his naked
glowing body to mine . . . Oh insupportable delight! oh superhu-
man rapture! what pain could stand before a pleasure so trans-
porting? I felt no more the smart of my wounds below; but
curling round him like the tendril of a vine, as if I fear'd any part
of him should be untouch'd or unpress'd by me; I return'd his
strenuous embraces and kisses with a fervour and gust only
known to true love, and which mere lust could never rise to.

Yes even at this time, that all the tyranny of the passions is
fully over, and that my veins roll no longer but a cold tranquil
stream, the remembrance of those passages that most affected
me in my youth, still chears, and refreshes me: Let me proceed
then—my beauteous youth was now glew'd to me in all the folds
and twists that we could make our bodies meet in: when no

longer able to rein in the fierceness of refresh'd desires, he gives his steed the head, and gently insinuating his thighs between mine, stopping my mouth with kisses of humid fire, makes a fresh irruption, and renewing his thrusts, pierces, tears, and forces his way up the torn tender folds of the sheath, that yielded him admission with a smart little less severe than when the breach was first made: I stifled however my cries, and bore him with the passive fortitude of an heroine: soon his thrusts more and more furious, cheeks flush'd with a deeper scarlet, his eyes turn'd up in the fervent fit, and rolling nothing but their whites, some dying sighs, and an agonizing shudder, announced the approaches of that extatic pleasure, I was yet in too much pain, to come in for my share of.

Nor was it till after a few enjoyments had numb'd and blunted the sense of the smart, and giving me to feel the titillating inspersion[31] of balsamic sweets, drew from me the delicious return, and brought down all my passion, that I arriv'd at excess of pleasure, through excess of pain; but when successive engagements had broke and inur'd me, I began to enter into the true unallay'd relish of that pleasure of pleasures, when the warm gush darts through all the ravish'd inwards; what floods of bliss! what melting transports! what agonies of delight! too fierce, too mighty for nature to sustain: well has she therefore, no doubt, provided the relief of a delicious momentary dissolution, the approaches of which are intimated by a dear delirium, a sweet thrill, on the point of emitting those liquid sweets in which enjoyment itself is drown'd, when one gives the languishing stretch-out, and dies at the discharge.

How often, when the rage and tumult of my senses has subsided after the melting flow, have I, in a tender meditation, ask'd myself coolly the question, if it was in nature for any of its creatures to be so happy as I was? or, what were all the fears of my future fate, put in the scale of one night's enjoyment of any thing so transcendently the taste of my eyes, and heart, as that delicious, fond, matchless youth?

Thus we spent the whole afternoon, till supper-time, in a continued circle of love-delights, kissing, turtle-billing,[32] toying, and all the rest of the feast. At length supper was served in, before which *Charles* had, for I do not know what reason, slipt his cloaths on, and sitting down by the bed-side, we made table and table-cloth of the bed and sheets, whilst he suffer'd nobody to attend or serve but himself. He ate with a very good appetite, and seem'd charm'd to see me eat. For my part, I was so enchanted with my fortune, so transported with the comparison of the delights I now swarm in, with all the insipidity of my past scenes of life, that I thought them sufficiently cheap at even the price of my ruin, or the risque of their not lasting. The present possession was all my little head could find room for.

We lay together that night, when after playing repeated prizes of pleasure, nature overspent, and satisfy'd, gave us up to the arms of sleep: those of my dear youth encircl'd me, the consciousness of which made even that sleep more delicious.

Late in the morning I wak'd first; and observing my lover slept profoundly, softly disengag'd myself from his arms, scarcely daring to breathe, for fear of shortening his repose: my cap, my hair, my shift were all in disorder, from the rufflings I had undergone; and I took this opportunity to adjust, and set them as well as I could: whilst every now and then, looking at the sleeping youth with inconceiveable fondness and delight; and reflecting on all the pain he had put me to, tacitly own'd that the pleasure had over-paid me for my sufferings.

It was then broad day. I was sitting up in the bed, the cloaths of which were all tost, or roll'd off, by the unquietness of our motions, from the sultry heat of the weather; nor could I refuse myself a pleasure that sollicited me so irresistibly, as this fair occasion of feasting my sight with all those treasures of youthful beauty I had enjoy'd, and which lay now almost entirely naked, his shirt being trussed up in a perfect wisp, which the warmth of the room and season made me easy about the consequence of. I hung over him enamour'd indeed! and devour'd all his naked charms with only two eyes, when I could have wish'd them at least a hundred, for the fuller enjoyment of the gaze.

Oh! could I paint his figure as I see it now still present to my transported imagination! a whole length of an all-perfect manly beauty in full view. Think of a face without a fault, glowing with all the opening bloom, and vernal freshness of an age, in which beauty is of either sex, and which the first down over his upper lip scarce began to distinguish.

The parting of the double ruby pout of his lips, seem'd to exhale an air sweeter and purer than what it drew in: Ah! what violence did it not cost me to refrain the so tempted kiss?

Then a neck exquisitely turn'd, grac'd behind and on the sides with his hair playing freely in natural ringlets, connected his head to a body of the most perfect form, and of the most vigorous contexture, in which all the strength of manhood was conceal'd and soften'd to appearance, by the delicacy of his complexion, the smoothness of his skin, and the plumpness of his flesh.

The platform of his snow-white bosom, that was laid out in a manly proportion, presented on the vermillion summit of each pap, the idea of a rose about to blow.

Nor did his shirt hinder from observing that symmetry of his limbs, that exactness of shape, in the fall of it towards the loins, where the waist ends, and the rounding swell of the hips commences, where the skin, sleek, smooth, and dazzling white, burnishes on the stretch over firm, plump-ripe flesh, that crimped and run into dimples at the least pressure, or that the touch could not rest upon, but slid over as on the surface of the most polish'd ivory.

His thighs finely fashion'd, and with a florid glossy roundness gradually tapering away to the knee, seem'd pillars worthy to support that beauteous frame, at the bottom of which I could not without some remains of terror, some tender emotions too, fix my eyes on that terrible spit-fire machine, which had not so long before, with such fury broke into, torn, and almost ruin'd those soft tender parts of mine, which had not yet done smarting with the effects of its rage; but behold it now! crest-fall'n, reclining its half-capt vermillion head over one of his thighs, quiet, pliant, and to all appearance incapable of the mischiefs and cruelty it had committed. Then the beautiful growth of the hair, in short and soft curls round its root, its whiteness, branch'd veins, the supple softness of the shaft, as it lay foreshorten'd, roll'd and shrunk up into a squab thickness, languid, and born up from between the thighs, by its globular appendage, that wondrous treasure bag of nature's sweets, which rivell'd round, and purs'd up in the only wrinkles that are known to please, perfected the prospect; and all together form'd the most interesting moving picture in nature, and surely infinitely superior to those nudities furnish'd by the painters, statuaries, or any art, which are purchas'd at immense prices, whilst the sight of them in actual life is scarce sovereignly tasted by any but the few whom nature has endowed with a fire of imagination, warmly pointed by a truth of judgment to the spring-head, the originals of beauty of nature's unequall'd composition, above all the imitations of art, or the reach of wealth to pay their price.

But every thing must have an end. A motion made by this angelic youth, in the listlessness of going-off sleep, replac'd his shirt and cloaths in a posture that shut up that treasury from longer view.

I lay down then, and carrying my hands to that part of me, in which the objects just seen had begun to raise a mutiny, that prevail'd over the smart of them, my fingers now open'd themselves an easy passage; but long I had not the time to consider the wide difference *there,* between the maid, and the now finish'd woman, before *Charles* wak'd, and turning towards me, kindly enquir'd how I had rested? and scarce giving me time to answer, imprinted on my lips one of his burning rapture-kisses, which darted a flame to my heart, that from thence radiated to every part of me: and presently, as if he had proudly meant revenge for the survey I had smuggled of all his naked beauties, he spurns off the bed-cloaths, and trussing up my shift as high as it would go, took his turn to feast his eyes with all the gifts nature had bestow'd on my person; his busy hands too rang'd intemperantly over every part of me. The delicious austerity, and hardness of my yet unripe budding breasts, the whiteness and firmness of my flesh, the freshness and regularity of my features, the harmony of my limbs, all seem'd to confirm him in his satisfaction with his bargain: but, when curious to explore the havoc he had made in the tender center of his over-fierce attack, he not only directed his hands there, but with a pillow put under, placed me favourably for his wanton purpose of inspection; then, who can express the fire his eyes glisten'd, his hands glow'd with? whilst sighs of pleasure, and tender broken exclamations were all the praises he could utter. By this time, his machine stiffly risen at me, lifted and bore the flap of his shirt out, which presently fiercely removing, gave me to see it in its highest state and bravery: He feels it himself, seems pleas'd at its condition, and, smiling loves and graces, seizes one of my hands, and carries it, with a gentle compulsion, to this pride of nature, and its richest master-piece.

I struggling faintly, could not help feeling what I could not grasp, a column of the whitest ivory, beautifully streak'd with blue veins, and carrying, fully uncapt, a head of the liveliest vermillion: no horn could be harder, or stiffer; yet no velvet more smooth or delicious to the touch; presently he guided my hand lower, to that part, in which nature and pleasure keep their stores in concert, so aptly fasten'd and hung on to the root of their first instrument and minister, that not improperly he might be styl'd their purse-bearer too: there he made me feel, distinctly, through their soft cover, the contents, a pair of roundish balls, that seem'd to play within, and elude all pressure, but the tenderest, from without.

But now this visit of my soft warm hand, in those so sensible parts, had put every thing into such ungovernable fury, that disdaining all further preluding, and taking the advantage of my commodious posture, he made the storm fall where I scarce patiently expected, and where he was sure to lay it: presently then I felt the stiff intersertion between the yielding divided lips of the wound now open for life; where the narrowness no longer put me to intollerable pain, and afforded my lover no more difficulty than what heighten'd his pleasure, in the strict embrace of that tender warm sheath, round the instrument it was so deliciously adjusted to, and which, now cased home, so gorged me with pleasure, that it perfectly suffocated me, and took away my breath: then the killing thrusts! the unnumber'd kisses! every one of which was a joy inexpressible! and that joy lost in a crowd of yet greater blisses; but this was a disorder too violent in nature to lust long: the vessels so stir'd, and intensely heated, soon boil'd over, and for that time put out the fire: mean while all this dalliance and disport had so far consum'd the morning, that it became a kind of necessity to lay breakfast and dinner into one.

In our calmer intervals *Charles* gave the following account of himself, every tittle of which was true. He was the only son of a father, who having a small post in the revenue, rather over-liv'd his income, and had given this young gentleman a very slender education: no profession had he bred him up to, but design'd to provide for him in the army, by purchasing him an ensign's commission; that is to say, provided he could raise the money, or procure it by interest, either of which clauses was rather to be wish'd than hop'd for by him: on no better a plan, however, than this, had this improvident father suffer'd this youth, and a youth of great promise, to run up to the age of manhood, or near it at least, in next to idleness, and had besides taken no sort of pains to give him even the common premonitions against the vices of the town, and the dangers of all sorts which wait the unexperienc'd, and unwary, in it. He liv'd at home, and at discretion, with his father, who himself kept a mistress, and for the rest, provided *Charles* did not ask him for money, he was indolently kind to him: he might lie out when he pleas'd: any excuse would serve, and even his reprimands were so slight, that they carried with them rather an air of connivance at the fault, than any serious control or constraint. But, to supply his calls for money, *Charles*, whose mother was dead, had, by her side, a grand-mother who doated upon, and did not a little help spoil him. She had a considerable annuity to live upon, and very regularly parted with every shilling she could spare, to this darling of hers, to the no little heart-burn[33] of his father, who was vex'd, not that she by this means fed his son's extravagance; but that she preferred *Charles*

to himself; and we shall too soon see what a fatal turn such a mercenary jealousy could operate on the breast of a father.

Charles was however, by the means of his grand-mother's lavish fondness, very sufficiently enabl'd to keep a mistress so easily
contented as my love made me; and my good fortune, for such I
must ever call it, threw me in his way, in the manner above related, just as he was on the look-out for one.

As to his temper, the even sweetness of it made him seem
born for domestic happiness: tender, naturally polite, and
gentle-manner'd; it could never be his fault, if ever jars, or ani-
mosities ruffled a calm he was so qualify'd every way to maintain
or restore. Without those great or shining qualities that constitute a genius, or are fit to make a noise in the world, he had all
those humble ones that compose the softer social merit: plain
common sense, set off with every grace of modesty and good-
nature, made him, if not admir'd, what is much happier, universally belov'd and esteem'd. But, as nothing, but the beauties of
his person had at first attracted my regard, and fix'd my passion,
neither was I then a judge of that internal merit, which I had af-
terward full occasion to discover, and which perhaps, in that season of giddiness and levity, would have touch'd my heart very
little, had it been lodg'd in a person less the delight of my eyes,
and idol of my senses. But to return to our situation.

After dinner, which we eat a-bed in a most voluptuous disorder, *Charles* got up, and taking a passionate leave of me for a few
hours, he went to town, where concerting matters with a young
sharp lawyer, they went together to my late venerable mistress's,
from whence I had but the day before made my elopement, and
with whom he was determin'd to settle accounts in a manner that
should cut off all after-reckonings from that quarter.

Accordingly, they went; but by the way, the Templar,[34] his
friend, on thinking over *Charles*'s information, saw reason to give
their visit another turn, and instead of offering satisfaction, to
demand it.

On being let in, the girls of the house flock'd round *Charles*,
whom they knew, and from the earliness of my escape, and their

perfect ignorance of his ever having so much as seen me, not having the least suspicion of his being accessory to my flight, they were, in their way, *making up* to him; and as to his companion, they took him probably for a fresh cully: but the Templar soon check'd their forwardness by enquiring for the old lady, with whom he said, with a grave judge-like countenance, that he had some business to settle.

Madam was immediately sent for down, and the ladies being desir'd to clear the room, the lawyer ask'd her severely if she did not know, or had not decoy'd, under pretence of hiring as a servant, a young girl, just come out of the country, called *Frances* or *Fanny Hill,* describing me with all as particularly as he could from *Charles*'s description.

It is peculiar to vice to tremble at the enquiries of justice: and Mrs. *Brown,* whose conscience was not entirely clear upon my account, as knowing as she was of the town, as hackney'd as she was in buffing[35] through all the dangers of her vocation, could not help being alarm'd at the question, especially when he went on to talk of a Justice of Peace, *Newgate,* the *Old Baily,*[36] Indictments for keeping a disorderly house, Pillory, Carting,[37] and the whole process of that nature: She who, it is likely, imagin'd I had lodg'd an information against her house, look'd extremely blank, and began to make a thousand protestations, and excuses. However, to abridge, they brought away triumphantly my box of things, which had she not been under an awe, she might have disputed with them; and not only that, but a clearance and discharge of any demands on the house, at the expence of no more than a bowl of arrack-punch, the treat of which, together with the choice of the house-conveniences, was offer'd, and not accepted. *Charles* all the time acted the chance companion of the lawyer who had brought him there, as he knew the house, and appear'd in no wise interested in the issue, but he had the collateral pleasure of hearing all I had told him verified, so far as the bawd's fears would give her leave to enter into my history, which, if one may guess by the composition she so readily came into, were not small.

Phœbe, my kind tutress *Phœbe,* was at that time gone out, per-haps in search of me, or their cook'd up story had not, it is prob-able, pass'd so smoothly.

This negotiation had however taken up some time, which would have appear'd much longer to me, left as I was in a strange house, if the landlady, a motherly sort of woman, to whom *Charles* had liberally recommended me, had not come up and borne me company: We drank tea, and her chat help'd to pass away the time very agreeably, since he was our theme; but as the evening deepned, and the hour set for his return was elaps'd, I could not dispel the gloom of impatience, and tender fears which gather'd upon me, and which our timid sex are apt to feel in proportion to their love,

Long however I did not suffer, the sight of him over-paid me; and the soft reproach I had prepar'd for him, expir'd before it reach'd my lips.

I was still a-bed, yet unable to use my legs otherwise than awkwardly, and *Charles* flew to me, catches me in his arms, raised, and extending mine to meet his dear embrace, and gives me an account, interrupted by many a sweet parenthesis of kisses, of the success of his measures.

I could not help laughing at the fright the old woman had been put into, which my ignorance, and indeed my want of in-nocence, had far from prepar'd me for bespeaking: She had, it seems, apprehended that I had fled for shelter to some relation I had recollected in town, on my dislike of their ways and pro-ceeding towards me, and that this application came from thence. For, as *Charles* had rightly judg'd, not one neighbour had, at that still hour, seen the circumstance of my escape into the coach, or at least notic'd him; neither had any in the house the least hint or clue of suspicion of my having spoke to him, much less of my having clapt up such a sudden bargain with a perfect stranger: Thus the greatest improbability is not always what we should most mistrust.

We supp'd with all the gayety of two young giddy creatures at the top of their desires; and as I had most joyfully given up to

Charles the whole charge of my future happiness, I thought of nothing beyond the exquisite pleasure of possessing him.

He came to bed in due time, and this second night, the pain being pretty well over, I tasted, in full draughts, all the transports of perfect enjoyment. I swam, I bath'd in bliss, till both fell fast asleep, through the natural consequences of satisfi'd desires, and appeas'd flames; nor did we wake but to renew'd raptures.

Thus making the most of love, and life, did we stay at this lodging in *Chelsea* about ten days, in which time *Charles* took care to give his excursions from home a colourable gloss, and to keep his footing with his fond, indulgent grandmother, from whom he drew constant and sufficient supplies for the charge I was to him, and which was very trifling, in comparison with his former less regular course of pleasures.

Charles remov'd me then to a private ready-furnish'd lodging in *D——Street*, St. *James*'s, where he paid half a guinea a week for two rooms and a closet on the second floor, which he had been some time looking out for, and was more convenient for the frequency of his visits, than where he had at first plac'd me, in a house which I cannot say but I left with regret, as it was infinitely endear'd to me by the first possession of my *Charles*, and the circumstance of loosing there that jewel which can never be twice lost. The landlord however had no reason to complain of any thing, but of a procedure in *Charles* too liberal not to make him regret his loss of us.

Arriv'd at our new lodgings, I remember I thought them extremely fine, though ordinary enough even at that price; but had it been a dungeon that *Charles* had brought me to, his presence would have made it a little *Versailles*,

The landlady, Mrs. *Jones*, waited on us to our apartment, and with great volubility of tongue explain'd to us all its conveniences, "that her own maid should wait on us, —— that the best of quality had lodg'd at her house, —— that her first floor was let to a foreign secretary of an embassy, and his lady, — that I look'd like a very good-natur'd lady————". At the word "lady," I blush'd out of flatter'd vanity: this was too strong for a girl of my condition: for though *Charles* had had the precaution of dressing me in a less taudry flaunting style than were the cloaths I escap'd to him in, and of passing me for his wife that he had secretly married, and kept private, (the old story) on account of his friends. I dare swear this appear'd extremely apocryphal to a woman who knew the town so well as she did; but that was the least of her concern; It was impossible to be less scruple-ridden than she was: and the advantage of letting her rooms being her sole object, the truth itself would have far from scandaliz'd her, or broke her bargain.

A sketch of her picture and personal history will dispose you to account for the part she is to act in my concerns.

She was about forty-six years old, tall, meager, red-hair'd, with one of those trivial ordinary faces you meet with every where, and go about unheeded and unmention'd. In her youth she had been kept by a gentleman, who dying, left her forty pounds a year during her life, in consideration of a daughter he had by her; which daughter, at the age of seventeen, she sold, for not a very considerable sum neither, to a gentleman, who was going an *Envoy* abroad, and took his purchase with him, where he us'd her with the utmost tenderness, and it is thought was secretly married to her: but had constantly made a point of her not keeping up the least correspondence with a mother base enough to make a market of her own flesh and blood. However, as she had no nature, nor indeed any passion but that of money, this gave her no further uneasiness, than, as she thereby lost a handle of squeezing presents, or other after-advantages out of the bargain. Indifferent then by nature or constitution to every other pleasure but that of encreasing the lump, by any means whatever, she commenc'd a kind of private procuress, for which she was not amiss fitted by her grave decent appearance, and sometimes did a job in the match-making way; in short there was nothing that appear'd to her under the shape of gain, that she would not have undertaken. She knew most of the ways of the town, having not only herself been upon, but kept up constant intelligences in it, dealing, besides her practice in promoting a harmony between the two sexes, in private pawn-broking, and other profitable secrets. She rented the house she liv'd in, and made the most of it by letting it out in lodgings; and though she was worth, at least, near three or four thousand pounds, she would not allow herself even the necessaries of life, and pinn'd her subsistence entirely on what she could squeeze out of her lodgers,

When she saw such a young pair come under her roof, her immediate notions doubtless were how she should make the most money of us, by every means that money might be made, and which she rightly judg'd our situation and inexperience would soon beget her occasions of.

In this hopeful sanctuary, and under the clutches of this harpy,[38] did we pitch our residence. It will not be mighty material to you, or very pleasant to me, to enter into a detail of all the petty cut-throat ways and means with which she us'd to fleece us; all which *Charles* indolently chose to bear with, rather than take the trouble of removing, the difference of the expence being scarce attended to by a young gentleman who had no ideas of stint, or even economy, and a raw country girl who knew nothing of the matter.

Here, however, under the wings of my sovereignly belov'd, did I flow[39] the most delicious hours of my life; my *Charles* I had, and in him every thing my fond heart could wish or desire. He carried me to Plays, Operas, Masquerades, and every diversion of the Town, all which pleas'd me indeed, but pleas'd me infinitely the more for his being with me, and explaining every thing to me, and enjoying perhaps the natural impressions of surprize and admiration, which such sights, at the first never fail to excite in a *Country Girl* new to the delights of them: but to me they sensibly prov'd the power and full dominion of the sole passion of my heart over me, a passion in which soul and body were concenter'd, and left me no room for any other relish of life but love.

As to the men I saw at those places, or at any other, they suffer'd so much in the comparison my eyes made of them with my all-perfect *Adonis,* that I had not the infidelity even of one wandering thought to reproach myself with upon his account. He was the universe to me, and all that was not him, was nothing to me.

My love, in fine, was so excessive, that it arriv'd at annihilating every suggestion or kindling spark of jealousy, for one idea only tending that way gave me such exquisite torment, that my self-love, and dread of worse than death, made me for ever renounce and defy it: nor had I indeed occasion, for were I to enter here on a recital of several instances wherein *Charles* sacrific'd to me women of greater importance than I dare hint, (which considering his form was no such wonder), I might indeed give you full proof of his unshaken constancy to me, but would not you accuse me of warming up again a feast, that my vanity ought long ago to have been satisfy'd with?

In our cessations from active pleasure, *Charles* fram'd himself one, in instructing me, as far as his own lights reach'd; in a great many points of life, that I was, in consequence of my no-education, perfectly ignorant of: nor did I suffer one word to fall in vain from the mouth of my lovely teacher: I hung on every syllable he utter'd, and receiv'd as oracles all he said: whilst kisses were all the interruption. I could not refuse myself the pleasure of admitting, from lips that breath'd more than *Arabian* sweetness.[40]

I was in a little time enabl'd, by the progress I had made, to prove the deep regard I had paid to all that he had said to me; repeating it to him almost word for word; and to show that I was not entirely the parrot, but that I reflected upon, that I enter'd into it, I join'd my own comments, and ask'd him questions of explanation.

My country accent, and the rusticity of my gait, manners, and deportment, began now sensibly to wear off, so quick was my observation, and so efficacious my desire of growing every day worthier of his heart.

As to money, though he brought me constantly all he receiv'd, it was with difficulty he even got me to give it room in my bureau, and what cloaths I had, he could prevail on me to accept on, on no other foot, than that of pleasing him by the greater neatness in my dress, beyond which I had no ambition; I could have made a pleasure of the greatest toil, and work'd my fingers to the bone, with joy, to have supported him: guess then, if I could harbour any idea of being burdensome to him: and this disinterested turn in me was so unaffected, so much the dictate of my heart, that *Charles* could not but feel it, and if he did not love me as much as I did him, (which was the constant and only matter of sweet contention between us) he manag'd so at least as to give me the satisfaction of believing it impossible for man to be more tender, more true, more faithful than he was.

Our landlady, Mrs. *Jones*, came frequently up to my apartment from whence I never stirr'd on any pretext without *Charles:* nor was it long before she worm'd out, without much art, the secret of our having cheated the church of a ceremony; and in course of the terms we liv'd together upon: a circumstance which far from displeas'd her, considering the designs she had upon me, and which, alas! she will have too soon room to carry into execution. But in the mean time her own experience of life, let her see that any attempt however indirect, or disguis'd, to divert or break, at least presently, so strong a cement of hearts as ours was, could only end in losing two lodgers, of whom she made very competent advantages, if either of us came to smoak her commission,[41] for a commission she had from one of her customers, either to debauch or get me away from my keeper at any rate.

But the barbarity of my fate, soon sav'd her the task of disuniting us. I had now been eleven months with this life of my life, which had past in one continu'd rapid stream of delight: but nothing so violent was ever made to last. I was about three months gone with child by him, a circumstance which would have added to his tenderness, had he ever left me room to believe it could receive an addition, when the mortal, the unexpected blow of separation fell upon us. I shall gallop post over the particulars, which I shudder yet to think of, and cannot to this instant reconcile to myself how, or by what means I could outlive it.

Two live-long days had I linger'd through, without hearing from him, I who breath'd, who existed but in him, and had never yet seen twenty-four hours pass without seeing or hearing from him. The third day my impatience was so strong, my alarms had been so severe, that I perfectly sicken'd with them, and being unable to support the shock longer, I sunk upon the bed, and ringing for Mrs. *Jones*, who had far from comforted me under my anxieties, she came up and I had scarce breath and spirit enough to find words to beg of her if she would save my life, to fall upon some means of finding out instantly what was become of its only prop, and comfort: She pity'd me in a way that rather sharpen'd my affliction than suspended it, and went out upon this commission.

For she had not to go to *Charles*'s house, who liv'd but at an easy distance, in one of the streets that run into *Covent-Garden*. There she went into a public-house, and from thence sent for a maid servant, whose name I had given her, as the properest to inform her.

The maid readily came, and as readily, when Mrs. *Jones* enquir'd of her what was become of Mr. *Charles*, or whether he was gone out of town, acquainted her with the disposal of her master's son, which the very day after was no secret to the servants; such sure measures had he taken for the most cruel punishment of his child, for having more interest with his grand-mother than he had, though he made use of a pretence, plausible enough to get rid of him in this secret and abrupt manner, for fear her fondness should have interpos'd a bar to his leaving *England*, and proceeding on a voyage he had concerted for him, which pretext was, that it was indispensably necessary to secure a considerable inheritance, that devolv'd to him by the death of a rich merchant (his own brother) at one of the factories[42] in the South-Seas, of which he had lately receiv'd advice, together with a copy of the Will.

In consequence of which resolution to send away his son, he had, unknown to him, made the necessary preparations for fitting him out, struck a bargain with the captain of a ship, whose punctual execution of his orders he had secured by his interest with his principal owner and patron, and in short concerted his measures so secretly and effectually, that whilst his son thought he was going down the river that would take him a few hours, he was stopped on board of a ship, debar'd from writing, and more strictly watch'd than a state-criminal.

Thus was the idol of my soul torn from me, and forc'd on a long voyage without taking leave of one friend, or receiving one line of comfort, except a dry explanation and instructions from his father how to proceed, when he should arrive at his destin'd port, enclosing withal some letters of recommendation to a factor[43] there: all these particulars I did not learn minutely till some time after.

The maid at the same time added, that she was sure this usage of her sweet young master, would be the death of his grand-mama, as indeed it prov'd true, for the old lady on hearing it, did not survive the news a whole month, and as her fortune con-sisted in an annuity, out of which she had laid up no reserves, she left nothing worth mentioning to her so fatally envied darling, but absolutely refus'd to see his father before she died.

When Mrs. *Jones* return'd, and I observ'd her looks, they seem'd so unconcern'd and even nearest to pleas'd, that I half flatter'd myself, she was going to set my tortur'd heart at ease, by bringing me good news; but this indeed was a cruel delusion of hope: the barbarian, with all the coolness imaginable, stabs me to the heart, in telling me succinctly that he was sent away at least on a four years voyage, (here she stretch'd maliciously) and that I could not expect in reason ever to see him again: and all this with such pregnant circumstances, that I could not escape giving them credit, as in general they were indeed too true!

She had hardly finish'd her report, before I fainted away, and after several successive fits, all the while wild and senseless, I miscarried of the dear pledge of my *Charles*'s love: but the wretched never die when it is fittest that they should die, and women are hard-liv'd to a proverb.

The cruel and interested care taken to recover me, sav'd an odious life: which instead of the happiness and joys it had overflow'd in, all of a sudden presented no view before me of any thing but the depth of misery, horror, and the sharpest affliction.

Thus I lay six weeks, in the struggles of youth and constitution against the friendly efforts of death, which I constantly invok'd to my relief and deliverance, but which proving too weak for my wish, I recover'd at length, but into a state of stupefaction and despair that threaten'd me with a loss of my senses, and a mad-house.

Time, however, that great comforter in ordinary, began to assuage the violence of my suffering, and to numb my feeling of them. My health return'd to me, though I still retain'd an air of grief, dejection, and languor, which taking off from the ruddinesss of my country complexion, render'd it rather more delicate and affecting.

The landlady had all this time officiously provided, and seen that I wanted for nothing, and as soon as she saw me retriev'd into a condition of answering her purpose; one day after we had dined together, she congratulated me on my recovery, the merit of which she took entirely to herself, and all this by way of introduction to a most terrible, and scurvy epilogue: "You are now, says she, Miss *Fanny,* tolerably well, and you are very welcome to stay in these lodgings as long as you please; you see I have ask'd you for nothing this long time, but truely I have a call to make up a sum of money which must be answer'd"; and, with that, presents me with a bill for arrears of rent, diet, apothecary's charges, nurse, *&c.* sum total twenty-three pounds seventeen and six-pence: towards discharging of which I had not in the world (which she well knew) more than seven guineas, left by chance of my dear *Charles*'s common stock with me: at the same time she desir'd me to tell her what course I would take for payment. I burst out into a flood of tears, and told her my condition, that I would sell what few cloaths I had, and that for the rest, would pay her as soon as possible: but my distress being favourable to her views, only stiffen'd her the more.

She told me very coolly, that she was indeed sorry for my misfortunes, but that she must do herself justice, though it would go to the very heart of her to send such a tender young creature to prison:—At the word prison! every drop of my blood chill'd, and my fright acted so strongly upon me, that turning as pale and faint as a criminal at the first sight of his place of execution, I was on the point of swooning: my landlady, who wanted only to terrify me to a certain point, and not to throw me into a state of body inconsistent with her designs upon it, began to sooth me again, and told me, in a tone compos'd to more pity and gentleness, that it would be my own fault if she was forc'd to proceed to such extremities, but she believ'd there was a friend to be found in the world, who would make up matters to both our satisfactions, and that she would bring him to drink tea with us that very afternoon, when she hop'd we would come to a right understanding in our affairs. To all this, not a word of answer: I sat mute, confounded, terrify'd.

Mrs. *Jones*, however, judging rightly that it was her time to strike whilst the impressions were so strong upon me, left me to myself, and to all the terrors of an imagination, wounded to death by the idea of going to a prison, and, from a principle of self-preservation, snatching at every glimpse of redemption from it.

In this situation I sat near half an hour, swallow'd up in grief and despair, when my landlady came in, and observing a death-like dejection in my countenance, still in pursuance of her plan, put on a false pity, and bidding me be of good heart, things, she said, would not be so bad as I imagin'd, if I would be but my own friend: and closed with telling me she had brought a very honourable gentleman to drink tea with me, who would give me the best advice how to get rid of all my troubles: upon which, without waiting for a reply, she goes out, and returns with this very honourable gentleman, whose very honourable procuress she had been on this as well as other occasions.

The gentleman on his entering the room made me a very civil bow, which I had scarce strength, or presence of mind enough to return a curtsey to: when the landlady taking upon her to do all the honours of this first interview; for I had never, that I remember'd, (seen the gentleman before) sets a chair for him, and another for herself. All this while not a word on either side: a stupid stare was all the face I could put on this strange visit.

The tea was made, and the landlady, unwilling, I suppose, to lose any time, observing my silence and shyness before this entire stranger: "Come Miss *Fanny*," says she in a coarse familiar style, and tone of authority, "hold up your head, child, and do not let sorrow spoil that pretty face of yours: What! sorrows are only for a time: Come, be free, here is a worthy gentleman who has heard of your misfortunes, and is willing to serve you—you must be better acquainted with him; do not you now stand upon your punctilio's, and this and that, but make your market while you may."

At this so delicate, and eloquent harangue, the gentleman, who saw I look'd frighted and amaz'd, and indeed incapable of answering, took her up for breaking things in so abrupt a manner, as rather to shock than incline me to an acceptance of the good he intended me: then addressing himself to me, told me he was perfectly acquainted with my whole story, and every circumstance of my distress, which he own'd was a cruel plunge for one of my youth and beauty to fall into;—that he had long taken a liking to my person, for which he appeal'd to Mrs. *Jones*, there present, but finding me so deeply engag'd to another, he had lost all hopes of succeeding, till he heard the sudden reverse of fortune that had happen'd to me, on which he had given particular orders to my landlady to see that I should want for nothing, and that had he not been forc'd abroad to the *Hague* on affairs he could not refuse himself to, he would himself have attended me during my sickness;—that on his return, which was but the day before, he had, on learning my recovery, desir'd my landlady's good offices to introduce him to me, and was as angry at least, as I was shock'd, at the manner in which she had conducted herself towards obtaining him that happiness, but that to show me how much he disown'd her procedure, and how far he was from taking an ungenerous advantage of my situation, and from exacting any security for my gratitude, he would, before my face, that instant, discharge my debt entirely to my landlady, and give me her receipt in full, after which I should be at liberty either to reject or grant his suit, as he was much above putting any force upon my inclinations.

Whilst he was exposing his sentiments to me, I ventur'd just to look up to him, and observe his figure, which was that of a very well looking gentleman, well made, of about forty, dressed in a suit of plain cloaths, with a large diamond ring on one of his fingers, the lustre of which play'd in my eyes, as he wav'd his hand in talking, and rais'd my notions of his importance: in short, he might pass for what is commonly call'd a comely black man,[44] with an air of distinction natural to his birth and condition.

To all his speeches, however, I answer'd only in tears that flow'd plentifully to my relief, and choaking up my voice, excus'd me from speaking, very luckily, for I should not have known what to say.

The sight however mov'd him, as he afterwards told me, irresistibly, and by way of giving me some reason to be less powerfully afflicted, he drew out his purse, and calling for pen and ink, which the landlady was prepar'd for, paid her every farthing of her demand, independent of a liberal gratification, which was to follow unknown to me, and taking a receipt in full, very tenderly forc'd me to secure it, by guiding my hand, which he had thrust it into, so as to make me passively put it into my pocket.

Still I continued in a state of stupidity, or melancholic despair, as my spirits could not yet recover from the violent shocks they had receiv'd, and the accommodating landlady had actually left the room, and me alone with this strange gentleman before I observ'd it, and then observ'd it without alarm, for I was now lifeless, and indifferent to every thing.

The gentleman, however, no novice in affairs of this sort, drew near me, and under the pretence of comforting me, first with his handkerchief dried my tears as they ran down my cheeks; presently, he ventur'd to kiss me; on my part neither resistance nor compliance; I sat stock-still; and now looking on myself as bought by the payment that had been transacted before me, I did not care what became of my wretched body: and wanting life, spirits, or courage to oppose the least struggle, even that of the modesty of my sex, I suffer'd tamely whatever the gentleman pleased, who proceeding insensibly from freedom to freedom, insinuated his hand between my handkerchief and bosom, which he handled at discretion: finding thus no repulse and that every thing favour'd, beyond expectation, the completion of his desires, he took me in his arms, and bore me without life or motion to the bed, on which laying me gently down, and having me at what advantage he pleas'd, I did not so much as know what he was about, till recovering from a trance of lifeless insensibility, I found him buried in me, whilst I lay passive and innocent of the least sensation of pleasure: a death cold corpse could scarce have had less life or sense in it. As soon as he had thus pacified a passion, which had too little respected the condition I was in, he got off, and after recomposing the disorder of my cloaths, employ'd himself with the utmost tenderness to calm the transports of remorse and madness at myself, with which I was seiz'd, too late I confess, for having suffer'd on that bed the embraces of an utter stranger: I tore my hair, wrung my hands, and beat my breast like a mad-woman: but when my new master, for in that light I then view'd him, applied himself to appease me, as my whole rage was levell'd at myself, no part of which I thought myself permitted to aim at him, I begg'd him with more submission than anger, to leave me alone, that I might at least enjoy my affliction in quiet; this he positively refus'd, for fear, as he pretended, that I should do myself a mischief.

Violent passions seldom last long, and those of women least of any. A dead still calm succeeded this storm, which ended in a profuse shower of tears.

Had any one, but a few instants before, told me that I should have ever known any man but *Charles*, I would have spit in his face, or had I been offer'd infinitely a greater sum of money than that I saw paid for me, I had spurn'd the proposal in cold blood: but our virtues and our vices depend too much on our circumstances; unexpectedly beset as I was, betray'd by a mind weakned by a long severe affliction, and stunn'd with the terrors of a goal, my defeat will appear the more excusable, since I certainly was not present at, or a party in any sense, to it. However, as the first enjoyment is decisive, and he was now over the bar, I thought I had no longer a right to refuse the caresses of one that had got that advantage over me, no matter how obtain'd: conforming my-self then to this maxim, I consider'd myself as so much in his power, that I endur'd his kisses and embraces without affecting struggles, or anger, not that they as yet gave me any pleasure, or prevail'd over the aversion of my soul, to give myself up to any sensation of that sort: what I suffer'd, I suffer'd out of a kind of gratitude, and as matter of course after what had pass'd.

He was however so regardful as not to attempt the renewal of those extremities which had thrown me just before into such vi-olent agitations; but, now secure of possession, contented him-self with bringing me to temper by degrees, and waiting at the hand of time for those fruits of his generosity and courtship, which he since often reproach'd himself with having gather'd much too green, when yielding to the invitations of my inability to resist him, and overborn by desires, he had wreak'd his passion on a mere lifeless spiritless body, dead to all purposes of joy, since taking none, it ought to have been suppos'd incapable of giving any. This is however certain, my heart never thoroughly forgave him the manner in which I had fall'n to him, although, in point of interest, I had reason to be pleas'd that he found in my person—wherewithal to keep him from leaving me as easily as he had had me.

The evening was in the mean time so far advanc'd, that the maid came in to lay the cloth for supper, when I understood with joy, that my landlady, whose sight was present poison to me, was not to be with us.

Presently a neat and elegant supper was introduc'd, and a bot-tle of burgundy, with the other necessaries, were set on a dumb-waiter.

The maid quitting the room, the gentleman insisted, with a tender warmth, that I should sit up in the elbow chair by the fire, and see him eat, if I cou'd not be prevail'd on to eat myself. I obey'd, with a heart full of affliction, at the comparison it made between those delicious tete-a-tetes with my ever dear youth, and this forc'd situation, this new awkward scene, impos'd and obtruded on me by cruel necessity.

At supper, after a great many arguments us'd to comfort, and

reconcile me to my fate, he told me that his name was *H*———,
brother to the earl of *L*———, and that having, by the suggestions
of my landlady, been led to see me, he had found me perfectly to
his taste, had given her a commission to procure me at any rate,
and that he had at length succeeded as much to his satisfaction,
as he passionately wish'd it might be to mine, adding withal
some flattering assurances that I should have no cause to repent
my knowledge of him.

I had now got down at least half a partridge, and three or four
glasses of wine, which he compell'd me to drink by way of
restoring nature, but whether there was any thing extraordinary
put into the wine, or whether there wanted no more to revive the
natural warmth of my constitution, and give fire to the old train,
I began no longer to look with that constraint, not to say disgust,
on Mr. *H*——— which I had hitherto done, but withal there was
not the least grain of love mix'd with this softening of my sentiments: any other man would have been just the same to me as
Mr. *H*———, that stood in the same circumstances, and had done
for me, and with me, what he had done.

There are not, on earth at least, eternal griefs; mine were, if
not at an end, at least suspended: my heart, which had been so
long overloaded with anguish and vexation, began to dilate and
open to the least gleam of diversion, or amusement. I wept a little, and my tears reliev'd me: I sigh'd, and my sighs seem'd to
lighten me of a load that opprest me: my countenance grew, if
not cheerful, at least more compos'd, and free.

Mr. *H*——— who had watched, perhaps brought on this
change, knew too well not to seize it: He thrust the table imper-
ceptibly from between us, and bringing his chair to face me, he
soon began, after preparing me by all the endearments of assurances, and protestations, to lay hold of my hands, to kiss me, and
once more to make free with my bosom, which being at full liberty from the disorder of my loose dishabil, now panted and
throb'd less with indignation than with fear and bashfulness, at
being used so familiarly by still a stranger: but he soon gave me
greater occasion to exclaim, by stooping down and slipping his
hand above my garters; thence he strove to regain the pass which

he had before found so open, and unguarded: but now he could not unlock the twist of my thighs: I gently complain'd, and begg'd him to let me alone; told him I was not well: however, as he saw there was more form and ceremony in my resistance, than good earnest, he made his conditions for desisting from pursuing his point, that I should be put instantly to bed, whilst he gave certain orders to the landlady, and that he would return in an hour, when he hop'd to find me more reconcil'd to his passion for me, than I seem'd at present. I neither assented nor deny'd, but in my air and manner of receiving this proposal, gave him to see that I did not think myself enough my own mistress to refuse it.

Accordingly he went out and left me, when a minute or two after, before I could recover myself into any composure for thinking, the maid came in with her mistress's service, and a small silver porrenger of what she call'd a bridal posset,[45] and desir'd me to eat it as I went to bed, which consequently I did, and felt immediately a heat, a fire run like a hue-and-cry through ev'ry part of my body; I burnt, I glow'd, and wanted even little of wishing for any man.

The maid, as soon as I was lain down, took the candle away, and wishing me a good night, went out of the room, and shut the door after her.

She had hardly time to get down stairs before Mr. *H*—— open'd my room door softly, and came in, now undressed, in his night-gown and cap, with two lighted wax-candles, and bolting the door, gave me, though I expected him, some sort of alarm. He came a tip-toe to the bed-side, and saying with a gentle whisper, "pray, my dear, do not be startl'd,—I will be very tender and kind to you." He then hurry'd off his cloaths, and leap'd into bed, having given me openings enough, whilst he was stripping, to observe his brawny structure, strong made limbs, and rough shaggy breast.

The bed shook again when it receiv'd this new load. He lay on the outside, where he kept the candles burning, no doubt for the satisfaction of ev'ry sense; for as soon as he had kiss'd me, he roll'd down the bed-cloaths, and seem'd transported with the

view of all my person at full length, which he cover'd with a pro-
fussion of kisses, sparing no part of me. Then, being on his knees
between my thighs, he drew up his shirt, and bared all his hairy
thighs, and stiff staring truncheon, red-topt, and rooted into a
thicket of curls, which cover'd his belly to his navel, and gave it
the air of a flesh-brush: and soon I felt it joining close to mine,
when he had drove the nail up to the head, and left no partition
but the intermediate hair on both sides.

I had it now, I felt it now: and beginning to drive, he soon gave
nature such a powerful summons down to her favourite quarters,
that she could no longer refuse repairing thither: all my animal
spirits then rush'd mechanically[46] to that center of attraction,
and presently, inly warm'd, and stirr'd as I was beyond bearing, I
lost all restraint, and yielding to the force of the emotion, gave
down, as mere woman, those effusions of pleasure, which in the
strictness of still faithful love, I could have wish'd to have held
up.

Yet oh! what an immense difference did I feel between this
impression of a pleasure merely animal, and struck out of the
collision of the sexes, by a passive bodily effect, from that sweet
fury, that rage of active delight which crowns the enjoyments of
a mutual love-passion, where two hearts tenderly and truly
united, club to exalt the joy, and give it a spirit and soul that bids
defiance to that end, which mere momentary desires generally
terminate in, when they die of a surfeit of satisfaction.

Mr. *H*—— whom no distinctions of that sort seem'd to dis-
tract, scarce gave himself or me breathing time from the last encounter, but as if he had talk'd himself to prove that the
appearances of his vigour, were not signs hung out in vain, in a
few minutes he was in a condition for renewing the onset, to
which preluding with a storm of kisses, he drove the same
course as before with unbated fervour, and thus in repeated engagements, kept me constantly in exercise till dawn of morning,
in all which time, he made me full sensible of the virtues of his
firm texture of limbs, his square shoulders, broad chest, compact
hard muscles, in short a system of manliness, that might pass for
no bad image of our ancient sturdy barons, when they weilded

the battle-ax, whose race is now so thoroughly refin'd and fritter'd away into the more delicate modern-built frame of our pap-nerv'd softlings, who are as pale, as pretty, and almost as masculine as their sisters.[47]

Mr. *H——*, content however with having the day break upon his triumphs, resign'd me up to the refreshment of a rest we both wanted, and we soon dropt into a profound sleep.

Tho' he was some time awake before me, yet did he not offer to disturb a repose he had given me so much occasion for; but on my first stirring, which was not till past ten o'clock, I was oblig'd to endure one more trial of his manhood.

About eleven, in came Mrs. *Jones*, with two basins of the richest soup, which her experience in these matters had mov'd her to prepare. I pass over the fulsome compliments, the cant of this decent procuress, with which she saluted us both, but tho' my blood rose at the sight of her, I suppress my emotions, and gave all my concern to reflections on what would be the consequence of this new engagement.

But Mr. *H——*, who penetrated my uneasiness, did not long suffer me to languish under it, and acquainted me, that having taken a solid sincere affection to me, he would begin by giving me one leading mark of it, in removing me out of a house which must for many reasons be irksome and disagreeable to me, into convenient lodgings, where he would take all imaginable care of me; and desiring me not to have any explanations with my land-lady, or be impatient till he returned, he dress'd and went out, having left me a purse with two and twenty guineas in it, being all he had about him, as he exprest it, to keep my pocket till farther supplies.

As soon as he was gone, I felt the usual consequence of the first launch into vice; (for my love attachment to *Charles* never appear'd to me in that light.) I was instantly born away down the stream, without the power of making back to the shore. My dreadful necessities, my gratitude, and above all, to say the plain truth, the dissipation, and diversion I began to find in this new acquaintance, from the black corroding thoughts my heart had been a prey to, ever since the absence of my dear *Charles*, concurr'd to stun all contrary reflections. If I now thought of my first, my only charmer, it was still with the tenderness and regret of the fondest love, embitter'd with the consciousness that I was no longer worthy of him. I could have beg'd my bread with him all over the world, but, wretch that I was! I had neither the virtue or courage requisite not to outlive my separation from him.

Yet, had not my heart been thus preingag'd, Mr. *H*—— might probably have been the sole master of it, but the place was full, and the force of conjunctures alone had made him the possessor of my person, the charms of which had, by the bye, been his sole object, and passion, and were of course no foundation for a love either very delicate, or very durable. He did not return till six in the evening, to take me away to my new lodgings, and my move-ables being soon pack'd, and convey'd into a hackney-coach, it cost me but little regret to take my leave of a landlady whom I thought I had so much reason not to be over-pleas'd with, and as for her part, she made no other difference of my staying, or going, but what that of the profit created.

We soon got to the house appointed for me, which was that of a plain tradesman, who, on the score of interest, was entirely at Mr. *H*——'s devotion, and who let him the first floor very gen-teelly furnish'd for two guineas a week, of which I was instated mistress, with a maid to attend me.

He staid with me that evening, and we had a supper from a neighbouring tavern, after which, and a gay glass or two, the maid put me to bed, Mr. *H*—— soon follow'd, and notwith-standing the fatigues of the preceding night, I found no quarter nor remission from him. He piqu'd himself, as he told me, on doing the honours of my new apartment.

The morning being pretty well advanc'd, we got to breakfast: and the ice now broke, my heart, no longer engross'd by love, began to take ease, and to please itself with such trifles as Mr. *H*——'s liberal liking led him to make his court to the usual van-ity of our sex. Silks, laces, earrings, pearl-necklace, gold watch, in short all the trinkets and articles of dress were lavishly heap'd upon me, the sense of which, if it did not create returns of love, forc'd a kind of grateful fondness something like love, a distinction it would be spoiling the pleasure of nine tenths of the keepers in the town to make, and is I suppose the very good reason why so few of them ever do make it.

I was now establish'd the kept mistress, in form, well lodg'd, with a very sufficient allowance, and lighted up with all the lustre of dress.

Mr. *H*—— continu'd kind and tender to me, yet, with all this I was far from happy; for, besides my regrets for my dear youth, which though often suspended, or diverted, still return'd upon me in certain melancholic moments with redoubl'd violence, I wanted more society, more dissipation.

As to Mr. *H*——, he was so much my superior in every sense, that I felt it too much to the disadvantage of the gratitude I ow'd him, thus he gain'd my esteem, though he could not raise my taste; I was qualify'd for no sort of conversation with him, except one sort, and that is a satisfaction which leaves tiresome intervals, if not fill'd up by love, or other amusements.

Mr. *H*——, so experienc'd, so learned in the ways of women, numbers of whom had past through his hands, doubtless soon perceiv'd this uneasiness, and without approving or liking me the better for it, had the complaisance to indulge me.

He made suppers at my lodgings, where he brought several companions of his pleasures, with their mistresses, and by this means I got into a circle of acquaintance that soon strip'd me of all the remains of bashfulness and modesty which might be yet left of my country-education, and were, to a just taste, perhaps, the greatest of my charms.

We visited one another in form, and mimick'd, as near as we could, all the miseries, the follies, and impertinences of the women of quality, in the round of which they trifle away their time, without its ever entering into their little heads, that on earth there cannot subsist any thing more silly, more flat, more insipid and worthless, than, generally consider'd, their system of life is: they ought to treat the men as their tyrants indeed! were they to condemn them to it.

But tho', amongst the kept mistresses (and I was now acquainted with a good many, besides some useful matrons, who
live by their connexions with them) I hardly knew one that did
not perfectly detest their keepers, and of course, made little or
no scruple of any infidelity they could safely accomplish, I had
still no notion of wronging mine: for besides that no mark of
jealousy on his side started me the hint, or gave me the provocation to play him a trick of that sort, and that his constant generosity, politeness, and tender attentions to please me, forc'd a
regard to him, that, without affecting my heart, insur'd him my
fidelity, no object had yet presented, that could overcome the habitual liking I had contracted for him: and I was on the eve of obtaining from the movements of his own voluntary generosity, a
modest provision for life, when an accident happen'd which
broke all the measures he had resolv'd upon in my favour.

I had now liv'd near seven months with Mr. *H*——, when one
day returning to my lodgings, from a visit in the neighbourhood,
where I us'd to stay longer, I found the street-door open, and the
maid of the house standing at it talking with some of her acquaintance, so that I came in without knocking; and as I past by,
she told me Mr. *H*—— was above. I stept up stairs into my own
bed-chamber, with no other thought than of pulling off my hat,
&c. and then to wait upon him in the dining-room, into which
my bed-chamber had a door, as is common enough. Whilst I was
untying my hat-strings, I fancy'd I heard my maid *Hannah*'s
voice, and a sort of tustle, which raising my curiosity, I stole
softly to the door, where a knot in the wood had been slipt out,
and afforded a very commanding peep-hole to the scene then in
agitation, the actors of which had been too earnestly employ'd,
to hear my opening my own door, from the landing place of the
stairs, into my bed-chamber.

The first sight that struck me, was Mr. *H*—— pulling and
hauling this course country-strammel[48] towards a couch that
stood in the corner of the dining-room; to which the girl made
only a sort of an awkward hoidening resistance, crying out so
loud that I who listen'd at the door could scarce hear her, "Pray,

Sir, don't—let me alone—I am not for your turn.—You cannot, sure, demean yourself with such a poor body as I—. Lord, Sir, my mistress may come home.—I must not indeed. I will cry out—" All which did not hinder her from insensibly suffering herself to be brought to the foot of the couch; upon which a push of no mighty violence serv'd to give her a very easy fall, and my gentleman having got up his hands to the strong-hold of her *virtue,* she no doubt thought it was time to give up the argument, and that all further defence would be vain; and he throwing her petticoats over her face, which was now as red as scarlet, discover'd a pair of stout, plump, substantial thighs, and tolerably white; he mounted them round his hips, and coming out with his drawn weapon, stuck it in the cloven spot, where he seem'd to find a less difficult entrance than perhaps he had flatter'd himself with (for by the way this Blouze[49] had left her place in the country for a bastard) and indeed all his motions shew'd he was lodg'd pretty much at large. After he had done, his *dearee* gets up, drops her petticoats down, and smooths her apron and handkerchief. Mr. *H*—— look'd a little silly, and taking out some money, gave it her, with an air indifferent enough, biding her be a good girl, and say nothing.

Had I lov'd this man, it was not in nature for me to have had patience to see the whole scene through: I should have broke in and play'd the jealous princess with a vengance; but that was not the case, my pride alone was hurt, my heart not, and I could easier win upon myself to see how far he would go, till I had no uncertainty upon my conscience.

The least delicate of all affairs of this sort being now over, I retir'd softly into my closet, where I began to consider what I should do: my first scheme naturally was to rush in and upbraid them: this indeed flatter'd my present emotions and vexations, as it would have given immediate vent to them; but on second thoughts, not being so clear as to the consequence to be apprehended from such a step, I began to doubt whether it was not better to dissemble my discovery, till a safer season, when Mr. *H*—— should have perfected the settlement he had made over-

tures to me of, and which I was not to think such a violent explanation, as I was indeed not equal to the management of, could
possibly forward, and might destroy. On the other hand, the
provocation seem'd too gross, too flagrant, not to give me some
thoughts of revenge, the very start of which idea restor'd me to
perfect composure, and delighted as I was with the confus'd plan
of it in my head, I was easily mistress enough of myself to support the part of ignorance I had prescrib'd to myself; and as all
this circle of reflections was instantly over, I stole a tip-toe to the
passage-door, and opening it with a noise, past for having that
moment come home; and after a short pause, as if to pull off my
things, I open'd the door into the dining-room, where I found
the dowdy blowing the fire, and my faithful shepherd walking
about the room, and whistling, as cool and unconcern'd, as if
nothing had happen'd; I think, however, he had not much to brag
of having out-dissembled me; for I kept up, nobly, the character
of our sex for art, and went up to him with the same open air of
frankness, as I had ever receiv'd him. He staid but a little while,
made some excuse for not being able to stay the evening with
me, and went out.

As for the wench, she was now spoil'd at least for my servant;
and scarce eight and forty hours were gone round, before her insolence, on what had pass'd between Mr. H—— and her, gave me
so fair an occasion to turn her away at a minute's warning, that
not to have done it would have been the wonder; so that he could
neither disapprove it, nor find in it the least reason to suspect my
original motive. What became of her afterwards I know not; but
generous as Mr. H—— was, he undoubtedly made her amends:
tho' I dare answer, that he kept up no farther commerce with her
of that sort; as his stooping to such a coarse morsel, was only a
sudden sally of lust, on seeing a wholesome-looking, buxom
country wench, and no more strange than hunger, or even a
wimsical appetite's making a flying meal of neck-beef, for
change of diet.

Had I consider'd this escape of Mr. H—— in no more than
that light, and contented myself with turning away the wench, I
had thought and acted right; but, flush'd as I was with imaginary

wrongs, I should have held Mr. *H——* to have been too cheaply off, if I had not push'd my revenge farther, and repaid him, as exactly as I could for the soul of me, in the same coin.

Nor was this worthy act of justice long delaid: I had it too much at heart. Mr. *H——* had, about a fortnight before, taken into his service a tenant's son, just come out of the country, a very handsome young lad, scarce turn'd of nineteen, fresh as a rose, well shap'd, and clever-limb'd; in short, a very good excuse for any woman's liking, even tho' revenge had been out of the question; any woman, I say, who was disprejudic'd, and had wit and spirit enough to prefer a point of pleasure to a point of pride.

Mr. *H——* had clap'd a livery upon him; and his chief employ was, after being shewn my lodgings, to bring and carry letters or messages between his master and me; and as the situation of all kept-ladies is not the fittest to inspire respect even to the meanest of mankind, and perhaps less of it from the most ignorant, I could not help observing, that this lad, who was, I suppose, acquainted with my relation to his master by his fellow servants, used to eye me, in that bashful confus'd way, more expressive, more moving, and readier catch'd at by our sex, than any other declarations whatever: my figure had, it seems, struck him, and modest and innocent as he was, he did not himself know that the pleasure he took in looking at me was love, or desire; but his eyes, naturally wanton, and now enflam'd by passion, spoke a great deal more than he durst have imagin'd they did. Hitherto indeed I had only taken notice of the comeliness of the youth, but without the least design: My pride alone would have guarded me from a thought that way, had not Mr. *H——*'s condescension with my maid, where there was not half the temptation in point of person, set me a dangerous example; but now I began to look on this stripling as every way a delicious instrument of my design'd retaliation upon Mr. *H——*, of an obligation for which I should have made a conscience to die in his debt.

In order then to pave the way for the accomplishment of my scheme, for two or three times that the young fellow came to me with messages, I manag'd so, as without affectation, to have him admitted to my bed-side, or brought to me at my toilet, where I was dressing; and by carelessly shewing, or letting him see, as if without meaning or design, sometimes my bosom rather more bare than it should be; sometimes my hair, of which I had a very fine head, in the natural flow of it while combing; sometimes a neat leg, that had unfortunately slipt its garter, which I made no scruple of tying before him; easily gave him the impressions favourable to my purpose, which I could perceive to sparkle in his eyes, and glow in his cheeks. Then certain slight squeezes by the hand, as I took letters from him, did his business compleatly.

When I saw him thus mov'd, and fir'd for my purpose, I inflam'd him yet more, by asking him several leading questions; such as, had he a mistress?—was she prettier than me?—could he love such a one as I was?—and the like; to all which the blushing simpleton answer'd to my wish, in a strain of perfect nature, perfect undebauch'd innocence, but with all the awkwardness and simplicity of country-breeding.

When I thought I had sufficiently ripen'd him for the laudable point I had in view; one day that I expected him at a particular hour, I took care to have the coast clear for the reception I design'd him: and, as I had laid it, he came to the dining-room door, tapped at it, and on my bidding him come in. He did so, and shut the door after him: I desir'd him then to bolt it on the inside, pretending it would not otherwise keep shut.

I was then lying at length on that very couch, the scene of Mr. *H*——'s polite joys, in an undress, which was with all the art of negligence flowing loose, and in a most tempting disorder, no stays, no hoop—no incumbrance whatever: on the other hand, he stood at a little distance, that gave me a full view of a fine featur'd, shapely, healthy, country lad, breathing the sweets of fresh blooming youth: his hair, which was of a perfect shining black, play'd to his face in natural side-curls, and was set out with a smart tuck-up behind: new buck-skin breeches, that clipping close, shew'd the shape of a plump well made thigh, white stockings, garter-laced livery, shoulder-knot, altogether compos'd a figure in which the beauties of pure flesh and blood, appear'd under no disgrace from the lowness of a dress, to which a certain spruce neatness seems peculiarly fitted.

I bid him come towards me, and give me his letter, at the same time throwing down carelessly, a book I had in my hands. He colour'd, and came within reach of delivering me the letter, which he held out awkwardly enough for me to take, with his eyes rivetted on my bosom, which was, through the design'd disorder of my handkerchief, sufficiently bare, and rather shaded than hid.

I, smiling in his face, took the letter, and immediately catching gently hold of his shirt-sleeve, drew him towards me, blushing, and almost trembling: for surely his extreme bashfulness, and utter inexperience, call'd for at least all these advances to encourage him. His body was now conveniently inclin'd towards me, and just softly chucking his smooth beardless chin, I ask'd him, *If he was afraid of a lady?*—and with that took and carrying his hand to my breasts, I prest it tenderly to them. They were now finely furnish'd, and raised in flesh, so that panting with desire, they rose, and fell, in quick heaves, under his touch: at this the boy's eyes began to lighten with all the fires of inflam'd nature, and his cheeks flush'd with a deep scarlet: tongue-tied with joy, rapture, and bashfulness, he could not speak, but then his looks, his emotion, sufficiently satisfy'd me that my train had taken, and that I had no disappointment to fear.

My lips, which I threw in his way, so as that he could not escape kissing them, fix'd, fir'd and embolden'd him, and now glancing my eyes towards that part of his dress which cover'd the essential object of enjoyment, I plainly discover'd the swell and commotion there, and as I was now too far advanc'd to stop in so fair a way, and was indeed no longer able to contain myself, or wait the slower progress of his maiden bashfulness, (for such it seem'd, and really was) I stole my hand upon his thighs, down one of which, I could both see and feel a stiff hard body, confin'd by his breeches, that my fingers could discover no end to. Curious then and eager to unfold so alarming a mystery, playing as it were with his buttons, which were bursting ripe from the active force within, those of his waist-band and foreflap flew open at a touch, when out *it* started; and now, disengag'd from the shirt, I saw with wonder and surprize, what? not the play-thing of a boy, not the weapon of a man, but a may-pole of so enormous a standard, that had proportions been observ'd, it must have belong'd to a young giant: its prodigious size made me shrink again: yet! I could not without pleasure behold, and even ventur'd to feel, such a length! such a breadth of animated ivory, perfectly well turn'd and fashion'd, the proud stiffness of which distended its skin, whose smooth polish, and velvet-softness, might vie with that of the most delicate of our sex, and whose exquisite whiteness was not a little set off by a sprout of black curling hair round the root, through the jetty sprigs of which, the fair skin shew'd as, in a fine evening, you may have remark'd the clear light æther, through the branch-work of distant trees, over topping the summit of a hill: then the broad and blueish-casted incarnate of the head, and blue serpentines of its veins, altogether compos'd the most striking assemblage of figure and colours in nature; in short, it stood an object of terror and delight.

But what was yet more surprising, the owner of this natural curiosity (through the want of occasions in the strictness of his home-breeding, and the little time he had been in town not having afforded him one) was hitherto an absolute stranger, in practice at least, to the use of all that manhood he was so nobly stock'd with; and it now fell to my lot to stand his first trial of it, if I could resolve to run the risks of its disproportion to that tender part of me, which such an oversiz'd machine was very fit to lay in ruins.

But it was now of the latest to deliberate, for by this time, the young fellow, over-heated with the present objects, and too high-mettl'd to be longer curb'd in by that modesty and awe which had hitherto restrain'd him, ventur'd, under the stronger impulse and instructive promptership of nature alone, to slip his hands, trembling with eager impetuous desires, under my petti-coats, and seeing, I suppose, nothing extremely severe in my looks to stop, or dash him, he feels out and seizes gently the center-spot of his ardours: oh then! the fiery touch of his fingers determines me, and my fears melting away before the growing intolerable heat, my thighs disclose of themselves, and yield all liberty to his hand: and now a favourable movement giving my petticoats a toss, the avenue lay too fair, too open to be missed; he is now upon me: I had placed myself with a jet under him, as commodious, and open as possible to his attempts, which were untoward enough, for his machine meeting with no inlet, bore and batter'd stiffly against me in random pushes, now above, now below, now beside his point, till burning with impatience from its irritating touches, I guided gently with my hand, this furious fescue[50] to *where* my young novice was now to be taught his first lesson of pleasure. Thus he nick'd at length the warm and insufficient orifice: but he was made to find no breach practicable, and mine, though so often enter'd, was still far from wide enough to take him easily in.

By my direction, however, the head of his unwieldy machine was so critically pointed, that feeling him fore-right[51] against the tender opening, a favourable motion from me, met his timely thrust, by which the lips of it, strenuously dilated, gave way to his thus assisted impetuosity, so that we might both feel that he had gain'd a lodgment: persuing then his point, he soon, by violent, and to me most painful piercing thrusts, wedges himself at least so far in, as to be now tolerably secure of his entrance: here he stuck; and I now felt such a mixture of pleasure and pain, as there is no giving a definition of: I dreaded, alike, his splitting me farther up, or his withdrawing: I could not bear either to keep, or part with him. The sense of pain, however, prevailing, from his prodigious size and stiffness, acting upon me in those continu'd rapid thrusts with which he furiously persu'd his penetration, made me cry out gently, "Oh, my dear, you hurt me!" This was enough to check the tender respectful boy, even in his mid-career: and he immediately drew out the sweet cause of my complaint, whilst his eyes eloquently express'd at once his grief for hurting me, and his reluctance at dislodging from quarters, of which the warmth and closeness had given him a gust of plea-

sure that he was now desire-mad to satisfy, and yet too much a
novice not to be afraid of my withholding his relief, on account
of the pain he had put me to.

But I was myself far from being pleas'd with his having too
much regarded my tender exclaims, for now more and more fir'd
with the object before me, as it still stood with the fiercest erection, unbonneted, and displaying its broad vermillion head, I
first gave the youth a re-encouraging kiss, which he repaid me
with a fervour that seem'd at once to thank me, and bribe my farther compliance, and I soon replac'd myself in a posture to receive, at all risks, the renew'd invasion, which he did not delay an
instant; for being presently remounted, I once more felt the
smooth hard gristle, forcing an entrance, which he atchiev'd
rather easier than before: pain'd, however, as I was, with his efforts of gaining a complete admission, which he was so regardful
as to manage by gentle degrees, I took care not to complain. In
the mean time, the soft strait passage gradually loosens, yields,
and, stretch'd to its utmost bearing, by the stiff, thick, in-driven
engine, sensible at once to the ravishing pleasure of the *feel,* and
the pain of the distension, let him in about half way, when all the
most nervous activity he now exerted to further his penetration,
gain'd him not an inch of his purpose; for whilst he hesitated
there, the crisis of pleasure overtook him, and the close com-
pressure of the warm surrounding fold, drew from him the
extatic gush, even before mine was ready to meet it, kept up by
the pain I had endur'd in the course of the engagement, from the
unsufferable size of his weapon, tho' it was not as yet in above
half its length.

I expected then, but without wishing it, that he would draw;
but was pleasingly disappointed, for he was not to be let off so.
The well-breath'd youth, hot-mettl'd, and flush with genial
juices, was now fairly in for making me know my driver: as soon
then as he had made a short pause, waking as it were out of the
trance of pleasure, (in which every sense seem'd lost for a while,
whilst, with his eyes shut, and short quick breathings, he had
yielded down his maiden tribute); he still kept his post, yet un-
sated with enjoyment, and solacing in these so new delights, till

his stiffness, which had scarce perceptibly remitted, being throughly recover'd to him, who had not once unsheath'd, he proceeded afresh to cleave and open to himself an entire entry into me, which was not a little made easy to him by the balsamic injection, with which he had just plentifully moisten'd the whole internals of the passage. Redoubling then the active energy of his thrusts, favour'd by the fervid appetency of my motions, the soft oil'd wards can no longer stand so effectual a picklock, but yield, and open him an entrance. And now with conspiring nature, and my industry, strong to aid him, he pierces, penetrates, and at length, winning his way inch by inch, gets entirely in, and finally, a home-made thrust, sheaths it up to the guard; on the information of which, from the close jointure of our bodies, (insomuch that the hair on both sides perfectly interweav'd, and incurl'd, together), the eyes of the transported youth sparkl'd with more joyous fires, and all his looks and motions acknowledg'd excess of pleasure, which I now began to share, for I felt him in my very vitals! I was quite sick with delight! stir'd beyond bearing with its furious agitations within me, and gorg'd and cram'd even to a surfeit: thus I lay gasping, panting, under him, till his broken breathings, faultering accents, eyes twinkling with humid fires, lunges more furious, and an increased stiffness gave me to hail the approaches of the second period:—it came,—and the sweet youth, overpower'd with the extasy, died away in my arms, melting in a flood, that shot in genial warmth into the innermost recesses of my body, every conduit of which, dedicated to that pleasure, was on flow to mix with it. Thus we continu'd for some instants, loft, breathless, senseless of every thing, and in every part, but those favourite ones of nature, in which all that we enjoy'd of life and sensation, was now totally concenter'd.

When our mutual trance was a little over, and the young fellow had withdrawn that delicious stretcher, with which he had most plentifully drown'd all thoughts of revenge, in the sense of actual pleasure, the widen'd wounded passage refunded a stream of pearly liquids, which flow'd down my thighs, mix'd with streaks of blood the marks of the ravage of that monstrous machine of his, which had now triumph'd over a kind of second maiden-head. I stole, however, my handkerchief to those parts, and wip'd them as dry as I could, whilst he was re-adjusting, and buttoning up.

I made him now sit down by me, and as he had gather'd courage from such extreme intimacy, he gave me an aftercourse of pleasure, in a natural burst of tender gratitude and joy, at the new scenes of bliss I had open'd to him; scenes positively so new, that he had never before had the least acquaintance with that mysterious mark, the cloven stamp of female distinction, tho' nobody better qualify'd than he to penetrate into its deepest recesses, or do it nobler justice; but when by certain motions, certain unquietnesses of his hands, that wander'd not without design, I found he languish'd for satisfying a curiosity, natural enough, to view and handle those parts which attract and concenter the warmest force of imagination, charm'd as I was to have any occasion of obliging and humouring his young desires, I suffer'd him to proceed as he pleas'd, without check or controul, to the satisfaction of them.

Easily then reading in my eyes the full permission of myself to all his wishes, he scarce pleas'd himself more than me, when having insinuated his hands under my petticoat and shift, he presently remov'd those bars to the sight, by slyly lifting them upwards, under favour of a thousand kisses, which he thought, perhaps, necessary to divert my attention to what he was about. All my drapery being now roll'd up to my waist, I threw myself into such a posture upon the couch, as gave up to him, in full view, the whole region of delight, and all the luxurious landscape round it. The transported youth, devour'd every thing with his eyes, and try'd with his fingers to lay more open to his sight the secrets of that dark and delicious deep: he opens the folding lips, the softness of which yielding entry to any thing of a hard body, close round it, and oppose the sight: and feeling further, meets with, and wonders at, a soft fleshy excrescence, which, limber and relax'd after the late enjoyment, now grew, under the touch and examination of his fiery fingers, more and more stiff and considerable, till the titilating ardours of that so sensible part, made me sigh, as if he had hurt me. On which he withdrew his curious probing fingers, asking me pardon, as it were, in a kiss that rather increas'd the flame *there*.

Novelty ever makes the strongest impressions, and in plea-sures especially: no wonder then, that he was swallow'd up in raptures of admiration of things so interesting by their nature, and now seen and handled for the first time. On my part, I was richly overpaid for the pleasure I gave him, in that of examining the power of those objects thus abandon'd to him, naked, and free to his loosest wish, over the artless, natural stripling: his eyes streaming fire, his cheeks glowing with a florid red, his fervid frequent sighs, whilst his hands convulsively squeez'd, opened, press'd together again the lips and sides of that deep flesh-wound, or gently twich'd the over-growing moss; and all proclaim'd the excess, the riot of joys, in having his wantonness thus humour'd. But he did not long abuse my patience, for the objects before him had now put him by all his, and coming out with that formidable machine of his, he lets the fury loose, and pointing it directly to the pouting-lipt mouth, that bid him sweet defiance in dumb-shew, squeezes in the head, and driving with refresh'd rage, breaks in, and plugs up the whole passage of that soft-pleasure-conduit, where he makes all shake again, and put once more all within me into such an uproar, as nothing could still, but a fresh inundation from the very engine of those flames, as well as from all the springs with which nature floats that re-cevoir of joy, when risen to its flood-mark.

I was now so bruised, so batter'd, so spent with this over-match, that I could hardly stir, or raise myself, but lay palpitat-ing, till the ferment of my senses subsiding by degrees, and the hour striking at which I was oblig'd to dispatch my young man, I tenderly advis'd him of the necessity there was for parting, which I felt as much displeasure at as he could do, who seem'd eagerly dispos'd to keep the field, and to enter on a fresh action: but the danger was too great: and after some hearty kisses of leave, and recommendations of secrecy, and discretion, I forc'd myself to force him away, not without assurances of seeing him again, to the same purpose, as soon as possible, and thrust a guinea into his hands: not more; lest being too flush of money, a suspicion or discovery, might arise from thence, having every thing to fear from the dangerous indiscretion of that age in which young fellows would be too irresistable, too charming, if we had not that terrible fault to guard against.

Giddy and intoxicated as I was with such satiating draughts of pleasure, I still lay on the couch, supinely stretch'd out, in a delicious languor diffus'd over all my limbs, hugging myself for being thus reveng'd to my heart's content, and that in a manner so precisely alike, and on the identical spot, in which I had receiv'd the suppos'd injury: no reflections on the consequences ever once perplex'd me, nor did I make myself one single reproach for having, by this step, completely enter'd myself of a profession more decry'd than disus'd. I should have held it ingratitude to the pleasure I had receiv'd, to have repented of it; and since I was now over the bar, I thought by plunging over head and ears into the stream I was hurried away by, to drown all sense of shame or reflection.

Whilst I was thus making these laudable dispositions, and whispering to myself a kind of tacit vow of incontinency, enters Mr. H——. The consciousness of what I had been doing, deepen'd yet the glowing of my cheeks, flushed with the warmth of the late action, which, join'd to the piquant air of my dishabill, drew from Mr. H—— a compliment on my looks, which he was proceeding to back the sincerity of with proofs, and that with so brisk an action, as made me tremble for fear of a discovery from the condition those parts were left in from their late severe handling: the orifice dilated and inflam'd, the lips swollen with their uncommon distension, the ringlets press'd down, crush'd and uncurl'd with the overflowing moisture that had wet every thing round it; the different feel and state of things, in short, would hardly have pass'd, upon one of Mr. H——'s nicety and experience, unaccounted for but by the real cause; but here the woman sav'd me: I pretended a violent disorder of my head, and a feverish heat, that indispos'd me too much to receive his embraces.

He gave into this, and good naturedly desisted. Soon after, an old lady coming in, made a third, very *a propos* for the confusion I was in, and Mr. *H——*, after bidding me take care of myself, and recommending me to my repose, left me much at ease, and reliev'd by his absence.

In the close of the evening, I took care to have prepar'd for me a warm bath of aromatick and sweet herbs; in which, having fully lav'd, and solaced myself, I came out voluptiously refresh'd in body and spirit.

The next morning, waking pretty early after a night's perfect rest and composure, it was not without some dread and uneasiness, that I thought of what innovation that tender soft system of mine might have sustain'd from the shock of a machine so siz'd for its destruction.

Struck with this apprehension, I scarce dar'd to carry my hand thither, to inform myself of the state and posture of things.

But I was soon agreeably cur'd of my fears.

The silky hair that cover'd round the borders, now smooth'd, and reprun'd, had resum'd its wonted curl and trimness; the fleshy pouting lips, that had stood the brunt of the engagement, were no longer swoln or moisture-drench'd: and neither they, nor the passage into which they open'd, that had suffer'd so great a dilatation, betray'd any the least alteration, outward or inwardly, to the most curious research, notwithstanding also the laxity that naturally follows the warm bath.

This continuation of that grateful stricture which is in us, to the men, the very jet of their pleasure, I ow'd, it seems, to a happy habit of body, juicy, plump, and furnish'd towards the texture of those parts, with a fullness of soft springy flesh, that yeilding sufficiently as it does, to almost any distension, soon recovers itself so as to retighten that strict compression of its mantlings and folds which form the sides of the passage, wherewith it so tenderly embraces, and closely clips any foreign body introduc'd into it, such as my exploring finger then was.

Finding then every thing in due tone and order, I remember'd my fears, only to make a jest of them to myself. And now, palpably mistress of any size of man, and triumphing in my double achievement of pleasure and revenge, I abandon'd myself entirely to the ideas of all the delight I had swam in. I lay stretching out, glowingly alive all over, and tossing with burning impatience for the renewal of joys that had sinn'd but in a sweet excess: nor did I lose my longing, for about ten in the morning, according to expectation, *Will*, my new humble sweet-heart, came with a message from his master, Mr. *H———*, to know how I did. I had taken care to send my maid on an errand into the city, that I was sure would take up time enough; and from the people of the house I had nothing to fear, as they were plain good sort of folks, and wise enough to mind no more of other people's business than they could well help.

All dispositions then made, not forgetting that of lying in bed to receive him; when he was enter'd the door of my bed-chamber, a latch that I govern'd by a wire, descended, and secur'd it.

I could not but observe that my young minion was as much spruc'd out as could be expected from one in his condition; a desire of pleasing that could not be indifferent to me, since it prov'd that I pleas'd him, which I assure you was now a point I was not above having in view.

His hair trimly dress'd, clean linen and above all, a hale, ruddy, wholesome country look, made him out as pretty a piece of woman's meat as you should see, and I should have thought any one much out of taste, that could not have made a hearty meal of such a morsel as nature seem'd to have design'd for the highest diet of pleasure.

And why should I here suppress the delight I receiv'd from this amiable creature, in remarking each artless look, each motion of pure undissembled nature, betray'd by his wanton eyes, or shewing transparently the glow and suffusion of blood through his fresh, clear skin, whilst even his sturdy, rustic pressures, wanted not their peculiar charm? Oh! but say you, this was a young fellow in too low a rank of life to deserve so great a display. May be so! but was my condition, strictly consider'd, one jot more exalted? or had I really been much above him, did not his capacity of giving such exquisite pleasure sufficiently raise and enoble him, to *me* at least? Let who would, for me, cherish, respect, and reward the painter's, the statuary's, the musician's arts, in proportion to the delight taken in them; but at my age, and with my taste for pleasure, a taste strongly constitutional to me; the talent of pleasing, with which nature has endow'd a handsome person, form'd to me the greatest of all merits; compared to which the vulgar prejudices in favour of titles, dignities, honours, and the like, held a very low rank indeed! Nor perhaps would the beauties of the body be so much affected to be held cheap, were they in their nature to be bought and deliver'd; but for me, whose natural philosophy all resided in the favourite center of sense, and who was rul'd by its powerful instinct, in taking pleasure by its right handle, I could scarce have made a choice more to my purpose.

Mr. *H*——'s loftier qualifications of birth, fortune, and sense, laid me under a sort of subjection and constraint, that were far from making harmony in the concert of love; nor had he perhaps thought me worth softening that superiority to; but with this lad I was more on that level which love delights in.

We may say what we please, but those we can be the easiest and freest with, are ever those we like, not to say love the best.

With this stripling, all whose art of love was the action of it, I could without check of awe or restraint, give a loose to joy, and execute every scheme of dalliance my fond fancy might put me on, in which he was, in every sense, a most exquisite companion. And now my great pleasure lay in humouring all the petulances, all the wanton frolic of a raw novice just flesh'd, and keen on the burning scent of his game, but unbroken to the sport: and to carry on the figure, who could better *thread the wood* than he, or stand fairer for the heart of the hunt?

He advanc'd then to my bedside, and whilst he faulter'd out his message, I could observe his colour rise, and his eyes lighten with joy, in seeing me in a situation as favourable to his loosest wishes, as if he had bespoke the play.

I, smil'd, and put out my hand towards him, which he kneel'd down to (a politeness taught him by love alone, that great master of it), and greedily kiss'd. After exchanging a few confus'd questions and answers, I ask'd him if he would come to bed to me for the little time I could venture to detain him. This was just asking a person dying with hunger, to feast upon the dish on earth the most to his palate. Accordingly, without farther reflection, all his cloaths were off in an instant; when blushing still more at this new liberty, he got under the bed-cloaths I held up to receive him, and was now in bed with a woman for the first time in his life.

Here began the usual tender preliminaries, as delicious perhaps as the crowning act of enjoyment itself; which they often beget an impatience of, that makes pleasure destructive of itself, by hurrying on the final period, and closing that scene of bliss, in which the actors are generally too well pleas'd with their parts, not to wish them an eternity of duration.

When we had sufficiently graduated our advances towards the main point, by toying, kissing, clipping, seeing my breasts, now round and plump, feeling that part of me I might call a furnace-mouth, from the prodigious intense heat his fiery touches had rekindled there; my young sportsman, embolden'd by every freedom he could wish, wantonly takes my hand, and carries it to that enormous machine of his, that stood with a stiffness! a hardness! an upward bent of erection! and which, together with its bottom dependence, the inestimable bulse[52] of lady's jewels, form'd a grand show out of goods indeed! Then its dimensions, mocking either grasp or span, almost renew'd my terrors. I could not conceive how, or by what means, I could take, or put such a bulk out of sight. I stroak'd it gently, on which the mutinous rogue seem'd to swell, and gather a new degree of fierceness and insolence; so that finding it grew not to be trifl'd with any longer, I prepar'd for rubbers[53] in good earnest.

Slipping then a pillow under me, that I might give him the fairest play, I guided officiously with my hand, this furious battering-ram, whose ruby head presenting nearest the resemblance of a heart, I applied to its proper mark, which lay as finely elevated as we could wish; my hips being born up, and my thighs at their utmost extension, the gleamy warmth that shot from it, made him feel that he was at the mouth of the indraught, and driving foreright, the powerfully divided lips of that pleasure-thirsty channel receiv'd him. He hesitated a little; then, settled well in the passage, he makes his way up the streights of it, with a difficulty nothing more than pleasing, widening as he went, so as to distend and smooth each soft furrow: our pleasure increasing deliciously, in proportion as our points of mutual touch increas'd, in that so vital part of me, in which I had now taken him, all indriven, and compleatly sheath'd, and which cram'd as it was, stretch'd spliting ripe, gave it so gratefully strait an accommodation! so strict a fold! a suction so fierce, that gave and took unutterable delight! We had now reach'd the closest point of union; but when he backen'd to come on the fiercer, as if I had been actuated by a fear of losing him, in the height of my fury, I twisted my legs round his naked loins, the flesh of which, so firm, so springy to the touch, quiver'd again under the pressure; and now I had him *every way* encircled and begirt; and having drawn him home to me, I kept him fast there, as if I had sought to unite bodies with him at that point. This bred a pause of action, a pleasure stop; whilst that delicate glutton, my neither-mouth, as full as it could hold, kept palating, with exquisite relish, the morsel that so deliciously ingorg'd it. But nature could not long endure a pleasure that so highly provok'd without satisfying it; persuing then its darling end, the battery recommenc'd with redoubled exertion; nor lay I unactive on my side, but encountring him with all the impetuosity of motion I was mistress of, the downy cloathing of our meeting mounts, was now of real use to break the violence of the tilt; and soon, too soon indeed! the high-wrought agitation, the sweet urgency of this to-and-fro friction, rais'd the titilation on me to its height, so that finding myself on the point of going, and loath to leave the tender partner of my joys behind me, I employ'd all the forwarding motions and arts my experience suggested to me, to promote his keeping

me company to our journey's end. I not only then tightened the
pleasure-girth round my restless inmate, by a secret spring of
suction and compression, that obeys the will in those parts, but
stole my hand softly to that store-bag of nature's prime sweets,
which is so pleasingly attach'd to its conduit-pipe, from which
we receive them; there feeling, and most gently indeed squeezing those tender globular reservoirs, the magic touch took instant effect, quicken'd, and brought on upon the spur, the
symptoms of that sweet agony, the melting moment of dissolution, when pleasure dies by pleasure, and the mysterious engine
of it overcomes the titillation it has rais'd in those parts, by plying them with the stream of a warm liquid, that is itself the highest of all titillations, and which they thirstily express, and draw
in like the hot-natured leach, who, to cool itself, tenaciously attracts all the moisture within its sphere of exsuction: chiming
then to me, with exquisite consent, as I melted away, his oily balsamic injection mixing deliciously with the sluices in flow from
me, sheath'd and blunted all the stings of pleasure, whilst it flung
us into an extacy, that extended us fainting, breathless, entranced. Thus we lay, whilst a voluptuous languor possest, and
still maintain'd us motionless, and fast lock'd in one another's
arms. Alass! that these delights should be no longer-liv'd! for now
the point of pleasure, unedg'd by enjoyment, and all the brisk
sensations flatten'd upon us, resign'd us up to the cool cares of
insipid life. Disingaging myself then from his embrace, I made
him sensible of the reasons there were for his present leaving
me; on which, tho' reluctantly, he put on his cloaths with as little
expedition, however, as he could help, wantonly interrupting
himself between whiles, with kisses, touches, and embraces, I
could not refuse myself too; yet he happily return'd to his master before he was miss'd; but at taking leave, I forc'd him (for he
had sentiments enough to refuse it) to receive money enough to
buy a silver watch, that great article of subaltern finery, which he
at length accepted of as a remembrance he was carefully to preserve of my affections.

And here, Madam, I ought perhaps to make you an apology
for this minute detail of things, that dwelt so strongly upon my

memory after so *deep* an impression. But besides that this intrigue bred one great revolution in my life, which historical truth requires I should not sink upon you; may I not presume that so exalted a pleasure ought not to be ungratefully forgotten or suppress'd by me, because I found it in a character in low life, where, by the bye, it is oftner met with, purer and more unsophisticate, than amongst the false ridiculous refinements with which the great suffer themselves to be so grosly cheated by their pride: the great! than whom, there exist few amongst those they call the vulgar, who are more ignorant of, or who cultivate less, the art of living than they do: they, I say, who for ever mistake things the most foreign to the nature of pleasure itself, whose capital favourite object is enjoyment of beauty, wherever that rare invaluable gift is found, without distinction of birth or station.

As love never had, so now revenge had no longer any share in my commerce with this handsome youth. The sole pleasures of enjoyment were now the link I held to him by: for though nature had done such great matters for him in his outward form, and especially in that superb piece of furniture she had so liberally enrich'd him with; though he was thus qualify'd to give the senses their richest feast, still there was something more wanting to create in me, and constitute the passion of love. Yet *Will* had very good qualities too, gentle, tractable, and above all grateful: silentious, even to a fault; he spoke at any time very little, but made it up emphatically with action; and to do him justice, he never gave me the least reason to complain either of any tendency to encroach upon me for the liberties I allow'd him, or of his indiscretion in blabing them. There is then a fatality in love, or have lov'd him I must; for he was really a treasure, a bit for the *bonne bouche* of a duchess: and, to say the truth, my liking for him was so extreme, that it was distinguishing very nicely to deny that I lov'd him.

My happiness, however, with him did not last long, but found an end from my own imprudent neglect. After having taken even superfluous precautions against a discovery, our success in repeated meetings embolden'd me to omit the barely necessary ones.——About a month after our first intercourse, one fatal morning (the season Mr. *H*—— rarely, or never visited me in) I was in my closet, where my toilette stood, in nothing but my shift, a bed-gown, and under-petticoat. *Will* was with me, and both ever too well dispos'd to baulk an opportunity: for my part, a warm whim, a wanton toy had just taken me, and I had challeng'd my man to execute it on the spot, who hesitated not to comply with my humour; I was sat in the arm-chair, my shift and petticoat up, my thighs wide spread, and mounted over the arms of the chair, presenting the fairest mark to *Will*'s drawn weapon, which he stood in act to plunge into me, when, having neglected to secure the chamber door, and that of the closet standing ajar, Mr. *H*—— stole in upon us, before either of us was aware, and saw us precisely in these convicting attitudes.

I gave a great scream, and drop'd my petticoat: the thunder-struck lad stood trembling and pale, waiting his sentence of death. Mr. *H*—— look'd sometimes at one, sometimes at the other, with a mixture of indignation and scorn, and, without saying a word, spun upon his heel, and went out.

As confus'd as I was, I heard him very distinctly turn the key, and lock the chamber-door upon us, so that there was no escape but through the dining-room, where he himself was walking about with distemper'd strides, stamping in a great chafe, and doubtless debating what he should do with us.

In the mean time poor *William* was frighten'd out of his senses, and as much need as I had of spirits to support myself, I was oblig'd to employ them all to keep his a little up: The misfortune I had now brought upon him, endear'd him the more to me, and I could have joyfully suffer'd any punishment he had not shar'd in. I water'd plentifully with my tears the face of the frighten'd youth, who sat, not having strength to stand, as cold and as lifeless as a statue.

Presently Mr. *H*—— comes in to us again, and made us go before him into the dining-room, trembling and dreading the issue: Mr. *H*—— sat down on a chair, whilst we stood like criminals under examination; and, beginning with me, ask'd me with an

even firm tone of voice, neither soft nor severe, but cruelly indifferent, what I could say for myself for having abus'd him in so
unworthy a manner, with his own servant too, and how he had
deserv'd this of me.

Without adding to the guilt of my infidelity that of an audacious defence of it, in the old style of a common kept Miss, my
answer was modest, and often interrupted by my tears, in substance as follows: that I had never had a single thought of wronging him (which was true) till I had seen him taking the last
liberties with my servant-wench, (here he colour'd prodigiously)
and that my resentment at that which I was over-aw'd from giving a vent to by complaints, or explanations with him, had driven
me to a course that I did not pretend to justify; but that as to the
young man, he was entirely faultless, for that in the view of making him the instrument of my revenge, I had downright seduc'd
him to what he had done, and therefore hop'd, whatever he
determin'd about me, he would distinguish between the guilty
and the innocent; and that, for the rest, I was entirely at his
mercy.

Mr. *H*——, on hearing what I said, hung his head a little; but
instantly recovering himself, he said to me, as near as I can retain, to the following purpose:

"Madam, I take shame to myself, and confess you have fairly
turn'd the tables upon me.———It is not with one of your cast
of breeding and sentiments that I should enter into a discussion
of the very great difference of the provocations: be it sufficient
that I allow you so much reason on your side, as to have changed
my resolutions, in consideration of what you reproach me with:
and I own too, that your clearing that rascal there is fair and honest in you: renew with you I cannot; the affront is too gross: I give
you a week's warning, to go out of these lodgings: whatever I
have given you, remains to you; and as I never intend to see you
more, the landlord will pay you fifty pieces on my account, with
which, and every debt paid, I hope you will own I do not leave
you in a worse condition than what I took you up in, or than you
deserve of me.———Blame yourself only that it is no better."

Then, without giving me time to reply, he addrest himself to the young fellow.

"For you, spark, I shall for your father's sake take care of you: the town is no place for such an easy fool as thou art; and to-morrow you shall set out under the charge of one of my men, well recommended, in my name, to your father, not to let you return and be spoilt here."

At these words he went out, after my vainly attempting to stop him, by throwing myself at his feet: he took me off, though he seem'd greatly mov'd too, and took *Will* away with him, who, I dare swear, thought himself very cheaply off.

I was now once more adrift, and left upon my own hands, by a gentleman whom I certainly did not deserve. And all the letters, arts, friends entreaties that I employ'd within the week of grace in my lodging, could never win on him so much as to see me again. He had irrevocably pronounc'd my doom, and submission to it was my only part. Soon after he married a lady of birth and fortune, to whom I have heard he prov'd an irreproachable husband.

As for poor *Will*, he was immediately sent down to the country, to his father, who was an easy[54] farmer, where he was not four months before an innkeeper's buxom young widow, with a very good stock both in money and trade, fancy'd, and perhaps pre-acquainted with his secret excellencies, marry'd him; and I am sure there was at least one good foundation for their living happily together.

Though I should have been charm'd to see him before he went, such measures were taken by Mr. *H*——'s orders that it was impossible; otherwise I should certainly have endeavour'd to detain him in town, and would have spar'd neither offers nor expence to have procur'd myself the satisfaction of keeping him with me, he had such powerful holds upon my inclinations as were not easily to be shaken off or replac'd; as to my heart, it was quite out of the question: glad however I was from my soul that nothing worse, and, as things turn'd out, probably nothing better could have happen'd to him.

As to Mr. *H*——, though views of conveniency made me at first exert myself to regain his affection, I was giddy and thoughtless enough to be much easier reconcil'd to my failure than I ought to have been; but as I never had lov'd him, and his leaving me gave me a sort of liberty that I had often long'd for, I was soon comforted; and flattering myself that the stock of youth and beauty I was going into trade with, could hardly fail of procuring me a maintenance, I saw myself under a necessity of trying my fortune with them, rather with pleasure and gayety, than with the least idea of despondence.

In the mean time, several of my acquaintance amongst the sisterhood, who had soon got wind of my misfortune, flock'd to insult me with their malicious consolations: most of them had long envied me the affluence and splendour I had been maintain'd in; and though there was scarce one of them that did not at least deserve to be in my case, and would probably sooner or later come to it, it was equally easy to remark, even in their affected pity, their secret pleasure at seeing me thus disgrac'd and discarded, and their secret grief that it was still no worse with me. Unaccountable malice of the human heart! and which is not confin'd to the class of life they were of.

But as the time approach'd for me to come to some resolution how to dispose of myself, and I was considering round where to shift my quarters to, Mrs. *Cole*, a middle-aged discret sort of woman, who had been brought into my acquaintance by one of the misses that visited me, upon learning my situation, came to offer her cordial advice and service to me; and as I had always taken to her more than to any of my female acquaintance, I listen'd the easier to her proposals; and as it happen'd, I could not have put myself into worse, or into better hands in all *London;* into worse, because keeping a house of conveniency, there were no lengths in lewdness she would not advise me to go in compliance with her customers, no schemes of pleasure, or even unbounded debauchery, she did not take even a delight in promoting: into better, because no body having had more experience of the wicked part of the town than she had, was fitter to advise and guard one against the worst dangers of our profession; and what was rare to be met with in those of her's, she contented herself with a moderate living profit upon her industry and good offices, and had nothing of their greedy rapacious turn. She was really too a gentlewoman born, and bred, but through a train of accidents reduc'd to this course, which she pursued partly through necessity, partly through choice, as never woman delighted more in encouraging a brisk circulation of the trade, for the sake of the trade itself, or better understood all the mysteries and refinements of it, than she did; so that she was consummately at the top of her profession, and dealt only with customers of distinction: to answer the demands of whom she kept a competent number of her daughters in constant recruit: so she call'd those whom their youth and personal charms recommended to her adoption and management: several of whom, by her means, and through her tuition and instructions, succeeded very well in the world.

This useful gentlewoman, upon whose protection I now threw myself, having her reasons of state, respecting Mr. *H———*, for not appearing too much in the thing herself, sent a friend of her's, on the day appointed for my removal, to conduct me to my new lodgings, at a brush-makers in *R——— street, Covent-Garden*, the very next door to her own house, where she had no conveniences to lodge me herself; lodgings, that by having been for several successions tenanted by ladies of pleasure, the landlord of them was familiariz'd to their ways; and provided, the rent was duly paid, every thing else was as easy and as commodious as one could desire.

The fifty guineas promis'd me by Mr. *H———*, at his parting with me, having been duly paid me, all my cloaths and moveables chested up, which were at least of two hundred pounds value, I had them convey'd into the coach, where I soon follow'd them, after taking a civil leave of the landlord and his family, with whom I had never liv'd in a degree of familiarity enough to regret the removal; but still, the very circumstance of its being a removal, drew tears from me. I left too a letter of thanks for Mr.

H——, from whom I concluded myself, as I really was, irretrievably separated.

My maid I had discharged the day before, not only because I had her of Mr. *H*——, but that I suspected her of having some how or other been the occasion of his discovering me, in revenge perhaps for my not having trusted her in it.

We were soon got to my lodgings, which, though not so handsomely furnish'd, nor so showy as those I left, were to the full as convenient, and at half price, though on the first floor. My trunks were safely landed, and stow'd in my apartments, where my neighbour and now governante, Mrs. *Cole*, was ready with my landlord to receive me, to whom she took care to set me out in the most favourable light, that of one from whom there was the clearest reason to expect the regular payment of his rent: all the cardinal virtues attributed to me would not have had half the weight of that recommendation alone.

I was now settled in lodgings of my own, abandon'd to my own conduct, and turn'd loose upon the town, to sink or swim, as I could manage with the current of it: and what were the consequences, together with the number of adventures which befell me in the exercise of my new profession, will compose the matter of another letter; for, surely, it is high time to put a period to this.

I am,

MADAM,

Yours, &c. &c. &c.

Volume II

Madam,

If I have delay'd the sequel of my history, it has been purely to afford myself a little breathing time, not without some hopes that, instead of pressing me to a continuation, you would have acquitted me of the task of pursuing a confession, in the course of which, my self-esteem has so many wounds to sustain.

I imagined indeed, that you would have been cloy'd and tired with the uniformity of adventures and expressions, inseparable from a subject of this sort, whose bottom or ground-work being, in the nature of things, eternally one and the same, whatever variety of forms and modes, the situations are susceptible of, there is no escaping a repetition of near the same images, the same figures, the same expressions, with this further inconvenience added to the disgust it creates, that the words *joys, ardours, transports, extasies,* and the rest of those pathetic terms so congenial to, so received in the *practise of pleasure,* flatten, and lose much of their due spirit and energy, by the frequency they indispensibly recur with, in a narrative of which that *practise* professedly composes the whole basis: I must therefore trust to the candour of your judgment for your allowing for the disadvantage I am necessarily under, in that respect, and to your imagination and sensibility the pleasing task of repairing it, by their supplements, where my descriptions flag or fail: the one will readily place the pictures I present before your eyes, the other give life to the colours where they are dull, or worn with too frequent handling.

What you say besides, by way of encouragement concerning the extreme difficulty of continuing so long in one strain, in a mean temper'd with taste, between the revoltingness of gross, rank, and vulgar expressions, and the ridicule of mincing metaphors and affected circumlocutions, is so sensible, as well as good-natur'd, that you greatly justify me to myself for my compliance with a curiosity that is to be satisfied so extremely at my expence.

———

Resuming now where I broke off in my last; I am, in my way, to remark to you, that it was late in the evening before I arriv'd at my new lodgings, and Mrs. *Cole,* after helping me to range, and secure my things, spent the whole evening with me in my apartment, where we supped together, in giving me the best advice and instruction with regard to this new stage of my profession I was now to enter upon, and passing thus from a private devotee to pleasure, into a public one, to become a more general good, with all the advantages requisite to put my person out to use, either for interest, or pleasure, or both. But then she observ'd, as I was a kind of new face upon the town, that it was an establish'd rule, and mystery of trade, for me to pass for a maid, and dispose of myself as such on the first good occasion, without prejudice however, to such diversions as I might have a mind to in the interim, for that nobody could be a greater enemy than she was to the losing of time. That she would, in the mean time, do her best to find out a proper person, and would undertake to manage this nice point for me, if I would accept of her aid and advice to such good purpose, that in the loss of a fictitious maiden-head, I should reap all the advantages of a native one.

As a great delicacy of sentiments did not extremely belong to my character at that time, I confess, against myself, that I perhaps too readily closed with a proposal which my candor and ingenuity gave me some repugnance to: but not enough to contradict the intention of one to whom I had now throughly abandon'd the direction of all my steps. For Mrs. *Cole* had, I do not know how, unless by one of those unaccountable invincible simpathies, that nevertheless form the strongest links, especially of female friendship, won and got intire possession of me. On her side, she pretended that a strict resemblance, she fancied she saw in me to an only daughter, whom she had lost at my age, was the first motive of her taking to me so affectionately as she did: it might be so: there exist as slender motives of attachments, that gathering force from habit, and liking, have proved often more solid, and durable, than those founded on much stronger reasons: but this I know, that tho' I had had no other acquaintance with her, than seeing her at my lodgings, when I liv'd with Mr. *H——*, where she had made errands to sell me some millinary ware, she had by degrees insinuated herself so far into my confidence, that I threw myself blindly into her hands, and came at length to regard, love, and obey her implicitly: and to do her justice, I never experienc'd at her hands other than a sincerity of tenderness, and care for my interest, hardly heard of in those of her profession. We parted that night, after having settled a perfect unreserv'd agreement; and the next morning Mrs. *Cole* came, and took me with her to her house, for the first time.

Here, at the first sight of things, I found every thing breathe an air of decency, modesty, and order.

In the outer parlour, or rather shop, sat three young women, very demurely employ'd on millinary work, which was the cover of a traffic in more precious commodities: but three beautifuller creatures could hardly be seen: two of them were extremely fair, the eldest not above nineteen, and the third, much about that age, was a piquant brunette, whose black sparkling eyes, and perfect harmony of features, and shapes, left her nothing to envy in her fairer companions: Their dress too, had the more design in it, the less it appeared to have, being in a taste of uniform correct

neatness, and elegant simplicity. These were the girls that composed the small, and domestic stock, which my governess train'd
up with surprising order and management, considering the
giddy, wildness of young girls once got upon the loose. But then
she never continued any in her house, whom after a due novici-
ate, she found untractable, or unwilling to comply with the rules
of it. Thus had she insensibly formed a little family of love, in
which the members found so sensibly their account in a rare al-
liance of pleasure with interest, and of a necessary outward decency, with unbounded secret liberty, that Mrs. *Cole,* who had
pick'd them as much for their temper as their beauty, govern'd
them with ease to herself, and them too.

To these pupils then of hers, whom she had prepar'd, she presented me as a new boarder, and one that was to be immediately
admitted to all the intimacies of the house; upon which these
charming girls gave me all the marks of a welcome reception,
and indeed of being perfectly pleas'd with my figure, that I could
possibly expect from any of my own sex; but they had been effectually brought to sacrifice all jealousy, or competition of
charms, to a common interest; and consider'd me as a partner,
that was bringing no despicable stock of goods into the trade of
the house: they gather'd round me, view'd me on all sides; and, as
my admission into this joyous troop made a little holiday, the
shew of work was laid aside, and Mrs. *Cole* giving me up, with
special recommendation, to their caresses and entertainment,
went about her ordinary business of the house.

The sameness of our sex, age, profession, and views, soon created as unreserv'd a freedom and intimacy as if we had been for
years acquainted. They took and shew'd me the house, their respective apartments, which were furnish'd with every article of
conveniency and luxury, and above all, a spacious drawing-
room, where a select revelling band usually met, in general parties of pleasure; the girls supping with their sparks, and acting
their wanton pranks with unbounded licentiousness, whilst a defiance of awe, modesty, or jealousy, were their standing rules, by
which, according to the principles of their society, whatever
pleasure was lost on the side of sentiment, was abundantly made

up to the senses, in the poignancy of variety, and the charms of ease and luxury. The authors and supporters of this secret institution,[1] would, in the height of their humour, style themselves the restorers of the liberty of the golden age, and its simplicity of pleasures, before their innocence became so unjustly branded with the names of guilt, and shame.

As soon then as the evening began, and the shew[2] of a shop was shut, the academy open'd, the mask of mock-modesty was compleatly taken off, and all the girls deliver'd over to their respective calls of pleasure, or interest, with their men: and none of that sex were promiscuously admitted, but only such as Mrs. *Cole* was previously satisfied of their character and discretion. In short, this was the safest, politest, and at the same time the most thorough house of accommodation in town, every thing being conducted so, that decency made no intrenchment[3] upon the most libertine pleasures, in the practice of which too, the choice familiars of the house had found the secret so rare and difficult, of reconciling even all the refinements of taste and delicacy, with the most gross and determinate gratifications of sensuality.

After having consum'd the morning in the indearments and instructions of my new acquaintance, we went to dinner, when Mrs. *Cole,* presiding at the head of her cluck,[4] gave me the first idea of her management and address, in inspiring these lively amiable girls with so sensible a love, and respect for her. There was no stiffness, no reserve, no airs of pique, or little jealousies, but all was unaffectedly gay, chearful, and easy.

After dinner, Mrs. *Cole,* seconded by the young ladies, acquainted me, that there was a chapter[5] to be held that night in form, for the ceremony of my reception into the sisterhood, and in which, with all due reserve to my maiden-head, that was to be occasionally cooked up for the first proper chapman, I was to undergo a ceremonial of initiation, they were sure I should not be displeased with.

Embark'd as I was, and moreover captivated with the charms of my new companions, I was too much prejudiced in favour of any proposal they could make, to so much as hesitate an assent, which therefore readily giving, in the style of a *charte blanche,* I receiv'd fresh kisses of compliment from them all, in approval of my docility and good-nature. "Now I was a sweet girl,—" "I came into things with a good grace,—" "I was not affectedly coy—" "I should be the pride of the house—" and the like.

This point thus adjusted, the young women left Mrs. *Cole* to talk and concert matters with me, when she explain'd to me, that I should be introduc'd that very evening to four of her best friends, one of whom she had, according to the custom of the house, favour'd with the preference of engaging me in the first party of pleasure, assuring me at the same time, that they were all young gentlemen agreeable in their persons, and unexceptionable in every respect; that united and holding together by the band of common pleasures, they composed the chief support of her house, and made very liberal presents to the girls that pleased and humour'd them, so that they were properly speaking the founders, and patrons of this little Seraglio. Not but that she had, at proper seasons, other customers to deal with, whom she stood less upon punctilio with, than with these: for instance, it was not on one of them she could attempt to pass me for a maid; they were not only too knowing, too much town-bred, to bite at such a bait, but they were such generous benefactors to her, that it would be unpardonable to think of it.

Amidst all the flutter and emotion which this promise of pleasure, for such I conceived it, stir'd up in me, I preserv'd so much of the woman as to feign just reluctance enough, to make some merit of sacrificing it to the influence of my patroness, whom I likewise, still in character, reminded of its perhaps being right for me to go home and dress in favour of my first impressions.

But Mrs. *Cole,* in opposition to this, assured me that the gentlemen I should be presented to, were, by their rank and taste of things, infinitely superior to the being touch'd with any glare of dress, or ornaments, such as silly women rather confound, and overlay, than set off their beauty with; that these veteran voluptuaries knew better than not to hold them in the highest contempt, they with whom the pure native charms alone could pass current, and who would at any time leave a sallow, washy, painted dutchess on her own hands, for a ruddy, healthy, firm-flesh'd country-maid: and as for my part, that nature had done enough for me, to set me above owing the least favour to art; concluding withall, that for the instant occasion, there was no dress like an undress.

I thought my governess too good a judge of these matters, not to be easily over-rul'd by her: after which she went on preaching very pathetically the doctrine of passive obedience, and non re-sistance to all those arbitrary tastes of pleasure, which are by some stil'd the refinements, and by others, the depravations of it; between whom it was not the business of a simple girl, who was to profit by pleasing, to decide, but to conform.

Whilst I was edifying by these wholesome lessons, tea was brought in, and the young ladies, returning, join'd company with us.

After a great deal of mix'd chat, frolick, and humour, one of them, observing that there would be a good deal of time on hand before the assembly-hour, proposed, that each girl should enter-tain the company with that critical period of her personal history, in which she first exchanged the maiden state for womanhood. The proposal was approv'd, with one only restriction of Mrs. *Cole*, that she, on the account of her age, and I on the account of my titular maidenhood, should be excused, at least till I had under-gone the forms of the house.[6] This obtained me a dispensation, and the promotress of this amusement was desired to begin.

Her name was *Emily* ——, a girl fair to excess, and whose limbs were if possible too well-made, since their plump fulness was rather to the prejudice of that delicate slimness of shape re-quired by the nicer judges of beauty: her eyes were blue, and stream'd inexpressible sweetness, and nothing could be prettier than her mouth, and lips, which closed over a range of the even-est, whitest teeth. Thus she began.

"Neither my extraction, nor the most critical adventure of my life, are sublime enough to impeach me of any vanity in the ad-vancement of the proposal you have approved of. My father and mother were, and for ought I know, are still, farmers in the country, not above forty miles from town. Their barbarity to me, in favour of a son, on whom only they vouchsafed to bestow their tenderness, had a thousand times determined me to fly their house, and throw myself on the wide world; but at length an accident forced me on this desperate step, at the age of fifteen. I had broken a China-bowl, the pride and idol of both their hearts, and as an unmerciful beating was the least I had to depend on at their hands, in the silliness and timidity of those tender years, I left the house, and at all adventures took the road to *London*. How my loss was resented I do not know, for till this instant I have not heard a syllable about them. My whole stock was two broadpieces[7] of my god-mother's, a few shillings, silver shoe-buckles, and thimble. Thus equipp'd, with no more cloaths than the ordinary ones I had on my back, and frighten'd at every foot, or noise I heard behind me, I hurried on: and I dare swear, walked a dozen miles before I stopp'd thro' mere weariness and fatigue. I sat down on a stile, where I wept bitterly, and yet was still rather under encreased impressions of fear on the account of my escape; which made me dread worse than death, the going back to face my unnatural parents. Refresh'd by this little repose, and relieved by my tears, I was proceeding onward, when I was overtaken by a sturdy country lad, who was going to *London,* to see what he could do for himself there, and, like me, had given his friends the slip. He could not be above seventeen, was ruddy, well featur'd enough, with uncomb'd flaxen hair, a little flapp'd hat, a kersey[8]-frock, yarn stockings; in short, a perfect plough-boy. I saw him come whistling behind me, with a bundle tied to the end of a stick: his travelling equipage. We walk'd by one another for some time without speaking, at length we join'd company, and agreed to keep together till we got to our journey's end. What his designs or ideas were I know not: the innocence of mine I can solemnly protest. As night drew on, it became us to look out for some inn, or shelter; to which perplexity another was added, and that was, what we should say for ourselves, if we were question'd: after some puzzle, the young fellow started a proposal, which I thought the finest that could be; and what was that? why that we should pass for husband and wife: I never once dream'd of consequences. We came presently, after having agreed on this notable expedient, to one of those hedge-accommodations[9] for foot-passengers, at the door of which stood an old crazy beldam, who, seeing us trudge by, invited us to lodge there. Glad of any cover, we went in, and my fellow-traveller taking all upon him, call'd for what the house afforded, and we supp'd together as man and wife, which considering our figures, and ages, could not have past on any one, but such as any thing could pass on. But when bed-time came on, we had neither of us the courage to contradict our first account of ourselves; and what was extremely pleasant, the young lad seem'd as perplex'd as I was, how to evade the lying together, which was so natural for the state we had pretended to: whilst we were in this quandary, the landlady takes the candle, and lights us to our apartment, through a long yard, at the end of which it stood, separate from the body of the house. Thus we suffer'd ourselves to be conducted, without saying a word in opposition to it, and there, in a wretched room, with a bed answerable, we were left to pass the night together, as a thing quite in course. For my part, I was so incredibly innocent, as not even then to think much more harm of going into bed with the young man, than with one of our dairy-wenches: nor had he perhaps any other notions than those of innocence, till such a fair occasion put them into his head. Before either of us undressed, however, he put out the candle; and the bitterness of the weather made it a kind of necessity for me to get into bed: slipping then my cloaths off, I crept under the bed-cloaths, where I found the young stripling already nestled, and the touch of his warm flesh rather pleased than alarmed me. I was indeed too much disturb'd with the novelty of my condition, to be able to sleep; but then I had not the least thought of harm: but oh! how powerful are the instincts of nature, and how little is there wanting to set them in action. The young man sliding his arm under my body, drew me gently towards him, as if to keep himself and me warmer; and the heat I felt from joining our breasts, kindled another that I had hitherto never felt, and was even then a stranger to the nature off. Embolden'd, I suppose, by my easiness, he ventur'd to kiss me, and I insensibly return'd it, without knowing the consequence of returning it: for on this encouragement, he slipp'd his hand all down from my breast, to that part of me, where the sense of feeling is so exquisitely critical, as I then experienc'd by its instant taking fire upon the touch, and glowing with a strange tickling heat: there he pleas'd himself and me, by feeling till growing a little too bold, he hurt me and made me complain: then he took my hand, which he guided, not unwillingly on my side, between the twist of his closed thighs, which were extremely warm; there he lodg'd and press'd it, till raising it by degrees, he made me feel the proud distinction of his sex from mine. I was frighten'd at the novelty, and drew back my hand; yet, press'd and spurr'd on by sensations of a strange pleasure, I could not help asking him, what that was for? He told me, he would show me, if I would let him; and without waiting for my answer, which he prevented by stopping my mouth with kisses I was far from disrelishing, he got a-top of me, and inserting one of his thighs between mine, open'd them so as to make way for himself, and fix'd me to his purpose; whilst I was so much out of my usual sense, so subdu'd by the present power of a new one, that, between fear and desire, I lay utterly passive, till the piercing pain rouz'd, and made me cry out: but it was too late; he was too firm fix'd in the saddle for me to compass flinging him, with all the struggles I could use, some of which only serv'd to further his point, and at length an omnipotent thrust murther'd at once my maidenhead, and almost me: I now lay a bleeding witness of the necessity impos'd on our sex, to gather the first honey off the thorns.

"But the pleasure rising, as the pain subsided, I was soon reconcil'd to fresh trials, and before morning, nothing on earth could be dearer to me than this rifler of my virgin-sweets. He was every thing to me now. How we agreed to join fortunes, how we came up to town together, where we lived some time, till necessity parted us, and drove me into this course of life, in which I had been long ago batter'd and torn to pieces before I came to this age, as much through my easiness, as through my inclination, had it not been for my finding refuge in this house; these are all circumstances which pass the mark I proposed, so that here my narrative ends."

In the order of our sitting, it was *Harriet*'s turn to go on. Amongst all the beauties of our sex that I had before or have since seen, few indeed were the forms that could dispute excellence with her's; it was not delicate, but delicacy itself incarnate. Such was the simmetry of her small, but exactly fashion'd limbs. Her complexion, fair as it was, appear'd yet more fair, from the effect of two black eyes, the brilliancy of which gave her face more vivacity than belong'd to the colour of it, which was only defended from paleness, by a sweetly pleasing blush in her cheeks, that grew fainter and fainter, till at length it died away insensibly into the overbearing white. Then her miniature features join'd to finish the extreme sweetness of it, which was not belied by that of a temper turn'd to indolence, languor, and the pleasures of love. Press'd to subscribe her contingent,[10] she smil'd, blush'd a little, and thus complied with our desires.

"My father was neither better nor worse than a miller, near the city of *York;* but both he and my mother dying whilst I was an infant, I fell under the care of a widow, and childless aunt, house-keeper to my lord *N*——, at his seat in the county of — —, where she brought me up with all imaginable tenderness. I was not seventeen, as I am not now eighteen, before I had, on the account of my person purely, (for fortune I had notoriously none) several advantageous proposals: but whether nature was slow in making me sensible of her favourite passion, or that I had not seen any of the other sex who had stirr'd up the least emotion or curiosity to be better acquainted with it, I had till that age preserv'd a perfect innocence even of thought: whilst my fears of I did not well know what, made me no more desirous of marrying than of dying. My aunt, good woman, favour'd my timorousness, which she look'd on as a childish affection, that her own experience might probably assure her would wear off in time, and gave my suiters proper answers for me.

"The family had not been down at this seat for years, so that it was neglected, and committed entirely to my aunt, and two more old domestics, to take care of it.

"Thus I had the full range of a spacious lonely house, and

gardens, situate at above half a mile distance from any other habitation, except perhaps a straggling cottage, or so.

"Here, in tranquility, and innocence, I grew up, without any memorable accident, till one fatal day I had, as I had often done before, left my aunt fast asleep, and secure for some hours, after dinner: and resorting to a kind of antient summer-house, at some distance from the house, I carry'd my work with me, and sat over a rivulet, which its door and window fac'd upon. Here I fell into a gentle-breathing slumber, which stole upon my senses, as they fainted under the excessive heat of the season, at that hour: a cane-couch, with my work-basket for a pillow, were all the conveniences of my short repose; for I was soon awak'd and alarm'd by a flounce, and noise of splashing in the water, I got up to see what was the matter; and what indeed should it be but the son of a neighbouring gentleman, as I afterwards found, (for I had never seen him before,) who had stray'd that way with his gun, and heated by his sport, and the sultriness of the day, had been tempted by the freshness of the clear stream; so that presently stripping, he jump'd into it on the other side which border'd on a wood, some trees whereof, inclin'd down to the water, form'd a pleasing, shady recess, commodious to undress, and leave his cloaths under.

"My first emotions, at the sight of this youth naked in the water, were, with all imaginable respect to truth, those of surprize and fear: and in course I should immediately have run out, had not my modesty, fatally for itself, interposed the objection of the door and window being so situated, that it was scarce possible to get out, and make my way along the bank to the house, without his seeing me: which I could not bear the thought of, so much asham'd and confounded was I at having seen him. Condemn'd then to stay till his departure should release me, I was greatly embarrass'd how to dispose of myself: I kept sometime, betwixt terror and modesty, even from looking through the window, which being an old-fashion'd casement, without any light behind me, could hardly betray any one's being there to him from within; then the door was so secure, that without violence, or my own consent, there was no opening it, from without.

"But now, by my own experience, I found it too true, that objects which afright us, when we cannot get from them, draw our eyes as forcibly as those that please us. I could not long withstand that nameless impulse, which, without any desire of this novel sight, compell'd me towards it: embolden'd too by my certainty of being at once unseen and safe, I ventur'd by degrees to cast my eyes on an object so terrible and alarming to my virgin modesty as a naked man: But as I snatch'd a look, the first gleam that struck me, was in general, the dewy lustre of the whitest skin imaginable, which the sun playing upon, made the reflection of it perfectly beamy. His face, in the confusion I was in, I could not well distinguish the lineaments of, any farther than that there was a great deal of youth and freshness in it. The frolic, and various play of all his fine polish'd limbs, as they appear'd above the surface, in the course of his swimming, or wantoning with the water, amus'd and insensibly delighted me: sometimes he lay motionless on his back, water-born, and dragging after him a fine head of hair, that floating swept the stream in a bush of black curls. Then the overflowing water would make a separation between his breast and glossy white belly; at the bottom of which, I could not escape observing so remarkable a distinction, as a black mossy tuft; out of which appear'd to emerge a round, softish, limber, white, something, that play'd every way, with every the least motion or whirling eddy. I cannot say but that part chiefly, by a kind of natural instinct, attracted, detain'd, captivated my attention: it was out of the power of all my modesty to command my eye away from it, and seeing nothing so very dreadful in its appearance, I sensibly look'd away all my fears: but as fast as they gave way, new desires and strange wishes took place, and I melted as I gazed. The fire of nature, that had so long lain dormant, or conceal'd, began to break out, and make me feel my sex for the first time. He had now chang'd his posture, and swam prone on his belly, striking out with his legs and arms, finer modell'd than which could not have been cast, whilst his floating locks play'd o'er a neck and shoulders, whose whiteness they delightfully set off. Then the luxuriant swell of flesh that rose from the small of his back, and terminates its double cope at where the thighs are sent off, perfectly dazzl'd one with its watery glistening gloss.

"By this time I was so affected by this inward revolution of sentiments, so soften'd by this sight, that now, betray'd into a sudden transition from extreme fears to extreme desires, I found these last so strong upon me, the heat of the weather too perhaps conspiring to exalt their rage, that nature almost fainted under them: not that I so much as knew precisely what was wanting to me; my only thought was, that so sweet a creature as this youth seem'd to me, could only make me happy; but then the little likelihood there was of compassing an acquaintance with him, or perhaps of ever seeing him again, dash'd my desires, and turn'd them into torments. I was still gazing with all the powers of my sight on this bewitching object, when, in an instant, down he went. I had heard of such things as a cramp seizing on even the best swimmers, and occasioning their being drown'd; and imagining this so sudden eclipse to be owing to it: the inconceivable fondness this unknown had given birth to, distracted me with the most killing terrors, insomuch, that my concern giving me wings, I flew to the door, open'd it, ran down to the banks of the canal, guided thither by the madness of my fears for him, and the intense desire of being an instrument to save him, though I was ignorant how, or by what means to effect it; but was it for fears, and a passion so sudden as mine to reason? All this took up scarce the space of a few moments. I had then just life enough to reach the green borders of the water-piece, where wildly looking round for the young man, and missing him still, my fright and concern sunk me down in a deep swoon, which must have lasted me some time; for I did not come to myself, till I was rouz'd out of it by a sense of pain that pierced me to the vitals, and awak'd me to the most surprising circumstance of finding myself not only in the arms of this very same young gentleman I had been so sollicitous to save; but taken at such an advantage in my unresisting condition, that he had actually completed his entrance into my body so far, that weakened as I was by all the preceding conflicts of mind I had suffer'd, and struck dumb by the violence of my surprize, I had neither the power to cry out, nor the strength to disengage myself from his strenuous embraces, before, urging his point, he had forced his way into me, and completely triumph'd over my virginity, as he might now as well see by the streams of blood that follow'd his drawing out, as he had felt by the difficulties he had met with in consummating his penetration. But the sight of the blood, and the sense of my condition, had (as he told me afterwards) since the ungovernable rage of his passion was somewhat appeas'd, now wrought so far on him, that at all risques, even of the worst consequences, he could not find in his heart to leave me, and make off, which he might easily have done. I still lay all discompos'd in bleeding ruin, palpitating, speechless, unable to get off, and frighten'd, and fluttering like a poor wounded partridge, and ready to faint away again at the sense of what had befallen me. The young gentleman was by me, kneeling, kissing my hand, and with tears in his eyes, beseeching me to forgive him, and offering all the reparation in his power. It is certain, that could I, at the instant of regaining my senses, have call'd out, or taken the bloodiest revenge, I would not have stuck at it: the violation was attended too with such aggravating circumstances! though he was ignorant of them, since it was to my concern for the preservation of his life, that I owed my ruin.

"But how quick is the shift of passions from one extreme to another! and how little are they acquainted with the human heart who dispute it! I could not see this amiable criminal, so suddenly the first object of my love, and as suddenly of my just hate, on his knees, bedewing my hand with his tears, without relenting: He was still stark-naked, but my modesty had been already too much wounded, in essentials to be so much shock'd as I should have otherwise been with appearances only: in short, my anger ebb'd so fast, and the tide of love return'd so strong upon me, that I felt it a point of my own happiness to forgive him: the reproaches I made him were murmur'd in so soft a tone, my eyes met his with such glances, expressing more languor than resentment, that he could not but presume his forgiveness was at no desperate distance; but still he would not quit his posture of submission, till I had pronounced his pardon in form; which, after the most fervent entreaties, protestations, and promises, I had not the power to with-hold. On which, with the utmost marks of a fear of again offend-ing, he ventured to kiss my lips, which I neither declined, or resented: but on my mild expostulations with him upon the bar-barity of his treatment, he explain'd the mystery of my ruin, if not entirely to the clearance, at least much to the alleviation of his guilt, in the eyes of a judge so partial in his favour as I was grown. It seems that the circumstance of his going down, or sinking, which in my extreme ignorance I had mistaken for something very fatal, was no other than a trick of diving, which I had not ever heard, or at least attended to, the mention of; and he was so long-breath'd at it, that in the few moments in which I ran out to save him, he had not yet emerged, before I fell into the swoon, in which, as he rose, seeing me extended on the bank, his first idea was, that some young woman was upon some design of frolick or diversion with him, for he knew I could not have fallen asleep there without his having seen me before; agreeable to which no-tion he had ventured to approach, and finding me without sign of life, and still perplex'd as he was what to think of the adventure, he took me in his arms at all hazards, and carried me into the summer-house, of which he observed the door open: there he laid me down on the couch, and tried, as he protested in good faith, by several means to bring me to myself again, till fired, as he said be-yond all bearing, by the sight and touch of several parts of me, which were unguardedly exposed to him, he could no longer gov-ern his passion, and the less, as he was not quite sure that his first idea of this swoon being a feint, was not the very truth of the case: seduced then by this flattering notion, and overcome by the pres-ent, as he stiled them, super-humane temptations, combined with the solitude, and seeming security of the attempt, he was not enough his own master not to make it. Leaving me then just only whilst he fastened the door, he return'd with redoubled eagerness to his prey, when, finding me still entranced, he ventured to place me as he pleased, whilst I felt, no more than the dead, what he was about, till the pain he put me to, rouzed me just time enough to be witness of a triumph I was not able to defeat, and now scarce regretted: for, as he talked, the tone of his voice sounded, methought, so sweetly in my ears, the sensible nearness of so new and interesting an object to me, wrought so powerfully upon me, that, in the rising perception of things in a new and pleasing light, I lost all sense of the past injury. The young gentleman soon discern'd the symptoms of a reconciliation in my softened looks, and hastening to receive the seal of it from my lips, press'd them tenderly to pass his pardon in the return of a kiss so melting fiery, that the impression of it being carried to my heart, and thence to my new-discover'd sphere of Venus, I was melted into a softness, that could refuse him nothing. When now he managed his caresses and endearments so artfully as to insinuate the most soothing consolations for the past pain, and the most pleasing expectations of future pleasure; but whilst mere modesty kept my eyes from seeking his, and rather declin'd them, I had a glimpse of that instrument of the mischief which was now, obviously even to me, who had scarce had snatches of a comparative observation of it, resuming its capacity to renew it, and grew greatly alarming with its encrease of size, as he bore it no doubt designedly, hard and stiff, against one of my hands carelessly dropt; but then he employ'd such tender prefacing, such winning progressions, that my returning passion of desire being now so strongly prompted by the engaging circumstances of the sight and incendiary touch of his naked glowing beauties; I yielded at length to the force of the present impressions, and he obtained of my tacit blushing consent, all the gratifications of pleasure left in the power of my poor person to bestow, after he had cropt its richest flower, during my suspension of life, and abilities to guard it.

"Here, according to the rule laid down, I should stop; but I am so much in motion, that I could not if I would. I shall only add, however, that I got home without the least discovery, or suspicion of what had happened. I met my young ravisher several times after, whom I now passionately lov'd, and who, though not of age to claim a small but independent fortune, would have married me; but as the accidents that prevented it, and their consequences which threw me on the publick, contain matter too moving and serious to introduce at present, I cut short here."

Louisa, the brunette whom I mentioned at first, now took her turn to treat the company with her history. I have already hinted to you the graces of her person, than which nothing could be more exquisitely touching; I repeat touching, as a just distinction from striking, which is ever a less lasting effect, and more generally belongs to the fair complexions; but leaving that decision to every one's taste, I proceed to give you *Louisa's* narrative, as follows.

———

"According to my practical maxims of life, I ought to boast of my birth, since I owe it to pure love, without marriage; but this I know, it was scarce possible to inherit a stronger propensity to that cause of my being, than I did: I was the rare production of the first essay of a journeyman cabinet-maker, on his master's maid; the consequence of which was a big belly, and the loss of her place. He was not in circumstances to do much for her; and yet, after all this blemish, she found means, after she had dropt her burthen, and disposed of me at a poor relation's in the country, to repair it by marrying a pastry cook here in *London,* in thriving business; on whom she soon, under favour of the compleat ascendant he had given her over him, passed me for a child she had by her first husband. I had, on that footing been taken home, and was not six years old when this father-in-law died, and left my mother in tolerable circumstances, and without any children by him. As to my natural father, he had betaken himself to the sea; where, when the truth of things came out, I was told that he died, not immensely rich you may think, since he was no more than a common sailor. As I grew up, under the eye of my mother, who kept on the business, I could not but see in her severe watchfulness, the marks of a slip, which she did not care should be hereditary; but we no more choose our passions than our features or complexion, and the bent of mine was so strong to the forbidden pleasure, that it got the better, at length, of all her care and precaution. I was scarce twelve years old, before that part of me which she wanted so much to keep out of harms way, made me feel its impatience to be taken notice of, and come into play: already had it put forth the signs of forwardness in the sprout of a soft down over it, which had often flatter'd, and I might also say, grown under my constant touch, and visitation: so pleas'd was I with what I took to be a kind of title to womanhood, that state I pined to be entered of, for the pleasures I conceiv'd where annex'd to it: and now the growing importance of that part to me, and the new sensations in it, demolish'd at once all my girlish play-things and amusements: nature now pointed me strongly to more solid diversions, while all the stings of desire settled so fiercely in that little centre of them, that I could not mistake the spot I wanted a play-fellow in.

"I now shun'd all company in which there was no hopes of coming at the object of my longings, and used to shut myself up, to indulge in solitude some tender meditation on the pleasures, I strongly perceiv'd the overture of, in feeling and examining what nature assur'd me must be the chosen avenue, the gates for the unknown bliss to enter at, that I panted after.

"But these meditations only encreased my disorder, and blew the fire that consum'd me. It was yet worse when yeilding at length to the insupportable irritations of the little fairy charm that tormented me; I searched it with my fingers, teazing it to no end. Sometimes, in the furious excitations of desire, I threw my self on my bed, spread my thighs abroad, and lay as it were expecting the long'd-for relief, till finding my illusion, I shut and squeez'd them together again, burning and fretting. In short, this dev'lish thing, with its impetuous girds[11] and itching fires, led me such a life, that I could neither, night or day, be at peace with it or myself. In time, however, I thought I had gained a prodigious prize, when figuring to myself, that my fingers were something of the shape of what I pined for, I worked my way in for one of them with great agitation and delight; yet not without pain too did I deflour myself as far as it could reach; proceeding with such a fury of passion, in this solitary and last shift of pleasure, as extended me at length breathless on the bed, in an amorous melting trance.

"But frequency of use dulling the sensation, I soon began to perceive that this finger-work was but a paultry shallow expedient, that went but a little way to relieve me, and rather rais'd more flame than its dry insignificant titilation could rightly appease.

"Man alone, I almost instinctively knew, as well by what I had industiously picked up at weddings and christenings, was possess'd of the only very remedy that could reduce this rebellious disorder; but watch'd, and overlook'd as I was, how to come at it, was the point, and that to all appearance, an invincible one: not that I did not rack my brains and invention how at once to elude my mother's vigilance, and procure myself the satisfaction of my impetuous curiosity, and longings for this mighty and untasted pleasure. At length, however, a singular chance did at once the work of a long course of alertness. One day that we had dined at an acquaintance's over the way, together with a gentlewoman-lodger that occupied the first floor of our house, there started an indispensible necessity for my mother's going down to *Greenwich* to accompany her: the party was settled, when I do not know what genius wispered me to plead a head-ach that I certainly had not, against my being included in a jaunt that I had not the least relish for: the pretext however passed, and my mother, with much reluctance, prevailed with herself to go without me; but took particular care to see me safe home, where she consign'd me into the hands of an old trusty maid-servant who served in the shop, for we had not a male creature in the house.

"As soon as she was gone, I told the maid I would go up and lie down on our lodger's bed, mine not being made, with a charge to her at the same time not to disturb me, as it was only rest I wanted. This injunction probably proved of eminent service to me. As soon as I was got into the bed-chamber, I unlaced my stays, and threw myself on the out-side of the bed cloaths in all the loosest undress. Here I gave myself up to the old insipid privy shifts of self-viewing, self-touching, self-enjoying, *in fine* to all the means of *self-knowledge* I could devise, in search of the pleasure that fled before me, and tantalized me with that unknown something that was out of my reach; thus all only served to enflame myself, and to provoke violently my desires, whilst the one thing needful to their satisfaction was not at hand, and I could have bit my fingers for representing it so ill. After then wearying and fatiguing myself with grasping of shadows, whilst that more sensible part of me disdain'd to content itself with less than realities, the strong yearnings, the urgent struggles of nature towards the melting relief, and the extreme self-agitations I had us'd to come at it, had wearied and thrown me into a kind of unquiet sleep, for if I toss'd and threw about my limbs in proportion to the distraction of my dreams, as I had reason to believe I did, a by-stander could not have help'd seeing all for love: and one there was, it seems; for waking out of my very short slumber, I found my hand lock'd in that of a young man, who was kneeling at my bed-side, and begging my pardon for his boldness, but that being son to the lady to whom this bed-chamber, he knew, belong'd, he had slipp'd by the servant of the shop, as he suppos'd, unperceiv'd; when finding me asleep, his first ideas were to withdraw; but that he had been fix'd and detain'd there by a power he could better account for, than resist. What shall I say? my emotions of fear and surprize were instantly subdu'd by those of the pleasure I bespoke in great presence of mind from the turn this adventure might take: he seem'd to me no other than a pitying angel, dropt out of the clouds; for he was young and perfectly handsome, which was more than even I had ask'd for; *Man,* in general, being all that my utmost desires had pointed at. I thought then I could not put too much encouragement into my eyes and voice; I regretted no leading advances: no matter for his after-opinion of my forwardness, so it might bring him to the point of answering my pressing demands of present ease; it was not now with his thoughts, but his actions, that my business immediately lay. I rais'd then my head, and told him in a soft tone that tended to prescribe the same key to him, that his mama was gone out, and would not return till late at night: which I thought no bad hint; but, as it prov'd, I had nothing of a novice to deal with: the impressions I had made on him, from the discoveries I had betray'd of my person in the disorder'd motions of it, during his view of me asleep, had, as he afterwards told me, so fix'd, and charmingly prepar'd him, that, had I known his dispositions, I had more to hope for from his violence, than to fear

from his respect; and even less than the extreme tenderness
which I threw into my voice, and eyes, would have serv'd to encourage him to make the most of the opportunity. Finding then
that his kisses imprinted on my hand were taken as tamely as he
could wish, he rose to my lips, and glewing his to them, made me
so faint with overcoming joy, and pleasure, that I fell back, and
he with me, in course, on the bed, upon which I had, by insensibly shifting from the side to near the middle, invitingly made
room for him: He is now lain down by me, and the minutes being
too precious to consume in untimely ceremony, or dalliance, my
youth proceeds immediately to those extremities, which all my
looks, flushings, and palpitations had assur'd him he might attempt without the fear of repulse: those rogues, the men, read us
admirably on these occasions! I lay then at length panting for the
imminent attack, with wishes far beyond my fears, and for which
it was scarce possible for a girl barely thirteen, but tall and well
grown, to have better dispositions. He threw up my petticoat and
shift, whilst my thighs were by an instinct of nature unfolded to
their best; and my desires had so thoroughly destroy'd all modesty in me, that even their being now naked, and all laid open to
him, was part of the prelude that pleasure deepen'd my blushes
at, more than shame; but when his hand, and touches, naturally
attracted to their center, made me feel all their wantonness, and
warmth in, and round it, oh! how immensely different a sense of
things did I perceive there, than when under my own insipid
handling and now his waistcoat was unbutton'd, and the confinement of the breeches burst through, when out starting to view
the amazing, pleasing object of all my wishes, all my dreams, all
my love, the king member indeed! I gaz'd at, I devour'd it, length
and breadth with my eyes intently directed to it, till his getting
upon me, and placing it between my thighs, took from me the
enjoyment of its sight, to give me a far more grateful one, in its
touch, in that part, where its touch is so exquisitely affecting: applying it then to the minute opening, for such at that age it certainly was, I met with too much good will, I felt with too great a
rapture of pleasure the first insertion of it, to heed much the
pain that follow'd: I thought nothing too dear to pay for this the

richest treat of the senses; so that, split up, torn, bleeding, mangled, I was still superiourly pleas'd, and hugg'd the author of all this delicious ruin: but when soon after he made his second attack, sore, and red-raw as every thing was, the smart was soon put away by the sovereign cordial; all my soft complainings were silenc'd, and the pain melting fast away into pleasure, I abandon'd myself over to all its transports, and gave it the full possession of my whole body and soul; for now all thought was at an end with me; I liv'd but in what I felt only: and who could describe those feelings, those agitations, yet exalted by the charm of their novelty, and surprize? when that part of me which had so long hunger'd and thirsted for the dear morsel that now so delightfully cramm'd it, forc'd all my vital sensations to fix their home there, during the stay of my new and belov'd guest; who too soon paid me for his hearty welcome, in a dissolvent, richer far than that I have heard of some queen treating her paramour with, in liquefy'd pearl, and ravishingly pour'd into me, where now myself too much melted to give it a dry reception, I hail'd it with the warmest confluence of sweets on my side, amidst all those extatic raptures, not unfamiliar I presume to this good company. Thus however, I arriv'd at the very top of all my wishes, by an accident unexpected indeed, but not so wonderful: for this young gentleman was just arriv'd in town from college, and came familiarly to his mother at her apartment, where he had once before been, though, by mere chance, I had not seen him: so that we knew one another by hear-say only, and finding me stretch'd on his mother's bed, he readily concluded, from her description, who it was—, the rest you know. This affair had however no ruinous consequences; the young gentleman escaping then, and many more times, undiscover'd; but the warmth of my constitution that made the pleasures of love a kind of necessary of life to me, having betray'd me into indiscretions fatal to my private fortune, I fell at length to the publick, which it is probable I might have met with the worst of ruin, if my better fate had not thrown me into this safe and agreeable refuge."

Here *Louisa* ended: and these little histories having brought the time for the girls to retire, and to prepare for the revels of the evening, I staid with Mrs. *Cole,* till *Emily* came and told us the company was met, and waited for us.

Mrs. *Cole* on this, taking me by the hand, with a smile of encouragement, led me up stairs, preceded by *Louisa,* who was come to hasten us, and lighted us with two candles, one in each hand.

On the landing-place of the first pair of stairs, we were met by a young gentleman, extremely well dress'd, and a very pretty figure, to whom I was to be indebted for the first essay of the pleasures of the house. He saluted me with great gallantry, and handed me into the drawing room, the floor of which was overspread with a Turky-carpet, and all its furniture voluptuously adapted to every demand of the most study'd luxury; now too it was by means of a profuse illumination, enliven'd by a light scarce inferior to, and perhaps more favourable to joy, more tenderly pleasing, than that of broad sunshine.

On my entrance into the room, I had the satisfaction to hear a buzz of approbation run through the whole company, which now consisted of four gentlemen, including my particular, (this was the cant-term of the house for one's gallant for the time) the three young women, in a neat flowing dishabille, the mistress of the academy, and myself. I was welcom'd and saluted by a kiss all round, in which however it was easy to discover, in the superior warmth of that of the men, the distinction of the sexes.

Aw'd, and confounded as I was, at seeing myself surrounded, caress'd, and made court to by so many strangers, I could not immediately familiarize myself to all that air of gaiety, and joy, which dictated their compliments, and animated their caresses. They assur'd me that I was so perfectly their taste, as to have but one fault against me, which I might easily be cur'd of: and that was my modesty: this, they observ'd, might pass for a beauty the more with those who wanted it for a heightener; but their maxim was, that it was an impertinent mixture, and dash'd the cup so as to spoil the sincere draught of pleasure: they consider'd it accordingly as their mortal enemy, and gave it no quarter wherever they met with it: this was a prologue not unworthy of the revels that ensu'd.

In the midst of all the frolic and wantonnesses, which this joyous band had presently and all naturally run into, an elegant supper was serv'd in, and we sat down to it, my spark elect placing himself next to me, and the other couples without order, or ceremony. The delicate cheer, and good wine, soon banish'd all reserve; the conversation grew as lively as could be wish'd, without taking too loose a turn: these professors of pleasure knew too well, to stale the impressions of it, or evaporate the imagination in words, before the time of action. Kisses however were snatch'd at times, or where a handkerchief round the neck interpos'd its feeble barrier, it was not extremely respected: the hands of the men went to work with their usual petulance, till the provocations on both sides rose to such a pitch, that my particular's proposal for beginning the country-dances was receiv'd with instant assent: for, as he laughingly added, he fancied the instruments were in tune. This was a signal for preparation, that the complaisant Mrs. *Cole*, who understood life, took for her cue of disappearing; no longer so fit for personal service herself, and content with having settled the order of battle, she left us the field to fight it out at discretion.

As soon as she was gone, the table was remov'd from the middle, and became a side-board; a couch was brought into its place, of which when I whisperingly enquired the reason of my particular, he told me, that as it was chiefly on my account that this convention was met, the parties intended at once to humour their taste of variety in pleasures, and by an open publick enjoyment, to see me broke of any taint of reserve or modesty, which they look'd on as the poison of joy: that though they occasionally preached pleasure, and lived up to the text, they did not enthusiastically set up for its missionaries, and only indulg'd themselves in the delights of a practical instruction of all the pretty women they lik'd well enough to bestow it upon, and fell properly in the way of it; but that as such a proposal might be too violent, too shocking for a young beginner; the older standers were to set an example, which he hop'd I would not be averse to follow, since it was to him I was devolv'd in favour of the first experiment; but that still I was perfectly at my liberty to refuse the

party, which being in its nature one of pleasure, suppos'd an exclusion of all force, or constraint.

My countenance expressed, no doubt, my surprise, as my silence did my acquiescence. I was now embark'd, and thoroughly
determined on any voyage the company would take me on.

The first that stood up, to open the ball, were a cornet of
horse[12] and that sweetest of olive-beauties, the soft and amorous
Louisa. He led her to the couch, "nothing loth," on which he gave
her the fall; and extended her at her length with an air of rough-
ness and vigour, relishing high of amourous eagerness and impatience. The girl spreading herself to the best advantage, with
her head upon the pillow, was so concenter'd in what she was
about, that our presence seem'd the least of her care or concern.
Her petticoats thrown up with her shift, discover'd to the company the finest turn'd legs and thighs that could be imagin'd, and
in a broad display, that gave us a full view of that delicious cleft
of flesh, into which the pleasingly hair-grown mount over it
parted, and presented a most inviting entrance, between two
close ledges, delicately soft and pouting. Her gallant was now
ready, having disincumbered himself from his cloaths overloaded with lace, and presently his shirt remov'd, shew'd us his
forces in high plight, bandied,[13] and ready for action: but giving
us no time to consider dimensions, and proving the stiffness of
his weapon, by his impatience of delay, he threw himself instantly over his charming antagonist, who receiv'd him as he
push'd at once dead at mark, like a heroine without flinching, for
surely never was girl constitutionally truer to the taste of joy, or
sincerer in the expressions of its sensations than she was: we
could observe the pleasure lighten in her eyes as he introduc'd
its plenipotentiary instrument into her, till at length, having
indulg'd her its utmost reach, its irritations grew so violent, and
gave her the spurs so furiously, that collected within herself, and
lost to every thing but the enjoyment of her favourite feelings,
she retorted his thrusts with a just concert of springy heaves,
keeping time so exactly with the most pathetic sighs, that one
might have number'd the strokes in agitation by their distinct

murmurs, whilst her active limbs kept wreathing and intertwist-
ing with his in convulsive folds: Then the turtle-billing kisses,
and the poignant painless love-bites, which they both exchang'd
in a rage of delight, all conspiring towards the melting period; it
soon came on, when *Louisa,* in the ravings of her pleasure frensy,
impotent of all restraint, cry'd out: "Oh Sir!—Good Sir!—pray
do not spare me! ah! ah!—I can no more." And all her accents
now faltering into heart-fetch'd sighs, she clos'd her eyes in the
sweet death, in the instant of which she was deliciously
embalm'd by an injection, of which we could easily see the signs,
in the quiet, dying, languid posture of her late so furious driver,
who was stopp'd of a sudden, breathing short, panting; and for
that time, giving up the spirit of pleasure.

As soon as he was dismounted, *Louisa* sprung up, shook her
petticoats, and running up to me, gave me a kiss, and drew me to
the side-board, to which she was herself handed by her gallant,
where they made me pledge them in a glass of wine, and toast a
droll health of *Louisa*'s proposal in high frolic, that of "the
miraculous thing which wets where it tickles, and tickles where
it wets."

By this time the second couple was ready to enter the lists,
which were a young baronet, and that delicatest of charmers, the
winning tender *Harriet.* My gentle esquire came to acquaint me
with it, and brought me back to the scene of action.

And surely, never did one of her profession accompany her
dispositions for the bare-fac'd part she was engag'd to play, with
such a peculiar grace of sweetness, modesty, and yielding coyness as she did. All her air and motions breath'd only unreserv'd,
unlimited complaisance, without the least mixture of impudence, or prostitution. But what was yet more surprising, her
spark-elect, in the midst of the dissolution of a publick open enjoyment, doated on her to distraction, and had, by dint of love
and sentiments, touched her heart, though for a while the restraint of their engagement to the house, laid him under a kind
of necessity of complying with an institution which himself had
had the greatest share in establishing.

Harriet then was led to the vacant couch by her gallant, blushing as she look'd at me, and with eyes made to justify any thing, tenderly bespeaking of me the most favourable construction of the step she was thus irresistibly drawn into.

Her lover, for such he was, sat her down at the foot of the couch, and passing his arms round her neck, preluded with a kiss fervently applied to her lips, that visibly gave her life and spirit to go through with the scene; and as he kiss'd, he gently inclin'd his head, till it fell back on a pillow dispos'd to receive it, and leaning himself down all the way with her, at once countenanc'd and endear'd her fall to her: there as if he had guess'd our wishes, or meant to gratify at once his pleasure and his pride, in being the master, by title of present possession, of beauties delicate beyond imagination, he discover'd her breasts, to his own touch, and our common view; but oh! what delicious manuals of love-devotion! how inimitably fine-moulded! small, round, firm, and excellently white: then the grain of their skin so soothing, so flattering to the touch! and their nipples, that crown'd them the sweetest buds of beauty! when he had feasted his eyes with the touch and perusal, feasted his lips with kisses of the highest relish imprinted in those all-delicious twin orbs, he proceeded downwards.

Her legs still kept the ground; and now with the tenderest attention not to shock, or alarm her too suddenly, he, by degrees, rather stole than roll'd up her petticoats, at which, as if a signal had been given, *Louisa* and *Emily* took hold of her legs, in pure wantoness, and yet in ease too, to her, kept them stretch'd wide abroad. Then lay expos'd, or to speak more properly, display'd the greatest parade in nature of female charms. The whole company, who, except myself, had often seen them, seem'd as much dazzled, surpris'd, and delighted, as any one could be who had now beheld them for the first time. Beauties so excessive could not but enjoy the priviledges of eternal novelty. Her thighs were so exquisitely fashion'd, that either more in, or more out of flesh than they were, they would have declin'd from that point of perfection they presented. But what infinitely enrich'd and adorn'd them, was the sweet intersection, form'd where they met, at the bottom of the smoothest, roundest, whitest belly, by that central furrow which nature had sunk there, between the soft relievo[14] of two pouting ridges, and which in this girl was in perfect sim-metry of delicacy and miniature with the rest of her frame: no! nothing in nature could be of a beautifuller cut: then the dark umbrage of the downy sprig-moss that over-arch'd it, bestow'd on the luxury of the landscape, a touching warmth, a tender fin-ishing, beyond the expression of words, or even the paint of thought.

Her truly enamour'd gallant, who had stood absorb'd and engross'd by the pleasure of the sight, long enough to afford us time to feast ours, no fear of glutting! addressed himself at length to the materials of enjoyment, and lifting the linen veil that hung between us and his master-member of the revels, ex-hibited one whole eminent size proclaim'd the owner a true woman's hero. He was besides, in every other respect, an accomplish'd gentleman, and in the bloom and vigour of youth: standing then between *Harriet*'s legs, which were supported by her two companions at their widest extension, with one hand he gently disclos'd the lips of that luscious mouth of nature, whilst with the other, he stoop'd his mighty machine to its lure, from the heighth of its stiff stand-up towards his belly; the lips kept open by his fingers, receiv'd its broad shelving head of coral hue; and when he had nestled it in, he hover'd there a little, and the girls then deliver'd over to his hips the agreeable office of sup-porting her thighs: and now, as if he meant to spin out his plea-sure, and give it the more play for its life, he pass'd up his instrument so slow, that we lost sight of it inch by inch, till at length it was wholly taken into the soft laboratory of love, and the mossy mounts of each fairly met together. In the mean time, we could plainly mark the prodigious effect the progressions of this delightful energy wrought in this delicious girl, gradually heightening her beauty as they heighten'd her pleasure. Her countenance, and whole frame, grew more animated; the faint blush of her cheeks gaining ground on the white, deepen'd into a florid vivid vermilion glow: her naturally brilliant eyes now sparkled with tenfold lustre: her languor was vanish'd, and she appear'd quick spirited, and alive all over. He had now fix'd, nail'd, this tender creature with his home driven wedge, so that she lay passive per force, and unable to stir, till beginning to play a strain of arms[15] against this vein of delicacy, as he urg'd the to-and-fro constriction; he awaken'd, rouz'd, and touch'd her so to the heart, that, unable to contain herself, she could not but reply to his motions, as briskly as her nicety of frame would admit of, till the raging stings of the pleasure, rising towards the point, made her wild with the intolerable sensations of it, and she now threw her legs and arms about at random, as she lay lost in the sweet transport: which on his side again declar'd itself by quicker, eagerer thrusts, convulsive grasps, burning sighs, swift laborious breathings, eyes darting humid fires; all faithful tokens of the imminent approaches of the last gasp of joy: it came on at length: the baronet led the extasy, which she critically join'd in, as she felt the melting symptoms from him, in the nick of which, glewing more ardently than ever his lips to hers, with eyes lifted up in a trance, he shew'd all the signs of that agony of bliss being strong upon him, in which he sent his soul distil'd in liquid sweets, up the body of that charming creature, and gave her the finishing titillation; inly thril'd with which, we saw plainly, that she answer'd it down with all the effusion of spirit and matter she was mistress of, whilst a general soft shudder ran through all her limbs, which she gave a stretch-out of, and lay motionless, breathless, dying with dear delight; and in the height of its expression, showing through the nearly clos'd lids of her eyes, just the edges of their black, the rest being roll'd strongly upwards in her extasy: then her sweet mouth appear'd languishingly open, with the tip of her tongue leaning negligently towards the lower range of her white teeth, whilst the natural ruby-colour of her lips glow'd with heighten'd life; was this a subject not to dwell upon? and accordingly her lover still kept on her, with an abiding delectation, till compress'd, squeez'd, and distill'd to the last drop, he flipp'd out at last, and took leave with one fervent kiss, expressing satisfy'd desires, but unextinguish'd love.

As soon as he was off, I ran to her, and sitting down on the couch by her, rais'd her head, which she declin'd gently, and hung in my bosom, to hide her blushes and confusion at what had past, till by degrees she recompos'd herself, and accepted of a restorative glass of wine from my spark, who had left me to fetch it her, whilst her own was re-adjusting his affairs, and buttoning up, after which he led her, leaning languishingly upon him, to our stand of view round the couch.

And now *Emily*'s partner had taken her out for her share in the dance, when this transcendently fair and sweet-tempered creature readily stood up: and if a complexion to put the rose and lily out of countenance, extreme pretty features, and that florid health and bloom for which the country-girls are so lovely, might pass her for a beauty, she certainly was one, and one of the most striking of the fair ones.

Her gallant began first, as she stood, to disingage her breasts, and restore them to the liberty of nature, from the easy confinement of no more than a pair of jumps[16]; but on their coming out to view, we thought a new light was added to the room, so superiourly shining was their whiteness; then they rose in so happy a swell as to compose her a well-form'd fullness of bosom, that had such an effect on the eye as to seem flesh hardening into marble, of which it emulated the polish'd glass, and far surpass'd even the whitest, in the life and lustre of its colours, white vein'd with blue. Refrain who could from such provoking enticements to it in reach? He touch'd her breasts first lightly, when the glossy smoothness of the skin eluded his hand, and made it slip along the surface: he press'd them, and the springy flesh that fill'd them, thus pitted by force, rose again reboundingly with his hand, and on the instant effac'd the dint of the pressure: and alike indeed was the consistence of all those parts of her body throughout, where the fullness of flesh compacts and constitutes all that fine firmness which the touch is so highly attach'd to. When he had thus largely pleas'd himself with this branch of dalliance, and delight, he truss'd up her petticoat and shift, in a wisp to her waist, where being tuck'd in, she stood fairly naked on every side: a blush at this overspread her lovely face, and her eyes, downcast to the ground, seem'd to beg for quarter, when she had so great a right to triumph in all the treasures of youth and beauty that she now so victoriously display'd. Her legs were perfectly well shap'd, and her thighs, which she kept pretty close, showed so white, so round, so substantial, and abounding in firm flesh, that nothing could offer a stronger recommendation to the luxury of the touch, which he accordingly did not fail to indulge himself in: then gently removing her hand, which in the first emotion of natural modesty, she had carried thither, he gave us rather a glimpse than a view of that soft narrow chink, running its little length downwards, and hiding the remains of it between her thighs: but plain was to be seen the fringe of light-brown curls, in beauteous growth over it, that with their silky gloss created a pleasing variety from the surrounding white, whose lustre too, their gentle embrowning shade considerably raised. Her spark then endeavour'd, as she stood, by disclosing her thighs, to gain us a compleater sight of that central charm of attraction, but not obtaining it so conveniently in that attitude, he led her to the foot of the couch, and bringing to it one of the pillows, gently inclin'd her head down, so that as she lean'd with it over her crossed hands, straddling with her thighs wide spread, and jutting her body out, she presented a full back-view of her person, naked to her waist. Her posteriours, plump, smooth, and prominent, form'd luxuriant tracts of animated snow, that splendidly fill'd the eye, till it was commanded down the parting or separation of those exquisitely white cliffs, by their narrow vale, and was there stopt, and attracted by the embower'd bottom cavity, that terminated this delightful vista, and stood moderately gaping from the influence of her bended posture, so that the agreeable interior red of the sides of the orifice came into view, and with respect to the white that dazzl'd round it, gave somewhat the idea of a pink-flash in the glossiest white satin. Her gallant, who was a gentleman about thirty, of an immense fortune, somewhat inclin'd to a fatness that was in no sort displeasing, improving the hint thus tender'd him of this mode of enjoyment, after settling her well in this posture and encouraging her with kisses and caresses to stand him through, drew out his affair ready erected, and whose extreme length, rather disproportion'd to its breadth, was the more surprising, as that excess is not often the case of those of his corpulent habit; making then the right and direct application, he drove it up to the guard, whilst the round bulge of those Turkish beauties of her's tallying with the hollow made by the bent of his belly and thighs, as they curv'd inwards, brought all those parts, surely not undelightfully, into warm touch, and close conjunction: his hands he kept pass'd round her body, and employ'd in toying with her enchanting breasts: as soon too as she felt him as home as he could reach, she lifted her head a little from the pillow, and turning her neck, without much straining, but her cheeks glowing with the deepest scarlet, and a smile of the tenderest satisfaction, met the kiss he press'd forward to give her, as they were thus close join'd together: when leaving him to pursue his delights, she hid again her face and blushes, with her hands and pillow, and thus stood passively and as favourably too as she could, whilst he kept laying at her with repeated thrusts, and making the meeting flesh on both sides re-sound again with the violence of them: then ever as he backen'd from her, we could see between them part of his long white-staff foamingly in motion, till, as he went on again, and closed with her, the interposing hillocks took it out of sight: sometimes he took his hands from the semi-globes of her bosom, and transferr'd the pressure of them to those larger ones, the present subjects of his soft blockade, which he squeez'd, grasp'd, and play'd with, till at length a pursuit of driving so hotly urg'd, brought on the heigth of the fit, with such symptoms of over-powering pleasure, that his fair partner became now necessary to support him, panting, fainting, and dying as he discharg'd, which she no sooner felt the killing sweetness of, than unable to keep her legs, and yielding to the mighty intoxication, she reel'd, and falling forward on the couch, made it a necessity for him, if he would preserve the warm pleasure-hold, to fall upon her, where they perfected, in a continu'd conjunction of body, and extatic flow, their scheme of joys for that time.

As soon as he had disengag'd, the charming *Emily* got up, and we crowded round her with congratulations, and other officious little services; for it is to be noted, that though all modesty and reserve were banish'd the transaction of these pleasures, good manners and politeness were inviolably observ'd: here was no gross ribaldry, no offensive or rude behaviour, or ungenerous reproaches to the girls for their compliance with the humours, and desires of the men. On the contrary, nothing was wanting to soothe, encourage, and soften the sense of their condition to them. Men know not in general how much they destroy of their own pleasure, when they break through the respect and tenderness due to our sex, and even to those of it who live only by pleasing them. And this was a maxim perfectly well understood by these polite voluptuaries, these profound adepts in the great art and science of pleasure, who never shew'd these votaries of theirs a more tender respect than at the time of those exercises of their complaisance, when they unlock'd their treasures of conceal'd beauty, and show'd out in the pride of their native charms, ever-more touching surely than when they parade it in the artificial ones of dress and ornament.

The frolic was now come round to me, and it being my turn of subscription to the will and pleasure of my particular-elect, as well as that of the company, he came to me, and saluting me very tenderly, with a flattering eagerness, put me in mind of the compliances my presence there authoriz'd the hopes of, and at the same time repeated to me, that if all this force of example had not surmounted any repugnance I might have to concur with the humours and desires of the company, that though the play was bespoke for my benefit, and great as his own private disappointment might be, he would suffer any thing sooner than be the instrument of imposing a disagreeable task on me.

To this I answer'd, without the least hesitation, or mincing grimace, that had I not even contracted a kind of engagement to be at his disposal without the least reserve, the example of such agreeable companions would alone determine me, and that I was in no pain about any thing but my appearing to so great a disadvantage after such superior beauties: and take notice, that I thought as I spoke. The frankness of the answer pleas'd them all: my particular was complimented on his acquisition, and, by way of indirect flattery to me, openly envied.

Mrs. *Cole,* by the way, could not have given me a greater mark of her regard than in managing for me the choice of this young gentleman for my master of the ceremonies; for independent of his noble birth, and the great fortune he was heir to; his person was even uncommonly pleasing, well shap'd and tall; his face mark'd with the small-pox, but no more than what added a grace of more manliness to features, rather turn'd to softness, and delicacy, was marvellously enliven'd by eyes which were of the clearest sparkling black; in short, he was one whom any woman would, in the familiar style, readily call a very pretty fellow.

I was now handed by him to the cockpit[17] of our match, where, as I was dress'd in nothing but a white morning gown, he vouchsafed to play the male-*Abigail*[18] on the occasion, and spar'd me the confusion that would have attended the forwardness of undressing myself: my gown then was loosen'd in a trice, and I divested of it: my stays next offer'd an obstacle which quickly gave way, *Louisa* very readily furnishing a pair of scissors to cut the lace: off went that shell; and dropping my upper-coat, I was now reduc'd to my under-one, and my shift, the open bosom of which gave the hands, and eyes all the liberty they could wish: here I imagin'd the stripping was to stop; but I reckon'd short: my spark, at the desire of the rest, tenderly beg'd, that I would not suffer the small remains of a covering to rob them of a full view of my whole person: and for me, who was too flexibly obsequious to dispute any point with them, and who consider'd the little more that remain'd as very immaterial, I readily assented to whatever he pleas'd. In an instant, then, my under petticoat was untied, and at my feet, and my shift drawn over my head, so that my cap, slightly fasten'd, came off with it, and brought all my hair down (of which be it again remember'd without vanity, that I had a very fine head) in loose disorderly ringlets, over my neck and shoulders, to no unfavourable set-off of my skin.

I now stood before my judges in all the truth of nature, to whom I could not appear a very disagreeable figure, if you please to recollect what I have before said of my person, which time, that at certain periods of life, robs us every instant of our charms, had, at that of mine, then greatly improv'd into full and open bloom, for I wanted some months of eighteen: my breasts, which in the state of nudity are ever capital points, now in no more than grateful plenitude, maintain'd a firmness and steady independence of any stay or support, that dared and invited the test of the touch. Then I was as tall, as slim-shap'd as could be consistent with all that juicy plumpness of flesh ever the most grateful to the senses of sight and touch, which I owed to the health and youth of my constitution. I had not, however, so thoroughly renounc'd all innate shame, as not to suffer great confusion at the state I saw myself in: but the whole troop round me, men and women, reliev'd me with every mark of applause and satisfaction, every flattering attention to raise, and inspire me with even sentiments of pride on the figure I made, which my friend gallantly protested, infinitely out-shone all other *birth-day* finery[19] whatever, so that had I leave to set down, for sincere, all the compliments these connoisseurs over-whelm'd me with upon this occasion, I might flatter myself with having pass'd my examination, with approbation of the learned.

My friend however, who for this time had alone the disposal of me, humour'd their curiosity, and perhaps his own, so far that he plac'd me in all the variety of postures and lights imaginable, pointing out every beauty under every aspect of it, not without such parentheses of kisses, such inflammatory liberties of his roving hands, as made all shame fly before them, and a blushing glow give place to a warmer one of desire, which led me even to find some relish in the present scene.

But in this general survey, you may be sure, the most material spot of me was not excus'd the strictest visitation: nor was it but agreed, that I had not the least reason to be diffident of passing even for a maid, on occasion; so inconsiderable a flaw had my preceding adventures created there, and so soon had the blemish of an over-stretch been repair'd and worn out, at my age, and in my naturally small make in that part.

Now, whether my partner had exhausted all the modes of regaling the touch, or sight, or whether he was now ungovernably wound up to strike, I know not; but briskly throwing off his cloaths the prodigious heat bred by a close room, a great fire, numerous candles, and even the inflammatory warmth of these scenes, induc'd him to lay aside his shirt too, when his breeches, before loosen'd, now gave up their contents to view, and shewed in front, the enemy I had to engage with, stifly bearing up the port of its head unhooded, and glowing red: then I plainly saw what I had to trust to: it was one of those just true-siz'd instruments of which the masters have a better command, than the more unweildy, inordinate siz'd ones are generally under. Straining me then close to his bosom, as he stood up fore-right against me, and applying to the obvious niche its peculiar idol, he aim'd at inserting it, which, as I forwardly favour'd, he effected at once by canting up my thighs over his naked hips, and made me receive every inch, and close home; so that stuck upon the pleasure-pivot, and clinging round his neck, in which and his hair, I hid my face burningly flushing with my present feelings as much as with shame, my bosom glew'd to his, he carried me once round the couch, on which he then, without quitting the middle-fastness, or dischannelling, laid me down, and began the pleasure-grist, but so provokingly predispos'd and prim'd as we were, by all the moving sights of the night, our imagination was too much heated, not to melt us of the soonest, and accordingly I no sooner felt the warm spray darted up my inwards from him; but I was punctually on flow to share the momentary extasy; but I had yet greater reason to boast of our harmony; for finding that all the flames of desire were not yet quench'd within me: but that rather, like wetted coals, I glow'd the fiercer for this sprinkling: my hot-mettled spark sympathysing with me, and loaded for a double-fire, recontinu'd the sweet battery with undying vigour: greatly pleas'd at which, I gratefully endeavour'd to accommodate all my motions to his best advantage and delight; kisses, squeezes, tender murmurs, all came into play, till our joys growing more turbulent and riotous, threw us into a fond disorder, and as they raged to a point, bore us far from ourselves into an ocean of boundless pleasures, into which we both plung'd to-

gether in a transport of taste: now all the impressions of burning desire, from the lively scenes I had been spectatress of,
ripen'd by the heat of this exercise, and collecting to a head,
throb'd and agitated me with insupportable irritations: I perfectly fever'd and madden'd with their excess: I did not now
enjoy a calm of reason enough to perceive, but I, extatically indeed! *felt* the policy and power of such rare and exquisite
provocatives as the examples of the night had proved towards
thus exalting our pleasures: which, with great joy, I sensibly
found my gallant shar'd in, by his nervous and home expressions[20] of it: his eyes flashing eloquent flames, his action infuri-
ated with the stings of it, all conspiring to raise my delight by
assuring me of his; lifted then to the utmost pitch of joy that
human life can bear undestroy'd by excess, I touched that
sweetly critical point, when scarce prevented by the spermatic
injection from my partner spurting liquid fire up to my vitals, I
dissolv'd, and breaking out into a deep drawn sigh, sent my
whole sensitive soul down to that passage where escape was denied it, by its being so deliciously plugged and choak'd up. Thus
we lay a few blissful instants, overpower'd, still, and languid; till,
as the sense of pleasure stagnated, we recover'd from our
trance, and he slipt out of me, not, however, before he had
protested his extreme satisfaction, by the tenderest kiss and
embrace, as well as by the most cordial expressions.

The company who had stood round us in a profound silence,
when all was over, help'd me to hurry on my cloaths in an instant,
and complimented me on the sincere homage they could not escape observing had been done (as they term'd it) to the sover-
eignty of my charms, in my receiving a double payment of
tribute at one juncture: but my partner, now dress'd again,
signaliz'd, above all, a fondness unbated by the circumstance of
recent enjoyment: the girls too kiss'd and embrac'd me, assuring
me, that for that time, or indeed any other, unless I pleas'd, I was
to go through no farther publick trials, and that I was now consummately initiated, and one of them.

As it was an inviolable law for every gallant to keep to his partner, for the night especially, and even till he relinquish'd possession over to the community, in order to preserve a pleasing property, and to avoid the disgusts and indelicacy of another arrangement, the company, after a short refection[21] of biskets and wine, tea and chocolate, served in at, now, about one in the morning, broke up, and went off in pairs. Mrs. *Cole* had prepar'd my spark and me an occasional field-bed, to which we retired, and there ended the night in one continued strain of pleasure, sprightly and uncloy'd enough for us not to have form'd one wish for its ever knowing an end. In the morning, after a restorative breakfast in bed, he got up, and with very tender assurances of a particular regard for me, left me to the composure and refreshment of a sweet slumber; waking out of which, and getting up to dress before Mrs. *Cole* should come in, I found in one of my pockets a purse of guineas, which he had slipt there; and just as I was musing on a liberality I had certainly not expected, Mrs. *Cole* came in, to whom I immediately communicated the present, and naturally offer'd her whatever share she pleas'd; but assuring me that the gentleman had very nobly rewarded her, she would on no terms, no entreaties, no shape I could put it in, receive any part of it. Her denial, she observ'd, was not affectation or grimace, and proceeded to read me such admirable lessons on the economy of my person and my purse, as I became amply paid for my *general* attention and conformity to, in the course of my acquaintance with the town. After which, changing the discourse, she fell on the pleasures of the preceding night, where I learn'd, without much surprise, as I began to enter her character, that she had seen every thing that had passed, from a convenient place, manag'd solely for that purpose, and of which she readily made me the confidante.

She had scarce finish'd with this, when the little troop of love, the girls my companions, broke in, and renew'd their compliments and caresses; I observ'd with pleasure, that the fatigues and exercises of the night, had not usurp'd in the least on the life of the complexion, or the freshness of their bloom: this I found by their confession, was owing to the management and advice of our rare directress. They went down then to figure it,[22] as usual, in the shop; whilst I repair'd to my lodgings; where I employ'd myself till I return'd to dinner, at Mrs. *Cole's*.

Here I staid, in constant amusement, with one or other of these charming girls, till about five in the evening: when seiz'd with a sudden drowsy fit, I was prevailed on to go up and doze it off on *Harriet's* bed, who left me on it to my repose. There then I lay down in my cloaths, and fell fast asleep, and had now enjoy'd by guess, about an hour's rest; when I was pleasingly disturb'd by my new and favourite gallant, who enquiring for me, was readily directed where to find me. Coming then into my chamber, and seeing me lie alone, with my face turn'd from the light towards the inside of the bed, he, without more ado, just slipp'd off his breeches, for the greater ease and enjoyment of the naked touch; and softly turning up my petticoat and shift behind, open'd himself the prospect of the back avenue to the genial seat of pleasure; where, as I lay at my side-length, inclining rather face downward, I appear'd full fair, and liable to be entered: laying himself then gently down by me, he invested me behind, and giving me to feel the warmth of his body, as he applied his thighs and belly close to me, and the endeavours of that machine, whose touch has something so exquisitely singular in it, to make its way good into me, I wak'd, pretty much startled at first; but seeing who it was, dispos'd myself to turn to him, when he gave me a kiss; and desiring me to keep my posture, just lifted up my upper thigh, and ascertaining the right opening, soon drove it up to the farthest; satisfied with which, and solacing himself with lying so close in full touch of flesh in those parts, he suspended all motion, and thus steep'd in pleasure, kept me lying on my side, in to him, spoon-fashion, as he term'd it, from the snug indent of the back-part of my thighs, and all upwards, into the space of the bending between his thighs and belly; till after some time, that restless, and turbulent inmate, impatient by nature of longer quiet, urg'd him to action, which now prosecuting, with all the usual train of toying, kissing, and the like, ended at length in the liquid proof on both sides, that we had not been exhausted, or at least were quickly recruited of last night's draughts of pleasure on us.

With this noble and agreable youth, liv'd I in perfect joy and constancy: he was full bent on keeping me to himself, for the honey-month[23] at least; but his stay in *London* was not even so long, his father who had a great post in *Ireland,* taking him abruptly with him, on his repairing thither. Yet even then I was near keeping hold of his affection, and person, for he had propos'd, and I had consented to follow his order to go to *Ireland* after him, as soon as he should be settled there; but meeting with an agreeable and advantageous match in that kingdom, he chose the wiser part, and forbore sending for me, but at the same time took care that I should receive a magnificent present, which did not however compensate for all my deep regret on my loss of him.

This event also created a chasm in our little society, which Mrs. *Cole,* on the foot of her usual caution, was in no haste to fill up: but then it redoubl'd her attention to procure me in the advantages of the traffick for a counterfeit maidenhead, some consolation for the sort of widowhood I had been left in, and this was a scheme she had never lost prospect of, and only waited for a proper person to bring it to bear with.

But I was, it seems, fated to be my own caterer in this, as I had been in my first trial of the market.

I had now pass'd near a month in the enjoyment of all the pleasures of familiarity and society with my companions, whose particular favourites, (the Baronet excepted, who soon after took *Harriet* home) had all, on the terms of community establish'd in the house, sollicited the gratification of their taste for variety in my embraces; but I had with the utmost art and address, on various pretexts, eluded their pursuit, without giving them cause to complain: and this reserve I used neither out of dislike to them, or disgust of the thing, but my true reason was my attachment to my own, and my tenderness of invading the choice of my companions, who outwardly exempt, as they seem'd, from jealousy, could not but in secret like me the better for the regard I had for, without making a merit of it to, them. Thus easy, and belov'd by the whole family did I go on, when one day, that, about five in the afternoon, I stepp'd over to a fruiterer's shop, in *Covent-Garden,* to pick some table-fruit for myself and the young women, I met with the following adventure.

Whilst I was chaffering[24] for the fruit I wanted, I observ'd my-self follow'd by a young gentleman, whose rich dress first at-tracted my notice; for the rest, he had nothing remarkable in his person, except that he was pale, thin-made, and ventur'd himself upon legs rather of the slenderest. Easy was it to perceive, with-out seeming to perceive it, that it was me he wanted to be at, by his making a full set at, and keeping his eyes fix'd on, me, till he came to the same basket that I stood at, and cheapening, or rather giving the first price ask'd for the fruit, began his ap-proaches. Now most certainly I was not at all out of figure to pass for a modest girl. I had neither the feathers, nor *fumet* of a tawdry town-miss[25]; a straw hat, a white gown, clean linen, and above all, a certain natural and easy air of modesty (which the appearances of never forsook me, even on those occasions that I most broke in upon it, in practice) where all signs that gave him no opening to conjecture my condition. He spoke to me, and this address from a stranger throwing a blush into my cheeks, that still set him wider off the truth, I answer'd him, with an awk-wardness and confusion the more apt to impose, as there was re-ally, a mixture of the genuine in them. But when proceeding on the foot of having broke the ice, to join discourse, he went into other leading questions, I put so much innocence, simplicity, and even childishness, into my answers, that on no better foundation, liking my person as he did, I will answer for it, that he would have been sworn for my modesty. There is, in short, in the men, when once they are caught, by the eye especially, a fund of culli-bility,[26] that their lordly wisdom little dreams of, and in virtue of which the most sagacious of them are seen so often our dupes. Amongst other queries he put to me one was, whether I was mar-ried, or no. I replied, that I was too young, to think of that this many a year. To that of my age, I answer'd, and sunk a year upon him, passing myself for not seventeen. As to my way of life, I told him I had serv'd an apprenticeship to a millener in *Preston,* and was come to town after a relation that I found on my arrival was dead, and I now liv'd journey-woman to a millener in town. That last article indeed was not much on the side of what I pretended to pass for; but it did pass, under favour of the growing passion I had inspir'd him with. After he had next got out of me, very dextrously as he thought, what I had no sort of design to make a reserve of, my own, my mistress's name, and place of abode, he loaded me with fruit, all the rarest and dearest he could pick out, and sent me home pondering on what might be the consequence of this adventure.

As soon then as I came to Mrs. *Cole*'s I related to her all that had passed, on which she very judiciously concluded, that, if he did not come after me, there was no harm done, and that, if he did, as her presage suggested to her he would, his character, and his views should be well sifted, so as to know whether the game was worth the springes[27]; that in the mean time nothing was easier than my part in it, since no more rested on me than to follow her cue and promptership throughout, to the last act.

The next morning, after an evening spent on his side, as we afterwards learnt, in perquisitions into Mrs. *Cole*'s character in the neighbourhood, (than which nothing could be more favourable to her designs upon him,) my gentleman came in his chariot to the shop, where Mrs. *Cole* alone had an inkling of his errand; asking then for her, he easily made a beginning of acquaintance by bespeaking some millenary ware, when as I sat without lifting up my eyes, and pursuing the hem of a ruffle with the utmost composure, and simplicity of industry, Mrs. *Cole* took notice that the first impressions I made on him ran no risque of being destroy'd by those of *Louisa,* and *Emily,* who were then sitting at work with me. After vainly endeavouring to catch my eyes in rencounter[28] with his, as I held my head down, affecting a kind of consciousness of guilt, for having, by speaking to him, given him encouragement and means of following me home, and after giving Mrs. *Cole* direction when to bring herself the things home, and the time he should expect them at, he went out, taking with him some goods, that he paid for liberally, for the better grace of his introduction.

The girls all this time did not in the least smoak the mystery of this new customer, but Mrs. *Cole,* as soon as we were conveniently alone, insur'd me, in virtue of her long experience in these matters, that for this bout my charms had not miss'd fire, for that by his eagerness, his manner, and looks, she was sure he had it; the only point now in doubt was his character, and circumstances, which her knowledge of the town would soon gain her sufficient acquaintance with, to take her measures upon.

And effectively, in a few hours, her intelligence serv'd her so well, that she learn'd that this conquest of mine was no other than Mr. *Norbert,* a gentleman originally of a great fortune, which, with a constitution naturally not the best, he had greatly impair'd by his over-violent pursuit of the vices of the town, in the course of which having worn out and stal'd all the more common modes of debauchery, he had fallen into a taste of maiden-hunting, in which chase he had ruin'd a number of girls, sparing no expence to compass his ends, and generally using them well till tir'd, or cool'd by enjoyment, or springing a new face, he could with more ease disembarrass himself of the old ones, and resign them up to their fate, as his sphere of achievements of that sort lay only amongst such as he could proceed with by way of bargain and sale.

Concluding from these premises, Mrs. *Cole* observ'd that a character of this sort was ever lawful prize; that the sin would be, not to make the best of our market of him; and that she thought such a girl as me only too good for him at any rate, and on any terms.

She went then, at the hour appointed to his lodgings in one of our inns of court,[29] which were furnish'd in a taste of grandeur that had a special eye to all the conveniences of luxury and pleasure. Here she found him in ready waiting, and after finishing her business of pretence, and a long circuit of discussions concerning her trade, which she said was very bad, the qualities of her servants, prentices, journey-women, the discourse naturally landed at length on me, when Mrs. *Cole* acting admirably the good old prating gossip, who lets every thing escape her, when her tongue is set in motion, cook'd him up a story so plausible of me, throwing in every now and then such strokes of art, with all the simplest air of nature, in praise of my person and temper, as finish'd him finely for her purpose, whilst nothing could be better counterfeited than her innocence of his; but when now fir'd, and on edge, he proceeded to drop hints of his design and views upon me, after he had with much confusion and pains brought her to the point (she kept as long aloof from as she thought proper) of understanding him, without now affecting to pass for a dragoness of virtue, by flying out into those violent and ever suspicious passions, she stuck with a better grace and effect to the character of a plain, honest, good sort of a woman, that knew no harm, and that getting her bread in an honest way, was made of easy and flexible stuff enough to be wrought upon to his ends, by his superior skill and address; but however, she managed so artfully that three or four meetings took place, before he could obtain the least favourable hope of her assistance, without which, he had, by a number of fruitless messages, letters, and other direct trials of my disposition, convinc'd himself there was no coming at me, all which too rais'd at once my character and price with him.

Regardful, however, of not carrying these difficulties to such a length as might afford time for starting discoveries, or incidents, unfavourable to her plan, she at last pretended to be won over by mere dint of entreaties, promises and above all, by the dazzling sum she took care to wind him up to the specification of, when it was now even a piece of art to feign, at once a yielding to the allurements of a great interest, as a pretext for her yielding at all, and the manner of it such, as might persuade him she had never before dipp'd her virtuous fingers in an affair of that sort.

Thus she led him through all the gradations of difficulty, and obstacles, necessary to enhance the value of the prize he aim'd at, and in conclusion, he was so struck with the little beauty I was mistress of, and so eagerly bent on gaining his ends of me, that he left her even no room to boast of her management in bringing him up to her mark, he drove so plum[30] of himself into every

thing tending to make him swallow the bait: not that in other respects, Mr. *Norbert* was not clear-sighted enough, not that he did
not perfectly know the town, and even by experience, the very
branch of imposition now in practice upon him; but we had his
passion to friend so much, he was so blinded, and hurried on by
it, that he would have thought any undeception a very ill office
done to his pleasure. Thus concurring, even precipitantly, to the
point she wanted him at, Mrs. *Cole* brought him at last to hug
himself on the cheap bargain, he consider'd the purchase of my
imaginary jewel, was to him, at no more than three hundred
guineas to myself, and an hundred to the brokeress; being a slender recompence for all her pains, and all the scruples of conscience she had now sacrificed to him for this the first time of her
life; which sums were to be paid down on the nail, upon livery of
my person, exclusive of some no inconsiderable presents that
had been made in the course of the negotiation: during which, I
had occasionally, but sparingly, been introduc'd into his company, at proper times and hours, in which it is incredible how little it seem'd necessary to strain my natural disposition to
modesty higher, in order to pass it upon him for that of a very
maid: all my looks and gestures ever breathing nothing but that
innocence which the men so ardently require in us, for no other
end than to feast themselves with the pleasure of destroying it,
and which they are so grievously, with all their skill, subject to
mistakes in.

When the articles of the treaty had been fully agreed on, the
stipulated payments duly secur'd, and nothing now remain'd but
the execution of the main point, which center'd in the surrender
of my person up to his free disposal and use, Mrs. *Cole* manag'd
her objections, especially to his lodgings, and insinuations so
nicely, that it became his own mere motion, and urgent request,
that this copy of a wedding should be finish'd at her house: at
first, indeed, she did not care, not she, to have such doings in
it,—she would not for a thousand pounds have any of the servants, or 'prentices know it—her precious good name would be
gone for ever,—with the like excuses: however, on superior ob-

jections to all other expedients, whilst she took care to start none but those that were most liable to them, it came round at last to the necessity of her obliging him in that conveniency, and of doing a little more where she had already done so much.

The night then was fix'd, with all possible respect to the eagerness of his impatience, and in the mean time Mrs. *Cole* had omitted no instructions, nor even neglected any preparation that might enable me to come off with honour, in regard to the appearance of virginity, except that, favour'd as I was by nature, with all the narrowness of stricture in that part requisite to conduct my designs, I had no occasion to borrow those auxiliaries of art that create a momentary one, easily discover'd by the test of a warm bath: and as to the usual bloody symptoms of defloration, which, if not always, are generally attendants on it, Mrs. *Cole* had made me the mistress of an invention of her own, which could hardly miss its effect, and of which more in its place.

Every thing then being dispos'd and fix'd for Mr. *Norbert*'s reception, he was at the hour of eleven at night, with all the mysteries of silence and secrecy, let in by Mrs. *Cole* herself, and introduc'd into her bed-chamber, where, in an old-fashion'd bed of her's, I lay, fully undress'd, and panting, if not with the fears of a real maid, at least with those perhaps greater, of a dissembled one, which gave me an air of confusion and bashfulness that maiden-modesty had all the honour of, and was indeed scarce distinguishable from it, even by less partial eyes than those of my lover, so let me call him, for I ever thought the term *cully* too cruel a reproach to the men, for their abus'd weakness for us.

As soon as Mrs. *Cole,* after the old gossipery,[31] on those occasions, us'd to young women abandon'd for the first time to the will of man, had left us alone in her room, which, by-the-bye, was well lighted up, at his previous desire, that seem'd to bode a stricter examination than he afterwards made; Mr. *Norbert,* still dress'd, sprung towards the bed, where I had got my head under the cloaths, and defended them a good while before he could even get at my lips, to kiss them: so true it is, that a false virtue, on this occasion, ever makes a greater rout and resistance, than a true one! from thence he descended to my breasts, the feel of which I disputed tooth and nail with him, till tir'd with my resistance, and thinking probably to give a better account of me, when got into bed to me; he hurry'd his cloaths off in an instant, and came into bed.

Mean while, by the glimpse I stole of him, I could easily discover a person far from promising any such doughty performances as the storming of maidenheads generally requires, and whose flimzy consumptive texture, gave him more the air of an invalid that was press'd, than of a volunteer, on such hot service.

At scarce thirty, he had already reduc'd his strength of appetite down to a wretched dependance on forc'd provocatives, very little seconded by the natural powers of a body jaded, and wrack'd off to the lees[32] by constant repeated overdraughts of pleasure, which had done the work of sixty winters on his springs of life; leaving him at the same time all the fire and heat of youth in his imagination, which serv'd at once to torment and to spur him down the precipice.

As soon as he was in bed, he threw off the bed-cloaths, which I suffer'd him to force from my hold, and I now lay as expos'd as he could wish, not only to his attacks, but his visitation[33] of the sheets, where, in the various agitations of my body, through my endeavours to defend myself, he could easily assure himself there was no preparation, or stain of blood, though to do him justice, he seem'd less strict an examinant than I had apprehended from so experienc'd a practitioner. My shift then he fairly tore open, finding I made too much use of it to barricade my breasts, as well as the more important avenue: yet in every thing else he proceeded with all the marks of tenderness and regard to me, whilst the art of my play was, to shew none for him: I acted then all the niceties, apprehensions, and terrors, supposable for a girl perfectly innocent, to feel, at so great a novelty as a naked man in bed with her for the first time. He scarce even obtain'd a kiss but what he ravish'd; I put his hand away twenty times from my breasts, where he had satisfy'd himself of their hardness and consistence with passing for hitherto unhandled goods: but when grown impatient for the main point, he now threw himself upon me, and first trying to examine me with his finger, sought to make himself further way, I complain'd of his usage bitterly, "I thought he would not have serv'd a body so. I was ruin'd.—I did not know what I had done.—I would get up, so I would."—And at the same time kept my thighs so fast lock'd, that it was not for a strength like his to force them open, or do any good. Finding thus my advantages, and that I had both my own and his motions at command, the deceiving him became so easy, that it was perfect playing upon velvet[34]: in the mean time, his machine, which was one of those sizes that slip in and out without being minded, kept pretty stifly bearing against that part, which the shutting my thighs barr'd access to; but finding, at length, he could do no good by mere dint of bodily strength, he resorted to intreaties and arguments; to which I only answer'd, with a tone of shame and timidity, "that I was afraid it would kill me—Lord!—I would not be serv'd so.—I was never so us'd in all my born days.—I wonder'd he was not asham'd of himself, so I did.—" With such silly infantine moods of repulse and complaint as I judg'd best adapted to express the characters of innocence, and afright. Pretending however to yield at length to the vehemence of his insistence, in action and words, I sparingly disclos'd my thighs so, that he could just touch the cloven inlet with the tip of his instrument, but as he fatigu'd and toil'd to get it in, a twist of my body, so as to receive it obliquely, not only thwarted his admission, but giving a scream, as if he had pierced me to the heart, I shook him off me, with such violence that he could not with all his might to it, keep the saddle: vex'd indeed at this he seem'd, but not in the style of any displeasure with me for my skittishness; on the contrary, I dare swear, he held me the dearer, and hugg'd himself for the difficulties that even hurt his instant pleasure: fired, however, now, beyond all bearance of delay, he remounts, and begg'd of me to have patience, stroaking and soothing me to it by all the tenderest endearments and protestations of what he would moreover do for me, at which feigning to be something soften'd, and abating of the anger that I had shewn at his hurting me so prodigiously, I suffer'd him to lay my thighs aside, and make way for a new trial; but I watch'd the directions and management of his point so

well, that no sooner was the orifice in the least open to it; but I
gave such a timely jerk, as seem'd to proceed, not from the evasion of his entry, but from the pain his efforts at it put me to: a
circumstance too that I did not fail to accompany with proper
gestures, sighs, and cries of complaint, of which, "that he had
hurt me—he kill'd me—I should die—" were the most frequent
interjections. But now, after repeated attempts, in which he had
not made the least impression, towards gaining his point, at least
for that time, the pleasure rose so fast upon him that he could
not check or delay it, and in the vigour and fury, which the approaches of the height of it inspir'd him, he made one fierce
thrust that had almost put me by my guard, and lodg'd it so far
that I could feel the warm inspersion just within the exterior orifice, which I had the cruelty not to let him finish there, but threw
him out again, not without a most piercing loud exclamation, as
if the pain had put me beyond all regard of being overheard. It
was easy then to observe that he was more satisfy'd, more highly
pleas'd with the suppos'd motives of his baulk of consummation,
than he would have been at the full attainment of it. It was on
this foot that I salv'd[35] to myself all the falsity I employ'd to procure him that blissful pleasure in it, which most certainly he
would not have tasted in the truth of things. Eas'd however, and
reliev'd by one discharge, he now apply'd himself to soothe, encourage, and put me into humour, and patience to bear his next
attempt, which he began to prepare and gather force for, from all
the incentives of the touch and sight, which he could think of, by
examining every individual part off my whole body, which he
declar'd his satisfaction with, in raptures of applause, kisses universally imprinted, and sparing no part of me, in all the eagerest
wantonnesses of feeling, seeing and toying: his vigour however
did not return so soon, and I felt him more than once pushing at
the door, but so little in a condition to break in, that I question
whether he had the power to enter, had I held it ever so open; but
this he then thought me too little acquainted with the nature of
things to have any regret or confusion about, and he kept fatiguing himself and me for a long time before he was in any state of
stiffness to resume his attempts with any prospect of success!

and then I breath'd him so warmly, and kept him so at bay, that before he had made any sensible progress in point of penetration, he was deliciously sweated, and weary'd out indeed! so that it was deep in the morning before he had atchiev'd his second let-go, about half way of entrance, I all the time crying and complaining of his prodigious vigour, and the immensity of what I appear'd to suffer splitting up with. Tir'd however at length, with such athletic drudgery, my champion began now to give out, and to gladly embrace the refreshment of some rest; kissing me then with much affection, and recommending me to my repose, be presently fell fast asleep: which as soon as I had well satisfied myself of, I, with much composure of body, so as not to wake him by any motion, with much ease and safety too, play'd off Mrs. *Cole*'s device for perfecting the signs of my virginity.

In each of the head bed-posts, just above where the bed-steads are inserted into them, there was a small drawer so artfully adapted to the mouldings of the timber-work, that it might have escap'd even the most curious search, which drawers were easily open'd or shut, by the touch of a spring, and were fitted each with a shallow glass tumbler, full of a prepar'd fluid blood; in which lay soak'd, for ready use, a sponge; that requir'd no more than gently reaching the hand to it, taking it out, and properly squeezing between the thighs, when it yielded a great deal more of the red liquid than would save a girl's honour: after which, replacing it, and touching the spring, all possibility of discovery, or even of suspicion, was taken away; and all this was not the work of the fourth part of a minute, and of which ever side one lay, the thing was equally easy and practicable, by the double care taken to have each bed-post provided alike. True it is, that had he wak'd, and caught me in the fact, it would at least have cover'd me with shame and confusion; but then, that he did not, was, with the precautions I took, a risk of a thousand to one in my favour.

At ease now, and out of all fear of any doubt or suspicion, on his side, I address'd myself in good earnest to my repose; but could obtain none, and in about half an hour's time, my gentle-man wak'd again, and turning towards me, I feign'd a sound sleep, which he did not long respect; but girding himself again to renew the onset, he began to kiss and caress me, when now mak-ing as if I just wak'd, I complain'd of the disturbance, and of the cruel pain that this little rest had stolen my senses from. Eager, however, for the pleasure, as well as honour of consummating an entire triumph over my virginity; he said, and did every thing that could overcome my resistance, and bribe my patience to the end, which now I was ready to listen to, from being secure of the bloody proofs I had prepar'd of his victorious violence, though I still thought it good policy not to let him in yet a while. I answer'd then only to his importunities, in sighs and moans, that I was so hurt, I could not bear it. I was sure he had done me a mischief; that he had, he was such a sad[36] man! Turning at this, down the cloaths, and viewing the field of battle by the glimmer of a dying taper, he saw plainly my thighs, shift, and sheets, all yet wet, and stain'd with what he readily took for virgin gore,[37] proceeding from his last half-penetration; convinc'd, and trans-ported at which, nothing could equal his joy and exultation. The illusion was complete: no other conception enter'd his head but that of his having been at work upon an unopen'd mine: which idea, upon so strong an evidence, redoubled at once his tender-ness for me, and his ardour for breaking it wholly up. Kissing me then with the utmost rapture, he comforted me, and begg'd my pardon for the pain he had put me to, observing withal, that it was only a thing in course; but the worst was certainly past, and that with a little courage and constancy I should get it once well over, and never after experience any thing but the greatest plea-sure. By little and little I suffer'd myself to be prevail'd on, and giving, as it were, up the point to him, I made my thighs, insen-sibly spreading them, yield him liberty of access, which improv-ing, he got a little within me, when, by a well-manag'd reception, I work'd the female screw[38] so nicely, that I kept him from the easy mid-channel direction, and by dexterous wreathings and contortions creating an artificial difficulty of entrance, made him win it inch by inch, with the most laborious struggles, I all the time sorely complaining, till at length, with might and main, winding his way in, he got it completely home, and giving my virginity, as he thought, the *coup de grace,* furnish'd me the cue of setting up a terrible outcry, whilst he, triumphant, and like a cock, clapping his wings over his down-trod mistress, pursu'd his pleasure, which presently rose in virtue of this idea of a complete victory, to a pitch that made me soon sensible of his melting period, whilst I now lay acting the deep wounded, breathless, frighten'd, undone, no longer, maid.

You will ask me perhaps, whether all this time I enjoy'd any perception of pleasure? I assure you, little or none; till just towards the latter end, a faintish sense of it came on mechanically, from so long a struggle, and frequent fret in that ever sensible part: but, in the first place, I had no taste for the person I was suffering the embraces of, on a purely mercenary account, and then I was not entirely delighted with myself for the jade's part I was playing, whatever excuses I might have to plead for being brought into it: but then this insensibility kept me so much the mistress of my mind and motions, that I could the better manage so close a counterfeit, through the whole scene of deception.

Recover'd at length to more shew of life, by his tender condolances, kisses, and embraces, I upbraided him, and reproach'd him for my ruin, in such natural terms, as added to his satisfaction with himself, for having accomplish'd it; and guessing, by certain observations of mine, that it would be rather favourable to him, to spare him, when he sometime after, feebly enough, came on again to the assault, I resolutely withstood any further endeavours, on a pretext that flatter'd his prowess, of my being so violently hurt and sore, that I could not possibly endure a fresh trial: he then graciously granted me a respite, and the morning soon after advancing, I got rid of farther importunity, till *Mrs. Cole,* being rang for by him, came in, and was made acquainted in terms of the utmost joy and rapture, with his triumphant certainty of my virtue, and the finishing stroke he had given it, in the course of the night; of which he added, she would see proof enough, in bloody characters, on the sheets.

You may guess how a woman of her turn of address and experience, humour'd the jest, and play'd him off with mix'd exclamations of shame, anger, compassion for me, and of her being pleas'd that all was so well over; in which last, I believe, she was perfectly sincere. And now, as the objection which she had represented as an invincible one, to my lying the first night at his lodgings (which were studiously calculated for a freedom of intrigues) on the account of my maiden fears and terrors, at the thoughts of going to a gentleman's chambers, and being alone with him in bed, was surmounted, she pretended to persuade me, in favour to him, that I should go there to him, whenever he pleas'd, and still keep up all the necessary appearances of working with her, that I might not lose, with my character, the prospect of getting a good husband, and at the same time her house would be kept the safer from scandal. All this seem'd so reasonable, so considerate to Mr. *Norbert*, that he never once perceiv'd, that she did not want him to resort to her house, lest he might in time discover certain inconsistencies with the character she had set out with to him; besides that this plan greatly flatter'd his own ease, and views of liberty.

Leaving me then to my much wanted rest, he got up, and Mrs. *Cole*, after settling with him all points relating to me, got him undiscover'd out of the house. Aftar which, and I was awake, she came in, and gave me due praises on my success; behaving too with her usual moderation, and disinterestness, she refus'd any share of the sum I had thus earn'd, and put me into such a secure and easy way of disposing of my affairs, which now amounted to a kind of little fortune, that a child of ten years old might have kept the account, and property of them safe in its hands.

I was now restor'd again to my former state of a kept mistress, and us'd punctually to wait on Mr. *Norbert* at his chambers, whenever he sent a messenger for me, which I constantly took care to be in the way of, and manag'd with so much caution that he never once penetrated the nature of my connexions with Mrs. *Cole*, but indolently given up to ease, and the town dissipations, the perpetual hurry to them hinder'd him from looking into his own affairs, much less into mine.

In the mean time, if I may judge from my own experience, none are better paid, or better treated, during their reign, than the mistresses of those who, enervate by nature, debaucheries, or age, have the least employment for the sex: sensible that a woman must be satisfy'd some way, they ply her with a thousand little tender attentions, presents, caresses, confidences, and exhaust their invention in means and devices to make up for the capital deficiency: and even towards lessening that, what arts, what modes, what refinements of pleasure have they not recourse to, to raise their lanquid powers, and press nature into the service of their sensuality? But here is their misfortune, that when by a course of teazing, worrying, handling, wanton postures, lascivious motions, they have at length accomplish'd a flashy enervate enjoyment, they have at the same time lighted up a flame in the object of their passion, that not having the means themselves to quench, drives her for relief, into the next person's arms, who can finish their work: and thus they become bawds to some secret favourite, tried, and approv'd of for a more vigorous, and satisfactory execution; for with women, of our turn especially, however well our hearts may be dispos'd, there is a controuling part, or queen-seat in us, that governs itself by its own maxims of state, amongst which not one is stronger in practise with it, than, in matter of its dues, never to accept the will for the deed.

Mr. *Norbert,* who was much in this ungracious case, though he profess'd and shew'd to like me extremely, could but seldom consummate the main-joy itself with me, without such a length and variety of preparations as were at once wearisome and inflammatory.

Sometimes he would strip me stark naked on a carpet, by a good fire; when he would contemplate me almost by the hour, disposing me in all the figures and attitudes of body, that it was susceptible of being view'd in: kissing me in every part, the most secret and critical one so far from excepted, that it receiv'd most of that branch of homage, then his touches were so exquisitely wanton, and luxuriously diffus'd, and penetrative at times, that he made me perfectly rage with titillating fires, when, after all, and when with much ado, he had gain'd a short-liv'd erection, he would perhaps melt it away in a washy sweat, or a premature abortive effusion, that provokingly mock'd my eager desires; or, if carried home, how faulter'd and unnervous[39] the execution! how insufficient the sprinkle of a few heat-drops to extinguish all the flames he had kindled.

One evening I cannot help remembering, that returning home from him with a spirit he had rais'd in a circle his wand had prov'd too weak to lay, as I turn'd the corner of a street, I was overtaken by a young sailor. I was then in that spruce, neat, and plain dress, which I ever affected, and perhaps might have in my trip a certain air of restlessness unknown to the composure of cooler thoughts. However he seiz'd me as prize, and, without ceremony, threw his hands round my neck, and kiss'd me bois-terously, and sweetly. I look'd at him with a beginning of anger and indignation at his rudeness, that soften'd away into other sentiments as fast I view'd him: for he was tall, manly-carriag'd, handsome of body and face, so that I ended my stare, with ask-ing him in a tone turn'd to tenderness, what he meant: at which, with the same frankness, and vivacity as he had begun with me, he propos'd treating me with a glass of wine: now, certain it is, that had I been in a calmer state of blood than I was; had I been less under the dominion of unappeas'd irritations and desires, I should have refus'd him without hesitation: but I do not know how it was, my pressing calls, his figure, the occasion, and if you will, the powerful combination of all these with a start of cu-riosity, to see the end of an adventure so novel to me as being thus treated like a common street-plyer,[40] made me give a silent consent: in short, it was not my head that I now obey'd. I suffer'd myself then to be tow'd along as it were by this man-of-war, who took me under his arm as familiarly as if he had known me all his life-time, and led me into the next convenient tavern, where we were shown into a little room on one side of the passage. Here, scarce allowing himself patience till the drawer brought in the wine call'd for, he fell directly on board me: when untucking my

handkerchief, and giving me a smacking buss, he laid my breasts
bare at once, which he handled with that keenness of gust that
abridges a ceremonial ever more tiresome than pleasing on such
pressing occasions; and now hurrying towards the main-point,
we found no conveniency for our purpose; two or three disabled
chairs, and a ricketty table composing the whole furniture of the
room.

Without more ado, he plants me with my back standing
against the wall, and my petticoats up; and coming out with a
splitter indeed, made it shine, as he brandish'd it, in my eyes, and
going to work with an impetuosity and eagerness, bred very
likely by a long fast at sea, went to give me the taste of it: I straddled, I humour'd my posture, and did my best in short to buckle
to it; I took part of it in too; but still things did not jee⁴¹ to his
thorough liking: changing then in a trice his system of battery,
he leads me to the table, and with a master-hand lays my head
down on the edge of it, and with the other canting up my petticoat and shift, bares my naked posteriours to his blind, and furious guide: it forces his way between them, and I feeling pretty
sensibly that it was going by the right door, and knocking des-
perately at the wrong one, I told him of it: "Pooh," says he, "my
dear, any port in a storm." Altering, however directly, his course,
and lowering his point, he fix'd it right, and driving it up with a
delicious stiffness, made all foam again, and gave me the *tout*
with such fire, and spirit, that in the fine disposition I was in,
when I submitted to him, and stirr'd up so fiercely as I was, I got
the start of him, and went away into the melting swoon, and
squeezing him, whilst in the convulsive grasp of it, drew from
him such a plenteous bedewal of balmy sweets, as join'd to my
own effusion, prefectly floated those parts, and drown'd in a del-
uge all my raging conflagration of desire.

When this was over, how to make my retreat was my concern;
for though I had been so extremely pleas'd with the difference
between this warm broadside pour'd so briskly into me, and the
tiresome pawing and toying, to which I had ow'd the unappeas'd
flames that had driven me into this step; now I was grown cooler,
I began to apprehend the danger of contracting an acquaintance

with this, however agreeable, stranger; who, on his side, spoke of passing the evening with me, and continuing our intimacy, with an air of determination that made me afraid of its being not so easy to get away from him as I could wish: in the mean time I carefully conceal'd my uneasiness, and readily pretended to consent to stay with him, telling him, I should only step to my lodgings, to leave a necessary direction, and then instantly re-turn. This he very glibly swallow'd, on the notion of my being one of those unhappy street-errants, who devote themselves to the pleasure of the first ruffian that will stoop to pick them up, and of course, that I would scarce bilk myself of my hire by my not returning, to make the most of the job. Thus he parted with me, not before, however, he had order'd, in my hearing, a supper, which I had the barbarity of disappoint him of my company to.

But when I got home, and told Mrs. *Cole* my adventure, she represented so strongly to me the nature and dangerous conse-quences of my folly, the risques to my health, in being so open-legg'd, and free of my flesh, that I not only took resolutions never to venture so rashly again, which I inviolably preserv'd; but pass'd a good many days in continual uneasiness lest I should have met with other reasons, besides the pleasure of that ren-counter, to remember it: but these fears wrong'd my pretty sailor, for which I gladly make him this reparation.

I had now liv'd with Mr. *Norbert* near a quarter of a year, in which space I circulated my time very pleasantly, between my amusements at Mrs. *Cole*'s, and a proper attendance on that gen-tleman, who paid me profusely for the unlimited complaisance with which I passively humour'd every caprice of pleasure, and which had won upon him so greatly, that finding, as he said, all that variety in me alone, which he had sought for in a number of women, I had made him lose his taste for inconstancy, and new faces. But what was yet at least as agreeable to me as his fondness and attachment, as well as much more flattering; the love I had inspir'd him with, bred a deference to me that was of great ser-vice to his health. For having by degrees, and with most pathetic representations, brought him to some husbandry[42] of it, and to ensure the duration of his pleasures by moderating their use, and correcting those excesses in them he was so addicted to, and which had shatter'd his constitution, and destroy'd his powers of life, in the very point, for which he seem'd chiefly desirous to live; he was grown more delicate, more temperate, and all in course more healthy; his gratitude for which was taking a turn very favourable for my fortune, when once more the caprice of it, dash'd the cup from my lips.

His sister, lady *L*——, for whom he had a great affection, desiring him to accompany her down to *Bath,* for her health, he could not refuse her such a favour, and accordingly, though he counted on staying away from me no more than a week at farthest, he took his leave of me, with an ominous heaviness of heart, and left with me a sum far above the state of his fortune, and very inconsistent with the intended shortness of his journey, but it ended in the longest that can be, and is never but once taken; for, arriv'd at *Bath,* he was not there two days before he fell into a debauch of drinking with some gentlemen, that threw him into a high fever, which carry'd him off in four days time, never once out of a delirium. Had he been in his senses to make a will, perhaps he might have made favourable mention of me in it. Thus, however, I lost him; and as no condition of life is more subject to revolutions than that of a woman of pleasure, I soon recover'd my chearfulness, and now beheld myself once more struck off the list of kept-mistresses, and return'd into the bosom of the community, from which I had been in some manner taken.

Mrs. *Cole* still continuing her friendship, offer'd me her assistances and advice towards another choice; but I was now in a state of ease and affluence enough to look about me at leisure; and as to any constitutional calls of pleasure, their pressure or sensibility was greatly lessen'd by a consciousness of the ease with which they were to be satisfy'd at Mrs. *Cole's* house, where *Louisa* and *Emily* still continu'd in the old way; and my great favourite *Harriet,* us'd often to come and see me, and entertain me, with her head and heart full of the happiness she enjoy'd with her dear baronet, whom she lov'd with tenderness and constancy, even though he was her keeper; and what is yet more, had made her independent by a handsome provision for her, and hers.

I was then in this vacancy from any regular employ of my person, in my way of business, when one day Mrs. *Cole,* in the course of the constant confidence we liv'd in, acquainted me that there was one Mr. *Barvile,* a gentleman who us'd her house, just come to town, whom she was not a little perplex'd about providing a suitable companion for; which was indeed a point of difficulty, as he was under the tyranny of a cruel taste; that of an ardent desire, not only of being unmercifully whipp'd himself, but of whipping others, in such sort, that tho' he paid extravagantly those who had the courage and complaisance to submit to his humour; there were few, delicate as he was in the choice of his subjects, who would exchange turns with him so terribly at the expence of their skin: but what yet increas'd the oddity of this strange fancy, was the gentleman's being young; whereas it generally attacks, it seems, such as are, through age, oblig'd to have recourse to this experiment, for quickening the circulation of their sluggish juices, and determining a conflux of the spirits of pleasure towards those flagging, shrivelly parts, that rise to life only by virtue of those titillating ardours created by the discipline of their opposites, with which they have so surprising a consent.

This Mrs. *Cole* could not well acquaint me with, in any expectation of my offering my service; for sufficiently easy as I was in my circumstances, it must have been the temptation of an immense interest indeed, that could have induced me to embrace such a job; neither had I ever express'd, or indeed felt, the least impulse or curiosity to know more of a taste, that promis'd so much more pain than pleasure, to those that stood in no need of such violent goads: what then should move me to subscribe myself voluntarily to a party of pain, foreknowing it such? Why, to tell the plain truth; it was a sudden caprice, a gust of fancy for trying a new experiment, mix'd with the vanity of approving my personal courage to Mrs. *Cole,* that determin'd me, at all risques, to propose myself to her, and relieve her from any farther look-out; accordingly, I at once pleas'd and surpris'd her, with a frank and unreserv'd tender of my person to her, and her friend's absolute disposal on this occasion.

My good temporal mother, was however so kind as to use all the arguments she could imagine to dissuade me: but as I found they only turn'd on a motive of tenderness to me, I persisted in my resolution, and thereby acquitted my offer of any suspicion of its not having been sincerely made, or out of compliment only: acquiescing then thankfully in it, Mrs. *Cole* assur'd me, that bating[43] the pain I should be put to, she had no scruple to engage me in this party, which she assur'd me I should be liberally paid for, and which the secresy of the transaction, preserv'd safe from the ridicule that otherwise vulgarly attended it: that for her part, she consider'd pleasure of one sort or other, as the universal port of destination, and every wind that blew thither a good one, provided it blew nobody any harm: that she rather compassionated, than blam'd those unhappy persons, who are under a subjection they cannot shake off, to those arbitrary tastes that rule their appetites of pleasure with an unaccountable control: tastes too, as infinitely diversify'd, as superior to, and independent of all reasoning, as the different relishes or palates of mankind in their viands[44]; some delicate stomachs nauseating plain meats, and finding no favour but in high season'd, luxurious dishes; whilst others again pique themselves upon detesting them.

I stood now in no need of this preamble of encouragement, or justification: my word was given, and I was determin'd to fulfil my engagements; accordingly the night was set, and I had all the necessary previous instructions how to act and conduct myself. The dining-room was duly prepar'd and lighted up, and the young gentleman posted there in waiting for my introduction to him.

I was then, by Mrs. *Cole,* handed in, and presented to him in a loose dishabille, fitted, by her direction, to the exercise I was to go through, all in the finest linen, and a thorough white-uniform: gown, petticoat, stockings, and satin slippers, like a victim led to the sacrifice; whilst my dark auburn hair, falling in drop-curls over my neck, created a pleasing distinction of colour from the rest of my dress.

As soon as Mr. *Barvile* saw me, he got up with a very visible air of pleasure and surprise, and after saluting me, ask'd Mrs. *Cole* if it was possible that so fine, and delicate a creature, would voluntary submit to such sufferings, and rigours, as were the subject of this assignation. She answer'd him properly, and now reading in his eyes, that she could not too soon leave us together, she went out, after recommending him to use moderation with so tender a novice.

But whilst she was employing his attention, mine had been taken up with examining the figure and person of this unhappy young gentleman, who was thus unaccountably condemn'd to have his pleasure lash'd into him, as boys have their learning.

He was exceeding fair, and smooth complexion'd; and appear'd to me no more than twenty at most, tho' he was three years older than what my conjectures gave him; but then he ow'd this favourable mistake to a habit of fatness, which spread through a short, squab stature, and a round, plump, fresh-colour'd face, gave him greatly the look of a *Bacchus*,[45] had not an air of austerity, not to say sterness, very unsuitable even to his shape of face, dash'd that character of joy, necessary to complete the resemblance. His light-brown hair was pretty thick, uncurl'd, and look'd as if it had been trimm'd with a bowl-dish, as we are told the *Roundheads* were in *Oliver*'s times.[46] His dress was extremely neat, but plain, and far inferior to the ample fortune, he was in full possession of: this too was a taste in him, and not avarice.

As soon as Mrs. *Cole* was gone, he seated me near him, when now his face chang'd upon me, into an expression of the most pleasing sweetness and good humour, the more remarkable for its sudden shift from the other extreme, which I found afterwards, when I knew more of his character, was owing to an habitual state of conflict with, and dislike of himself, for being enslav'd to so peculiar a gust,[47] by the fatality of a constitutional ascendant, that render'd him incapable of receiving any pleasure, till he submitted to these extraordinary means of procuring it at the hands of pain, whilst the constancy of this repining consciousness, stamp'd at length that cast of sourness and severity on his features which was in fact, very foreign to the natural sweetness of his temper.

After then a competent preparation by apologies, and encouragement to go through my part with spirit and constancy, he stood up near the fire, whilst I went to fetch the instruments of discipline, out of a closet hard by: these were several rods, made each of two or three strong twigs of birch tied together, which he took, handled, and view'd with as much pleasure as I did with a kind of shuddering presage.

Next we took from the side of the room a long broad bench, made easy to lie at length on by a soft cushion in a callico-cover: and every thing being now ready, he took his coat and waistcoat off; and, at his motion and desire, I unbutton'd his breeches, and rolling his shirt up rather above his waist, tuck'd it in securely there; when directing naturally my eyes to that humoursome master-movement, in whose favour all these dispositions were making, it seem'd almost shrunk into his belly, scarce showing its tip above the sprout of hairy curls that cloath'd those parts, as you may have seen a wren peep its head out of the grass.

Stooping then to untie his garters, he gave them me for the use of tying him down to the legs of the bench, a circumstance no farther necessary than as I suppose it made part of the humour[48] of the thing, since he prescribed it to himself, amongst the rest of the ceremonial.

I led him then to the bench, and according to my cue, plaid at forcing him to lie down: which, after some little shew of reluctance, for form-sake, he submitting to, was straitway extended flat upon his belly, on the bench, with a pillow under his face; and as he thus tamely lay, I tied him slightly hand and foot, to the legs of it; which done, his shirt remaining truss'd up over the small of his back, I drew his breeches quite down to his knees; and now he lay, in all the fairest, broadest display of that part of the backview, in which a pair of chubby, smooth-cheek'd, and passing[49] white posteriours rose cushioning upwards from two stout, fleshful thighs, and ending their cleft, or separation, by an union at the small of the back, presented a bold mark, that swell'd, as it were, to meet the scourge.

Seizing now one of the rods, I stood over him, and, according to his direction, gave him, in one breath, ten lashes with much good-will, and the utmost nerve and vigour of arm that I could put to them, so as to make those fleshy orbs quiver again under them, whilst himself seem'd no more concern'd, or to mind them, than a lobster would a flea-bite: in the mean time, I view'd intently the effects of them, which to me at least appear'd surprisingly cruel: every lash had skimm'd the surface of those white cliffs, which they deeply redden'd, and lapping round the side of the furthermost from me, cut, especially into the dimple of it, such livid weals, as the blood either spun out from, or stood in large drops on; and from some of the cuts I pick'd out even the splinters of the rod, that had stuck in the skin: nor was this raw work to be wonder'd at, considering the greenness of the twigs, and the severity of the infliction, whilst the whole surface of his skin was so smooth-stretch'd over the hard and firm pulp of flesh that fill'd it, as to yield no play, or elusive swagging under the stroke, which thereby took place the more plum, and cut into the quick.

I was however already so mov'd at the piteous sight, that I from my heart repented the undertaking, and would willingly have given over, thinking he had full enough; but, he encouraging, and beseeching me earnestly to proceed, I gave him ten more lashes, and then resting, survey'd the encrease of bloody appearances, and at length, steel'd to the sight, by his stoutness in suffering, I continu'd the discipline, by intervals, till I observ'd him wreathing and twisting his body in a way that I could plainly perceive was not the effect of pain, but of some new and powerful sensation; curious to dive into the meaning of which, in one of my pauses of intermission, I approach'd, as he still kept working, and grinding his belly against the cushion under him; and first, stroking the untouch'd and unhurt side of the flesh-mount next me, then softly insinuating my hand under his thigh, felt the posture things were in forwards, which was indeed surprising;

for that machine of his, which I had by its appearance, taken for an impalpable, or at best a very diminutive subject, was now, in virtue of all that smart and havock of his skin behind, grown not only to a prodigious stiffness of erection, but to a size that frighted even me: a non-pareil thickness indeed! the head of it alone fill'd the utmost capacity of my grasp: and when, as he heav'd and wriggled to and fro, in the agitation of his strange pleasure, it came into view, it had some thing of the air of a round fillet of the whitest veal, like its owner, squab, and short in proportion to its breadth; but when he felt my hand there, he begg'd I would go on briskly with my jerking, or he should never arrive at the last stage of pleasure.

Resuming then the rod, and the exercise of it, I had fairly worn out three bundles, when after an increase of struggles, and motion, and a deep sigh or two, I saw him lie still and motionless: and now he desir'd me to desist, which I instantly did, and proceeding to untie him, I could not but be amaz'd at his passive fortitude, on viewing the skin of his butcher'd, mangl'd posteriours, late so white, smooth, and polish'd, now all one side of them, a confus'd cut-work of weals, livid flesh, gashes and gore, insomuch that when he stood up, he could scarce walk; in short, he was in sweetbriars.[50]

Then I plainly perceiv'd on the cushion, the marks of a plenteous effusion of white liquid, and already had his sluggard member run up to its old nestling-place, and ensconc'd itself again, as if asham'd to show its head, which nothing, it seems, could raise but stripes inflicted on its opposite neighbours, who were thus constantly oblig'd to suffer for his caprice.

My gentleman had now put on his cloaths, and recompos'd himself, when giving me a kiss, and placing me by him, he sat down himself as gingerly as possible, with the one side off the cushion, which was too sore for him to bear resting any part of his weight on.

Here he thank'd me extremely for the pleasure I had procur'd him, and seeing perhaps some marks in my countenance of terror, and apprehension of retaliation on my own skin, for what I had been the instrument of his suffering in his, he assur'd me, he was ready to give up to me any engagement I might deem myself under to stand him, as he had done me; but that if I proceeded in my consent to it, he would consider the difference of my sex, its greater delicacy, and incapacity to undergo pain. Rehearten'd at which, and piqu'd in honour,[51] as I thought, not to flinch so near the trial, especially, as I well knew Mrs. *Cole* was an eye-witness, from her stand of espial,[52] to the whole of our transactions, I was now less afraid of my skin, than of his not furnishing me an opportunity of signalizing my resolution.

Consonant to this disposition was my answer, but my courage was still more in my head, than in my heart, and as cowards rush into the danger they fear, in order to be the sooner rid of the pain of that sensation, I was entirely pleas'd with his hastening matters into execution.

He had then little to do, but to unloose the strings of my petticoat, and lift them, together with my shift, navel-high, where he just tuck'd them up loosely girt, and might be slipt up higher at pleasure: then viewing me round with great seeming delight, he laid me at my length, on my face, upon the bench, and when I expected he would tie me, as I had done him, and held out my hands, not without fear, and a little trembling; he told me, he would by no means terrify me unnecessarily with such a confinement; for that though he meant to put my constancy to some trial, the standing it was to be completely voluntary on my side, and therefore I was to be at full liberty to get up whenever I found the pain too much for me:——You cannot imagine how much I thought myself bound, by being thus allow'd to remain loose, and how much spirit this confidence in me, gave me, so that I was, even from my heart, careless how much my flesh might suffer in honour of it.

All my back parts naked half way up, were now fully at his mercy: and first, he stood at a convenient distance, delighting himself with a gloating survey of the attitude I lay in, and of all the secret stores I thus expos'd to him in fair display: then springing eagerly towards me, he cover'd all those naked parts with a fond confusion of kisses; and now taking hold of the rod, rather wanton'd with me, in gentle inflictions on those tender trembling masses of my flesh behind, than any way hurt them, till by degrees he began to tingle them with smarter lashes, so as to provoke a red colour into them, which I knew, as well by the flagrant glow I felt there, as by his telling me, they now emulated the native roses of my other cheeks: when he had then amus'd himself with admiring, and toying with them, he went on to strike harder, and more hard; so that I needed all my patience not to cry out, or complain at least: at last he twigg'd me so smartly as to fetch blood in more than one lash: at sight of which, he flung down the rod, flew to me, kiss'd away the starting drops, and sucking the wounds, eas'd a good deal of my pain: but now raising me on my knees, and making me kneel with them strad-dling wide, that tender part of me naturally the province of pleasure, not of pain, came in for its share of suffering, for now, eying it wistfully, he directed the rod so that the sharp ends of the twigs lighted there, so sensibly, that I could not help winch-ing,[53] and writhing my limbs with smart; so that my contorsions of body must necessarily throw it into an infinite variety of pos-tures, and points of view, fit to feast the luxury of the eye: but still I bore every thing without crying out: when presently giving me another pause, he rush'd, as it were, on that part, whose lips, and round-about, had felt his cruelty, and by way of reparation, glews his own to them: then he open'd, shut, squeez'd them, pluck'd softly the overgrowing moss, and all this in a style of wild passionate rapture, and enthusiasm, that express'd excess of pleasure, till betaking himself to the rod again, encourag'd by my passiveness, and infuriate with this strange taste of delight, he made my poor posteriours pay for the ungovernableness of it; for now shewing them no quarter, the traytor cut me so, that I wanted but very little of fainting away, when he gave over; and yet I did not utter one groan, or angry expostulation; but in my heart I resolv'd nothing so seriously, as never to expose myself again to the like severities.

You may guess then in what a curious pickle those flesh-cushions of mine were, all sore, raw, and in fine, terribly clawed off; but so far from feeling any pleasure in it, that the recent smart made me pout a little; and not with the greatest air of satisfaction, receive the compliments, and after-caresses of the author of my pain.

As soon as my cloaths were huddled on, in a little decency, a supper was brought in by the discreet Mrs. *Cole* herself, which might have piqued the sensuality of a cardinal, accompanied with a choice of the richest wines; all which she set before us, and went out again, without having by a word, or even by a smile, given us the least interruption, or confusion, in those instants of secrecy, that we were not yet ripe for the admission of a third to.

I sat down then, still scarce in charity with my butcher; for such I could not help considering him, and was moreover not a little piqued at the gay, satisfied air of his countenance, which I thought myself insulted by: but when the now necessary refreshment to me, of a glass of wine, and a little eating, (all the time observing a profound silence) had somewhat chear'd, and restor'd me to spirits; and as the smart began to go off, my good humour return'd accordingly, which alteration not escaping him, he said, and did every thing that could confirm me in, and indeed exalt, it.

But scarce was supper well over, before a change so incredible was wrought in me, such violent, yet pleasingly irksome sensations took possession of me, that I scarce knew how to contain myself: the smart of the lashes was now converted into such a prickly heat, such fiery tinglings, as made me sigh, squeeze my thighs together, shift and wriggle about my seat, with a furious restlessness; whilst these itching ardours thus excited in those parts on which the storm of discipline had principally fallen, detach'd legions of burning, subtile,[54] stimulating spirits, to their opposite spot, and center of assemblage, where their titillation rag'd so furiously, that I was even stinging-mad with them: no wonder then, that in such a taking, and devour'd by flames that lick'd up all modesty and reserve, my eyes now charg'd brimful of the most intense desire, fired on my companion very intelligible signals of distress: my companion, I say, who grew in them every instant more amiable, and more necessary to my urgent wishes, and hopes of immediate ease.

Mr. *Barvile,* no stranger, by experience, to these situations, soon knew the pass I was brought to; soon perceiv'd my extreme disorder; in favour of which, removing the table out of the way, he began a prelude that flatter'd me with instant relief, which I was not however so near as I imagin'd: for as he was unbutton'd to me, and tried to provoke, and rouse to action his unactive, torpid machine, he blushingly own'd, that no good was to be expected from it, unless I took in hand to re-excite its languid, loitering powers, by just refreshing the smart of the yet recent, blood-raw cuts, seeing it could, no more than a boy's top, keep up without lashing: sensible then, that I should work as much for my own profit as his, I hurried my compliance with his desire, and abridging the ceremonial, whilst he lean'd his head against the back of a chair, I had scarce gently made him feel the lash, before I saw the object of my wishes give signs of life, and presently, as it were with a magic touch, it started up into a noble size, and distinction indeed! hastening then to give me the benefit of it, he threw me down on the bench; but such was the refresh'd soreness of those parts behind, on my leaning so hard on them as became me to compass the admission of that stupendous head of his machine, that I could not possibly bear it: I got up then, and tried, by leaning forwards, and turning the crupper[55] on my assailant, to let him in at the back-avenue; but here it was likewise impossible to stand his bearing so fiercely against me in his agitations, and endeavours to enter that way, whilst his belly batter'd directly against the recent sore: what should we do now? both intolerably heated! both all in one fury! but pleasure is ever inventive for its own ends: he strips me in a trice, stark naked, and placing a broad settee-cushion on the carpet before the fire, oversets me gently topsy-turvy on it; and handling me only at the waist, whilst you may be sure I favour'd all his dispositions, brought my legs round his neck; so that my head was kept from the floor only by my hands, and the velvet cushion, which was now bespread with my flowing hair: thus I stood on my head and hands, supported by him in such manner, that whilst my thighs clung round him, so as to expose to his sight all my back-figure, including the theatre of his bloody pleasure, the center of my forepart fairly bearded the now worthy object of its rage, that now stood in fine condition to give me satisfaction for the injuries of its neighbours. But as this posture was certainly not the easiest, and our imagination, wound up to the height, could suffer no delay; he first, with the utmost eagerness and effort, just lip-lodg'd that broad, acorn-fashion'd head of his instrument; and still friended by the fury with which he had made that impression, he soon stuffed in the rest; when now, with a pursuit of thrusts fiercely urg'd, he absolutely overpower'd, and absorb'd all sense of pain and uneasiness, whether from my wounds behind, my most untoward posture, or the oversize of his stretcher, in an infinitely predominat delight: when now all my whole spirits of life and sensation, rushing impetuously to the cock-pit, where the prize of pleasure was hotly in dispute, and clustering to a point there, I soon receiv'd the dear relief of nature from these over-violent strains and provocations of it, harmonizing with which, my gallant spouted into me such a potent overflow of the oily balsamic injection, as soften'd and unedg'd all those irritating stings of a new species of titilation, which I had been so untolerably madden'd with, and restor'd the ferment of my senses to some degree of composure.

I had now achiev'd this rare adventure, ultimately much more to my satisfaction than I had bespoke the nature of it to turn out, nor was it much lessen'd, you may think, by my spark's lavish praises of my constancy and complaisance, which he gave weight to by a present that greatly passed my utmost expectation: besides his gratification to Mrs. *Cole.*

I was not however, at any time reintic'd to renew with him, or resort again to the violent expedient of lashing nature into more hast than good speed, which by the way, I conceive acts somewhat in the manner of a dose of *Spanish* flies,[56] with more pain perhaps, but less danger, and might be necessary to him; but was nothing less to, than to me, whose appetites wanted the bridle more than the spur.

Mrs. *Cole*, to whom this adventrous exploit had more and

more endear'd me, look'd on me now as a girl after her own heart, afraid of nothing; and, on a good account, hardy enough to fight all the weapons of pleasure through. Attentive then, in consequence of these favourable conceptions, to promote either my profit or pleasure, she had special regard for the first, in a new gallant of a very singular turn, that she procur'd for, and introduc'd to me.

This was a grave, staid, solemn, elderly gentleman, whose peculiar humour was a delight in combing fine tresses of hair, and as I was perfectly headed to his taste, he us'd to come constantly at my toilette hours, when I let down my hair as loose as nature; and abandon'd it to him, to do what he pleas'd with it; and accordingly he would keep me an hour, or more, in play with it, drawing the comb through it, winding the curls round his fingers, even kissing it as he smooth'd it, and all this led to no other use of my person, or any other liberties whatever, any more than if a distinction of sexes had not existed,

Another peculiarity of taste he had, which was to present me at once with a dozen pair of the whitest kid-gloves at a time: these he would divert himself with drawing on me, and then biting off their fingers ends; all which fooleries of a sickly appetite, the old gentleman paid more liberally for, than most others did for more essential favours. This lasted till a violent cough seizing and laying him up, deliver'd me from this most innocent, and most insipid trifler; for I never heard more of him, after his first retreat.

You may be sure a by-job of this sort interfer'd with no other pursuit, or plan of life, which I led in truth with a modesty and reserve that was less the work of virtue, than of exhausted novelty, a glut of pleasure, and easy circumstances, that made me indifferent to any engagements in which pleasure and profit were not eminently united; and such I could with the less impatience wait for at the hands of time and fortune, as I was satisfied I could never mend my pennyworths,[57] having evidently been serv'd at the top of the market, and even been pamper'd with dainties; besides that, in the sacrifice of a few momentary im-

pulses, I found a secret satisfaction in respecting myself, as well
as preserving the life and freshness of my complexion. *Louisa*
and *Emily* did not carry indeed their reserve as high as I did, but
still they were far from cheap or abandon'd, though two of their
adventures seem'd to contradict this general character, which for
their singularity I shall give you in course, beginning first with
Emily's.

Louisa and she went one night to a ball; the first in the habit of
a shepherdess, *Emily* in that of a shepherd: I saw them in their
dresses before they went, and nothing in nature could represent
a prettier boy than this last did; being so extremely fair and well
limb'd. They had kept together for some time, when *Louisa*
meeting with an old acquaintance of hers, very cordially gives
her companion the drop, and leaves her under the protection of
her boy's habit, which was not much, and of her discretion which
was, it seems, yet less. *Emily* finding herself deserted, saunter'd
thoughtlessly about a while, and as much for coolness and air, as
any thing else, pull'd off her mask, at length, and went to the
side-board, where, eyed and mark'd out by a gentleman in a very
handsome domino, she was accosted by, and fell into chat with,
him. The domino, after a little discourse, in which *Emily* doubtless distinguish'd her good nature and easiness more than her
wit, began to make violent love to her, and drawing her insensibly to some benches at the lower end of the masquerade-room,
got her to sit by him, where he squeez'd her hands, pinch'd her
cheeks, prais'd and play'd with her fair hair, admir'd her complexion, and all in a style of courtship dash'd with a certain
oddity, that not comprehending the mystery of, poor *Emily* attributed to his falling in with the humour of her disguise, and
being naturally not the cruellest of her profession, began to incline to a parley on essentials: but here was the stress of the joke:
He took her really for what she appear'd to be, a smock-fac'd[58]
boy, and she forgetting her dress, and of course ranging quite
wide of his ideas, took all those addresses to be paid to herself as
a woman, which she precisely ow'd to his not thinking her one:
however this double error was push'd to such a height on both

sides, that *Emily* who saw nothing in him but a gentle man of distinction by those points of dress, to which his disguise did not
extend, warm'd too by the wine he had ply'd her with, and the
caresses he had lavish'd upon her, suffer'd herself to be persuaded to go to a bagnio[59] with him; and thus loosing sight of
Mrs. *Cole*'s cautions, with a blind confidence put herself into his
hands to be carried wherever he pleas'd: or his part equally
blinded by his wishes, whilst her egregious simplicity favour'd
his deception more than the most exquisite art could have done,
he suppos'd, no doubt, that he had lighted on some soft simpleton fit for his purpose, or some kept minion broke to his hand,
who understood him perfectly well, and enter'd into his designs;
but be that as it would, he led her to a coach, went into it with
her, and brought her into a very handsome apartment, with a bed
in it, but whether it were a bagnio or not, she could not tell, having spoke to nobody but himself. But when they were alone together, and her *enamorato* began to proceed to those extremities
which instantly discover the sex, she remark'd that no description could paint up to the life, the mixture of pique, confusion,
and disappointment, that appear'd in his countenance, which
join'd to the mournful exclamation, "By heavens a woman!" This
at once open'd her eyes which had hitherto been shut in downright stupidity. However, as if he had meant to retrieve that escape, he still continu'd to toy with and fondle her, but with so
staring an alteration from extreme warmth into a chill and forc'd
civility, that even *Emily* herself could not but take notice of it,
and now began to wish she had paid more regard to Mrs. *Cole*'s
premonitions against ever engaging with a stranger: and now an
excess of timidity succeeded to an excess of confidence, and she
thought herself so much at his mercy and discretion, that she
stood passive throughout the whole progress of his prelude: for
now, whether the impressions of so great a beauty had even
made him forgive her, her sex, or whether her appearance or figure in that dress still humour'd his first illusion, he recover'd by
degrees a good part of his first warmth, and keeping *Emily* with
her breeches still unbuttoned, stript them down to her knees,
and gently impelling her to lean down, with her face against the

bed-side, placed her so, that the double-way between the double
rising behind, presented the choice fair to him, and he was so
fiercely set on a mis-direction, as to give the girl no small alarms
for fear of loosing a maiden-head she had not dreamt of; however her complaints, and a resistance gentle, but firm, check'd,
and brought him to himself again; so that turning his steed's
head, he drove him at length in the right road, in which his imagination having probably made the most of those resemblances
that flatter'd his taste, he got with much ado whip and spur to his
journey's end: after which he led her out himself, and walking
with her two or three streets length, got her a chair,[60] when making her a present not any thing inferior to what she could have
expected, he left her, well recommended to the chairmen, who
on her directions, brought her home.

This she related to Mrs. *Cole* and me, the same morning, not
without the visible remains of the fear and confusion she had
been in, still stamp'd on her countenance, Mrs. *Cole*'s remark was,
that her indiscretion proceeding from a constitutional facility,
there were little hopes of any thing curing her of it, but repeated
severe experience. Mine was that I could not conceive how it was
possible for mankind to run into a taste, not only universally odious, but absurd, and impossible to gratify, since, according to the
notions and experience I had of things, it was not in nature to
force such immense disproportions. Mrs. *Cole* only smill'd at my
ignorance, and said nothing towards my undeception, which was
not effected but by occular demonstration, some months after,
which a most singular accident furnish'd me, and I will here set
down, that I may not return again to so disagreeable a subject.

I had on a visit intended to *Harriet*, who had lodgings at
Hampton-Court, hired a chariot to go out thither, Mrs. *Cole* having
promis'd to accompany me: but some indispensible business in-
tervening to detain her, I was obliged to set out alone; and scarce
had I got a third of my way, before the axle-tree broke down, and
I was well off, to get out safe and unhurt, into a publick-house of
a tolerably handsome appearance, on the road. Here the people
told me that the stage[61] would come by in a couple of hours at
farthest, upon which, determining to wait for it, sooner than

loose the jaunt I had got so far forward on, I was carried into a very clean decent room up one pair of stairs, which I took possession of for the time I had to stay, in right of calling for sufficient to do the house justice.

Here, whilst I was amusing myself with looking out of the window, a single horse-chaise stopt at the door, out of which lightly leap'd two young gentlemen, for so they seem'd, who came in as it were only to bait[62] and refresh a little, for they gave their horse to be held in a readiness against they came out[63]: and presently I heard the door of the next room to me open, where they were let in and call'd about them briskly, and as soon as they were serv'd, I could just hear that they shut and fasten'd the door on the inside.

A spirit of curiosity far from sudden, since I do not know when I was without it, prompted me, without any particular suspicion, or other drift, or view, to see who they were, and examine their persons and behaviour. The partition of our rooms was one of those moveable ones that when taken down, serv'd occasionally to lay them into one, for the convenience of a large company; and now my nicest search could not shew me the shadow of a peep-hole, a circumstance which probably had not escap'd the review of the parties on the other side, whom much it stood upon not to be deceiv'd in it; but at length I observ'd a paper-patch of the same colour as the wainscot, which I took to conceal some flaw, but then it was so high, that I was oblig'd to stand on a chair to reach it, which I did as softly as possible, and with the point of a bodkin soon pierc'd it, and open'd myself espial-room sufficient: and now applying my eye close, I commanded the room perfectly, and could see my two young sparks romping, and pulling one another about, entirely to my imagination, in frolic, and innocent play.

The eldest might be, on my nearest guess, towards nineteen, a tall comely young man, in a white fustian frock, with a green velvet cape, and a cut bob wig.

The youngest could not be above seventeen, fair, ruddy, compleatly well made, and to say the truth, a sweet pretty stripling: He was, I fancy too, a country lad, by his dress, which was a green plush frock, and breeches of the same, white waistcoat and stockings, a jockey cap, with his yellowish hair long, and loose, in natural curls.

But after a look of circumspection which I saw the eldest cast every way round the room, probably in too much hurry and heat not to overlook the very small opening I was posted at, especially at the height it was, whilst my eye too close to it, kept the light from shining through, and betraying it; he said something to his companion that presently chang'd the face of things.

For now the elder began to embrace, to press, to kiss the younger, to put his hands in his bosom, and give such manifest signs of an amorous intention, as made me conclude the other to be a girl in disguise, a mistake that nature kept me in countenance[64] in, for she had certainly made one, when she gave him the male stamp.

In the rashness then of their age, and bent as they were to accomplish their project of preposterous pleasure, at the risque of the very worst of consequences,[65] where a discovery was nothing less than improbable, they now proceeded to such lengths as soon satisfied me, what they were.

For presently the eldest unbotton'd the other's breeches, and removing the linen barrier, brought out to view a white shaft, middle-siz'd, and scarce fledg'd, when after handling, and playing with it a little, with other dalliance, all receiv'd by the boy without other opposition, than certain wayward coyness, ten times more alluring than repulsive, he got him to turn round with his face from him, to a chair that stood hard by, when knowing, I suppose, his office, the Ganymede[66] now obsequiously lean'd his head against the back of it, and projecting his body, made a fair mark, still cover'd with his shirt, as he thus stood in a sideview to meet but fronting his companion, who presently unmasking his battery, produc'd an engine, that certainly deserv'd to be put to a better use, and very fit to confirm me in my disbelief of the possibility of things being push'd to odious extremities, which I had built on the disproportion of parts; but this disbelief I was now to be cur'd of, as by my consent all young men should likewise be, that their innocence may not be betray'd into such snares, for want of knowing the extent of their danger, for nothing is more certain than, that ignorance of a vice, is by no means a guard against it.

Slipping then aside the young lad's shirt, and tucking it up under his cloaths behind, he shew'd to the open air, those globular, fleshy eminences that compose the mount-pleasants of *Rome,* and which now, with all the narrow vale that intersects them, stood display'd, and expos'd to his attack: nor could I, without a shudder, behold the dispositions he made for it. First then, moistening well with spittle his instrument, obviously to render it glib, he pointed, he introduc'd it, as I could plainly discern, not only from its direction, and my losing sight of it; but by the writhing, twisting, and soft murmur'd complaints of the young sufferer; but, at length, the first streights of entrance being pretty well got through, every thing seem'd to move, and go pretty currently on, as in a carpet-road, without much rub, or resistance: and now passing one hand round his minion's hips, he got hold of his red-topt ivory toy, that stood perfectly stiff, and shewed, that if he was like his mother behind, he was like his father before; this he diverted himself with, whilst with the other, he wanton'd with his hair, and leaning forward over his back, drew his face, from which the boy shook the loose curls that fell over it, in the posture he stood him in, and brought him towards his, so as to receive a long-breath'd kiss, after which, renewing his driving, and thus continuing to harrass his rear, the height of the fit came on with its usual symptoms, and dissmiss'd the action.

All this, so criminal a scene, I had the patience to see to an end, purely that I might gather more facts, and certainty against them in my full design to do their deserts instant justice, and accordingly, when they had readjusted themselves, and were preparing to go out, burning as I was with rage, and indignation, I jump'd down from my chair, in order to raise the house upon them, with such an unlucky impetuosity, that some nail or ruggedness in the floor caught my foot, and flung me on my face with such violence, that I fell senseless on the ground, and must have lain there some time e'er any one came to my relief, so that they, alarm'd, I suppose, by the noise of my fall, had more than the necessary time to make a safe retreat, which they affected, as I learnt, with a precipitation no body could account for, till, when come to my self, and compos'd enough to speak, I acquainted those of the house with the transaction I had been evidence to.

When I came home again, and told Mrs. *Cole* this adventure, she very sensibly observ'd to me, that there was no doubt of due vengeance one time or other overtaking these miscreants, however they might escape for the present; and that, had I been the temporal instrument of it, I should have been, at least, put to a great deal more trouble and confusion than I imagine: that as to the thing itself, the less said of it was the better; but that though she might be suspected of partiality, from its being the common cause of woman-kind, out of whose *mouths* this practice tended to take something more precious than bread, yet she protested against any mixture of passion, with a declaration extorted from her by pure regard to truth, which was, "*that* whatever effect this infamous passion had in other ages, and other countries, it seem'd a peculiar blessing on our air and climate, that there was a plague-spot visibly imprinted on all that are tainted with it, in this nation at least; for that among numbers of that stamp whom she had known, or at least were universally under the scandalous suspicion of it, she could not name an exception hardly of one of them, whose character was not in all other respects the most worthless and despicable that could be, stript of all the manly virtues of their own sex, and fill'd up with only the very worst vices and follies of ours: that, in fine, they were scarce less execrable than ridiculous in their monstrous inconsistency, of loathing and contemning women, and all at the same time, apeing their manners, airs, lisp, skuttle, and, in general, all their little modes of affectation, which become them at least better, than they do these unsex'd male-misses."[67]

But here washing my hands of them, I replunge into the stream of my history, into which I may very properly ingraft a terrible sally[68] of *Louisa*'s, since I had some share in it myself, and have besides engag'd myself to relate it, in point of countenance to poor *Emily*. It will add too one more example to thousands, in confirmation of the maxim, that when women get once out of compass, there are no lengths of licentiousness they are not capable of running.

One morning then, that both Mrs. *Cole* and *Emily*, were gone out for the day, and only *Louisa* and I (not to mention the housemaid) were left in charge of the house; whilst we were loitering away the time, in looking through the shop-windows, the son of a poor woman who earned very hard bread indeed by mending of stockings, in a stall in the neighbourhood, offers us some nosegays rang'd round a small basket; by selling of which the poor boy eked out his mother's maintenance of them both: nor was he fit for any other way of livelihood, since he was not only a perfect changeling, or idiot, but stammer'd so that there was no understanding even those sounds that his half-a-dozen, at most, animal ideas prompted him to utter.

The boys, and servants in the neighbourhood, had given him the nick-name of *Good-natur'd Dick*, from the soft simpleton's doing every thing he was bid to do at the first word, and from his naturally having no turn to mischief; then, by the way, he was perfectly well made, stout, and clean-climb'd, tall of his age, as strong as a horse, and, with all, pretty featur'd; so that he was not absolutely such a figure to be snuffed at neither, if your nicety could, in favour of such essentials, have dispens'd with a face unwash'd, hair tangl'd for want of combing, and so ragged a plight, that he might have disputed points of shew, with e'er a heathen philosopher of them all.

This boy we had often seen, and bought his flowers, out of pure compassion, and nothing more: but just at this time, as he stood presenting us his basket, a sudden whim, a start of wayward fancy seiz'd *Louisa*, and without consulting me, she calls him in, and began to examine his nosegays culls out two, one for herself, another for me, and pulling out half-a-crown, very currently gives it him to change, as if she had really expected he could have chang'd it: but the boy scraching his head, made his signs explain his inability, in place of words, that he could not with all his struggling, articulate.

Louisa at this, says: "Well, my lad, come upstairs with me, and I will give you your due." Winking at the same time to me, and beckoning me to accompany her, which I did, securing first the street-door, that by this means, together with the shop, became wholly the care of the faithful house-maid.

As we went up, *Louisa* whisper'd me, that she had conceiv'd a strange longing to be satisfy'd, whether the general rule held good with regard to this changeling and how far nature had made him amends in her best bodily gifts, for her denial of the sublimer intellectual ones[69]; begging at the same time my assistance in procuring her this satisfaction: a want of complaisance was never my vice, and I was so far from opposing this extravagant frolic that now, bit with the same maggot, and my curiosity conspiring with hers, I enter'd plum into it, on my own account.

Consequently, as soon as we came into *Louisa*'s bed-chamber, whilst she was amusing him with picking out his nosegays, I undertook the lead, and began the attack: as it was not then very material to keep much measures with a mere natural,[70] I made presently very free with him, though at my first motion of meddling, his surpise and confusion made him receive my advances but awkwardly; nay, insomuch that he bashfully shy'd, and shy'd back a little, till encouraging him with my eyes, plucking him playfully by the hair, sleeking his cheeks, and forwarding my point by a number of little wantonness, I soon turn'd him familiar, and gave nature her sweetest alarm; so that arrouz'd, and beginning to feel himself, we could, amidst all the innocent laugh and grin I had provok'd him into, perceive the fire lighting in his eyes, and diffusing over his cheeks, blend its glow with that of his blushes; the emotion in short of animal pleasure glar'd distinctly in the simpleton's countenance; yet struck with the novelty of the scene, he did not know which way to look or move; but tame, passive, simpering, with his mouth half open, in stupid rapture, stood, and tractably suffer'd me to do what I pleas'd with him: his basket was dropt out of his hands, which *Louisa* took care of.

I had now, through more than one rent, discover'd and felt his thighs, the skin of which seem'd the smoother and fairer for the coarseness, and even dirt of his dress; as the teeth of Negroes seem the whiter for the surrounding black: and poor indeed of habit! poor of understanding! he was however abundantly rich in personal treasures, such as flesh, firm, plump, and replete with the sweet juices of youth, and robust well-knit limbs. My fingers too had now got within reach of the true, the genuine sensitive plant, which instead of shrinking from the touch, joys to meet it, and swells, and vegetates under it: mine pleasingly informing me that matters were so ripe for the discovery we meditated, that they were too mighty for the confinement they were ready to break; a waistband that I unskewer'd,[71] and a rag of shirt that I remov'd, and which could not have cover'd a quarter of it, reveal'd the whole of the idiot's standard of distinction, erect, in full pride and display: but such an one! it was positively of so tremendous a size, that prepar'd as we were to see something extraordinary, it still, out of measure surpass'd our expectation, and astonish'd even me, who had not been us'd to trade in trifles: in fine, it might have answer'd very well the making a show of: its enormous head seem'd in hue and size, not unlike a common sheep's heart; then you might have troll'd[72] dice securely along the broad back of the body of it: the length of it too was prodigious; then the rich appendage of the treasure-bag beneath, large in proportion, gather'd, and crisp'd up, round, in shallow furrows, help'd to fill the eye, and complete the proof of his being a natural, not quite in vain, since it was full manifest that he inherited, and largely too, the prerogative of majesty, which distinguishes that otherwise most unfortunate condition, and gives rise to the vulgar saying, "That a fool's bauble is a lady's play fellow." Nor wholly without reason; for, generally speaking, it is in love, as it is in war, where the longest weapon carries it. Nature, in short, had done so much to him in those parts, that she perhaps held herself acquitted for doing so little for his head.

For my part, who had sincerely no intention to push the joke further than simply satisfying my curiosity with the sight of it alone, I was content in spite of the temptation that star'd me in the face, with having rais'd a may-pole for another to hang a garland; for by this time, easily reading *Louisa*'s desires in her wishful eyes, I acted the commodious part, and made her, who sought no better sport, significant signs of encouragement to go through-stitch[73] with the adventure: intimating too that I would stay and see fair play; in which indeed I had in view to humour a new-born curiosity, to observe what appearances active nature would put on in a natural, in the course of this her darling operation.

Louisa, whose appetite was up, and who, like the industrious bee, was, it seems, not above gathering the sweets of so rare a flower, tho' she found it planted on a dung-hill, was but too read-ily dispos'd to take the benefit of my cession: urg'd then strongly by her own desires, and emboldened by me, she presently determin'd to risque a trial of parts with the idiot, who was by this time nobly inflam'd for her purpose, by all the irritations we had us'd to put the principles of pleasure effectually into mo-tion, and to wind up the springs of its organ to their supreme pitch: and it stood accordingly stiff and straining, ready to burst with the blood and spirits that swell'd it to a bulk! No! I shall never forget it.

Louisa then taking and holding the fine handle that so invit-ingly offer'd itself, led the ductile youth by that master-tool of his, as she stept backward towards the bed, which he joyfully gave way to, under the incitations of instinct, and palpably deliver'd up to the goad of desire.

Stopt then by the bed, she took the fall she lov'd, and lean'd to the most, gently backward upon it, still holding fast what she held, and taking care to give her cloaths a convenient toss up, so that her thighs duly disclos'd, and elevated, laid open all the out-ward prospect of the treasury of love: the rose-lipt ouverture[74] presenting the cock-pit so fair, that it was not in nature even for a natural to miss it: nor did he; for *Louisa*, fully bent on grappling with it, and impatient of dalliance or delay, directed faithfully the point of the battering piece, and bounded up with a rage of so voracious appetite, to meet, and favour the thrust of insertion, that the fierce activity on both sides, effected it, but effected it with such a pain of distention, that *Louisa* cry'd out violently, that she was hurt beyond all bearing, that she was kill'd: but it was too late; the storm was up, and force was on her to give way to it. For now the man-machine, strongly work'd upon by the sensual passion, felt so manfully his advantages, and superiority, felt withal the sting of pleasure so intolerable, that maddening with it, his joys began to assume a character of furiousness which made me tremble for the too tender *Louisa:* he seem'd at this juncture greater than himself; his countenance, before so void of meaning, or expression, now grew big with the importance of the act he was upon. In short, it was not now that he was to be play'd the fool with: but what is pleasant enough, I myself was aw'd into a sort of respect for him, by the comely terrors his emotions drest him in: his eyes shooting sparks of fire, his face glowing with ardours that gave all another life to it: his teeth churning; his whole frame agitated with a raging ungovernable impetuosity, all sensibly betraying the formidable fierceness with which the genial instinct acted upon him: butting then, and goring all before him, and mad, and wild, like an overdriven steer, he ploughs up the tender furrow, all insensible of *Louisa's* complaints: nothing can stop, nothing can keep out a fury like his; which having once got its head in, its blind rage soon made way for the rest, piercing, rending, and breaking open all obstruction. The torn, split, wounded girl cries, struggles, invokes me to her rescue, and endeavours to get from under the young savage, or shake him off, but alas, in vain! her breath might as soon have still'd, or stemm'd a storm in winter, as all her strength have quell'd his rough assault, or put him out of his course. And indeed all her efforts, and struggles were manag'd in such disorder, that they serv'd rather to entangle, and fold her the faster in the twine of his boisterous arms; so that she was tied to the stake, and oblig'd to fight the match out, if she died for it: for his part, instinct-ridden as he was, the expressions of his animal passion partaking something of ferocity, were rather worryings[75] than kisses, intermix'd with eager ravenous love-bites on her cheeks and neck; the prints of which did not wear out for some days after.

Poor *Louisa,* however, bore up at length better than could have been expected, and though she suffer'd, and greatly too, yet ever true to the good old cause, she suffer'd with pleasure, and enjoy'd her pain: and soon now, by dint of an enrag'd enforcement, the brute-machine, driven like a whirlwind, made all smoak again, and wedging its way up, to the utmost extremity, left her in point of penetration nothing either to fear, or to desire, and now,

"Gorg'd with the dearest morsel of the earth."

SHAKESPEAR.[76]

Louisa lay, pleas'd to the heart, pleas'd to her utmost capacity of being so, with every fibre in those parts, stretch'd almost to breaking, on a rack of joy, whilst the instrument of all this over-fulness, search'd her senses with its sweet excess, till the pleasure gain'd upon her so, its point stung her so home, that catching at length the rage from her furious driver, and sharing the riot of his wild rapture, she went wholly out of her mind into that favourite part of her body, the whole intenseness of which was so fervorously[77] fill'd, and employ'd: there alone she existed, all lost in those delirious transports, those extasies of the senses, which her winking eyes, the brighten'd vermilion of her lips, and cheeks, and sighs of pleasure deeply fetched, so pathetically express'd. In short, she was now as mere a machine, as much wrought on, and had her motions as little at her own command, as the natural himself, who thus broke in upon her, made her feel with a vengeance his tempestuous tenderness, and the force of mettle he batter'd with: their active loins quiver'd again with the violence of their conflict, till the surge of pleasure foaming, and raging to a height, drew down the pearly shower that was to allay this hurricane: the purely sensitive idiot then first shed those tears of joy that attend its last moments, not without an agony of delight, and even almost a roar of rapture, as the gush escap'd him, so sensibly too for *Louisa,* that she kept him faithful company, going off, in consent, with the old symptoms; a delicious delirium, a tremulous convulsive shudder, and the critical dying oh! And now, on his getting off, she lay pleasure-drench'd and regorging its essentials sweets: but quite spent, but gasping for breath, without other sensation of life than in those exquisite vibrations, that trembled yet on the strings of delight, which had been so ravishingly touch'd; and which nature had been too intensely stirr'd with, for the senses to be quickly at peace from.

As for the changeling, whose curious engine had been thus successfully play'd off, his shift of countenance and gesture had even something droll, or rather tragi-comic in it. There was now an air of sad, repining foolishness, superadded to his natural one of no meaning, and idiotism; as he stood with his label of manhood, now lank, unstiffen'd, becalm'd, and flapping against his thighs, down which it reached half-way, terrible even in its fall: whilst, under the dejection of spirit, and flesh, which naturally follow'd, his eyes, by turns cast down towards his struck standard, or piteously lifted to *Louisa,* seem'd to require at her hands what he had so sensibly parted from to her, and now ruefully missed; but the vigor of nature soon returning, dissipated this blast of faintness which the common law of enjoyment had subjected him to; and now his basket re-became his main concern, which I look'd for, and brought him, whilst *Louisa* restor'd his dress to its usual condition, and afterwards pleas'd him perhaps more by taking all his flowers off his hands, and paying him at his rate, for them, than if she had embarrass'd him by a present, that he would have been puzzled to account for, and might have put others on tracing the motives of it.

Whether she ever return'd to the attack, I know not, and to say the truth, I believe not; she had had her freak out,[78] and had pretty plentifully drowned her curiosity in a glut of pleasure, which as it happen'd had no other consequence, than that the lad, who retain'd only a confus'd memory of the transaction, would when he saw her, for some little time after, express a grin of joy, and familiarity, alter his idiot manner, and soon forgot her, probably in favour of the next woman tempted on the report of his parts to take him in.

Louisa too herself did not long outstay this adventure, at Mrs. *Cole*'s (to whom, by the bye, we took care not to boast of our exploit, till all fear of consequences was clearly over:) for, an occasion presenting itself of proving her passion for a young fellow, at the expence of her discretion, proceeding all in character, she pack'd up her toilette, at half a day's warning, and went with him abroad, since which I lost entirely sight of her, and it never fell in my way to hear what became of her.

But a few days after she had left us, two very pretty young gentlemen, who were Mrs. *Cole*'s especial favourites, and free of her academy, easily obtain'd her consent for *Emily*'s and my acceptance of a party of pleasure, at a little, but agreeable house, belonging to one of them, situate not far up the river *Thames*, on the *Surry* side.

Every thing being settled, and it being a fine summer-day, but rather of the warmest, we set out after dinner, and got to our rendezvous, about four in the afternoon, where landing at the foot of a neat, joyous pavilion, *Emily* and I were handed into it, by our Squires, and there drank tea with a chearfulness and gaiety, that the beauty of the prospect, the serenity of the weather, and the tender politeness of our sprightly gallants, naturally led us into.

After tea, and taking a turn in the garden, my particular, who was the master of the house, and had in no sense schem'd this party of pleasure for a dry one; propos'd to us, with that frankness which his familiarity at Mrs. *Cole*'s entitled him to, as the weather was excessive hot, to bathe together, under a commodious shelter that he had prepar'd expressly for that purpose, in a creek of the river, with which a side-door of the pavilion immediately communicated, and where we might be sure of having our diversion out, safe from interruption, and with the utmost privacy.

Emily, who never refus'd any thing, and I, who ever delighted in bathing, and had no exception to the person who propos'd it, or to those pleasures it was easy to guess it implied, took care, on this occasion, not to wrong our training at Mrs. *Cole*'s, and agreed to it, with as good a grace as we could. Upon which, without loss of time, we return'd instantly to the pavilion, one door of which open'd into a tent, pitch'd before it, that with its Marquise,[79] form'd a pleasing defence against the fun, or the weather, and

was besides as private as we could wish. The lining of it, im-
bossed cloth, represented a wild forest-foliage, from the top,
down to the sides, which, in the same stuff, were figur'd with
fluted pilasters, with their spaces between fill'd with flower-
vases, the whole having a gay effect upon the eye, wherever you
turn'd it.

Then it reach'd sufficiently into the water, yet contain'd convenient benches round it, on the dry ground, either to keep our
cloaths, or,—or,—in short, for more uses than resting upon.
There was a side-table too, loaded with sweatmeats, jellies, and
other eatables, and bottles of wine and cordials, by way of occasional relief from any rawness, or chill of the water, or from any
faintness from whatever cause: and, in fact, my gallant who understood *chère entière*[80] perfectly, and who for taste (even if you
would not approve this specimen of it) might have been comp-
troller of pleasures to a *Roman* emperor, had left no requisite
towards convenience, or luxury unprovided.

As soon as we had look'd round this inviting spot, and every
preliminary of privacy was duly settled: strip, was the word:
when the young gentlemen soon dispatch'd the undressing each
his partner, and reduc'd us to the naked confession of all those
secrets of person, which dress generally hides, and which the
discovery of, was, naturally speaking, not to our disadvantage.
Our hands indeed mechanically carried towards the most interesting part of us, skreen'd at first all from the tufted cliff downwards, till we took them away, at their desire, and employ'd
them, in doing them the same office, of helping them off with
their cloaths, in the process of which, there past all the little
wantonnesses, and frolic, that you may easily imagine.

As for my spark, he was presently undrest, all to his shirt, the
fore-lappet[81] of which, as he lean'd languishingly on me, he
smilingly pointed to me, to observe, as it bellied out, or rose, and
fell, according to the unruly starts of the motion behind it: but it
was soon fix'd; for now taking off his shirt, and naked as a Cupid,
he show'd it me at so upright a stand, as prepar'd me indeed for
his application to me for instant ease: but tho' the sight of its fine

size was fit enough to fire me; the cooling air, as I stood in this
state of nature, join'd to the desire I had of bathing first, enabled
me to put him off, and tranquillize him, with the remark, that a
little suspense would only set a keener edge on the pleasure:
leading then the way, and showing our friends an example of
continency, which they were giving signs of losing respect to, we
went, hand in hand, into the stream, till it took us up to our neck,
where, the no more than grateful coolness of the water, gave my
senses a delicious refreshment from the sultryness of the season,
and made me more alive, more happy in myself, and, in course,
more alert, and open to voluptuous impressions.

Here I lav'd and wanton'd with the water, or sportively play'd
with my companion, leaving *Emily* to deal with hers at discretion. Mine, at length, not content with making me take the
plunge over head and ears, kept splashing me, and provoking me
by all the little playful tricks he could devise, and which I strove
not to remain in his debt for. We gave, in short, a loose to mirth:
and now, nothing would serve him but giving his hands the re-
gale of going over every part of me, neck, breast, belly, thighs,
and all the sweet *et cetera*, so dear to the imagination; under the
pretext of washing, and rubbing them; as we both stood in the
water, no higher now than the pit of our stomachs, and which did
not hinder him from feeling and toying with that leak that distinguishes our sex, and is so wonderfully water-tight: for his fingers, in vain dilating and opening it, only let more flame than
water into it, be it said, without a figure: at the same time he
made me feel his own engine, which was so well wound up, as to
stand even the working in water, and he accordingly threw one
arm round my neck, and was endeavouring to get the better of
that harsher constriction bred by the surrounding fluid, and had
in effect won his way so far as to make me sensible of the pleasing stretch of those nether-lips, from the in-driving machine,
when, independent of my not liking that awkward mode of enjoyment, I could not help interrupting him, in order to become
joint-spectators of a plan of joy, in hot operation between *Emily*
and her partner, who impatient of the fooleries, and dalliance of

the bath, had led his nymph to one of the benches on the green bank, where he was very cordially proceeding to teach her the difference betwixt jest and earnest.

There setting her on his knee, and gliding one hand over the surface of that smooth polish'd, snow-white skin of hers, which now doubly shone with a dew-bright lustre, and presented to the touch something like what one would imagine of animated ivory, especially in those ruby-nippled globes, which the touch is so fond of, and delights to make love to; with the other, he was lusciously exploring the sweet secret of nature, in order to make room for a stately piece of machinery, that stood up-rear'd, between her thighs, as she continued sitting on his lap, and press'd hard for instant admission, which the tender *Emily*, in a fit of humour deliciously protracted, affecting to decline, and elude the very pleasure she sigh'd for, but in a style of waywardness so prettily put on, and managed, as to render it only ten times more poignant: then her eyes, all amidst the softest, dying languishment, express'd at once a mock-denial, and extreme desire, whilst her sweetness was zested with a coyness so pleasingly provoking, her moods of keeping him off, were so attractive, that they redoubl'd the impetuous rage with which he cover'd her with kisses, and kisses that whilst she seem'd to shy from or scuffle for, the cunning wanton contriv'd such sly returns of, as were doubtless the sweeter for the gust she gave them, of being stoln, or ravished.

Thus *Emily*, who knew no art but that which nature itself, in favour of her principal end, pleasure, had inspir'd her with; the art of yielding, coy'd it indeed, but coyed it to the purpose; for with all her straining, her wrestling, and striving to break from the clasp of his arms, she was so far wiser yet, than to mean it, that, in her struggles, it was visible, that she aim'd at nothing more than multiplying points of touch with him, and drawing yet closer the folds that held them every where entwin'd, like two tendrils of a vine intercurling together, so that the same effect, as when *Louisa* strove in good earnest to disengage from the idiot, was now produc'd by different motives.

Mean while, their emersion out of the cold water, had caused a general glow, a tender suffusion of heighten'd carnation over their bodies; both equally white, and smooth-skinn'd; so that as their limbs were thus amorously interwoven, in sweet confusion, it was scarce possible to distinguish who they respectively belonged to, but for the brawnier, bolder muscles of the stronger sex.

In a little time however, the champion was fairly in with her, and had tied at all points the true lover's knot, when now, adieu all the little refinements of a finessed reluctance! adieu the tender friendly feint! she was presently driven forcibly out of the power of using any art: and indeed, what art but must give way, when nature corresponding with her sweet assailant, invaded in the heart of her capital, and carried by storm, lay at the mercy of the proud conqueror, who had made his entry triumphantly, and completely? soon however to become a tributary! for the engagement growing hotter and hotter, at close quarters, she presently brought him to the pass of paying down the dear debt to nature, which she had no sooner collected in, but, like a duellist who has laid his antagonist at his feet, when he has himself received a mortal wound, *Emily* had scarce time to plume herself upon her victory, but shot with the same discharge, she, in a loud expiring sigh, in the closure of her eyes, the stretch-out of her limbs, and a remission of her whole frame, gave manifest signs that all was as it should be, and happily well over with her.

For my part, who had not with the calmest patience stood in the water all this time, to view this warm action, I lean'd tenderly on my gallant, and, at the close of it, seem'd to ask him with my eyes, what he thought of it; but he more eager to satisfy me by his actions, than by words, or looks, as we shoal'd[82] the water together towards the shore, shew'd me the staff of love so intensely set up, that had not even, charity beginning at home, in this case, urged me to our mutual relief, it would have been cruel indeed to have suffer'd the youth to burst with straining, when the remedy was so obvious, and so near at hand.

Accordingly we took to a bench, whilst *Emily* and her spark, who belonged it seems to the sea, stood at the side-board, drinking to our good voyage, for as the last observ'd, we were well under weigh, with a fair wind up channel, and fullfreighted: nor indeed were we long before we finished our trip to *Cythera,* and unloaded in the old haven; but as the circumstances did not admit of much variation, I shall spare you the description.

At the same time, allow me to place you here an excuse I am conscious of owing you, for having perhaps too much affected the figurative style; though surely it can pass no where more allowably than in a subject which is so properly the province of poetry, nay! is poetry itself, pregnant with every flower of imagination, and loving metaphors, even were not the natural expressions; for respects of fashion and sound necessarily forbid it.

Resuming now my history, you may please to know, that what with a competent number of repetitions, all in the same strain, (and by the bye, we have a certain natural sense that those repetitions are very much to the taste of) what with a circle of pleasures delicately varied, there was not a moment lost to joy all the time we staid there, till late in the night, we were re-escorted home by our 'squires, who deliver'd us safe to Mrs. *Cole,* with generous thanks for our company.

This too was *Emily'*s last adventure in our way; for scarce a week after, she was, by an accident too trivial to detail to you the particulars, found out by her parents, who were in very good circumstances, and who had been punish'd for their partiality to their son, in the loss of him, occasion'd by a circumstance of their over-indulgence to his appetite: upon which, the so long engross'd stream of fondness, running violently in favour of this lost, and inhumanly abandon'd child, whom, if they had not neglected all enquiry about, they might long before have recover'd, they were now so overjoy'd at their retrieval of her, that, I presume, it made them much the less strict in examining to the bottom of things; for they seem'd very glad to take for granted, in the lump, every thing that the grave and decent Mrs. *Cole* was pleas'd to pass upon them; and soon afterwards sent her, from the country, a handsome acknowledgment.

But it was not so easy to replace to our community the loss of so sweet a member of it, for, not to mention her beauty, she was one of those mild, pliant characters, that if one does not entirely esteem, one can scarce help loving, which is not such a bad compensation neither: owing all her weaknesses to good-nature, and an indolent facility that kept her too much at the mercy of first impressions, she had just sense enough to know that she wanted leading-strings,[83] and thought herself so much obliged to any who would take the pains to think for her, and guide her, that with a very little management, she was capable of being made a most agreeable, nay, a most virtuous wife; for vice, it is probable, had never been her choice, or her fate, if it had not been for occasion, or example, or had she not depended less upon herself, than upon her circumstances: this presumption her conduct afterwards verified; for presently meeting with a match, that was ready cut and dry for her, with a neighbour's son of her own rank, and a young man of sense and order, who took her as the widow of one lost at sea, (for so it seems one of her gallants, whose name she had made free with, really was) she naturally struck into all the duties of her domestic,[84] with as much simplicity of affection, with as much constancy and regularity, as if she had never swerv'd from a state of undebauch'd innocence from her youth.

These desertions had, however, now so far thinn'd Mrs. *Cole's* cluck, that she was left with only me, like a hen with one chicken; but tho' she was earnestly entreated and encourag'd to recruit her *corps*, her growing infirmities, and above all the tortures of a stubborn hip-gout, which she found would yield to no remedy, determin'd her to break up her business, and retire with a decent pittance into the country, where I promised myself, nothing so sure, as my going down to live with her, as soon as I had seen a little more of life, and improv'd my small matters into a competency that would create me an independence on the world; for I was now, thanks to Mrs. *Cole*, wise enough to keep that essential in view.

Thus I was then to lose my faithful preceptress, as did the Philosophers of the Town the White Crow of her profession[85]; for, besides that, she never ransomed[86] her customers, whose taste too she ever studiously consulted; besides that she never racked her pupils with unconscionable extortions, nor ever put their hand earnings, as she call'd them, under the contribution of poundage; she was a severe enemy to the reduction of innocence, and confin'd her acquisitions solely to those unfortunate young women, who, having lost it, were but the juster objects of compassion: amongst these indeed, she pick'd out such as suited her views, and taking them under her protection, rescu'd them from the danger of the public sinks of ruin and misery, to place or form them, well, or ill, in the manner you have seen. Having then settled her affairs, she set out on her journey, after taking the most tender leave of me, and, at the end of some excellent instructions, recommending me to myself, with an anxiety, perfectly maternal: in short, she affected me so much that I was not presently reconcil'd to myself for suffering her, at any rate, to go without me; but fate had it seems, otherwise dispos'd of me.

I had, on my separation from Mrs. *Cole,* taken a pleasant convenient house near *Marybone,* but easy to rent and manage, from its smallness, which I furnish'd neatly and modestly: there, with a reserve of eight hundred pounds, the fruit of my deference to Mrs. *Cole's* counsels, exclusive of cloaths, some jewels, some plate, I saw myself in purse for a long time, to wait without impatience for what the chapter of accidents might produce in my favour.

Here, under the new character of a young gentlewoman, whose husband was gone to sea, I had mark'd me out such lines of life and conduct, as leaving me at a competent liberty to pursue my views, either of pleasure or fortune, bounded me nevertheless strictly within the rules of decency, and discretion: a disposition in which you cannot escape observing a true pupil of Mrs. *Cole's.*

I was scarce however well warm in my new abode, when going out one morning pretty early to enjoy the freshness of it, in the pleasing outlet of the fields, accompanied only by a maid, whom I had newly hired; as we were carelessly walking among the trees, we were alarm'd with the noise of a violent coughing, turning our heads towards which, we distinguish'd a plain well-dress'd elderly gentleman, who, attack'd with a sudden fit, was so much overcome as to be forc'd to give way to it, and sit down at the foot of a tree, where he seem'd suffocating with the severity of it, being perfectly black in the face: not less mov'd than frighten'd with which I flew on the instant to his relief, and using the rote of practice[87] I had observ'd on the like occasion, I loosen'd his cravat, and clapp'd him on the back; but whether to any purpose, or whether the cough had had its course, I know not; but the fit went immediately off; and now recover'd to his speech, and legs, he returned me thanks, with as much emphasis as if I had sav'd his life: this naturally engaging a conversation, he acquainted me where he lived, which was at a considerable distance from where I met with him, and where he had stray'd insensibly on the same intention of a morning-walk.

He was, as I afterwards learn'd, in the course of the intimacy, which this little accident gave birth to, an old batchelor turn'd of sixty, but of a fresh, vigorous complexion, insomuch that he scarce mark'd five and forty, having never rack'd, or forc'd his constitution, by permitting his desires to over tax his ability.

As to his birth, and condition; his parents, honest and fail'd mechanicks, had by the best traces he could get of them, left him an infant orphan on the parish; so that it was from a charity school, that by honesty and industry he made his way into a merchant's compting-house,[88] from whence being sent to a house in *Cadiz,* he there, by his talents and activity, acquired a fortune, but an immense one; with which he return'd to his native country, where he could not, however, so much as fish one single relation out of the obscurity he was born in. Taking then a taste for retirement, and pleas'd to enjoy life, like a mistress, in the dark, he flow'd his days in all the ease of opulence, without the least parade of it, and rather studying the concealment, than the show of a fortune, looking down on a world he perfectly knew; himself, to his wish, unknown, and unmark'd by it.

But as I propose to devote a letter entirely to the pleasure of retracing to you all the particulars of my acquaintance with this ever, to me, memorable friend, I shall, in this, transiently touch on no more than may serve, as mortar, to cement, or form the

connexion of my history, and to obviate your surprise that one of
my high blood, and relish of life, should count a gallant of threescore such a catch.

Referring then to a more explicit narrative, to explain by what
progressions our acquaintance, certainly innocent, at first, insensibly changed nature, and ran into unplatonic lengths, as might
well be expected from one of my condition of life, and above all
from that principle of electricity which scarce ever fails of pro-
ducing fire, when the sexes meet: I shall only here acquaint you,
that as age had not subdued his tenderness for our sex, neither
had it robb'd him of the power of pleasing, since whatever he
wanted in the bewitching charms of youth, he atton'd for, or sup-
plemented with the advantages of experience, the sweetness of
his manners, and above all his flattering address in touching the
heart by an application to the understanding. From him, it was
that I first learn'd to any purpose, and not without infinite pleasure, that I had such a portion of me worth bestowing some regard on: from him I received my first essential encouragement,
and instructions how to put it into that train of cultivation,
which I have since pushed to the little degree of improvement
you see it at. He it was, who first taught me to be sensible that the
pleasures of the mind were superior to those of the body, at the
same time, that they were so far from obnoxious to, or incom-
patible with each other, that besides the sweetness in the variety,
and transition, the one serv'd to exalt and perfect the taste of the
other, to a degree that the senses alone can never arrive at.

Himself a rational pleasurist, as being much too wise to be
asham'd of the pleasures of humanity, lov'd me indeed, but lov'd
me with dignity, in a mean[89] equally remov'd from that sourness,
or frowardness which age is unpleasingly characteris'd by, and
from that childish silly dotage that so often disgraces it, and
which he himself used to turn into ridicule, and compare to an
old goat affecting the frisk of a young kid.

In short, every thing that is generally unamiable in his season
of Life, was, in him, repair'd by so many advantages, that he existed a proof manifest, at least to me, that it is not out of the

power of age to please, if it lays out to please, and if making just allowances, those in that class do not forget, that it must cost them more pains, and attention, than what youth, the natural spring-time of joy, stands in need of: as fruits out of season, require proportionably more skill and cultivation, to force them.

With this gentleman then, who took me home soon after our acquaintance commenc'd, I lived near eight months, in which time, my constant complaisance, my docility, my attention to deserve his confidence and love, and a conduct, in general, devoid of the least art, and founded on my sincere esteem, and regard for him, won, and attach'd him so firmly to me, that after having generously trusted me with a genteel, independent settlement, proceeding to heap marks of affection on me, he appointed me, by an authentick will, his sole heiress, and executrix; a disposition which he did not outlive two months, being taken from me by a violent cold that he contracted, as he unadvisedly ran to the window, on an alarm of fire, at some streets distance, and stood there naked-breasted, and expos'd to the fatal impressions of a damp night-air.

After acquitting myself of my duty towards my deceas'd benefactor, and paying him a tribute of unfeign'd sorrow, which a little time chang'd into the most tender, grateful memory of him, that I shall ever retain, I grew somewhat comforted by the prospect that now open'd to me, if not of happiness, at least of affluence, and independence.

I saw myself then, in the full bloom and pride of youth (for I was not yet nineteen) actually at the head of so large a fortune, as it would have been even the height of impudence in me, to have rais'd my wishes, much more my hopes, to: and that this unexpected elevation did not turn my head, I ow'd to the pains my benefactor had taken to form and prepare me for it, as I ow'd his opinion of my management of the vast possessions he left me, to what he had observ'd of the prudential economy I had learned under Mrs. *Cole*, of which the reserve he saw I had made, was a proof, and encouragement, to him.

But alas! how easily is the enjoyment of the greatest sweets in life, in present possession, poisoned by the regret of an absent one! but my regret was a mighty and a just one, since it had my only truly belov'd *Charles* for its object.

Given him up I had indeed compleatly, having never once heard from him since our separation; which as I found afterwards, had been my misfortune, and not his neglect, for he wrote me several letters which had all miscarried, but forgotten him I never had: and amidst all my personal infidelities, not one had made a pin's point impression on a heart impenetrable to the true love-passion, but for him.

As soon, however, as I was mistress of this unexpected fortune, I felt more than ever how dear he was to me: from its insufficiency to make me happy, whilst he was not to share it with me: my earliest care, consequently, was to endeavour at getting some account of him. But all my researches produc'd me no more light, than that his father had been dead some time, not so well as even with the world; and that *Charles* had reached his port of destination in the *South-Seas*, where finding the estate he was sent to recover, dwindled to a trifle, by the loss of two ships, in which the bulk of his uncle's fortune lay, he was come away with the small remainder, and might perhaps, according to the best advice, in a few months return to *England*, from whence he had, at the time of this my enquiry, been absent two years and seven months: a little eternity in love!

You cannot conceive with what joy I embraced the hopes thus given me of seeing the delight of my heart again; but as the term of months was assign'd it, in order to divert, and amuse my impatience for his return, after settling my affairs with much ease, and security, I set out on a journey for *Lancashire*, with an equipage suitable to my fortune, and with a design purely to revisit my place of nativity, for which I could not help retaining a great tenderness, and might naturally not be sorry to show myself there, to the advantage I was now in pass to do, after the report *Esther Davis* had spread of my being spirited away to the Plantations, for on no other supposition could she account for the suppression of myself to her, since her leaving me so abruptly at the inn. Another favourite intention I had, to look out for my relations, though I had none besides distant ones, and to prove a benefactress to them. Then Mrs. *Cole's* place of retirement lying in my way, was not amongst the least of the pleasures I had propos'd to myself in this expedition.

I had taken nobody with me but a discreet decent woman, to figure it as my companion, besides my servants, and was scarce got into an inn, about twenty miles from *London,* where I was to sup and pass the night, when such a storm of wind and rain sprang up, as made me congratulate myself on having got under shelter before it began.

This had continu'd a good half hour, when bethinking me of some directions to be given to the coachman, I sent for him, and not caring that his shoes should soil the very clean parlour, in which the cloth was laid, I stept into the hall kitchen, where he was, and where, whilst I was talking to him, I slantingly observ'd two horsemen driven in by the weather, and both wringing wet, one of whom was asking if they could be assisted with a change, till their cloaths could be dried; but heavens! who can express what I felt at the sound of a voice, ever present to my heart, and that it now rebounded at or when pointing my eyes towards the person it came from, they confirm'd its information; in spite of so long an absence, and of a dress one would have imagin'd studied for disguise: a horseman's great coat with a stand-up cape, and his hat flapp'd; but what could escape the piercing alertness of a sense surely guided by love? A transport then, like mine, was above all consideration, or schemes of surprize, and I, that instant, with the rapidity of the emotions that I felt the spur of, shot into his arms, crying out as I threw mine round his neck, "My life! My soul! My *Charles!*" And, without further power of speech swoon'd away, under the oppressing agitations of joy and surprise.

Recover'd out of my entrancement, I found myself in my charmer's arms, but in the parlour, surrounded by a crowd which this event had gather'd round us, and which immediately, on a signal from the discreet landlady, who currently took him for my

husband, clear'd the room, and desirably left us alone to the raptures of this re-union, my joy at which, had like to have prov'd,
at the expence of my life, its power superior to that of grief at
our fatal separation.

The first object then, that my eyes open'd on, were their
supreme idol, and my supreme wish, *Charles*, on one knee, holding me fast by the hand, and gazing at me in a transport of fondness. Observing my recovery, he attempted to speak, and give
vent to his impatience of hearing my voice again, to satisfy him
once more that it was *me:* but the mightiness, and suddenness of
the surprize continuing to stun him, choak'd his utterance: he
could only stammer out a few broken, half-form'd, faultering accents, which my ears greedily drinking in, spelt, and put together so as to make out their sense. "After so long!—so
cruel!—an absence,—my dearest *Fanny!*—Can it? can it be
you?"—stifling me at the same time with kisses, that stopping my
mouth, at once prevented the answer that he panted for, and
encreas'd the delicious disorder, in which all my senses were rap-
turously lost. Amidst, however, this croud of ideas, and all blissful ones, there obtruded only one cruel doubt, that poison'd
nearly all this transcendent happiness: and what was it, but my
dread of its being too excessive to be real. I trembled now with
the fear of its being no more than a dream, and of my waking out
of it into the horrors of finding it one: under this fond apprehension, imagining I could not make too much of the present prodigious joy, before it should vanish and leave me in the desert again,
nor verify its reality too strongly, I clung to him, I clasp'd him, as
if to hinder him from escaping me again. "Where have you been?
How could you—could you leave me?—Say you are still mine,—
that you still love me,—and thus! thus! (kissing him as if I would
consolidate lips with him) I forgive you—forgive my hard fortune in favour of this restoration.—"All these interjections
breaking from me, in that wildness of expression, that justly
passes for eloquence in love, drew from him all the returns my
fond heart could wish, or require. Our caresses, our questions,
our answers, for some time, observ'd no order; all crossing, or interrupting one another in sweet confusion, whilst we exchang'd

hearts at our eyes, and renew'd the ratifications of a love unabated by time or absence: not a breath, not a motion, not a gesture on either side, but what was strongly impressed with it. Our hands lock'd in each other, repeated the most passionate squeezes, so that their fiery thrill went to the heart again.

Thus absorpt, and concenter'd in this unutterable delight; I had not attended to the sweet author of it, being thoroughly wet, and in danger of catching cold, when, in good time, the landlady, whom the appearance of my equipage (which by the by *Charles* knew nothing of) had gain'd me an interest in, for me, and mine, interrupted us, by bringing in a decent shift of linen, and cloaths, which now, somewhat recover'd into a calmer composure by the coming in of a third person, I prest him to take the benefit of, with a tender concern, and anxiety, that made me tremble for his health.

The landlady leaving us again, he proceeded to shift, in the act of which, tho' he proceeded with all that modesty, which became these first solemner instants of our re-meeting, after so long an absence, I could not contain certain snatches of my eyes, lur'd by the dazzling discoveries of his naked skin, that escap'd him as he chang'd his linen, and which I could not observe the unfaded life, and complexion of, without emotions of tenderness and joy, that had himself too purely for their object, to partake of a loose, or mis-tim'd desire.

He was soon drest in these tempory cloaths, which neither fitted him, nor became the light my passion plac'd him in, to me at least: yet as they were on him, they look'd extremely well, in virtue of that magic charm which love put into every thing that he touch'd, or had relation to him; and where indeed was that dress that a figure like his would not give grace to? For now as I ey'd him more in detail, I could not but observe the even favourable alteration which the time of his absence had produc'd in his person.

There were still the same exquisite lineaments, still the same vivid vermilion, and bloom reigning in his face, but now the roses were more fully blown: the tant[90] of his travels, and a beard somewhat more distinguishable, had, at the expence of no more delicacy than what he could better spare, than not, given it an air of becoming manliness, and maturity, that symmetriz'd nobly with that air of distinction and empire,[91] with which nature had stamp'd it, in a rare mixture with the sweetness of it; still nothing had he lost of that smooth plumpness of flesh, which glowing with freshness, blooms florid to the eye, and delicious to the touch: then, his shoulders were grown more square, his shape more form'd, more portly, but still free, and airy. In short, his figure show'd riper, greater, and perfecter to the experienced eye, than in his tender youth; and now, he was not much more than two and twenty.

In this interval, however, I pick'd out of the broken, often pleasingly, interrupted account of himself, that he was, at that instant, actually on his road to *London,* in not a very paramount plight, or condition, having been wreck'd on the *Irish* coast, for which he had prematurely embark'd, and lost the little all he had brought with him from the *South-Seas,* so that he had not, till after great shifts and hardships, in the company of his fellow traveller, the captain, got so far on his journey; that so it was, (having heard of his father's death and circumstances,) he had now the world to begin again, on a new account: a situation, which he assur'd me, in a vein of sincerity, that flowing from his heart, penetrated mine, gave him no farther pain, than that he had it not in his power, to make me as happy as he could wish. My fortune, you will please to observe, I had not enter'd upon any overture of, reserving to feast myself with the surprize of it to him, in calmer instants. And as to my dress, it could give him no idea of the truth, not only as it was mourning, but likewise in a stile of plainness and simplicity, that I have ever kept to with studied art. He press'd me indeed tenderly to satisfy his ardent curiosity, both with regard to my past and present state of life, since his being torn away from me; but I had the address to elude his questions, by answers that shewing his satisfaction at no great distance, won upon him to wave his impatience, in favour of the thorough confidence he had in my not delaying it; but for respects I should in good time acquaint him with.

Charles however thus return'd to my longing arms, tender, faithful, and in health, was already a blessing too mighty for my conception! but, *Charles* in distress!—*Charles* reduc'd, and broke down to his naked personal merit, was such a circumstance, in favour of the sentiments I had for him, as exceeded my utmost desires: and accordingly, I seem'd so visibly charm'd, so out of time, and measure pleas'd at his mention of his ruin'd fortune, that he could account for it no way but that the joy of seeing him again, had swallow'd up every other sense, or concern.

In the mean time, my woman had taken all imaginable care of *Charles*'s travelling companion; and, as supper was coming in, he was introduc'd to me, when I receiv'd him, as became my regard for all of *Charles*'s acquaintance, or friends.

We four then supp'd together in the stile of joy, congratulation, and pleasing disorder, that you may guess. For my part, though all these agitations had left me not the least stomach, but for that uncloying feast, the sight of my ador'd youth, I endeavour'd to force it, by way of example for him, who, I conjectur'd, must want such a recruit after riding, and indeed, he eat like a traveller; but gaz'd at, and addressed me all the time like a lover.

After the cloth was taken away, and the hour of repose came on, *Charles* and I were, without further ceremony, in quality of man and wife, shown up together to a very handsome apartment, and, all in course, the bed, they said, to be the best in the inn.

And here, decency forgive me! if, once more I violate thy laws, and keeping the curtains undrawn, sacrifice thee for the last time, to that confidence, without reserve, with which I engaged to recount to you the most striking circumstances of my youthful disorders.

As soon then as we were in the room together, left to ourselves, the sight of the bed starting the remembrance of our first joys, and the thought of my being instantly to share it with the dear possessor of my virgin heart, moved me so strongly, that it was well I lean'd upon him, or I must have fainted again, under the overpowering sweet alarm. *Charles* saw into my confusion, and forgot his own, that was scarce less, to apply himself to the removal of mine.

But now the true refining passion had regain'd thorough possession of me, with all its train of symptoms; a sweet sensibility, a tender timidity, love-sick yearnings temper'd with diffidence and modesty, all held me in a subjection of soul, incomparably dearer to me than the liberty of heart which I had been long, too long! the mistress of, in the course of those grosser gallantries, the consciousness of which now made me sigh with a virtuous confusion and regret: no real virgin in short, in view of the nuptial bed, could give more bashful blushes to unblemish'd innocence, than I did to a sense of guilt; and indeed I lov'd *Charles* too truly not to feel severely, that I did not deserve him.

As I kept hesitating, and disconcerted under this soft distraction, *Charles*, with a fond impatience, took the pains to undress me, and all I can remember, amidst the flutter and discomposure of my senses, was, some flattering exclamations of joy and admiration, more especially at the feel of my breasts now set at liberty from my stays, and which panting and rising in tumultuous throbs, swell'd upon his dear touch, and gave it the welcome pleasure of finding them well-form'd, and unfail'd in firmness.

I was soon laid in bed, and scarce languish'd an instant for the darling partner of it, before he was undress'd and got between the sheets, with his arms clasp'd round me, giving and taking, with a gust inexpressible, a kiss of welcome, that my heart rising to my lips, stamp'd with its warmest impression, concurring to my bliss, with that delicate and voluptuous emotion which *Charles* alone had the secret to excite, and which constitutes the very life, the essence of pleasure.

Mean while, two candles lighted on a side-table near us, and a joyous wood-fire, threw a light into the bed, that took from one sense of great importance to our joys, all pretext of complaining of its being shut out of its share of them: and indeed, the sight of my idolized youth, was, alone from the ardour with which I had wish'd for it, without other circumstance, a pleasure to die of.

But as action was now a necessity to desires so much on edge as ours, *Charles*, after a very short prelusive dalliance, lifting up my linen and his own, laid the broad treasures of his manly chest close to my bosom, both beating with the tenderest alarms! when now, the sense of his glowing body in naked touch with mine, took all power over my thoughts out of my own disposal, and deliver'd up every faculty of my soul to the sensiblest of joys, that affecting me infinitely more with my distinction of the person, than of the sex, now brought my conscious heart deliciously into play; my heart, which, eternally constant to *Charles,* had never taken any part in my occasional sacrifices to the calls of constitution, complaisance, or interest. But, ah! what became of me, when, as the powers of solid pleasure thickened upon me, I could not help feeling the stiff stake that had been adorned with the trophies of my despoiled virginity, bearing hard and inflexible against one of my thighs, which I had not yet opened, from a true principle of modesty, revived by a passion too sincere to suffer any aiming at the false merit of difficulty, or my putting on an impertinent mock-coyness.

I have, I believe, somewhere before remark'd, that the feel of that favourite piece of manhood has, in the very nature of it, something inimitably pathetic.[92] Nothing can be dearer to the touch, or can affect it with a more delicious sensation. Think then! as a lover think, what must be the consummate transport of that quickest of our senses, in their central seat too! when after so long a deprival, it felt itself re-inflamed under the pressure of that peculiar scepter-member, which commands us all: but especially my darling elect from the face of the whole earth. And now, at its mightiest point of stiffness, it felt to me something so subduing, so active, so solid, and agreeable that I know not what name to give its singular impression; but the sentiment of consciousness of its belonging to my supremely beloved youth, gave me so pleasing an agitation, and work'd so strongly on my soul, that it sent all its sensitive spirits to that organ of bliss in me, dedicated to its reception: there concentering to a point, like rays in a burning-glass, they glow'd, they burnt with the intensest heat: the springs of pleasure were, in short, wound up to such a pitch! I panted now with so exquisitely keen an appetite for the imminent enjoyment, that I was even sick with desire, and unequal to support the combination of two distinct ideas, that delightfully distracted me! for all the thought I was capable of, was that I was now in touch at once with the instrument of pleasure, and the great-seal of love; ideas that mingling streams, pour'd such an ocean of intoxicating bliss on a weak vessel, all too narrow to contain it, that I lay overwhelm'd, absorpt, lost in an abyss of joy, and dying of nothing but immoderate delight.

Charles then rouz'd me somewhat out of this extatic distraction, with a complaint softly murmur'd amidst a crowd of kisses, at the position, not so favourable to his desires, in which I receiv'd his urgent insistance for admission, where that insistence was alone so engrossing a pleasure, that it made me inconsistently suffer a much dearer one to be kept out, but how sweet to correct such a mistake! my thighs now obedient to the intimations of love and nature, gladly disclose, and with a ready submission resign up the soft gateway to entrance at pleasure: I see! I feel the delicious velvet tip!—he enters might and main with— oh!—my pen drops from me here in the extasy now present to my faithful memory! Description too deserts me, and delivers over a task, above its strength of Wing, to the imagination: but it must be an imagination exalted by such a flame as mine, that can do justice to that sweetest, noblest of all Sensations that hailed and accompany'd the stiff insinuation all the way up, till it was at the end of its penetration, sending up, through my eyes, the Sparks of the love-fire that ran all over me, and blaz'd in every vein, and every pore of me: a system incarnate of joy all over.

I had now totally taken in love's true arrow from the point up to the feather, in that part, where making no new wound, the lips of the original one of nature, which had owed its first breathing to this dear instrument, clung, as if sensible of gratitude, in eager suction round it, whilst all its inwards embrac'd it tenderly, with a warmth of gust, a compressive energy that gave it, in its way, the heartiest welcome in nature, every fibre there gathering tight round it, and straining ambitiously to come in for its share of the blissful touch.

As we were giving then a few moments of pause to the delectation of the senses, in dwelling with the highest relish on this intimatest point of re-union, and chewing the cud of enjoyment, the impatience natural to the pleasure soon drove us into action. Then began the driving tumult on his side, and the responsive heaves on mine, which kept me up to him: whilst as our joys grew too mighty for utterance, the organs of our voice, voluptuously intermixing, became organs of the touch: And, oh, that touch, how delicious! how poignantly luscious!—And now! now! I felt! to the heart of me, I felt the prodigious keen edge, with which love, presiding over this act, points the pleasure: Love! that may be stiled the Attic salt[93] of enjoyment: and indeed, without it, the joy, great as it is, is still a vulgar one, whether in a king or a beggar: for it is undoubtedly love alone, that refines, ennobles, and exalts it.

Thus happy then, by the heart, happy by the senses, it was beyond all power, even of thought, to form the conception of a greater delight, than what I was now consummating the fruition of.

Charles, whose whole frame all convulsed with the agitation of his rapture, whilst the tenderest fires trembled in his eyes, all assured me of a perfect concord of joy, penetrated me so profoundly, touch'd me so vitally, took me so much out of my own possession, whilst he seem'd himself so much in mine, that in a delicious enthusiasm I imagin'd such a transfusion of heart and spirit, as that coaliting,[94] and making one body and soul with him, I was him, and he, me.

But all this pleasure tending, like life from its first instants, towards its own dissolution, liv'd too fast, not to bring on upon the spur its delicious moment of mortality; for presently the approach of the tender agony discover'd itself by its usual signals, that were quickly follow'd by my dear love's liquid emanation of himself, that spun out, and shot feelingly indeed! up the ravish'd indraught, where the sweetly soothing balmy titillaton open'd at the warm jerk, all the sluices of joy on my side, which extatically in flow, help'd to allay the prurient glow, and drown'd our pleasure for a while, soon however to be on float again! for *Charles*, true to nature's laws, in one breath expiring, and ejaculating, languish'd not long in the dissolving trance, but recovering spirit

again, soon gave me to feel that the true mettle springs of his instrument of pleasure, were by love, and perhaps by a long vacation, wound up too high to be let down by a single explosion; his
stiffness still stood my friend: resuming then the action afresh,
without dislodging, or giving me the trouble of parting from my
sweet tenant, we play'd over again the same opera, with the same
delightful harmony and concert: our ardours, like our love, knew
no remission: and, all as the tide serv'd, my lover, lavish of his
stores, and pleasure-milk'd, overflow'd me once more from the
fulness of those his oval reservoirs of the genial emulsion: whilst
on my side, a convulsive grasp in the instant of my giving down
my liquid contribution, render'd me sweetly subservient at once,
to the increase of his joy, and of its effusions, moving me so as to
make me exert all those springs of the compressive exsuction,
with which the sensitive mechanism of that part thirstily draws
and drains the nipple of Love, with much such an instinctive eagerness, and attachment, as, to compare great with less, kind nature engages infants at the breast, by the pleasure they find in the
motion of their little mouths and cheeks, to extract the milky
stream prepar'd for their nourishment.

But still there was no end of his vigour: this double-discharge,
had so far from extinguish'd his desires, for that time, that it had
not even calm'd them: and, at his age, desires are power: he was
proceeding then amazingly to push it to a third triumph, still
without uncasing: if a tenderness natural to true love, had not
inspir'd me with self-denial enough to spare, and not overstrain
him, and accordingly, entreating him to give himself and me
quarter,[95] I obtain'd at length a short suspension of arms, but not
before he had exultingly satisfy'd me that he gave out standing.

The remainder of the night, with what we borrow'd upon the
day, we employ'd with unweary'd fervour, in celebrating thus the
festival of our re-meeting; and got up pretty late in the morning,
gay, brisk, and alert, though rest had been a stranger to us, but
the pleasures of love had been to us, what the joy at victory is to
an army, repose, refreshment: every thing.

The journey into the country being now intirely out of the
question, and orders having been given over-night for turning

the horses heads towards *London,* we left the inn as soon as we had breakfasted, not without a liberal distribution of the tokens of my grateful sense of the happiness I had met with in it.

Charles and I were in my coach, the captain and my companion in a chaise[96] hir'd purposely for them, to leave us the conveniency of a *tête-à-tête.*

Here, on the road, as the tumult of my senses was tolerably compos'd, I had command enough of head, to break, properly, to him, the course of life that the consequences of my separation from him had driven me into, which, at the same time that he tenderly deplor'd with me, he was the less shock'd at, as on reflecting how he had left me circumstanc'd, he could not be entirely unprepar'd for it.

But when I open'd the state of my fortune to him, and with that sincerity, which from me, to him, was so much a nature in me, I begg'd of him his acceptance of it, on his own terms, I should appear to you perhaps too partial to my passion, were I to attempt the doing his delicacy justice. I shall content myself then with assuring you, that after his flatly refusing the unreserv'd, unconditional donation that I long persecuted him in vain to accept, it was at length, in obedience to his serious commands (for I stood out unaffectedly, till, he exerted the sovereign authority which love had given him over me) that I yielded my consent to wave the remonstrance I did not fail of making strongly to him, against his degrading himself, and incurring the reflexion, however unjust, of having, for respects of fortune, barter'd his honour for infamy and prostitution, in making one his wife, who thought herself too much honour'd in being but his mistress.

The plea of love then over-ruling all objections, *Charles,* entirely won with the merit of my sentiments for him, which he could not but read the sincerity of in a heart ever open to him, oblig'd me to receive his hand, by which means I was in pass, amongst other innumerable blessings, to bestow a legal parentage on those fine children you have seen by this happiest of matches.[97]

Thus, at length, I got snug into port, where, in the bosom of virtue, I gather'd the only uncorrupt sweets: where, looking back on the course of vice, I had run, and comparing its infamous blandishments with the infinitely superior joys of innocence, I could not help pitying, even in point of taste, those who, immers'd in a gross sensuality, are insensible to the so delicate charms of VIRTUE, than which even PLEASURE has not a greater friend, nor than VICE a greater enemy. Thus temperance makes men lords over those pleasures that intemperance enslaves them to: the one, parent of health, vigour, fertility, chearfulness, and every other desirable good in life, the other, of diseases, debility, barrenness, self-loathing, with only every evil incident to human nature.

You laugh perhaps at this tail-piece of morality,[98] express'd[99] from me by the force, of truth, resulting from compar'd experiences: you think it, no doubt, out of place; out of character: possibly too you may look on it as the paultry finesse of one who seeks to mask a devotee to Vice under a rag of a veil, impudently smuggled from the shrine of Virtue; just as if one was to fancy one's self compleatly disguis'd at a masquerade, with no other change of dress, than turning one's shoes into slippers: or, as if a writer should think to shield a treasonable libel, by concluding it with a formal prayer for the king. But, independent of my flattering myself that you have a juster opinion of my sense, and sincerity, give me leave to represent to you, that such a supposition is even more injurious to Virtue, than to me: since consistently with candour and good-nature it can have no foundation but in the falsest of fears, that its pleasures cannot stand in comparison with those of Vice, but let truth dare to hold it up in its most alluring light: then mark! how spurious, how low of taste, how comparatively inferior its joys are to those which Virtue gives sanction to, and whose sentiments are not above making even a sauce for the senses, but a sauce of the highest relish! whilst vices, are the harpies, that infect, and foul the feast. The paths of Vice are sometimes strew'd with roses, but then they are for ever infamous for many a thorn; for many a canker-worm: those of Virtue are strew'd with roses purely, and those eternally unfading ones.

If you do me then justice, you will esteem me perfectly consistent in the incense I burn to virtue: if I have painted vice all in its gayest colours, if I have deck'd it with flowers, it has been solely in order to make the worthier, the solemner sacrifice of it, to virtue.[100]

You know Mr. *C——— O———*, you know his estate, his worth, and good sense: can you, will you pronounce it ill meant, at least of him when anxious for his son's morals, with a view to form him to Virtue, and inspire him with a fixt, a rational contempt for vice, he condescended to be his master of the ceremonies, and led him by the hand thro' the most noted bawdy-houses in town, where he took care that he should be familiariz'd with all those scenes of debauchery, so fit to nauseate a good taste? The experiment, you will cry, is dangerous. True, on a fool: but are fools worth the least attention to?

I shall see you soon, and in the mean time think candidly[101] of me, and believe me ever.

Madam,

Yours, &c. &c. &c.

Notes

1. *destroy it without mercy:* Fanny's prefatory remarks resemble those of other fictional autobiographies of the period, invoking a willing audience who has called for an account of the narrator's past exploits. By noting that the task will be "ungracious" (i.e., wicked), Fanny establishes a moral distance between her present and past selves; by highlighting her own powers of observation and reflection, she authorizes herself as the ideal guide to take readers through the "whirl of loose pleasures" she experienced.

2. *souse:* Plunge.

3. *composed the whole system:* Fanny's lack of a formal education would have been typical for women and men of the laboring classes. She identifies it as "very vulgar" and later will describe periods in which she learns more and benefits from education as stages that lead to her elevation in status.

4. *unmark'd:* Those who survived smallpox were frequently severely scarred. As Fanny notes, scarring would have robbed her of the commodity that made it possible for her to become a woman of pleasure, her physical beauty. It was not until after the 1750s that

a safe and inexpensive system of smallpox inoculation was developed. See also p. 138

5. *dowlass shifts, and stuff gowns:* Dowlas is a kind of coarse linen cloth; stuff is thin woven wool cloth.

6. *vartue:* This spelling of "virtue" alludes directly to Henry Fielding's *Shamela* (1741), a parody of Samuel Richardson's *Pamela; or, Virtue Rewarded* (1740). In the original, the servant girl Pamela withstands the sexual advances of her master, eventually receiving the ultimate reward for her defense of her virtue when he marries her. Fielding's satirical *Shamela* presents the protagonist as a lascivious woman, who shamelessly barters her "virtue" for financial gain.

7. *liquorish:* Drunkenly.

8. *intelligence-office:* A place where information could be obtained about servants and those seeking to employ them.

9. *drawers:* A tapster at a tavern or public house.

10. *receipt of custom:* Presumably, the counter where fees for services were collected.

11. *manteel:* A mantle.

12. *squob-fat:* Variant of "squab"; short and stout.

13. *minuties: Minutie,* the French word for "minutia," was frequently used interchangeably with the latter. Fanny's addition of the "s" calls attention to it as an affectation.

14. *for which there is no accounting:* Here, as elsewhere in the novel, Fanny distances herself from homosexuality. Whereas she views lesbian sex in fairly benign terms as an "arbitrary taste," later she will describe male homosexuality as criminal, a distinction that registers the intolerance of the early eighteenth century for sodomy.

15. *white lute-string:* Lutestring is a glossy silk fabric, hence a silk dress.

16. *chapman:* Customer.

17. *could not conceal my strangeness to:* Alludes to a scene in Richardson's *Pamela,* in which her master dresses her in fine clothes. Fanny's attraction to the new finery indicates her readiness to go down the path of debauchery that her clothing signifies.

18. *buckles:* Curls.

19. *tushes:* Tusks.

20. *jakes:* A privy.

21. *jockey-ship:* Trickery, in this case using Fanny as bait.

22. *look'd goats and monkeys at me:* Lasciviously leering. Goats were emblematic of lechery, monkeys of mischief.

23. *no root in education:* An implicit argument for female education, since "native purity" without the aid of education cannot withstand the powerful influence of example and habituation. Later, Fanny will highlight learning as a central element in her reformation.

24. *over the left shoulder:* Cast away; put behind her.

25. *settle-bed:* A chaise longue or daybed.

26. *neck-beef-eater:* Neck-beef being an inferior cut of beef, the description here underscores the fleshiness of the man and this particular transaction. Note the emphasis throughout the scene on the bestial aspects of the body.

27. *Guido's touch:* Italian painter Guido Reni (1575–1642), master of the Bolognese school of painting.

28. *estray:* Stray; straggler.

29. *Adonis:* In Greek mythology, Adonis was a handsome youth with whom Aphrodite fell in love.

30. *imbrew'd:* Soaked.

31. *inspersion:* Sprinkling.

32. *turtle-billing:* Probably a variation of "turtledove," to be affectionately demonstrative.

33. *heart-burn:* State of jealous enmity.

34. *Templar:* Barrister, from the Temple, buildings originally occupied by the Knights Templar; but from before the Reformation also occupied by lawyers.

35. *buffing:* Brazening it out.

36. *Newgate, the Old Baily:* Newgate was the main prison in London, notoriously filthy and overcrowded. The Old Bailey Sessions House was London's principal criminal court.

37. *Pillory, Carting:* Two forms of punishment. The pillory involved putting the prisoner in stocks and displaying him or her for public

humiliation. Also, a prisoner could be carried through town in a cart to allow the public to throw insults and objects at the offender.

38. *harpy:* In Greek mythology, a harpy was a rapacious creature, with the body of a bird, and the head of a woman; hence a predatory and shrewish woman.

39. *flow:* Pass.

40. *Arabian sweetness:* Possibly an allusion to the *Arabian Nights Entertainments, or The Thousand and One Nights,* a collection of tales originally in Arabic that were translated by Antoine Galland between 1704 and 1717; an English version of the tales appeared from 1705 to 1708. Oriental tales were much in vogue during the eighteenth century, typically presenting a view of Asians as sensuous and voluptuous creatures.

41. *smoak her commission:* Variant of "smoke," here meaning to suspect her plot to get money from one of her customers for procuring Fanny for his sexual enjoyment.

42. *factories:* Trading stations for merchandise.

43. *factor:* An agent.

44. *black man:* Olive-skinned with dark hair.

45. *bridal posset:* Hot milk curdled with ale or wine and mixed with sugar and spices, typically given as a remedy for colds or other ailments; here, it is clearly intended to reduce Fanny's inhibitions and to put her in the mood for sex.

46. *mechanically:* Automatically, without conscious thought. One eighteenth-century understanding of sexuality held it to be a sort of natural attraction between men and women, resembling that of animals. Fanny deliberately contrasts this with the love-based union she found with Charles.

47. *almost as masculine as their sisters:* A dig at the alleged growing effeminacy of the aristocracy, here contrasted with the vigor and manliness of medieval barons.

48. *strammel:* A scrawny, unattractive person.

49. *Blouze:* Variant of "blowze"; a slattern.

50. *fescue:* Stick used as a pointer.

51. *fore-right:* Directly opposite.

52. *bulse:* Package of diamonds or gold dust.

53. *rubbers:* In games of chance or cards, rubbers referred to a set of

three or five rounds to be played for best two out of three or three out of five.

54. *easy:* Comfortably well off.

VOLUME TWO

1. *authors and supporters of this secret institution:* The libertines who visit Mrs. Cole's establishment resemble in their philosophy late-seventeenth-century proponents of free love, the most famous of which was John Wilmot, second earl of Rochester (1647–1680). Rochester experimented in living a life of sensation and pleasure, espousing the belief that all pleasure that did not harm anyone else should be pursued without reference to Puritanical notions of morality that only sought to curb the natural animal spirits.

2. *shew:* Appearance; sham.

3. *intrenchment:* Inroad; encroachment; intrusion.

4. *cluck:* Roost.

5. *chapter:* A meeting, typically with an ecclesiastic application, referring to an assembly of the members of a monastic order or a meeting of the canons of a collegiate or cathedral church. References to Fanny's ceremonial initiation and, as the scene progresses, to the recitation of catechism, clearly parody religious rites.

6. *forms of the house:* Training; instruction.

7. *broad-pieces:* After the introduction of the guinea in 1663, the twenty-shilling pieces of previous years were called broadpieces because they were thinner and broader than the new coins.

8. *kersey:* A coarsely woven, ribbed woolen jersey.

9. *hedge-accommodations:* Of the kind to be met with by the wayside; common, inferior quality.

10. *Press'd to subscribe her contingent:* To recount her accident, i.e., the story of her defloration.

11. *girds:* Sudden movements or jerks.

12. *cornet of horse:* Fifth commissioned officer in the cavalry, who carried the colors, or cornet.

13. *high plight, bandied:* In high form, curved.

14. *relievo:* Relief, in the sense of a sculpture in which carved figures contrast with a smooth background.

15. *strain of arms:* A piece of military music. One trope operating

throughout the orgy is that the couples are engaged in dancing or making music.

16. *jumps:* A less confining form of bust support than stays.

17. *cockpit:* A place where a contest is fought.

18. *Abigail:* A waiting woman or lady's maid.

19. *birth-day finery:* Initially, a birthday suit was a new outfit worn to celebrate the birthday of the sovereign; by the mid-eighteenth century, the phrase also signified nakedness. Here, both senses seem to be in operation.

20. *nervous and home expressions:* Vigorous and pointed.

21. *refection:* Refreshment.

22. *figure it:* To play a role; in this case the women pretend to be milliners as a cover for their nocturnal employments.

23. *honey-month:* Used interchangeably with honeymoon, the first period of a mutually satisfying relationship.

24. *chaffering:* Bargaining; haggling.

25. *neither the feathers, nor fumet of a tawdry town-miss:* Fanny keeps a low profile, and unlike a town-miss—a country girl who has found her ruin along with a modicum of disposable income—she does not deck herself out in feathers or scent (fumet).

26. *cullibility:* Gullibility. To cully could mean to fool, cheat, or take in; as a noun, "cully" designated a simpleton who was easily tricked (see also page 150).

27. *springes:* Snare or trap used to catch small birds.

28. *rencounter:* A coming together; collision.

29. *inns of court:* The four Inns of Court—the London law societies—are Lincoln's Inn, Gray's Inn, the Inner Temple, and the Middle Temple.

30. *plum:* Softly; easily.

31. *gossipery:* Small talk.

32. *wrack'd off to the lees:* Destroyed; ruined to the last drop.

33. *visitation:* Inspection.

34. *playing upon velvet:* Sporting slang: in a position of gaining the advantage with ease.

35. *salv'd:* "Salve," in the sense of a sophistical excuse or evasion.

36. *sad:* Deplorably bad.

37. *gore:* Blood.
38. *female screw:* A cylindrical cavity with ridges on the inside.
39. *unnervous:* Weak; lacking vigor.
40. *street-plyer:* Streetwalker; prostitute.
41. *jee:* Move; go. Note here that the sailor seeks to sodomize Fanny and she rebukes him. When he quips, "any port in a storm," he implies that as a sailor, he is familiar with anal intercourse when women are not available.
42. *husbandry:* Conservation; thrifty preservation.
43. *bating:* Except for; with the exception of.
44. *viands:* Victuals; food.
45. *Bacchus:* Dionysus, god of wine; his devotees were given to drunken revelry and sensual excess.
46. *Roundheads were in Oliver's times:* A Parliamentarian, one who opposed Royalists loyal to Charles I during the Civil War. The name came from the short haircuts of a group of apprentices who demonstrated against the king at Westminster in 1641. Oliver for Oliver Cromwell, who was protector of the realm during the Interregnum, the period between the execution of Charles I in 1649 and the Restoration of Charles II in 1660.
47. *gust:* Taste; inclination.
48. *humour:* The quality of action that the participant finds stimulating.
49. *passing:* Extremely; very.
50. *sweetbriars:* A species of rose with hooked prickles, pink blossoms, and a rich aroma. Here the metaphor indicates a kind of pleasure in pain.
51. *honour:* Fanny's definition of honor here differs significantly from that attributed to women of her day. Discussions of female honor during the eighteenth century almost always refer to sexual chastity. Fanny claims a more masculine brand of honor, in the sense of keeping one's word or acting with bravery.
52. *stand of espial:* Station for spying.
53. *winching:* Wincing.
54. *subtile:* Acute; keen.
55. *crupper:* Rump; hindquarters.

56. *Spanish flies:* Slang for a preparation made from the dried beetle cantharis and ingested as an aphrodisiac.

57. *mend my pennyworths:* Increase my value.

58. *smock-fac'd:* Pale, smooth, effeminate.

59. *bagnio:* A brothel.

60. *chair:* A light vehicle drawn by one horse, or possibly a sedan chair.

61. *stage:* Stagecoach.

62. *bait:* To have a light snack.

63. *readiness against they came out:* Kept ready so that the men can leave at a moment's notice.

64. *in countenance in:* Fanny mistakes the younger man for a girl, asserting nature has made a mistake in making this individual a male.

65. *worst of consequences:* The penalty for sodomy, at this time and into the nineteenth century, was death.

66. *Ganymede:* From Ganymede, a Trojan whom Zeus made his cup bearer; a boy kept by a pederast.

67. *male-misses:* Mrs. Cole expounds a theory that male homosexuals bear marks of effeminacy and are similarly marred in character. Partaking in none of the strengths of the conventional male and in all of the weaknesses of the female, the male miss, also known during this period as a "molly," is presented here as a monstrous figure.

68. *sally:* An audacious adventure; escapade.

69. *sublimer intellectual ones:* Eighteenth-century sexual folklore held that idiots were blessed with larger sexual organs in recompense for their limited mental capacities.

70. *natural:* One who is by nature deficient in intelligence.

71. *unskewer'd:* Unfastened.

72. *troll'd:* Rolled.

73. *through-stitch:* To go through with; to carry out.

74. *ouverture:* Opening.

75. *worryings:* Biting or tearing at the throat, as an animal might tear at its prey.

76. *Shakespeare: Romeo and Juliet* V.iii. 45–48. Romeo's speech as he opens the tomb to find Juliet, whom he believes to be dead:

> *Thou detestable maw, thou womb of death,*
> *Gorged with the dearest morsel of the earth,*
> *Thus I enforce thy rotten jaws to open,*
> *And in despite I'll cram thee with more food.*

77. *fervorously:* Full of fervor; ardent; warm.
78. *had her freak out:* Satisfied her whim.
79. *Marquise:* A canopy, in this case attached to the tent; a marquee.
80. *chère entière:* The enjoyment of pleasure; entertainment.
81. *fore-lappet:* The part of his shirt where the two sides of the fabric overlap.
82. *shoal'd:* Swam.
83. *leading-strings:* Strings attached to children to help them learn to walk.
84. *duties of her domestic:* Her household affairs.
85. *Philosophers of the Town the White Crow of her profession:* In his notes to the 1985 Penguin edition of the novel, Peter Wagner identifies this passage as alluding to the reading of oracles in ancient Greece and Rome. Augurs interpreted the sounds of birds and their flight patterns as having larger significance, and crows belonged to the second class of augurs. This reading does not seem consistent with the analogy in the passage—that Fanny loses Mrs. Cole, just as the philosophers lost their white crow.
86. *ransomed:* Blackmailed.
87. *practice:* Custom; habit.
88. *compting-house:* Counting-house.
89. *mean:* In a fair way.
90. *tant:* Tint.
91. *distinction and empire:* Dignity.
92. *pathetic:* Capable of arousing the emotions; moving; affecting.
93. *Attic salt:* Refined; delicate.
94. *coaliting:* Uniting; growing together.
95. *quarter:* A break or pause.
96. *chaise:* A carriage.
97. *happiest of matches:* This final view of Fanny as a wife and mother provides evidence of her complete reformation. The absence of a

religious conversion or any mention of divine providence is significant. Fanny finds her rewards on earth in the love of her husband and family: "health, vigour, fertility, chearfulness, and every other desirable good in life. . . ."

98. *tail-piece of morality:* Alludes to the convention of attaching a moral to the end of novels that detail the protagonist's criminal or lascivious past. By protesting her sincerity, Fanny calls attention to the fact that the moral part of her tale occupies just a small part of the text. Readers would note the difference between Fanny's assessment of morality as grounded in materialism and the majority of similar texts, which link virtue and religious principles.

99. *express'd:* Forced from.

100. *solemner sacrifice of it, to virtue:* Fanny's rationale for depicting vice in bright colors would not have found favor with conventional moralists of the period, who believed that authors should depict vice in the most ugly and severe manner possible in order to discourage readers from being seduced by more favorable pictures.

101. *candidly:* Without desiring to find fault.

FURTHER READING LIST

FOR *FANNY HILL*

Barker-Benfield, G. J. *The Culture of Sensibility: Sex and Society in Eighteenth-Century Britain.* Chicago: University of Chicago Press, 1992.

Braudy, Leo. "Fanny Hill and Materialism." *Eighteenth-Century Studies* 4 (1970): 21–40.

Bremner, Jan. *From Sappho to De Sade: Moments in the History of Sexuality.* New York: Routledge, 1989.

Copeland, Edward W. "Clarissa and Fanny Hill: Sisters in Distress." *Studies in the Novel* 4 (1972): 343–52.

Epstein, Julia. "Fanny's Fanny: Epistolarity, Eroticism, and the Trans-sexual Text," in *Writing the Female Voice: Essays on Epistolary Literature.* Edited by Elizabeth Goldsmith. Boston: Northeastern University Press, 1989.

Epstein, William H. *John Cleland: Images of Life.* New York: Columbia University Press, 1974.

Foxon, David F. *Libertine Literature in England, 1660–1745.* New York: University Books, 1965.

Kibbie, Ann Louise. "Sentimental Properties: *Pamela* and *Memoirs of a Woman of Pleasure.*" *ELH* 58, no. 3 (1991): 561–77.

Kopelson, Kevin. "Seeing Sodomy: Fanny Hill's Blinding Vision," in

Homosexuality in Renaissance and Enlightenment England. Edited by Claude J. Summers. New York: Haworth Press, 1992.

Graham, Rosemary. "The Prostitute in the Garden: Walt Whitman, Fanny Hill, and the Fantasy of Female Pleasure." *ELH* 64, no. 2 (1997): 569–97.

Markley, Robert. "Language, Power, and Sexuality in Cleland's *Fanny Hill.*" *Philological Quarterly* 63, no. 3 (1984): 343–56.

McCormick, Ian, ed. *Secret Sexualities: A Sourcebook of 17th and 18th Century Writing.* New York: Routledge, 1997.

Moore, Lisa L. "Domesticating Homosexuality: *Memoirs of a Woman of Pleasure,*" in *Dangerous Intimacies: Toward a Sapphic History of the British Novel.* Durham: Duke University Press, 1997.

Nussbaum, Felicity A. "One Part of Womankind: Prostitution and Sexual Geography in *Memoirs of a Woman of Pleasure.*" *Differences: A Journal of Feminist Cultural Studies* 7, no. 2 (1975): 17–40.

Sabor, Peter. "The Censor Censured: Expurgating *Memoirs of a Woman of Pleasure.*" *Eighteenth-Century Life* 9, no. 3 (1985): 192–201.

———. "From Sexual Liberation to Gender Trouble: Reading *Memoirs of a Woman of Pleasure* from the 1960s to the 1990s." *Eighteenth-Century Studies* 33, no. 4 (2000): 561–78.

Trumbach, Randolph. "Modern Prostitution and Gender in *Fanny Hill:* Libertine and Domesticated Fantasy," in *Sexual Underworlds of the Enlightenment.* Edited by G. S. Rousseau and Roy Porter. Chapel Hill: University of North Carolina Press, 1988.

Wagner, Peter. *Eros Revived: Erotica of the Enlightenment in England and America.* London: Secker and Warburg, 1988.

Whitley, Raymond K. "The Libertine Hero and Heroine in the Novels of John Cleland." *Studies in Eighteenth-Century Culture* 9 (1979): 387–404.

COMMENTARY

CHARLES REMBAR

IT SEEMS THERE WERE THESE
FIVE DISTRICT ATTORNEYS . . .

Memoirs of a Woman of Pleasure—the title used by the author, and by
G. P. Putnam's Sons two centuries later, and by almost nobody in between—is better known as *Fanny Hill.* When Putnam asked whether I
would defend it, I had never read the book. For that matter, I had not
read *Lady Chatterley's Lover* or *Tropic of Cancer* either, before the question of their defense came up. I may have been the only male of my
generation who had never seen any of the three. It appears quite certain I was the only one paid to read them.

Memoirs is, legally, a more vulnerable book than the other two. Had
it been the first to be tried, the prospect would have been hopeless. By
the time it came to court, in New York, it had the huge benefit of the
Chatterley decision. It also had the huge detriment of the New York
Tropic decision. (*Tropic* was still a year away from the Supreme Court.)

Fanny was vulnerable for two reasons. The first involves the dual tradition of literary censorship. The cases, quite apart from who wins, fall
into two lines that are fundamentally distinct, and in a sense opposed.
Both lines involve the same statutory prohibition, and the arguments of
the prosecution are superficially the same. But the underlying objections are different.

One tradition is represented most prominently by *Ulysses* and *Tropic
of Cancer,* the other by *Lady Chatterley's Lover* and *Fanny Hill.* For most
people *Ulysses* and *Tropic* are not enticing; *Lady Chatterley* and *Fanny* are.
In the one line of cases, the real complaint is that the books are offensive; in the other, that they arouse lust. In the one, public decency,
rather than private morality, is at stake; in the other, it is sin, rather than
the proprieties. The one book is attacked because it repels, the other because it attracts; the one because it disgusts, the other because it allures.

It is true that not a single word in *Memoirs,* standing alone, could possibly offend anyone. (Cleland's combinations, of course, are something
else.) Bad words may be offensive, but different readers will give different answers to the question whether they add to or detract from sexual

excitement. Most readers would be inclined to say Cleland did very well without the words. Their presence would have made a point for offensiveness (though it would not have been much of a point after the *Chatterley* and *Tropic* decisions), but it would hardly have added to the sin.

The taboo against illicit sex is much stronger and more deeply rooted than the taboo against bad manners. Where the book makes sex unattractive, the court is able to say that it will hardly affect anyone's morals. Thus Judge Woolsey concluded his famous opinion by disapproving the aphrodisiac and approving the emetic.

I disapproved of this approach and gave it very little scope even where it could be most telling—in the *Tropic of Cancer* cases. But whether I urged the point or not, it undoubtedly had its effect, and *Tropic*, though much rougher than *Ulysses*, was easier to defend than either *Chatterley* or *Fanny Hill*. As to these two, I felt obliged to concede—indeed, I asserted it before our opponents did—that the books were sexually stimulating. And from the point of view of those who contrived the anti-obscenity laws, and whose drives now fuel their enforcement, the concession was damning; the worst thing you can do is make sex look good. *Fanny Hill* did this more than anything else the courts had considered.*

The other reason the book was so vulnerable was the general impression people had of it. In literature, as in life, Fanny did not have much of a reputation. Nor did her creator. In the literary world—most of whose members had read the book as avid adolescents and not since—as well as in the public estimate, it was disreputable. A 1961 treatise, whose authors were both learned in the field and liberal in outlook, used it as an example of the "deliberately and flagrantly erotic." One of our own witnesses was later to testify that the work was known as pornography—a classic of pornography perhaps, if that helped.†

---

* Lenny Bruce, if he had wanted to win his cases, would ultimately have prevailed against his tormentors. In reality, offensiveness was the entire charge against him. Even though there was the additional difficulty that a performance rather than a book was involved, the value of his social comment and the absence of eroticism would have won for him on appeal.

† A past president of one of our most important bar associations telephoned me when the *Fanny Hill* case began and asked if I could lend him the book. He explained there had been a contraband volume in the Porcellian Club when he was at Harvard, but that he was never able to capture it. After he read the copy I sent him, he conveyed his gracious thanks and his sympathetic assurance that I had no chance of winning the case.

When I read it I was surprised. Cleland, I thought, was a very good writer, and *Memoirs* a pretty good book. It has style and grace and wit, and when I recalled the gross and clumsy and witless volumes that help to stock our bookstore shelves, I was quite ready, in fact eager, to go to court.

The publishers, however, were influenced by the general attitude. They were, in my judgment, too defensive. They planned to publish *Memoirs* as "A Literary Curiosity." I persuaded them to be less diffident. It struck me as much more than a curiosity, and in any event I could not see that being curious refuted the charge of being obscene. The caption on the dust jacket was changed from "A Literary Curiosity" to "The Classic Novel about Fanny Hill"—leaving it to the courts to decide the category in which the work had achieved the status.*

Fanny Hill was tried three times—in New York, in Boston and in Hackensack, New Jersey. The number of trials was pretty much a matter of the publisher's choice. Putnam, having seen what happened to Grove on *Tropic of Cancer,* decided not to indemnify the booksellers. Anybody who sold the book had to take care of himself.

Withholding indemnities does not, of course, insure against all legal expense. The publisher may itself be involved in litigation. If there is criminal prosecution, the case must be fought; conviction brings stigma, a fine for the corporation, and the risk of jail for its officers. If the authorities proceed by civil action, there is a choice: the publisher can accept an injunction where the action is brought, and write off that state as a market.

In New York, however, even a civil action would have to be defended. It was conceivable that the sale of a book forbidden in one place might go on elsewhere. But an injunction at the point of publication would make things difficult. Moreover, New York is itself a major part of the book market; the loss of sales would be by far the largest that a single adverse judgment could occasion. Finally, New York was Putnam's home and the center of the publishing world; in terms of

---

* I had not previously been Putnam's lawyer, and after the trial I asked Walter Minton, its president, why they had retained me. Minton said there were two reasons: one was the *Chatterley* and *Tropic* cases; the other was that we had several times met head-on when I represented authors he published and, he said, "I came away licking my wounds." I believe it was meant to be not a tribute to skill but a description of unremitting truculence. This is a note to young lawyers on how to endear themselves to future clients.

morale, a surrender in the heartland is devastating. So if there was trouble in New York, the publisher would have to litigate.

On the assumption that we lost in the New York courts, we would try to get to the United States Supreme Court, and there the matter would be settled, one way or the other, for the whole nation. But suppose we won in New York. By throwing away all arguments based on state law, we might, as with *Tropic* in Massachusetts, induce the state court to give us a victory, if it gave us any, on strictly federal grounds. The opposition would then be able to go to the Supreme Court.

But even when a litigant confines his position to a single ground, he does not avoid the possibility that a court will rule in his favor on another ground. We might have a decision of little use outside the immediate situation, and being the winner, we could not appeal. Besides, there is always the chance that a losing opponent will decide not to go farther, as had happened with *Tropic* in Boston.

In either of these events—a success based on state law or an opponent who decided he had had enough—the publishers would have a magnificent legal victory and a big practical problem. A New York decision against suppression would not stop prosecutors in other states. Unless the publisher were willing to give the indemnities and risk reenacting the Grove experience, the sale of the book might have to be restricted to the one state where it was cleared.

There was an intermediate course: the issue could be litigated in a few important states—important both for the prestige of their courts and for their share of the market. If the outcome in each case was favorable, prosecutors elsewhere might lose interest in the issue; meanwhile there would be substantial sales in these states. If the outcome in any of them was unfavorable, there would be an appeal to take to the Supreme Court.

Among the states right behind New York in pursuit of the book were New Jersey and Massachusetts. It was decided to turn and fight in those two jurisdictions, and to be careful not to sell the book in Chicago and Detroit and other hotbeds of morality. Hence the three concurrent cases on *Fanny Hill.**

---

* A federal case would have been preferable. For one thing, the decision of a federal court of appeals on a federal question usually has greater influence on a state court than the decision of the highest court of a sister state (though neither is controlling). For another, the chances of getting to the Supreme Court would be better; there would

New York did not keep us waiting. There was a 1941 act of the New York legislature that set up a special noncriminal procedure for the suppression of obscene material. The statute authorizes an injunction against any publication "of an indecent character." For the definition of "indecent character," it refers to Section 1141 of the Penal Law, under which Barney Rosset and Henry Miller were prosecuted in Brooklyn. (As mentioned earlier, all these statutory epithets come down to the concept of the legally obscene.)*

The idea was to afford an alternative to criminal prosecution—an enforcement device that would not send anybody to jail unless he went ahead and sold the book despite the injunction. With the nice whimsy to which codifiers of state legislation are addicted, this eminently civil action is found in Section 22-a of the New York Criminal Code.

It is a book-burning statute: if the book loses, all copies must be surrendered to the sheriff, who "shall be directed to seize and destroy the same." Moreover, the statute encounters the "doctrine of prior restraint"—that is, the doctrine that there should be no prior restraint. Prior to the trial, the court may issue a preliminary injunction, which stops distribution while the case is going on.†

For these reasons the validity of the statute was open to question. In an effort to shore it up, the New York legislature provided that the defendant might have a trial within one day after joinder of issue and that the court must render its decision within two days after the conclusion of the trial.‡

---

necessarily be a federal question. The government, we learned, had pondered whether to proceed against *Memoirs* and unfortunately had decided not to. This was consistent with its position on *Tropic*, although the renewed consideration of the subject indicated some feeling in Washington that *Memoirs* was a less defensible book.

* The "acquisition" or "possession" of the publication might also be enjoined. Ordinarily, it is distribution and sale that are the objects of official action. The fact that the statute also goes after readers is characteristic of the broad, sweeping, out-damned-spot spirit of legislation in this field. By way of comparison, consider wartime price controls, which never punished consumers, even though runaway inflation may be thought more of a threat to national survival than books about sex.

† Section 22-a says nothing about it, but the preliminary injunction is part of the traditional chancery suit for a permanent injunction, and the New York courts have construed the statute as implicitly authorizing provisional orders.

‡ "Joinder of issue" is the completion of the pleadings. Pleadings are the litigants' formal written statements of position. In modern practice, there are usually no more than

This, of course, contemplates an extraordinarily fast litigation; the procedure was designed to meet the charge that a preliminary injunction could cut off the sale at the outset and thus effect a prior restraint. The answer would be that if a restraint was imposed erroneously, it would not be for very long. A majority of the United States Supreme Court, speaking through Justice Felix Frankfurter, was impressed with the design, and the statute survived an attack on its constitutionality. (The decision came down the same day as *Roth*.)

The doctrine of prior restraint has a prestige it does not deserve. It plays a prominent part in the briefs of lawyers and the opinions of judges in First Amendment cases, and it has a considerable currency among laymen. The theory is that criminal punishment of dangerous expression (with the supposed safeguard of the jury system) is permissible because the word is already out, while legal restraints that operate in advance are abhorrent to the First Amendment guaranties.

The phrase "books on trial" has a fine rhetorical ring, and it is easy to feel noble when we allow anti-obscenity laws to act upon bad people and insist that books themselves must be kept inviolate. But in its final effect, a jail sentence after publication strikes at least as hard at freedom of speech as an injunction under a statute like 22-a. By and large, publishers would rather lose money than go to jail. If we consider only a single book, it may be argued that society's interests are served when the book comes out, even if the author or publisher is later punished. But if we consider the totality of expression, the jail sentence is the more baneful. Images of police and prosecutor, and

---

three: the plaintiff's complaint, the defendant's answer, and if the answer contains a counterclaim (a request for affirmative relief against the plaintiff), the plaintiff's reply. Pleadings are supposed to state the basic facts—not the evidence and not the law—on which each party will rely. (The word "pleading" is commonly and incorrectly used to mean legal argument; in the law, it means only these papers or the act of preparing them.)

Pleading was a very fancy art in the old days. The plaintiff served his Declaration, to which the defendant, if he did not Demur, responded with his Plea. This might be followed by the plaintiff's Replication. The defendant might thereupon make Rejoinder, which was sometimes met by plaintiff's Surrejoinder. Defendant could then serve a Rebutter, and plaintiff a Surrebutter. The forms were rigid, and a failure to follow the form prescribed for the particular category of grievance was often fatal.

Pleading is still an art, but it is now a freer one, and the courts will allow lawyers to correct their mistakes; ordinarily, the principal penalty for poor pleading is a waste of time and effort (which can also be fatal, but less often is).

prison itself, make a deep impression on authors and publishers, in no way matched by the sporting risks of the civil suit; anticipation does the censor's work. Moreover, prior restraint by injunction is not the same as the licensing John Milton fought, which meant a total suppression at the source, with no judicial review whatever. Except when used to describe an *ex parte* order,* or administrative as distinguished from judicial enforcement, "prior restraint" is an out-of-tune rallying cry.

But these were not the thoughts that formed the basis of Justice Frankfurter's opinion. Instead he emphasized the importance of allowing legislators wide choice of method ("It is not for this Court thus to limit the state in resorting to various weapons in the armory of the law") and pointed to the provisions for speed in the statute: the interference with freedom, he said, is nearly negligible. But the legislative scheme for instant litigation is illusory. It is ordinarily impossible for the defender of a book to bring the case to trial in a matter of days. Most trial judges have had little experience with constitutional problems; a thorough briefing has more than its usual significance. And the people who can make good witnesses are not available on short order.

As to the quick decision the statute calls for, suppose the judge politely asks the parties whether he may have longer than two days. Does the lawyer assume that an overworked judge's natural irritation at being pushed will have no bearing on the outcome? And even if that assumption is made, the fact is (up to now, anyway) that the less thought a judge gives to the matter, the greater the probability he will decide against the book.

Justice Frankfurter, writing at a time in his life when he was not at his brilliant best, loaded his statement of the case. Although the question presented to the Supreme Court was limited to the constitutionality of the procedure, and had nothing to do with whether the publications were obscene, his opinion described the materials that led to the suit and referred to appellants as "merchants of obscenity." It was none of the Court's business. The issue was the validity of an enforcement device—one that might be used, for example, against the

---

* An order made only after one side is heard. In some circumstances a court may act on the application of one party without giving the other an opportunity to oppose. The justification is usually some serious and continuing injury—a situation that gets worse with every passing moment and cannot wait for a two-sided hearing. In an obscenity case it would presumably be the headlong deterioration of moral fiber.

writings of Sigmund Freud. The procedure, and not the character of the books or the booksellers, was up for decision.

The case also presented the Justice with an opportunity to express, as he did on so many occasions, his confidence in the wisdom of state legislatures. In a sentence that expresses nostalgia for a curiously archaic legal concept, he said:

> If New York chooses to subject persons who disseminate obscene "literature" to criminal prosecution and also to deal with such books as deodands of old, or both, with due regard, of course, to appropriate opportunities for the trial of the underlying issue, it is not for us to gainsay its selection of remedies.

"Deodand"—adjective and noun—was part of the old common law. An animal or an inanimate object that caused the death of a human was deodand. Under the law, it was forfeited to the King, to be distributed in alms by his High Almoner—"for the appeasing," says Coke, "of God's wrath." The word is from *deo dandum,* "a thing to be given to God." Historically, God got cheated. Whether deodands went to the Crown or, as they did later, to the lord of the manor, their use for charitable purposes was subject to the corruption of the centuries.

Although the English common law was imported into the colonies and is the core of our legal system, deodands failed to make it across the sea. They have never been part of our law, an item with which to balance, say, the War with Mexico. But corrupt or not, un-American or not, they are a splendid example of unreason.

When the niceties of logic are applied to atavistic premises, the results are garish. The law of deodand made distinctions as to how much was to be forfeited. "Thus," says *Bouvier's Law Dictionary,* "if a man should fall from a cartwheel, the cart being stationary, and be killed, the wheel only would be deodand; while if he was run over by the same wheel in motion, not only the wheel but the cart and the load became deodand. And this, even though it belonged to the dead man." The widow and children have lost husband and father; it therefore follows that their cart and its contents must be taken from them. Taken from them and devoted (by the lord of the manor) to charitable purposes.

Blackstone, a true son of the eighteenth century, was romantic about reason, and his agile legal imagination could find reason even where it seems not to exist. Why should there be a distinction between the stationary cart and the moving cart, and the harsher penalty imposed where there is motion? Blackstone had a plausible answer: if the cart is in motion, chances are someone set it in motion. So negligence is involved, and the harsher penalty attaches because of the fault. This is a good idea, but not a true one.* The difficulty is that neither ownership nor control over the object that did the damage had any bearing on the legal outcome. If somebody stole your well-guarded sword and murdered a man with it, your sword would be forfeited. And the cart would be deodand even though the man who was killed was its owner and driver.

Probably the distinction is a product of anthropomorphism. A century later, Oliver Wendell Holmes, Jr., more logical than Blackstone, found a less logical basis for the concept. It was vengeance: deodand was institutionalized retaliation. Feelings of vengeance are not limited to human objects. Chairs over which we stumble get kicked; golf clubs that dub shots get broken. But the more an object moves, the more it resembles a living thing, and the more fitting the fury.

Blackstone's idea of where it began is disclosed in the opening sentence of his chapter: "In the blind days of popery. . . ." His historical view is foreshortened. Exodus, Chapter Twenty-one, verse 28, proclaims: "If an ox gore a man or a woman that they shall die, then the ox shall be surely stoned. . . ." And in this the Greeks were even more primitive than the Hebrews; the Greeks applied the concept to inanimate things. In Athens, under Draco's Laws, a statue that fell and killed a man was thrown into the sea.† The practical Normans were at least careful to get the benefit of the deodand; the Crown, not the sea, would have the prize.

Horses, oxen, carts, boats, millwheels and cauldrons were the commonest examples. But as late as 1840 a railway train that killed a man

---

* A good idea is fresh, ingenious and appealing. If it also happens to be true, it is a great idea. A great idea that has been around awhile is a truism. A while later it is a cliché.

† In the fourth century B.C., in one of the speeches of Aeschines:

We banish beyond our borders stocks and stones and steel, voiceless and mindless things, if they chance to kill a man; and if a man commits suicide, bury the hand that struck the blow afar from its body.

Holmes says Aeschines mentions this "quite as an everyday matter, evidently without thinking it at all extraordinary, only to point an antithesis to the honors heaped upon Demosthenes."

was declared deodand. (The company was allowed to keep the train by substituting money—two thousand pounds.) It was just twenty-eight years later that reason had a further triumph in *Queen v. Hicklin*.

It was this primitive notion that came to Justice Frankfurter's mind when he ruled that the New York censorship statute did not offend the Constitution. The Justice might as well have held state legislatures empowered to provide that First Amendment questions be decided in trial by ordeal. (And Barney Rosset, caught in the welter of *Tropic of Cancer* litigation, might have felt that in truth they were.)

The Supreme Court majority, relying on the appearance of expedition in the statute, was unrealistic. The statute permits the publisher to proceed at a pace the courts cannot accommodate. But the doctrine of prior restraint, on which those who attacked the statute were relying, is not realistic either. Proceedings like that provided by Section 22-a are, on the whole, an improvement on criminal prosecution.

———

This was the statute under which the authorities moved—suddenly and powerfully. An action under Section 22-a may be brought by a district attorney or by a corporation counsel.* But to meet and destroy *Fanny Hill*, the guardians of decency sent out the corporation counsel and five district attorneys. There are five counties within the city limits of New York, and the district attorney of each of them joined in the action. Such a display of unanimity in a field marked by difference of opinion could hardly fail to impress a court. It was all the more impressive in that only one of these six officials had proceeded against *Tropic of Cancer*. For good measure, the New York City police commissioner filed an affidavit expressing his agreement and asking for an injunction.

The massing of forces recalled an earlier litigation. The recollection brought with it both a small shudder and a warming ray of hope. I had returned from a World War II military career that involved an education in how to fly an airplane, maximum exposure to the bureaucratic weirdness of the wartime army, minimum exposure to danger, zero glory and a net negative contribution to the war effort. On my re-

---

* In New York City and certain other cities, the chief legal officer for noncriminal matters is called the corporation counsel. The title comes from the fact that in legal form a city is a corporation. The concept of the corporation was applied to ecclesiastical and municipal organizations long before it began to be used for business enterprises.

turn to civilian life, however, I encountered some serious fighting. I had been in the Office of Price Administration when I entered the service, and went back there after my discharge. My first assignment was a group of cases against most of the major oil companies. They were charged with violating price controls, and the cases were going on in various federal courts around the country. These great companies had staffs of "house counsel," lawyers on salary who form internal law offices for large business corporations. In addition, in each city, each company had on retainer a law firm, invariably one of the most imposing. Having evidently concluded that this double layer of high-priced legal talent (multiplied by the number of companies involved) was not enough, the defendants combined to bring in a specialist in oil litigation, somebody they evidently regarded as the champ. At the first few hearings, the parade of lawmanpower that pounded into court suggested a display of Soviet tanks crossing Red Square.

It was not that I was facing this legal horde unassisted; I had with me a recent graduate of Harvard Law School, very bright but not very experienced. He was a good four years younger than I and still had a trace of adolescent acne to certify his freshness at the bar.

The contrast turned out to be helpful. In their arguments, the defendants sought to create the impression that a powerful government agency, descended from the totalitarian New Deal, was persecuting patriotic businessmen who (Standard of Indiana, Texaco, *et al.*) were just trying to make an honest buck. The impression they in fact created was that a combination of powerful corporations was attempting to tyrannize a government reduced to sending boys to do a man's job. After they lost a few, the defendants got the point, and at the end they were represented (in court) by no more than a half dozen lawyers at a time. If we could do as well now . . .

The corporation counsel and the district attorneys started the action by moving for a preliminary injunction, which they did through an order to show cause. An order to show cause sounds like something more than it is. It is simply a motion, differing from an ordinary motion in that it is cast in the negative and comes on for argument sooner. The order directs the other side to show cause why the court should not do what the moving party is asking. But the other side has no greater burden of showing cause than when a motion is made in the regular way; it is still up to the moving party to convince the court it should act.

Newspapers frequently report the signing of an order to show cause as though it were a substantial victory. Ordinarily the only gain for the party getting the order is that his motion is heard three days earlier than it would have been. Occasionally, however, until the motion can be heard, the court will also put a stop to the conduct complained about. This temporary restraining order is a victory—a temporary one as its name indicates. But the order to show cause in itself has no effect other than to expedite the hearing of the motion.

The motion for preliminary injunction, toward which the corporation counsel's order to show cause was aimed, asks for a longer restraint—granted only after submission of papers and argument—that usually lasts through the trial.

In earlier 22-a actions, which involved various kinds of subliterature, the corporation counsel had obtained orders to show cause that included temporary restraining orders. But a higher court had frowned on the practice because of its *ex parte* nature. Accordingly, in our case, the corporation counsel departed from the traditional show-cause procedure; he gave us notice that he was going to ask the court to sign the order. This was intended to erase the judicial frown and refute the charge that the authorities were suppressing books without listening to both sides. The refutation was a little tinny. We got the notice late in the morning; the order, it told us, would be presented to the judge at two o'clock that afternoon. There was no time to prepare opposing papers. More important, since an order to show cause is granted or denied on the spot, the judge would have neither an opportunity to read the book nor time to consider the intricacies of the constitutional issues. If the order was to embody a temporary restraint, as the corporation counsel was asking, the court would be throttling the publication without giving the publisher any sort of a real hearing. This is exactly what happened.

At two o'clock the judge said he was not going to read the book: he could take the word of the corporation counsel and the five district attorneys that it was obscene. So while the plaintiffs' motion for a preliminary injunction was coming on, and while the judge (another one) would ponder it, and until the time when the motion would be decided, the publisher was enjoined from distributing the book, and the booksellers who were made parties to the action were enjoined from selling it—all without any judicial determination that the book ought to be suppressed.

Later a hearing on the preliminary injunction was held. The judge was a different one, but the result was not. A preliminary injunction was issued. *Fanny Hill*, the newspapers announced, was banned.

The ban, of course, would be lifted if we won at the trial. And at a full trial our chances would be better. But, it seemed, not much. There were a number of depressing elements. The Court of Appeals decision against *Tropic of Cancer* had come down, and the timing could hardly have been worse for *Fanny Hill*. The corporation counsel and the district attorneys started their action on July 8, 1963. On July 10 the *Tropic* decision was announced. The motion for preliminary injunction was heard on July 16 and decided on July 26. On August 20 the trial started.

As a matter of law, as I have said, *Memoirs* was harder to defend than *Tropic*. And aside from strict legal analysis, lower courts tend to follow what appears to be a trend in the higher courts. The general feeling now was that the Court of Appeals was opposed to "books like that." It would take an independent trial judge to go against the winds prevailing in the highest New York court. And independence apart, most judges of the New York Supreme Court were, as a matter of personal inclination, likely to be opposed to us. The decisions of the judges who had issued the temporary restraining order and the preliminary injunction were typical of the initial response of most members of the court.

These decisions were themselves an obstacle. "I find," said the justice granting the preliminary injunction, "that throughout its 298 pages, there is depicted in glowing terms a series of acts dealing with sex in a manner designed to appeal to the prurient interest. . . . The Court has considered the book as a whole in its impact on the average person in a community and I find that the book is patently offensive and utterly without any social value." This justice and the one who would preside at the trial sat on the same bench. Judges ordinarily do not like to overrule their brethren.

The extralegal considerations were no more auspicious. Political pressures were stronger than they had been. Mayor Wagner, during that July, had pledged to do something about "pornography." The mayor did not say exactly what he meant by the term. The Reverend Morton A. Hill of St. Ignatius Loyola filled it in for him. Father Hill said that *Fanny Hill* was an example. (The seemingly inevitable typo never took place; typesetters aren't what they used to be.) Later Father Hill went on a hunger strike, which ended only after the mayor designated Deputy Mayor Cavanaugh to head an anti-pornography drive.

Father Hill was not alone. Rabbi Julius Neumann, of Congregation Zichron Moshe, joined his fast. The flame, however, did not burn quite so pure for the rabbi; he hoped also to draw attention to Soviet anti-Semitism, which, he said, was "even more tragic" than the sale of pornographic books. These two clergymen worked together with the Reverend Robert E. Wittenberg of the Immanuel Lutheran Church. (The roster of religions was complete, an occasion if not for a Hallelujah at least for a Bingo.) They were all involved in Operation Yorkville, a group active in the anti-pornography struggle; the Operation exhibited a motion picture which showed what they were against.

My opponent in the case was Seymour Quel, one of the assistants to the corporation counsel. He was experienced, knowledgeable, courteous and—of chief interest to me—formidable. The trial was assigned to Justice Arthur Klein. Quel and I went to see him to work out a schedule. At one point during the conference the judge said, "I suppose I'll have to read the book before the trial. Do I have to be seen carrying that thing around with me?" This was mostly a joke, but only mostly.

Apparently Klein knew *Fanny Hill* and regarded it as not only notorious but embarrassing. Another depressing factor had been added. This did not mean, of course, that he would prejudge the case. But even the best judge cannot come to a trial with his mind *tabula rasa*. If he knows a book, or knows its reputation, he necessarily starts with some preconception—in this case that there was something shameful about the book.

Then we ran into difficulty getting witnesses. We had expected some difficulty, but not so much. In general, nobody wants to be a witness. For one thing, it takes time. There is the time spent in preparation, and the time spent in court. Courts do not make appointments to hear witnesses. In ordinary litigation in New York the lawyers hope to begin a trial on a particular date, but they may have to wait several days (because the last case took longer than the court estimated) and the witnesses have to wait along with them. And even when a trial is set for a certain day, it is not possible to forecast the hour when the turn of a particular witness will come, and so he usually has to be in court all day. Nor can it be said in advance whether the trial will last one day or two or three. It is not a matter of borrowing an hour or so, and the kind of people we wanted to testify were busy people.

But there is something more elemental, and even more of a problem, than the sacrifice of time. Courts are scary places. Being a witness is a scary business. I will return to this in a moment.

In this case, being a witness would take a real devotion to principle. D. H. Lawrence and Henry Miller are literary heroes. There is more of a consensus on Lawrence, but if Miller's laurel is not bestowed by acclamation, he wins it by virtue of the intensity of those who feel he should wear it. A critic could only enhance his reputation by taking the bold but socially approved (in the society of letters) step of going to court for *Lady Chatterley's Lover* or *Tropic of Cancer. Fanny Hill,* in any view, is another story.

That we should have impressive witnesses was particularly important here, and we needed a number of them. D. H. Lawrence was so great a name that two experts—Malcolm Cowley and Alfred Kazin— were enough. More would have created an imbalance of argument. For Henry Miller we had offered a wealth of literary endorsement, some of it elevating him to the highest place in the ranks of literature. Moreover, *Tropic of Cancer* was considered Miller's most representative writing. His best book, most people thought.

Poor John Cleland. That last could be said about *Memoirs:* it was his best book. But this was only because he had done nothing else worth mentioning. He had published very little, and his one other novel, *Memoirs of a Coxcomb,* was terrible—not terribly shocking, just terrible.*

As far as documentary evidence was concerned, there had been no critical writing about the book for the first 214 years of its existence. It was mentioned occasionally, but only under the heading of pornography. Nor were the current reviews much help. On the contrary, the two most prominent were so strongly against the book—one with some qualification, the other a ringing denunciation—that they were used by the corporation counsel. Other reviewers had some good things to say, but they all included a sentence or two that the opposition could make much of on cross-examination or rebuttal. And some reviewing jour-

---

* The writing in *Memoirs* is so clearly superior to Cleland's other work that it has been suggested it was written not by Cleland, but by his father, who was a friend of Alexander Pope's. Both extrinsic and intrinsic evidence, however—particularly its relationship to other novels of the 1740's—are such that *Memoirs* appears almost certainly to have been written close to the time it was published. Cleland was then about forty, and the hypothesis that his father was the author would involve an extraordinary instance of doing-the-boy's-homework.

nals ignored it altogether, possibly on the theory that there was no longer any news value, the original publication date of *Memoirs* having slipped by.

So the flesh-and-blood witnesses would by themselves have to carry the burden that in the other trials had been divided between them and the paper witnesses. We needed people with authoritative names and strong sentiments who could express those sentiments in court. It is one thing to state a brave opinion at a cocktail party, where brave statements are so splendidly orchestrated, or even in print, where your cross-examiners can only write letters. It is another to take an oath and state it from a witness chair, under the cold eye of the judge and the hot breath of the cross-examiner. And we needed more than two witnesses; two might be ticked off as eccentrics.

On the preliminary injunction we had submitted the affidavits of Louis Untermeyer, Maxwell Geismar, Dwight Macdonald, John Gassner and Norman Podhoretz—an all-star group that evidently made no impression on the judge who decided the motion. But the decision was not due to any weakness in the affidavits, and our affiants would have constituted a fine nucleus for the trial. Unfortunately, none of them was available. Untermeyer had gone to Japan, Geismar to the Adirondacks, a place just about as remote in travel time. Macdonald had testified in the Ralph Ginzburg trial, and in my judgment that appearance (which in all probability would be known to the other side) laid him open to cross-examination. Podhoretz and Gassner had commitments that stood in the way.

Walter Minton and I tried to get replacements. The bravest of those we asked, and the fairest as well, was Barbara Epstein, one of the two editors of *The New York Review of Books.* The thought of going to court alarmed her, but she agreed to do it. She also got in touch with John Hollander, who said he would testify. So did Eliot Fremont-Smith, Gerald Willen and Harry Karl. Some of these people have earned considerable recognition since that time, but they were then young and not widely known. Their testimony would be good, I thought, but their names would not impress the court. A week before the trial we still did not have the witnesses we needed.

Then three unexpected things happened. J. Donald Adams, in his "Page 2" piece in the *Sunday Times Book Review,* wrote a perceptive and favorable little article about *Memoirs,* and then offered to repeat in court what he had said in print. He would come in from his vacation.

Morris Ernst lent a hand, and met with Adams on Martha's Vineyard. Then Louis Untermeyer unexpectedly returned from the Far East. Finally—and really finally, when the trial had already begun—Eric Bentley said he would fly down from Cape Cod.

Now we had a fairly strong list of names. The only question was whether they would give us a fairly strong line of testimony. If they did, there would at least be a respectable record on appeal. (As it turned out, we had in addition a witness we did not expect.)

All of them had read my trial brief, so they had some understanding of the legal background and the issues. But in two instances there was no opportunity for the usual preparatory conference without which a lawyer is reluctant to chance what the witness may say. I did not see Untermeyer until just before his turn to testify, and I did not see Bentley at all. The others sounded good in advance, but courtrooms are special, and fine forthright statements in the lawyer's office often become diffident quavers on the witness stand.

This phenomenon, I think, has a great deal to do with the privilege against self-incrimination that the Fifth Amendment grants us.* The clause states that no person "shall be compelled in any criminal case to be a witness against himself." Its roots are commonly thought to lie in the use of torture to extract confession; the Star Chamber was only a century and a half gone when the Bill of Rights was appended to the Constitution. If the defendant's testimony may not be used unless he wants it to be, then the Star Chamber method is defeated.

But this was not all, I would think, that the authors of the Constitution had in mind. The privilege is a thin shield against a government bent on Inquisition. (Consider the Stalinist trials, where the induced voluntary confession, in terms of the Fifth Amendment, would be simply a waiver of the privilege.) But the Amendment has a value outside the context of tyranny. It defends against something less extreme than the rack and the wheel. Externally applied torture repudiated, torture remains in the situation. It is milder, and self-inflicted, but it is there—

---

* The Fifth Amendment also protects us from double jeopardy, from major accusation except upon indictment, and—the broadest of the rights in the Bill—from deprivation of life, liberty or property without due process of law. But it is the assurance that we will not be forced to condemn ourselves that has lately been heard of most, the phrase "criminal case" having been construed to cover proceedings outside court that might lead to prosecution, such as congressional hearings. "Take the Fifth" became part of the American idiom in the fifties, the numerologists apparently having taken over history.

often intense enough to affect the demeanor of a witness and the delivery of his testimony.

In our daily lives, we learn empirically that a direct, unhesitating, easy response usually marks the honest man, while hesitation, averted eyes, a tremulous voice and a groping for words identify the liar. Testifying in court is different from everyday conversation. The honest witness may hesitate, look away, speak with a tremor and mislay his vocabulary (while the well-coached perjurer reels off his tale). Jurymen, however, are not often in court and cannot make the appropriate discount. And the defendant, the man with most at stake, is most likely to be disturbed and unnatural. Hence it is simply unfair to make him testify unless he chooses to.

Everybody, almost everybody, is nervous in court—inexperienced lawyers especially, and witnesses who are parties most of all. But even experienced lawyers feel a tightening when the court is called to order, and all rise, and from a hidden chamber the man in the black robe goes to his high armored place.

The lawyer may have had lunch with the judge the day before, but he looks different up there on the bench. ("Bench" is an outrageous misnomer; it is an imposing seat of power. "Throne" would be closer.) Excluding the dishonest witness, who has good reason to feel anxiety, and the unprepared lawyer, who may be more anguished, the uneasiness remains.

Parties, witnesses and lawyers are all about to be put to the test, and whatever their interests in the outcome, the intensity of their feeling usually goes beyond anything appropriate. There is a residue of malaise, a stirring of submerged remorse. Fears come boiling up that have little to do with the matter at hand—forgotten crimes of childhood reach close to the surface—when we encounter the visible and majestic embodiment of authority in the courtroom. We are confronted at once with the twin and awful powers to inquire and to punish.

The eighteenth-century lawyers who drafted the Bill of Rights must have been aware of this. They understood in a general way, I believe, what has become explicit in this century. A defendant-witness may give every indication of guilt, and these indications can lead him to be judged guilty, although the guilt he betrays (and which betrays him) may have nothing to do with the accusation that brought him to court, or with transgression of any governmental law at all.

Judges themselves have confessed to an anticipatory apprehension.

And a judge will sometimes refer to his presiding at a trial—without any conscious punning—as his being "on trial." After all, he knows very well—though we may be confused—who it is inside that robe.

—

The pressures that bear on witnesses are a problem for litigants generally. We had some special problems—the high court's still steaming decision against *Tropic,* the paucity of witnesses to the eve of the trial, the strong opinion against us on the motion for injunction, the judge's hint of embarrassment and the infirmities of the book itself. The hot and sultry midsummer held a bleak and wintry prospect. About a week before the date of trial, I told Minton that it must be viewed, realistically, as an opportunity to build a good record for the appeal we would be taking.

The litigant at trial has two objectives. One is to convince the trial court; the other is to build a record for appeal. Their relative importance varies from case to case. In the present situation, it seemed pretty clear that we had to concentrate on making a record. Chances of winning in the lower court seemed to be roughly zero, give or take a percentage point.

But I spent most of the week writing our brief, and a lawyer working on a brief is in a sense singing in a shower; as the ideas come and the argument takes on tone and rhythm, it begins to sound good. You polish the draft and read your own paragraphs with a pleasured appreciation.

I allowed a discount for the shower effect, and still the brief seemed to make arguments that would be hard to reject—not impossible to reject, but hard, for a judge who wanted to act and sound like a judge. I revised my estimate; the trial would not be solely an effort to make a record. I told Minton I thought we had a ten percent chance of winning.

READING GROUP GUIDE

1. *Fanny Hill* is the first pornographic novel in English literature. Why do you think it surfaced in the mid-1700s? Do you think it complemented or contrasted with the London of that time?

2. Some modern critics compare *Fanny Hill* to Defoe's *Moll Flanders*. Is this an accurate comparison? Why or why not?

3. Some have argued that there are definite morals in this novel, as evidenced by the straight, truthful Fanny as opposed to Richardson's *Pamela,* in which sex is used to attract a husband. Is Fanny a moral woman?

4. When *Fanny Hill* was published, many opposed to the work were part of upper-class society. Why do you think that was? What is Cleland saying about the upper class in his descriptions of the lower class?

5. Some critics feel *Fanny Hill* has endured because of its uninhibited heroine. She has been described as "an ideal of both male and female fantasy: a woman who is extremely exciting to men, who delights in her own sexuality" (J. H. Plumb). Do you agree with this description? Do you agree with the critics' assessment?

6. Fanny "rewins" her domestic life and lover in the end, journeying from a lower-class prostitute to a virtuous, married lady. What is Cleland saying here? Was he simply giving a tidy ending to his book?

7. *Fanny Hill* lacks dramatic tension and events, and Cleland seems to lack the ability to weave narration with digression. Does this hurt the book?

8. As the second letter progresses, Fanny's exploits turn from the perverse to less wild escapades. How does this affect her and the story?

A NOTE ON THE TEXT

The text of this edition is based on the first London edition of the two volumes of *Memoirs of a Woman of Pleasure* (1748/9), provided by the Beinecke Rare Book and Manuscript Library, Yale University. Save for several small corrections, we have preserved the full text in whole.

MODERN LIBRARY IS ONLINE AT WWW.MODERNLIBRARY.COM

MODERN LIBRARY ONLINE IS YOUR GUIDE TO CLASSIC LITERATURE ON THE WEB

THE MODERN LIBRARY E-NEWSLETTER

Our free e-mail newsletter is sent to subscribers, and features sample chapter interviews with and essays by our authors, upcoming books, special promotio announcements, and news.

To subscribe to the Modern Library e-newsletter, send a blank e-mail to: sub_modernlibrary@info.randomhouse.com or visit www.modernlibrary.c

THE MODERN LIBRARY WEBSITE

Check out the Modern Library website at
www.modernlibrary.com for:

- The Modern Library e-newsletter
- A list of our current and upcoming titles and series
- Reading Group Guides and exclusive author spotlights
- Special features with information on the classics and other paperback series
- Excerpts from new releases and other titles
- A list of our e-books and information on where to buy them
- The Modern Library Editorial Board's 100 Best Novels and 100 Best Nonfiction Books of the Twentieth Century written in the English language
- News and announcements

Questions? E-mail us at modernlibrary@randomhouse.com
For questions about examination or desk copies, please visit
the Random House Academic Resources site at
www.randomhouse.com/academic